Empire of Israel:

A King to Rule

By Dale Ellis

The *Empire of Israel* series:

A King to Rule

A King to Fight

A King to Die

A King to Unite

Coming in 2020:

A King to Conquer

Table of Contents

Major Characters

The Israelites

Nathan is the protagonist of the story. At the tender age of twelve, he watched as Philistine soldiers from Gath murdered **Jotham**, his father, for daring to make Israelite weapons. Needing to protect **Miriam**, his mother, and **Leah**, his younger sister, Nathan joins the fight against the Philistine oppressors. Their cause seems hopeless until a group of *Monarchists* propose that the twelve tribes of Israel unite under a King and drive out all their enemies. An energized Nathan dedicates himself to building a strong Israelite kingdom and avenging his father.

Jonathan, Nathan's boyhood friend, is an impetuous and charismatic leader. Though their personalities are poles apart, they form an effective team. Jonathan's natural optimism lifts his friend out of despair while Nathan's caution tempers the other's recklessness. When Providence elevates him to be a Prince of Israel, Jonathan brings Nathan along as his armor bearer.

Saul, father of Jonathan, originally wanted nothing more in life than to be an honorable man. Handsome, tall and immensely talented, he was nonetheless overshadowed by his strong-willed father, **Kish**, the chief of their clan. Of course, the call of God to be Israel's King does change a man. A transformed Saul proves to be a capable king who can handle everything...except success.

Samuel has been the only man to hold tribal Israel's trinity of high offices. He grew from a child serving in the Tabernacle to become a priest and eventually recognized as a prophet of God.

6

During a time of national crisis, Samuel assumed the office of judge and led Israel to its last major military triumph. The aged Samuel lives in semi-retirement until new threats drive Israel to seek his counsel regarding a king.

Beker first rose to prominence as the opportunistic leader of Israel's anti-monarchist faction known as the *Highlanders*. Secure in their mountain strongholds, his followers oppose the revolutionary changes sought by the *Monarchists*. Blindsided by Saul's coronation, Beker deftly switches sides and becomes the indispensable right hand of the new king. Yet Beker continues to play his own game as he strives to become the power behind Israel's throne.

Helek serves as Beker's diplomatic henchman among the *Highlander* elite. He flatters, makes promises and pays bribes to preserve the *status quo*.

Elon works in the shadows as Beker's enforcer. Blackmail, threats and assassinations are his stock in trade. His reputation is such that a mere scowl is enough to intimidate even wealthy and powerful men.

Onan's roots in the powerful tribe of Judah are both a help and a hindrance to the *Monarchist* leader. Other tribes may support a *King of Israel* but fear a *Judean king over Israel*. Onan must win over influential non-Judean families such as Saul's.

Abner frequently chafes at being the cousin of a king. A natural leader, he must subordinate his own strong personality and ambitions to help King Saul overcome a shaky start to the family dynasty. Abner's desire to carve out his own place in the new kingdom leaves him vulnerable to cunning men such as Beker.

Gershon, the incumbent High Priest of Israel, believes the influence of the priesthood must be maintained for the glory of God and the benefit of the twelve tribes. Personally, he cares not whether Israel is ruled by the Patriarchs, a Judge or a King. Politically, Gershon will deal with whichever faction he feels will best serve the priesthood.

Each of the **Patriarchs** is recognized as the leader of his tribe. There is no central government as each of the twelve Israelite tribes prefers to attend to its own affairs. They assemble only during times of national crisis. The selection of a king who could diminish the power of the Patriarchs qualifies as a crisis.

Jephunneh, war chief of the tribe of Judah, boldly attacks his foes both on the battlefield and in the throne room. Impressed by Nathan's courage and leadership, Jephunneh becomes a valuable ally of the young man.

Laban walks a deadly tightrope to protect his people. His fellow Israelites living near Philistia must collaborate to survive. The Philistines draft Laban and other Judean fighters as scouts for an invasion of Saul's kingdom. These renegades face execution as traitors if captured by Saul's soldiers. The distrustful Philistines may simply murder them out of hand. Only Nathan and Prince Jonathan offer a chance at survival...and redemption.

The Philistines

Achish is the antagonist of the story. His princely claim on the crown of the Philistine Kingdom of Gath is tenuous at best. Simply being King Maoch's oldest son is not enough when competing against assorted half-brothers, royal bastards, jealous uncles and ambitious generals. Achish sees the battlefield as his best route to the throne, but it is a road fraught with peril. He must achieve enough military success to gain a strong following without threatening his suspicious father. A single misstep by Achish could result in either ignominious failure or execution for treason.

Maoch is the warrior king of the Philistine city-state of Gath and the father of Achish. His dream is to unite all five Philistine kingdoms under his rule and carve an empire out of Canaan. Sensing the growing weakness of his Egyptian overlords, Maoch makes an audacious move to expand Gath's territory. However, Maoch's political skills do not match his aggressiveness, which incites jealous rivals to plot his destruction.

Abimelek's official title is *Archon,* the chief administrator of Gath. He is also its spymaster and principal diplomat. Abimelek is kept busy filling in the gaps of King Maoch's bold, but crude, plans. Still, he recognizes Maoch's reach will one day exceed his grasp and that he must look to his own future. Abimelek can never be king, but he will settle for being the kingmaker.

Kaftor is the king of the Philistine city-state of Gaza, the traditional rival of Gath. His intelligence, greed and depravity all combine to make him the consummate schemer. Gaza is a formidable military power, but Kaftor leaves tactics to his generals. He steals more through negotiations than others gain by conquest. His best strategies depend on fear and rumors, while his weapon of choice is the assassin. Kaftor never goes to war unless his victory is already assured.

Phicol's boldness and shrewdness as a young officer caught the attention of King Maoch. After the bloodless acquisition of a profitable Egyptian trade route, Phicol is promoted to the governorship of a disputed Israelite territory. His small Philistine force must serve as bait to draw King Saul's fledgling army into a trap. If successful, Phicol can bring the entire land of Israel under the control of Gath.

Uruk's reputation as the best tracker in Philistia belies his little-known role as King Maoch's oldest confidant. He is the king's eyes, ears and voice in the field. Woe to the commander who disregards the advice of this simple scout! Maoch sends his old friend along with Phicol to ensure success.

Davon had no inkling of how his life would change after being assigned to babysit Prince Achish during the teenager's first battle. After the Israelites turned the tables on the Philistines, the young lieutenant and the future king jointly lead the survivors through hostile territory back to Gath. Davon becomes the strong right arm to Achish during the young man's rise to the throne of Gath.

Neighboring Kingdoms

Karaz served as a prominent general in the Hittite Empire, the ancient rival of Egypt and its Philistine vassals. His prosperous life fell apart after the Philistines murdered his family during a coup to place their own puppet on the Hittite throne. A devastated Karaz was forced to flee and become a vagabond mercenary. Destiny and vengeance come together when Karaz offers his services to an Israelite king with no crown, no wealth and no army. A chance to kill Philistines is reward enough.

Ahmose, brother-in-law to Egypt's current Pharaoh, battles both internal and external enemies to keep his relative on the throne. When Maoch of Gath brazenly seizes a valuable Egyptian trade route, Ahmose fears the unruly vassal conspires with ambitious Egyptian nobles. Not wanting to get bogged down in a provincial war, Ahmose risks taking an Egyptian army on a quick tour of Philistia to intimidate their kings. While a military solution must wait for better times, Ahmose initiates a political one.

Nahash, King of the Ammonites, has long coveted the fertile lands of the Jordan River Valley. When it appears that the new Israelite king wishes to provoke a conflict, Nahash is happy to oblige.

Malia commands a band of mercenaries from Crete in the employ of Kaftor, King of Gaza. He fights regular battles for a standard fee. However, civil wars and assassinations always cost extra. Working for a scoundrel like Kaftor means business will always be good.

Prologue

In those days there was no king in Israel; everyone did what was right in his own eyes.

From the Book of Judges, Chapter 21, verse 12

So all the children of Israel came out, from Dan to Beersheba, as well as from the land of Gilead, and the congregation gathered together as one man before the LORD at Mizpah. Now the children of Benjamin heard that the rest of Israel had gone up to Mizpah. Then the children of Israel said, "Tell us, how this wicked deed happened?" So the Levite, the husband of the woman who was murdered, answered and said, "My concubine and I went into Gibeah, which belongs to Benjamin, to spend the night. And the men of Gibeah rose against me, and surrounded the house at night because of me. They intended to kill me, but instead they raped my concubine and killed her. So I took hold of my concubine, cut her in pieces, and sent her throughout all the territory of Israel, because these men committed lewdness and outrage." So all the people arose as one man, and said, "Take ten men out of every hundred from all the tribes of Israel. When we come to Gibeah in Benjamin, we will repay all the vileness that those men have done in Israel."

From the Book of Judges, Chapter 20, verses 1, 3, 4, 5, 6 and 10

Abiram hobbled on swollen, blistered feet toward a rocky outcropping offering shade. The merciless sun overhead increased the agony of each step by making the stony trail feel hot enough to bake bread. Dust choked the Benjamite's throat.

Blood sucked from cracked lips provided his only moisture. His legs burned from evading the relentless horde intent on his destruction. Although his entire body screamed for just a moment's respite, Abiram kept moving. If he collapsed in the open, he might never rise again.

Despite his misery, Abiram smiled while crawling into a shady hollow surrounded by large stones. This crude refuge should conceal him from any pursuers, as long as they did not look too hard. Abiram's knees buckled as he tried to sit back against a rugged rock and he fell awkwardly on his rump. Abiram felt a cool breeze, closed his eyes and sighed contentedly. It was the most comfortable he had been all day.

Although his body rested, sleep eluded Abiram. Sweat flowing from his scalp loosened the encrusted blood on his brow. The salty, sticky liquid burned as it dripped into his eyes. Abiram jabbed his sword in the sand so he could use both hands to wipe away this new irritant. Eyes cleared, he then studied the nicked and battered blade that he had somehow clung to throughout his escape. Abiram was still wearing a boiled leather vest, but he had abandoned his helmet and shield many hours before. Thinking of these tools of war brought back the memories of the past three days. An army had come to punish the city of Gibeah in the land of Benjamin. Abiram belonged to one of the twenty-six militia regiments answering the call of their tribe to drive out the invaders. He had been shocked to learn Gibeah was not threatened by the Philistines, or the Canaanites, or even his people's most ancient foe, the Egyptians.

No, Benjamin had been invaded by their Israelite brethren.

The Benjamite leaders referred to the host arrayed against them as the *Alliance*. Abiram agreed that it seemed ludicrous to call them Israelites, since Benjamin was just as much a part of Israel as any other tribe. Abiram was neither surprised nor dismayed to learn the Alliance mustered ten soldiers for every Benjamite warrior. His tribe possessed not only better fighters, but also greater skill in battlefield maneuvers. The battle would also be fought on familiar ground where the Benjamites could use their knowledge of the terrain to good advantage.

On the first day of battle the Alliance selected a single tribe, Judah, to lead the assault against Gibeah. Abiram understood the logic behind this strategy. Judean soldiers could pin Benjamin's troops in place outside the city while the other tribes moved in for the kill. Benjamin won the day when the poorly coordinated Alliance forces reacted too slowly. The Benjamite regiments flowed swiftly around the flanks of the Judean vanguard and surrounded it. Tens of thousands of Judeans were slain before their relief arrived. The Benjamites then simply withdrew, allowing the panicked survivors to flee into the path of their allies, preventing a counterattack.

On the next day, the Alliance hurled their entire army eastward in a single massive thrust against Gibeah. Ten Benjamite regiments retreated into a carefully chosen valley which caused the larger force to bunch together. Eight other Benjamite regiments moved unseen through the hills to the north while eight more, including Abiram's regiment, crept through a gorge to the south. The Benjamite tactics were simple, but deadly. Like a snake with its head pinned down, the Alliance flanks became vulnerable. Abiram witnessed startled enemy companies wilt away one by one as his regiment struck from the south without warning. When the northern Benjamite formation attacked from a third direction, the Alliance army disintegrated. Thousands more fell to the swords of Benjamin before nightfall, reminding Abiram of lambs in a slaughter pen.

Abiram had been astounded when the Alliance forces rallied that morning for a third assault. If victory left him exhausted, Abiram wondered what those other poor losers must be feeling. When the day's combat commenced, Abiram's regiment was in reserve on a hill with a clear view of the action. The Alliance regiments came forward in a packed formation, similar to the previous day. Abiram shook his head ruefully at such stubbornness. He was preparing his weapons for an anticipated flanking move when excited shouts drew his attention back to the battlefield. He watched slack-jawed as the Alliance front ranks collapsed upon contact with the lead Benjamite regiments. A few casualties had sent the enemy fleeing in disarray. Abiram sensed this to be the turning point of the war. Unfortunately, he was correct.

At this fateful moment Benjamite discipline completely evaporated. The sight of their enemy's backs was too much for men like Abiram to resist. His nerves were worn raw by two days of bloody fighting. He and his comrades gave in to a primal urge to break ranks, pursue and kill. Their prey would not be allowed to rest or regroup. The invaders' only choice would be to flee to their homes or die on Benjamite soil.

Abiram ran for over a mile before stumbling into a mob of Benjamite warriors milling around in a field. His blood lust momentarily frustrated, Abiram scaled a nearby ridge to determine the cause of this ill-timed delay. His confidence was sorely shaken by the sight of thousands of Alliance soldiers waiting in well-formed ranks only a few hundred yards away. The panicked retreat was a ruse. Abiram felt dread as the enemy suddenly began cheering. He spun around when another Benjamite wailed in despair.

Abiram beheld a thick cloud of smoke hovering over the city of Gibeah.

The cunning behind the Alliance ambush was now painfully obvious to Abiram. While he and his companions were lured away by a feigned retreat, the remainder of the enemy army had captured Gibeah. The overly aggressive Benjamites were now trapped between two superior forces. Abiram watched as some officers attempted to organize the dispirited Benjamites, but he knew their efforts were futile. The different regiments were intermixed and few men understood the extent of the danger. However, the sound of *shofars* told Abiram the Benjamites were already doomed. Thousands of Alliance warriors now advanced in measured step while chanting their battle songs.

Abiram chose to fight from high ground rather than retreat with most of his comrades. Although most of the enemy flowed around the ridge, enough climbed up to slowly overwhelm the handful of Benjamites standing with Abiram. The next few minutes passed for him in a blur of clashing metal and spraying blood. When Abiram spotted an unexpected gap in the enemy formation, he followed the instincts of a mindless beast.

Abiram had run like a madman before collapsing in this miserable hole.

The sound of gravel crunching under foot shook Abiram out of his daze. His fingers instinctively sought his sword as he tried to make himself small within his rocky refuge. Abiram's ears detected more noises than a single man would make. At least two strangers were headed directly for his hiding place. Since the Alliance warriors seemed disinclined to take prisoners that day, he knew what he must do. Abiram summoned the last of his strength and lunged at his pursuers.

Abiram's clumsy attack drew no blood, but he still took two intruders completely by surprise. As Abiram drew back his sword, the nearer man fell on his back and scrambled away. The other stranger leveled half of a splintered javelin at Abiram's belly. They parried each other's weapon a few times while seeking an opening to strike. Then the other man took a step backwards and squinted at Abiram for several long seconds before holding the broken javelin over his head with both hands.

"Peace, Friend! We're Benjamites, too!"

"Prove it!"

"Use your eyes, Stupid. Do we look like victors?"

Abiram held his sword steady as he studied both men, as if through a haze. He recognized the hunted look of fugitives; in fact, the man on the ground was not even armed. As Abiram lowered his blade, the standing man jabbed the bronze tip of his javelin into the sand. The fallen man rose to his knees and held out a nearly depleted water skin. Abiram dropped his sword, grabbed the skin and greedily drank its last few sips. Abiram tossed the water skin back to its owner and slumped back down where he had been sitting. The other men crouched down in the hollow across from Abiram, although the javelin owner sat where he could still observe the trail. A moment of quiet passed before anyone spoke.

"Abiram."

"Shupham."

"Raphu."

Shupham tossed his water skin aside in disgust after confirming it was indeed empty. He spat out a mouthful of dirty saliva to clear his throat.

"Benjamin lost an entire army because some perverts in Gibeah couldn't keep their hands off a woman. We should let them burn that whole, cursed city."

Seeing Raphu remain silent, Abiram decided Shupham's remark was directed at him.

"Burn up the women and children too, Shupham?"

"No, Abiram, but we could have picked a few idiots for them to execute. No one would know the difference."

"We would know. Besides, you saw what the other tribes sent as their army. That bloodthirsty mob came for plunder, not justice. Killing a handful of imbeciles wouldn't satisfy them."

"It wouldn't have hurt to try."

"When someone brings an army that far, they use it. No, Shupham, it would have only shamed our tribe."

18

"Shame means little to anyone in Gibeah now, Abiram. They're all dead."

"Our Elders shouldn't have left it come to this."

"So what would you have done?"

"Demand the Patriarchs from the twelve tribes meet and judge the evidence. Keep all soldiers at home until the case is decided. What a farce! There were no witnesses, no suspects, and no evidence of murder...not even the dead woman's body. Her husband conveniently destroyed it."

"People's minds were already made up. A trial would have given the same results."

"A trial would have given everyone time to calm down, Shupham."

A derisive snort from Raphu interrupted Abiram.

"None of you get it, do you? Don't you understand what's really behind all of this?"

"Please, Raphu, enlighten me."

"That Levite belonged to the tribe of Ephraim."

"Meaning...what?"

"Ephraim is one of the biggest and wealthiest tribes. They share a common border with us. Our people have a peculiar talent for war. That makes Ephraim nervous, maybe a few other tribes too. A dead concubine from Ephraim provides an excuse to turn the rest of Israel against us."

"Ridiculous! Benjamin posed no threat to Ephraim."

"A thief assumes everyone else is a thief, Abiram."

"So you are saying this whole war was based on a lie?"

"Not necessarily. There are certainly enough degenerates in Gibeah to gang rape a woman to death. But if this incident had not occurred, another excuse would have been found to break us."

"Have you heard anything about an Ephraimite conspiracy, Shupham?"

"Oh, I've had to hear about it all afternoon, Abiram. However, we have bigger problems."

"What?"

Shupham pointed northward in answer to the question. Abiram pulled himself and felt his blood chill as he looked over the ridge. At least a dozen dirty, gray plumes stretched from horizon to horizon over the lands of Benjamin. Abiram knew only a large town or city could produce that much smoke. Tears filled his eyes when a fresh black column appeared while he attempted to count the others.

"Do they mean to exterminate our entire tribe? We are their brethren!"

"Apparently, we made the Alliance mad enough to forget that."

"We must go back! We must fight!"

"It's hopeless, Abiram."

"Raphu's right. The remnants of my regiment tried to defend the town of Gibeon. They blew through us like a sandstorm. I thought there were no other survivors until I met you two. You'll find only death there, Abiram."

"Then I will go alone. I want to kill more of those bastards."

"Abiram, you're in no shape to kill anyone but yourself. Why not just fall on your sword right here and save yourself a long walk?"

"So what should I do, Raphu?"

"Go to the *Refuge*."

"The Rock of Rimmon?"

"Come with us, Abiram. There's water, shelter and a place to defend. Any Benjamite survivors will head there eventually."

"How many?

"At least three. Does it matter?"

"But what could we do there?"

"Begin again."

Chapter 1 - The Blacksmith

Then the tribes of Israel sent men to the tribe of Benjamin, saying, "What is this wickedness that has occurred among you? Now therefore, deliver up the perverted men who are in Gibeah, that we may put them to death and remove the evil from Israel!" Instead, the children of Benjamin traveled from their cities to Gibeah, to go to battle against the children of Israel. At that time Benjamin numbered twenty-six thousand men who drew the sword, in addition to seven hundred select men from the city of Gibeah. Now the men of Israel numbered four hundred thousand men; all of these were men of war.

From the Book of Judges, Chapter 20, verses 12, 14, 15, and 17

Now there was no blacksmith to be found throughout all the land of Israel, for the Philistines said, "Lest the Hebrews make swords or spears."

From the Book of I Samuel, Chapter 13, verse 19

The Benjamite hill country near the town of Gibeah

Nathan slowed his breathing as he cautiously peered over the stony ledge. He searched anxiously for signs of the relentless band pursuing him and his companion. The afternoon sun beat down on the rocky foothills or *Shephelah*, as they were known to the Israelites who lived there. The oppressive heat was relieved only by a slight breeze from the great sea thirty miles to the west. Although his foes were still hidden, Nathan felt at ease as he surveyed the landscape. He reclined about ten feet above a ravine through which the narrow the trail passed. His friend Jonathan had a similar perch on the opposite side. Both were well concealed from anyone on the trail below, but still visible to each other. They had run for miles to lure their pursuers to this exact spot for an ambush. Even the time of day was perfect, for their adversaries must now stare into the late afternoon sun. As he slid back down, Nathan could feel his pulse racing. The hunted would soon become the hunters.

Suddenly Nathan's senses came fully alert. He heard distant voices, muffled by a small rise in the trail before it descended into the ravine. Nathan glanced to his left and saw Jonathan preparing for action. Gathering his weapons, Nathan edged over to the crest of the ridge. Tilting his head so only his right eye was exposed, Nathan counted a dozen figures coming down the ravine – all pre-teen boys. Nathan was surprised, but not because of his pursuers' youth.

After all, Nathan and Jonathan were both only twelve years old.

Nathan was expecting to see his opponents more spread out and seeking concealment as they advanced. Instead, the boys were moving openly in a compact group and talking loudly. *Could they be a diversion?* Nathan quickly rejected the thought since it was impossible to outflank his hiding place. Nathan looked across the ravine at his friend, but Jonathan merely shrugged in response. Both prepared to hurl their arsenal of small pebbles, carefully selected to sting, but not draw blood. By the rules of their game, any boys hit by a pebble were considered *wounded* and therefore eliminated from the *battle*. Nathan was almost disappointed. This would be too easy.

A stranger viewing this scene might think the boys engaged in mere play, but he would be wrong. Children played hide and seek. Young soldiers conducted war games. Stealth and ambush in mountainous terrain were the hallmarks of Israelite warfare. The boys sought to emulate the great warrior tradition for which their tribe of Benjamin was renowned. Nathan was especially proud of the exploits of his most notable ancestor, a great-great-grandfather named Abiram. Unfortunately, military prowess also bred arrogance. This combination nearly led to Benjamin's destruction a century before when the tribe went to war against the rest of Israel. Nathan knew his people were now the smallest of the Israelite tribes. However, like any little brother refusing to be bullied, Benjamites were a tough little band.

The other boys finally came close enough for their words to be understood. Unbelievably, they were yelling Nathan's name. Jonathan risked speaking in a low voice from across the ravine.

"Stay down, Nathan! It's a trick."

"Thanks, Donkey Boy. I'd have never guessed that."

"Keep it up, Nathan. One day, I'll repay."

"But it's what you are."

"My family breeds donkeys. You make it sound like one birthed me."

"There is a resemblance."

Nathan stifled a yelp of pain as he felt Jonathan skip a pebble off his skull. However, a sly grin from his friend was all it took to soothe Nathan's wounded pride. He thought Jonathan could charm a bee out of its honey. Jonathan's infectious enthusiasm had enticed Nathan into many adventures, as well as the occasional whipping. Nathan turned his attention back to their opponents' curious strategy. Although this particular ruse had never been used before, deception was certainly permitted. Then Nathan heard the words which would forever change his life.

"Nathan! The Philistines found the forge!"

Both Nathan and Jonathan immediately sprang to their feet. The war game was most definitely over. No adult would dare utter the word *forge*, much less scream it across the countryside. A boy could expect sore, red buttocks as punishment. Followed by Jonathan and the other boys, Nathan raced for his village. He soon outdistanced the others, and for good reason. The secret iron forge was vital not just for his village or even their tribe of Benjamin, but for the entire people of Israel. The Philistines had established a monopoly on iron making as a way to control their more numerous Israelite neighbors. All iron forges were confined to Philistia. The sale of iron swords, iron spear heads and iron arrowheads to non-Philistines was forbidden. Even the possession of iron files for sharpening tools was restricted. Philistine spies ruthlessly sought out any unauthorized activity. Having found a forbidden iron forge, Nathan knew the Philistine soldiers would execute its blacksmith.

The man they sought was his father, Jotham.

A handful of influential Benjamites were engaged in a conspiracy to obtain iron technology. Jotham had volunteered to journey to the land of the Hittites and apprentice as an iron maker. During the two year apprenticeship, a leader named Kish assumed responsibility for Jotham's family. Nathan had become fast friends with Jonathan, a grandson of Kish. A few months ago, Jotham returned home as a skilled blacksmith. Jonathan's father, Saul, coordinated the efforts to obtain both the materials and the labor to build Jotham his forge. Now everyone and everything associated with the forge was in danger.

As he approached his home, Nathan spotted a group of Philistine soldiers blocking the road, but he easily evaded them. The small village consisted of eight houses, a few storage sheds and a common sheep pen. Nathan crept along the stone sheep pen, until he was barely one hundred feet away from the village center. Peering over the three-foot high wall, Nathan counted nineteen Philistine soldiers. They were busy herding fourteen Israelite men flushed from the buildings toward the open square. Nathan clenched his teeth when he spotted his father among them. Frightened women and children huddled between the houses and wept. In the distance, Nathan could see men from the neighboring farms approaching with axes and scythes. He feared they would be too late.

Once all the local men were lined up, a Philistine officer stepped forward and shouted for quiet. Nathan could hear only the whispers of mothers calming their sobbing children. The enemy commander silently paced past the sullen Benjamites, studying each man in turn. Then the Philistine gave a simple order.

"Show me your hands."

Nathan instantly understood the Philistine's tactic. Ordinary men might possess the same strong, calloused hands as Jotham. But only a blacksmith's hands were burned from

26

working with molten iron or stained by the ingredients used in the smelting process. The Philistine officer sauntered down the line, examining each man's hands in turn. Jotham stood in ninth position with his hands firmly behind his back. His father did not move when the officer stopped before him. Nathan saw the Philistine's lip curl in anger.

"Show me your hands, dog!"

Jotham brought both hands from behind his back, but they were not empty. Nathan's father had concealed an iron dagger about 15 inches long in the sleeve of his tunic. Jotham now lunged toward the officer with his weapon. The startled man yelped and narrowly avoided tripping over his own feet in his haste to escape. The three nearest soldiers drew swords to defend their commander. Jotham was a brave and strong man, but he was inexperienced at fighting with blades. He managed to dodge the sword thrust of one Philistine and even sliced the man's arm. However, this move left him open to a killing blow from another soldier. As the sword was pulled from his belly, Jotham soundlessly fell to his knees and then over on his side. The dust around his body quickly became bloody mud. A brief moment of stunned silence was broken by the screams and cries of the village inhabitants.

Nathan leaped up and screamed as well, but his voice was lost in the clamor. He was climbing over the stone fence when a powerful set of arms grabbed him around the waist and threw him on his back. He looked up to see Jonathan pinning him to the ground. Nathan started to yell in protest when Jonathan clamped a firm hand over his mouth. Jonathan had always been taller and stronger, but Nathan in his rage nearly broke free. Something Jonathan said finally got through to him.

"Nathan! Think of your mother! Think of your sister!"

Images of his mother Miriam and his two-year-old sister Leah flooded Nathan's mind. He closed his eyes and willed himself to settle down. Jonathan sensed the change, relaxed his grip and moved to one side. Feeling calmer, Nathan opened his eyes and sat up.

"Nathan, your father's dead. He'd expect you to look after your mother and your sister. You can't do that if you're dead too."

Through tear-filled eyes, he looked at Jonathan. His friend was crying as well. The other boys had disappeared. Only Jonathan remained.

"A time will come when you can avenge your father. And I will be there at your side. I swear."

Jonathan stood up, reached down and pulled Nathan to his feet. They looked toward the square where the Philistine officer was loudly berating one of his soldiers. It seemed a good time to depart. Jonathan clapped Nathan on the shoulder.

"Let's find your family."

As a veteran sergeant in the Philistine army, Rapa knew how to handle officers. You let officers think that they were right. You made officers feel as if they were in charge. You never let an officer know how much you actually ran things behind his back. Most of the time it was for their own good. The situation he faced right now was a perfect example. Rapa kept all emotion from his face as he listened to his flustered captain.

"Rapa, I had orders to take that blacksmith alive! I was supposed to torture him until he gave up the names of everyone involved in this forge. I made this very clear to everyone, didn't I?"

Before Rapa could open his mouth, his captain rushed on.

"You had two squads of heavily armed men. Two! And you could not take a man alive armed only with a knife! The soldier that killed the blacksmith must be flogged!"

Rapa felt the Hebrew's weapon was rather large for a knife, but kept that thought to himself. The captain must have thought so too, judging from how the man had wet himself when the blacksmith pulled out that crude blade.

"Which soldier was that, Sir?"

The captain went silent as he tried to identify the man in question. Seeing the uncertainty of his captain, Rapa seized the initiative.

"No problem. I'll handle it for you. Now, what are your orders, Sir?"

The distracted captain began considering what to do next. Inwardly, the sergeant breathed a sigh of relief. Rapa already knew it was Gezar, one of the new conscripts who made up more than half the platoon. Prior to three months ago, Gezar had never handled anything deadlier than a fish net. Privately, Rapa was impressed by how Gezar had dispatched the blacksmith so skillfully. A soldier's first kill was always the hardest.

Rapa was also pleased with his handling of the captain. The busy officer was unlikely follow up on the matter. He would be too embarrassed to admit not knowing the name of one of his own men. Rather than being ordered to flog anyone, Rapa had instead secured his captain's permission to handle the matter himself. Oh, Rapa would deal very strongly with Gezar, but not flog him before the rest of the company. The last thing Rapa wanted was to go into battle with men who feared punishment for being too aggressive.

"Besides," Rapa thought as he stared at his captain's back, *"I didn't see you jump in there to disarm the blacksmith."*

"Very well, Rapa. The next best thing would be to arrest the blacksmith's family. They might know who was working with him. Round up the women and start questioning them. Hold their children, too. The answers will come faster that way."

Rapa's response was to look over the captain's shoulder.

"Ah, Sir?"

At first, the captain seemed oblivious to what attracted Rapa's attention. The sergeant could not believe the fool was unaware of how dangerous their situation was becoming. Every woman and child had vanished. There were only Hebrew men visible. Many more than lived in this village. Carrying scythes, axes, and other sharp farm implements. With each passing minute, more silent Hebrew men drifted into the village. A platoon of fifty Philistine soldiers had come in search of the Hebrew iron forge, but most were elsewhere. Two squads were blocking the roads and one squad was busy destroying the clandestine forge. There were fewer than twenty soldiers actually in the village. The Philistines were presently outnumbered two to one, with the odds growing steadily worse. Rapa exhaled in relief as his captain finally caught on.

"Rapa, our mission is finished. We have eliminated the forge and blacksmith as ordered. Form the men up to return to barracks."

"Yes, Sir."

Rapa smiled as he turned away. No extra handling was required.

Nathan initially panicked upon finding his small house undisturbed, but empty. Level-headed Jonathan calmly insisted this was actually a good thing. It meant Miriam and her young daughter were both safely hidden away. Nathan numbly followed Jonathan to his friend's home in Gibeah. Jonathan's father, Saul, immediately left to make inquiries. Jonathan's mother, Ahinoam, swept Nathan into the kitchen where a comforting plate of food was placed in his hands. As he numbly chewed, Nathan considered how swiftly his life had crumbled. An hour ago, he had been a young soldier in training. Now he was just a frightened little boy who barely felt Ahinoam stroking his hair. She assured him that his mother would head straight to this very house as soon as the threat had passed. Soon Nathan's fatigue overcame his fears.

Jonathan's gentle shaking woke Nathan from a fitful sleep a short time later. He was ashamed to be dozing off during such a crisis, even though it must be well past midnight. Clearing his head, Nathan recognized Miriam's voice from the next room. Saul's late night search had ended in success. In an instant, Nathan was tightly hugging his mother and his sleepy sister. After a brief, but heartfelt, reunion, Miriam handed her daughter over to Saul's wife, who discreetly took the toddler into the kitchen. Left alone with his mother, Nathan summoned his courage to answer her questions.

Miriam wept softly as Nathan described the death of her husband.

"What are your plans, Nathan?"

Miriam's question caught Nathan off-guard. It wasn't so much what his mother asked as how she asked it. He sensed their relationship had suddenly changed with his father's death. By tradition, the oldest son ascended to the family leadership. The intent of his mother's question now struck home. She was asking if he wished to take on his father's responsibilities. Of course if Nathan was not ready, Miriam was fully capable of running things until he matured. Yet, Nathan felt the urge to relieve as much of his mother's burden as possible. It required only a heartbeat to make his decision.

"I'll talk to Saul."

Miriam searched Nathan's face briefly before nodding her understanding. Her son was going to make arrangements for their care...and she approved. Nathan then left her and walked over to Jonathan's father.

"Saul, I need to speak with you."

"Nathan, you've had a trying day. Maybe it should wait until tomorrow?"

"It's about my family."

Saul looked thoughtfully at Nathan and seemed to realize at that moment he was no longer dealing with a mere boy. He nodded and led Nathan outside to a bench beside the house. Saul began to speak as if he were addressing an equal.

"What do you want to do, Nathan?"

"Take care of my family."

"Very commendable. What skills do you have?"

"I was going to be my father's apprentice, but..."

"I know. That's no longer possible. Let's get to the heart of the matter. Your father became a blacksmith at the behest of my people. That is why he died. Therefore, we bear some responsibility for his loss."

"I never meant to blame..."

"I know you didn't. However, I wish to offer assistance. Will you accept it?"

"Of course."

"Then sleep under my roof tonight. Your old home is no longer safe. Tomorrow I will rearrange the servant quarters so that your family can have the small house behind mine. I'll buy your old house from you, if you wish. We'll also discuss your wages. You may work for me until such time as you choose to move on."

"We will be most grateful."

"I still need to talk to my father, but I'm sure Kish will approve these arrangements."

Nathan felt a deep sense of relief as he reentered the house with Saul. At the very least, he would be able to provide food and shelter for his family. Nathan shuddered as he faced yet another dreadful task. Little Leah toddled over to Nathan and held out her arms in the universal request to be picked up. Secure in her brother's arms, she used her higher viewpoint to search the room. She finally gave Nathan a concerned look and voiced what was on her tiny heart.

"Abba?"

Nathan hugged his sister tightly as they cried together. The first of the nightmares came to Nathan shortly after that.

Chapter 2 - The Traitor

So, the children of Israel encamped against the city of Gibeah. Then the Benjamites came out of Gibeah, and on that day cut down twenty-two thousand men of the Israelites. The children of Israel wept before the LORD until evening, and asked the LORD "Shall I again battle against the children of my brother Benjamin?" And the LORD said, "Go up against him." And Benjamin went out against them from Gibeah on the second day, and cut down eighteen thousand more of the Israelites. Then all the children of Israel wept and fasted that day until evening. They offered burnt offerings and peace offerings before the LORD and asked, "Shall I yet again go out to battle against the children of my brother Benjamin, or shall I cease?" And the LORD said, "Go up, for tomorrow I will deliver them into your hand."

From the Book of Judges, Chapter 20, verses 19, 21, 23, 25, 26 and 28

A father of the fatherless, and a defender of widows, is God in his holy dwelling.

From Psalm 68, verse 5

Saul's home outside the town of Gibeah

Nathan looked on with pride as his father stoked the new iron forge for the first time. Jotham had brought their small family to the secluded location in the foothills for this special occasion. Miriam divided her attention between admiring her husband's skill and keeping curious little Leah away from the flames. Although his mother and sister might never return here, the forge represented Nathan's future occupation. After a few years of apprenticing with Jotham, Nathan could marry, move to a new village and start his own iron works. By then, they would have supplied their tribe of Benjamin with enough weapons to finally break the Philistine iron monopoly.

A man with no face suddenly materialized behind Jotham. Intent on his work, Nathan's father was oblivious to the dark figure's sword. Nathan tried to scream, but though his throat burned raw with the effort, no sound came from his mouth. He watched in horror as the unknown assailant skewered his father and allowed the body to fall lifeless on the dirt. The silent murderer now turned toward Nathan's newly widowed mother and orphaned sister, but the two seemed strangely unaware of Jotham's fate. Nathan lunged forward to their rescue, but felt himself pulled backwards by strong hands. He looked over his shoulder into the tearful eyes of Jonathan. Nathan pleaded with his friend, but the grip on his arms only tightened. When he turned back, his mother, sister and the mysterious figure had vanished. Nathan assumed that his family had fled with the killer in hot pursuit. He coiled his body before exploding in a mighty effort to break free.

The next thing Nathan knew, he was sprawled on a packed dirt floor beside a crude bed.

Nathan sat up and leaned against the bed in bewilderment, cold sweat dripping from his armpits. His clouded mind began separating nightmare from reality. Nathan relived his father's death but took comfort in the knowledge that his mother and sister were safe in Saul's household.

Though part fantasy, the dream drove home important truths to Nathan. First, the threat to his family remained. Second, his father's blood called out for justice...no, for vengeance. Israelite justice was an eye for an eye and a life for a life. Nathan would not be satisfied merely with the death of Jotham's murderer. He wanted vengeance tenfold, a hundredfold, a thousandfold, on everything Philistine. It was an improbable quest for a twelve-year-old boy, yet honor demanded it. He was still brooding when Jonathan peeked through the door at sunrise.

"Leave me be, Jonathan."

"There's food ready."

"Not hungry."

"Yes, you are."

"You don't know what I need, Donkey Boy."

"True, but I doubt hunger is it. And mother makes a great breakfast."

"You never listen to me."

"I never listen to anyone. Eat breakfast, and I promise never to ask another favor."

"You always say that. It's never true."

"At least I'm predictable. C'mon, Nathan. If you come to breakfast, you can call me some more funny names."

Jonathan's impish grin finally broke through Nathan's moodiness. It reminded him of his father's smile. Jotham would have considered sulking in the dark to be cowardly. He extended his hand, and Jonathan pulled him to his feet. Nathan followed his friend into the kitchen where Jonathan's mother Ahinoam had food waiting. Nathan sat down at the table between Miriam and Leah, just as his father would have done. Ahinoam tried to engage her guests in conversation, with little success. Then Nathan recognized the voices of Saul and Kish coming through the window. Their angry words caused everyone inside to stop talking.

"But Father, Jotham died for our cause!"

"He wasn't the first, Saul. He won't be the last."

"There's still his family."

"They are in God's hands, not mine."

"You never used to hide behind pious words. Has age tightened your purse strings?"

"Watch your tongue, Saul. I already employ more men around here than we really need. We also share our bounty with the neighbors."

"While keeping the best for ourselves."

"Our family is not responsible for every beggar in Benjamin!"

"It's only three people, Father. They will earn their keep."

"Fine, Saul. You house them. You feed them. You pay them."

After the two men walked out of earshot, everyone resumed eating in awkward silence. Once the meal was finished, Ahinoam suggested Jonathan take Nathan out to tend the donkeys. Sensing the two mothers wished to speak in private, Nathan agreed to help. In truth, Nathan wanted something to do. Physical labor had a marvelous capacity to help his mind focus. Nathan methodically reexamined the previous day's events while carrying fodder and water to the impatient animals. After an hour, he finally asked Jonathan the question weighing most heavily on his mind.

"How did the Philistines find the iron forge?"

Nathan recognized his future plans depended on this answer. Much thought had gone into the selection of the forge's location. Some old Canaanite ruins along a stream in a small valley became the chosen site. The forge could be built behind the old walls without attracting the same attention as new construction. There was ample water and storage available. The valley could be accessed from the surrounding hills through several secluded routes. Ore and fuel could be brought in and iron taken out. Only close examination would reveal the forge's smoke was not from one of the nearby homesteads. A lookout was constantly maintained from the valley rim. If any threat were spotted, Jotham was to douse the fires and blend in with his neighbors. Nathan could find no flaw in the planning. Yet, Jonathan replied without hesitation.

"The Philistines did not find the forge, Nathan. They were led to it."

Nathan dropped his bucket and stared at Jonathan in wonder. The swift answer indicated that his friend had been considering the same question. Nathan blurted out his first thought.

"A traitor?"

"Perhaps a traitor, Nathan, but definitely a spy."

"Who could have done such a thing?"

"That, my Friend, is what we must find out."

Nathan turned his fallen bucket upside down to sit on while considering this sudden revelation. It not only explained the discovery of the forge, but also how the Philistines knew where to seek its blacksmith. Jonathan shoved a donkey aside and sat on the manger opposite Nathan.

"Suppose you are right, Jonathan."

"Aren't I always?"

"So many people were involved. I've no idea where to start."

"Fortunately, I do. Here's what I think, Nathan. Our spy must meet two requirements. He has visited the forge. He has dealings with the Philistines, probably at their outpost in Gibeon."

Nathan mulled over Jonathan's assumptions. The Philistine platoon had indeed come from the garrison at Gibeon. The next task would be to identify someone with access to both the forge and the Philistines. He immediately eliminated any of the local women. None, except his mother, had ever been to the forge and an Israelite woman speaking with a Philistine would attract attention. It couldn't have been a child, as Nathan was the only one with access. That left the men of Kish's family, the forge builders, the lookouts and the suppliers. Nathan clenched his fists in frustration.

"That still leaves more than twenty men, Jonathan. How do we find the spy?"

"Have at least a little faith in me, Nathan. It's simple. We watch the Philistine outpost at Gibeon. Anyone from the forge who shows up is our spy."

"He might never meet the Philistines again."

"I think he will."

"Why?"

"To collect his pay."

Nathan was sickened that one of their tribe might betray his father for money. He grew pessimistic.

"What if the spy did not work for money? The Philistines could've threatened his family."

"I doubt it, Nathan. We'd know if the Philistines started harassing people."

"Well, the spy might already have been paid."

"Philistines never pay for anything in advance. They'd want to see the forge first. Besides, your father's death has created uproar. Our spy would feel safer waiting a few days to collect his blood money."

"How long must we keep watch? The spy might never show up!"

"You have something more pressing to do, my Friend?"

The Philistine garrisoned town of Gibeon

As imperfect as Jonathan's logic might be, it was Nathan's only hope. The next step was to arrange a clandestine journey to Gibeon, some ten miles away. However, Nathan was now working for Saul, and his absence would raise questions. His mother would doubtless be incensed if his real reason became known. Once again, his friend's charm worked its wonders. Jonathan requested that he and Nathan be allowed to sojourn in the hills to grieve Jotham's death. Saul readily agreed and provided the boys with a donkey and provisions for a week. Nathan and Jonathan left the next morning, but once out of sight, they took the road to Gibeon.

By noon the boys had found a secluded site with a clear view of the Philistine outpost. They endured heat, dust and boredom for three days, but not a single Israelite ventured inside. It was on the fourth day that a familiar face came down the road. It was Micah the woodcutter. He had supplied wood to make charcoal for the forge. Nathan shook off his drowsiness and poked the napping Jonathan. Micah neared the path leading to the outpost...and continued right on past. A powerful wave of disappointment nearly caused Nathan to miss Micah tossing something backwards. A small shiny object bounced near the feet of the sentry at the gate. The Philistine waited until Micah entered Gibeon's marketplace before retrieving the mysterious item and taking it inside.

Nathan followed the woodcutter while Jonathan watched the Philistine outpost. A few minutes later, Micah sat on a stone bench beside a busy well, placed a sack between his feet and opened it. Nathan found a spot behind some watering camels where he could covertly observe the suspected spy. When the camels' thirst was finally quenched, the woodcutter still had not moved. Thankfully, Nathan remained concealed when a herd of donkeys replaced the departing camels. Then Nathan noticed a new arrival at the well. It was the Philistine officer his father had tried to stab.

Nathan's heart nearly stopped when a hand suddenly grabbed his shoulder from behind. He turned to see the smirking face of Jonathan. His friend gestured towards the Philistine.

"He left the garrison a few minutes ago and marched straight over here. Look at his right hand."

Nathan saw something clutched in the Philistine's fist. Strolling around the well, the officer seemed to stare at everyone except the woodcutter. This unwanted attention caused all the Israelites to turn away. Stopping in front of Micah, the Philistine put his hands behind his back. Nathan and Jonathan were probably the only people whose view was not blocked by the Philistine's body. The officer carefully fondled a small leather pouch with a drawstring. Seconds later, the pouch plunked into the woodcutter's open sack. The Philistine made another circuit around the well and left. Micah remained seated for nearly an hour before departing. Nathan started after the woodcutter, but was restrained by Jonathan. He angrily hissed at his friend.

"He's getting away!"

"We know where he lives, Nathan. Now we talk with my father."

Jonathan was shrewd enough to wait until they could be alone in a barn with his father. Nathan winced at the severe tongue lashing they both received. Saul then questioned them at length on the day's events. The older man gave them a final admonishment to do nothing and say nothing before shooing them from the barn. Nathan received a sly wink from Jonathan as they went out the door. Yet, the next few days rolled by quietly without any sign of unusual activity.

One week later, a tired Saul returned home well after dark. His wife brought the food she had saved for her husband from the evening meal. Saul ate alone and in silence. Afterwards, he asked Nathan and Jonathan to join him outside. The moonlight allowed Nathan to discern the anguish etched into Saul's face.

"I took five men to visit Micah tonight. We asked him about his business with the Philistines. Micah denied everything. So, two men held him down while the rest of us searched his house. Found the pouch of silver. Micah finally admitted the meeting, but claimed it concerned wood for the garrison. I threw the silver pieces in his lying face and asked how many years it took to cut that much wood. Micah confessed and begged for mercy."

Saul paused to look up at the stars overhead. The uncomfortable silence was broken by Jonathan.

"So what happened?"

"We filled the house with some of Micah's wood and burned it down."

"That hardly sounds like a fitting punishment."

"Micah was in the house at the time, Son."

Saul started to go back inside, then turned and faced the boys.

"Kish and I had a talk. What you two did was clever, but dangerous. You should have come to me from the very first. Did you even consider that Micah might be working for us against the Philistines? Kish employs men for things like that. Your childish attempts at spying could have endangered other lives."

"We hadn't thought of that, Father."

"And that's the worst part – not thinking. You two will be men soon. You both should know better. Kish and I have decided. We can't have you doing things like this on your own. It could disrupt other efforts against the Philistines."

Nathan felt a heavy weight in the pit of his stomach. Jonathan and he faced severe consequences for their reckless behavior. Nathan could think of nothing worse than entering manhood already in disgrace. Who knew how many years his vengeful ambitions would be delayed while he earned back that lost trust. When Nathan was finally able to look Saul in the eye, he was surprised to see a smile waiting for him.

"So, Kish and I talked things over. Both of you will work with us now... in the fight against the Philistines."

Chapter 3 - The Benjamite League

That night the Israelites set men in ambush all around the city of Gibeah. On the third day, the children of Israel attacked the city of Gibeah just as they had the previous two times. So the children of Benjamin went out after the Israelites and were drawn away from the city. Then Israel's men in ambush burst forth from their position in the plain of Geba. These ten thousand select Israelites captured the city of Gibeah after a fierce battle. The rest of the Benjamites did not know they were now cut off and that disaster was upon them. So the LORD defeated Benjamin before Israel. That day the children of Israel destroyed twenty-five thousand one hundred Benjamites who drew the sword. But six hundred men of Benjamin escaped through the wilderness to the Rock of Rimmon where they hid for four months. Meanwhile, the men of Israel turned back against the children of Benjamin, and struck them down with the edge of the sword—from every city, man and beast, all that were found. They also set fire to all the Benjamite cities they came to.

From the Book of Judges, Chapter 20, verses 29, 30, 31, 33, 34, 25, 47 and 48

Saul's home outside the town of Gibeah

The next morning Nathan awoke as a very frightened and confused twelve year-old. It required all his concentration merely to sit up and place his feet on the dirt floor. Sleep had not come easily the previous night, but that was not surprising. He and Jonathan had been in a state of euphoria after learning how their amateur sleuthing had exposed the traitor Micah and

46

brought about his execution. Nathan thought it especially fitting that the man responsible for his father's murder was sent into the flames of Hades by being burned to death. He had gone to sleep feeling a little less angry at God over Jotham's murder. That only made what happened last night all the more jarring.

Inexplicably, the nightmare of his father's death returned to haunt Nathan. The details were even more vivid and lurid than before, but the worst part was a new ending. This time, Jotham looked directly into his son's eyes and scowled as he lay bleeding out. The thought his father might be displeased with him was both perplexing and unbearable. Nathan had expected Micah's execution to bring him peace, not torment. His distress left him deaf to a cheery voice approaching his room.

"I'm not going to keep dragging you to breakfast, Nathan. It's time you started...hey! Hey. What's wrong?"

"The nightmare."

"Again? Pay no attention to it, my friend. Your father is avenged. Your family is safe. You won!"

Lips trembling, Nathan proceeded to recount every aspect of his nightmare in agonizing detail. Jonathan kneeled on the floor and placed his hands on Nathan's knees while listening in silence. When Nathan fell to sobbing at the end, he felt Jonathan's strong arms hugging him gently.

"Nathan, your father still loves you. Trust me."

"Then why did he look at me with such anger?"

"Well, he can't be mad at you, so it must be something else."

"All right then...what?"

"Perhaps Micah's death is not enough. Remember, that piece of dung didn't actually kill your father."

"Right. It was some cursed foot soldier. But I didn't even see his face, Jonathan, did you?"

"No, his back was to us."

"Then it's hopeless. There're over a hundred Philistines at Gibeon. I'd never be sure which one was the murderer."

"So kill them all."

"I'll say one thing for you, Donkey Boy. You don't think small."

"It runs in the family, Nathan. Besides, you don't have to kill them all at once."

"Oh, sure. They'll each patiently wait their turn for an Israelite boy to slit their Philistine throats."

"And I never said you had to do it alone."

"Wonderful. We can each kill fifty."

"I meant the Benjamite League, Wise Ass. Remember what my father said? We're going to become members!"

"Are we old enough, Jonathan?"

"Times are hard. The League's been taking anyone who's had his "Manhood" ceremony. We'll both be thirteen in a few months, so age won't be the problem."

"Implying there's a different problem."

"The League may be reluctant to attack the Gibeon garrison. That's more ambitious than the raids they usually pull off. However, we have an advantage. Both my father and grandfather are Benjamite League leaders."

"Then persuading the League will become a full-time job for me."

"You mean for us. And try to be more positive. Think of it as an adventure."

The origins of the Benjamite League stretched back many generations, to the time of Nathan's grandfather's grandfather. It was birthed by the near annihilation of the tribe of Benjamin during a civil war when its warriors stood alone against the entire Nation of Israel. Such was their fighting prowess, that *twice* the audacious Benjamites decimated an army ten times larger than their own. However, the other tribes learned invaluable lessons from these galling defeats. During the third battle, they managed to ambush and slaughter the smaller Benjamite force. The victors then swept across the land of Benjamin in a blood-crazed frenzy, avenging their previous losses by killing every living thing they found. When vengeance finally gave way to reason, six hundred warriors were all that remained of Benjamin. Feeling remorse for their rampage, the Israelite Elders decreed that enough virgins be procured to provide a wife for each surviving Benjamite man. Naturally, kidnapping six hundred girls from their families required additional acts of violence and treachery. Their collective conscience thus cleared, the triumphant eleven tribes went home leaving Benjamin to rebuild its devastated land and nurse bitter memories. The Benjamites became a very clannish people with a smoldering distrust of their Israelite brethren.

Out of desperation, the six hundred male survivors banded together in the Benjamite League, pledging to preserve the smallest of the Israelite tribes. Their initial goals were rather mundane: obtain food and shelter while fathering as many offspring as possible. The League's founders successfully achieved the latter goal, for tens of thousands of their descendants presently occupied the land of their inheritance. The League became the focal point of a Benjamite revival which promoted tribal unity as the best means of survival. It also ensured their military traditions were passed on to subsequent generations. The leaders of the League resolved to never again be victimized...by anyone.

Unfortunately, zeal rarely survives a few generations of peace and prosperity. Clan loyalties surpassed tribal allegiance over time and the League's influence waned. This cultural shift came at a very inopportune moment for Benjamin; for nothing attracts the attention of the greedy more than someone else's good fortune...and few peoples were greedier than the Philistines. The five kings of Philistia had made numerous attempts over the years to dispossess the Israelites from their lands. A crushing defeat at hands of the Israelite judge Samuel a generation before had temporarily disrupted, but failed to halt, the Philistine expansion. Smarting from their humiliating loss, the Philistines grew ever more clever and patient. They offered seductive incentives to their neighbors for cooperation and were careful never to steal enough to unite all of Israel against them. Naturally, a wily predator always goes after the weakest animal in the herd first.

That predatory logic led Maoch, King of Gath, to target Benjamin for annexation. Gath had been encroaching on Benjamin's boundaries for several decades by slowly pushing forward trading outposts and planting garrisons. These Philistine incursions caused some Benjamite leaders, such as Jonathan's grandfather Kish, to revive the League as a fighting force. Sadly, the old unity was absent. A few valiant men responded to the League's call to arms, but most Benjamites were content to make small concessions to avoid war with a more advanced military power. Whenever a handful of patriots resisted, the Philistines provided just enough retaliation to discourage others from coming to their aid. Fewer men answered the League's call with each passing year.

It was at this low tide of the League's fortunes that two young members were added to its roster. Saul brought Nathan and Jonathan into Kish's band soon after each reached his thirteenth year. Jonathan was the first to go through the time-honored ceremony where a priest blessed his passage into manhood. Nathan had his turn a month later, but it was a bittersweet occasion. The participation of the boy's father was an important part of the ceremony, but Jotham could not be there for Nathan. Saul thoughtfully filled in so that Nathan did not have to stand alone before the priest.

Nathan was initially excited at the prospect of taking the field against the hated Philistines until Saul explained the painful reality. Nathan and Jonathan would receive regular training with sling, spear and bow, but their time as warriors was still several years off. In fact, neither boy would even be allowed to carry a personal weapon. A crestfallen Nathan realized the dreams of drenching his hands in Philistine blood would have to wait. According to Saul, it was a simple matter of numbers.

"Tell me, Nathan, how many warriors make up an *eleph*?

"Seventy?"

"Close enough. In my youth, our clan raised sixteen *elephs* of warriors for Samuel, just over a thousand men. There are two other clans in Kish's district besides ours. Guess how many *elephs* my father can count on today."

"Uh, forty?"

"Not even one."

"None?"

"Jonathan tells me you want to attack Gibeon, to avenge your father. Did you know the League planned to do that last year?"

"What happened?"

"Fewer than fifty poorly armed men responded to Kish's summons and the attempt was quietly abandoned. It's not something my father wants widely known."

"Have our people become cowards, Saul?"

"No, just discouraged. Our men are brave, but not foolish. They refuse to die for nothing. They need hope, and that only comes from victory."

"If enough men fight, we will have victory!"

"But until there is victory, our numbers will remain small. That is our dilemma."

"Jonathan and I have hope. We will fight."

"Unfortunately, two more inexperienced fighters won't make a difference."

"But I thought you needed us, Saul."

"We have plans for you and my son. Important plans. Can you read or write?"

"No."

"Then that's where your training starts. A Levite comes by one day a week to teach Jonathan from the writings of Moses. I'll make arrangements to include you."

"My family...I can't afford it."

"Consider it part of your wages."

"I don't need to read to kill Philistines."

"Benjamin needs trained leaders more than a few dead Philistines. Trust me, Nathan; you'll kill far more this way."

And that was Nathan's dilemma, for he did indeed trust Saul. He just didn't always believe him.

Although Nathan would never admit it, reading proved to be surprisingly enjoyable. His Levite tutor had cleverly drawn Nathan's first lessons from the most exciting passages of Israelite history. He found writing to be more of a chore, but saw it offered definite benefits. Once Nathan had mastered tracing his alphabet in the dirt, he advanced to a stylus and clay tablets. It would be a long time before he would be entrusted with expensive leather scrolls, but Nathan was content to wait. His tutor had piqued his interest with a pithy bit of wisdom.

Scrolls never forget.

Education turned out to be only a small part of Nathan's and Jonathan's lives. In the coming weeks, the Benjamite League's two youngest members became its busiest. Kish made regular use of Nathan and Jonathan as messengers, lookouts and scouts. Their youth proved to be a significant advantage for these missions, as they drew less attention than grown men. And lacking arms, the boys could plead innocence when questioned by the Philistines. Nathan earned great respect for his skills in tracking Philistine patrols, tax collectors and spies. Nevertheless, he recognized merely watching the enemy would not save his people. And his dreaded nightmare still returned from time to time. Being busy definitely helped Nathan sleep peacefully for days at a time, but the fearful visions still haunted many of his nights.

A few months of assignments gave Nathan more exposure to other Benjamites than in his previous thirteen years. He found the fickleness of his fellow tribesmen sometimes as troublesome as anything the Philistines did. The League's tactics seemed to drive away almost as many adherents as they attracted. Executing the traitorous woodcutter Micah was a prime example. Many Benjamites believed the League's action was excessive and withdrew their support from Kish's *eleph*. On the other hand, these same people eagerly sought the League's assistance if personally oppressed. When three Philistine soldiers molested a teenage girl from Gibeah, no one complained when Kish's band provided immediate retribution. The rising sun revealed the mutilated corpses of the rapists hanging from Gibeah's main gate. The Philistine response was both swift and brutal. All Israelite crops and storage barns along the highway between Gibeon and Gibeah were burned. The entire region teetered on the brink of starvation for months, but the Philistines never touched another woman from Gibeah. Nathan was greatly vexed by his neighbors' willingness to suffer for the purity of their daughters, and their apathy toward the death of his father. The relationship between his people and the Philistines proved to be very complex.

Saul once confided to Nathan that the Philistines' greatest threat to Benjamin was not military, but economic. The Philistines possessed a vast commercial empire due to their seafaring heritage. A fortune in trade goods passed through the ports of their coastal kingdoms each year. The Israelites grew ever more dependent on their rivals both to import certain items and to export Israelite wares. The Philistines used their wealth and military might to maintain profitable monopolies, such as the iron trade. Nathan always grew bitter thinking how his father had died to benefit a gang of foreign merchants. Philistine commerce directly impacted Kish's recruiting efforts because the Philistines excluded known members of the Benjamite League from the profitable traffic in trade goods. Nathan heard Kish grumble that the Philistines would never conquer Israel. They would simply buy it.

Nathan determined to make the Philistines pay a higher price than they ever dreamed.

Chapter 4 - The First Move

Now these are the nations which the LORD left in the land, that He might test Israel by them. (This was also so that future generations of Israel might be taught to know war.) Namely, five lords of the Philistines, all the Canaanites, the Sidonians, and the Hivites.

From the Book of Judges, Chapter 3, verses 1 to 3

The Royal Palace of the Philistine Kingdom of Gath

When Maoch crossed his palace courtyard that morning, he had no inkling one of his border garrisons had turned a young Benjamite boy into a blood enemy. Not that the King of Gath would have cared. Acquiring enemies was inevitable for a king. When people got in his way, as Jotham had, they died. Maoch was a cunning, ambitious and ruthless tyrant with dreams of greatness. Today he was just one member of the *Sarney*, a council made up of the five kings of Philistia. His capital of Gath differed little from the other principal Philistine cities of Gaza, Ashkelon, Ashdod and Ekron. Maoch believed that Philistia could be much more than it was, but not with five separate rulers. The Philistine position in Canaan was too precarious for that luxury.

Some might question whether Maoch even deserved the title of *king*. He and his four peers were supposedly sworn vassals of the Egyptian Empire. By treaty, their Canaanite holdings belonged to Pharaoh. It was an arrangement forced on Maoch's ancestors after their failed invasion of Egypt. In return for land, the Philistines served as a buffer between Egypt and the Hittite Empire. Survival, much less prosperity, was a constant challenge. No Philistine city-state counted more than thirty thousand pure-blood citizens, meaning the other Canaanite inhabitants vastly outnumbered them. However, two factors allowed Philistia to dominate Canaan's Mediterranean coast. First, their more numerous neighbors were divided into dozens of petty kingdoms and squabbling tribes. Second, the Philistine kings possessed the most advanced military units in the region. Maoch concluded long ago that a bold leader could shape Philistia into an empire to rival either the Egyptians or the Hittites. That thought hurried his steps toward a meeting which might bring Maoch's imperial dreams closer to fruition.

As Maoch strode into his private chamber, he was met by Abimelek, his chief administrator or *Archon*. As Gath's *Archon*, Abimelek was a frequent visitor to this cloistered room. The man might be the king's most trusted advisor, but Maoch knew better than to completely trust anyone, including his own sons. Maoch remembered all too well how he had risen to the throne of Gath.

Waiting behind the *Archon* was a Gath merchant named Lakzig, a man who trafficked in iron products, particularly weapons. The merchant had been escorted here by Maoch's bodyguards through a hidden passage to mask Lakzig's other occupation as one of Abimelek's spies. The king rarely met any of Abimelek's shadowy minions, but today was special. Lakzig's information was so vital that Maoch insisted on questioning the spy face to face.

The king gestured to his bodyguards who closed the doors as they silently departed. Once Maoch was seated, Abimelek and Lakzig prostrated themselves on the floor before rising to a kneeling position. Abimelek then prompted Lakzig to begin his report.

"My King, during a recent trip up the Nile, I carried samples of iron weapons to a number of Egyptian nobles selected by Abimelek. I left Memphis three weeks ago..."

Maoch held up his hand to stop the spy in mid-sentence.

"Are the rumors about the Egyptian outpost at Rafah true?"

Lakzig looked at Abimelek in fearful confusion. The *Archon* impatiently prompted the spy to skip ahead in his tale. Lakzig swallowed deeply while rapidly re-organizing his thoughts to accommodate the king's request.

"Yes, Lord, they are. The Egyptian garrison at Rafah is being reduced... again."

"How many soldiers will remain?"

"A company of infantry and a half squadron of chariots. 120 men, more or less."

Maoch held up one finger to silence Lakzig while he put this recent intelligence into context. Rafah was the closest Egyptian outpost to Gath. Sitting astride the major coastal trade route between Africa and Asia, the Egyptian garrison at Rafah provided security to many rich caravans. The Egyptians also collected hefty revenues from merchants for the privilege of doing business in Egypt. At its peak, Rafah was garrisoned by over four hundred infantry backed by three full squadrons of chariots. Every few months, a company of infantry and a squadron of chariots rotated back to Egypt. Maoch's interest was piqued a year ago when Abimelek determined fewer Egyptians were being sent to Rafah than were returning to Egypt. Up to now, the reductions were negligible. However, if Lakzig's reports were accurate, Rafah's strength had just been slashed drastically.

"Why are the Egyptians doing this now?"

"Civil war, my Lord. A faction in Thebes plots to replace Pharaoh with a young nephew. Pharaoh is recalling loyal troops from the borders to his capital in Memphis."

"Could Pharaoh fall?"

"It is possible, my King. The Royal Court at Memphis is afraid. The Egyptian nobles are more concerned with ending up on the stronger side than honoring their oaths. Meanwhile, Pharaoh is scraping together several field divisions from his outlying garrisons. He intends to move them about to protect his power."

The king rose without a word and walked to a balcony just off the meeting chamber. Lakzig appeared confused by the king's seemingly erratic behavior, but Abimelek was accustomed to Maoch's mercurial attention span. Judging the interview to be over, Abimelek discreetly dismissed Lakzig.

The *Archon* returned to find his king still gazing out over the city of Gath. He had served Maoch for nearly two decades, and yet the impulsive king still managed to surprise him. Now that they were alone, Abimelek rested his plump body in a chair and waited for Maoch to disclose his latest scheme. When

Abimelek judged enough time had passed, he coughed discreetly.

"The longer your moods last, Maoch, the riskier the enterprise."

"Egypt is but a pale reflection of its former glory, Abimelek. Her chaos is our opportunity."

"Becoming entangled in Egypt's internal affairs is hazardous for small states like ours. We have always been content to bide our time while Egypt feeds on itself. Our strategy is working. Why take risks now?"

"Rafah is ripe for the taking. A vital trade route would come under my control. Our coffers would swell with taxes from the caravans."

"Setting aside the Egyptians for a moment, Maoch, think about the other Philistine kings. Will the *Sarney* allow you to drag Philistia into a war with Egypt? I doubt it."

"Rafah will be mine before the *Sarney* even hears about it."

"Then consider this, Maoch. Both Gaza and Ashkelon are closer to Rafah than Gath is. They may feel entitled to it."

"And what if they do? Ashkelon suffers from a poor harvest. The King of Gaza is a schemer, not a warrior. Neither will move on Rafah while the Egyptians are still there. No, the timing is perfect for us."

"Even a crippled Egypt is more than Gath can take on alone, Maoch. My diplomatic skills may not save us this time."

"You're becoming an old woman, Abimelek. Ask yourself this: why should I fight the Egyptians when they are perfectly willing to war among themselves? Now is a time for cunning. We won't be so crude as to attack the Egyptians at Rafah. We will merely *displace* them."

"This *old woman* wonders how many soldiers are required for this *displacement*?"

"Surprisingly few, Abimelek. It's just a question of using them properly. We've already planned it out."

"We?"

"Phicol, the First Regiment commander, and I have devised the necessary tactics."

"I know of Phicol. He's aggressive like you, Maoch. However, provisioning even a small expedition in the field requires much preparation, perhaps weeks."

"I need only set Phicol and fifty chariots in motion tomorrow."

The Egyptian garrison at Rafah

Meni wondered whom he had offended at the Royal Court to be placed in such an awful predicament. Being appointed the new Egyptian commander at Rafah was supposed to be a high point of his military career. The first shock had come when he had arrived two months ago with a single company of replacements only to learn that the entire garrison of three hundred soldiers was returning to Memphis. Meni was expected to hold Egypt's most isolated outpost with only one hundred twenty-seven men and ten chariots. The next jolt came three weeks later when the monthly supplies failed to arrive from Pelusium. Meni had immediately dispatched a chariot westward to request a resupply. Meanwhile, he tried to cover the shortfall by purchasing food locally. However, knowledge of the outpost's predicament caused prices to soar, quickly depleting the garrison's wealth. After two more weeks of fruitless waiting, Meni sent three more of his precious chariots for help. Now on half rations, his impoverished soldiers scavenged the countryside, only to have the locals disappear with their food.

Meni even began accepting food in lieu of gold from the passing caravans. However, this stopgap measure provided little relief as caravans carried barely enough provisions to get to their next destination. Since Rafah's mission was to protect the trade route traffic, Meni could ill afford to starve the caravans. Newly collected tolls replenished Rafah's treasury, but there was no food to buy. Having been robbed once, people refused to bring out their hidden caches, even when offered gold.

When assistance finally arrived, it came from the east, not the west, in the form of fifty Philistine chariots from Gath. Their commander, Phicol, reported that Arabu raiders were ravaging the land. Phicol regretted his soldiers carried only enough food for themselves. Naturally, they would share a little with their Egyptian allies while Phicol requested supplies from Gath. Meni warily noted that each Philistine chariot carried two soldiers in addition to the usual driver and archer. Meni's soldiers were not only outnumbered nearly two to one, but the Philistines possessed much greater mobility. Ten days later, supplies arrived from Gath... escorted by fifty more heavily armed Philistine chariots. Meni discovered to his dismay that the new provisions would last his men only a week at half rations.

All of Meni's suspicions were being confirmed. His supposed allies were slowly starving his command to death. Worse, the second contingent of Philistines had camped between his barracks and Rafah's only water source. Cut off from water, the Egyptians would die from thirst long before they starved. Attempting to drive off the superior Philistine force would be futile. Their foes could simply withdraw and wait until the Egyptians were too weak to resist. Meni's only option was to escape Rafah while his men still had the strength. He was doomed no matter what he did. Even if his men survived, Meni faced execution for abandoning his post.

Chapter 5 - The Countermove

Trusting in Egypt is like using a cracked stick as a staff. For if a man leans on it for support; the staff will splinter and pierce his hand. So is Pharaoh, king of Egypt, to all who trust on him.

From II Kings, Chapter 18, verse 1

The LORD foils the plans of the nations; He thwarts the goals of their people.

From Psalm 33, verse 10

The Egyptian garrison at Rafah

Ahmose, brother-in-law to Pharaoh, lay back on a well-worn couch in his tent, swirled the wine in his cup and counted the drops of sweat rolling down the face of the nervous officer standing before him. The unfortunate man was Meni, commander of the beleaguered Egyptian garrison at Rafah. Meni was initially relieved by Ahmose's unexpected appearance at Rafah with an expeditionary force of some ten thousand soldiers. For weeks, the starving Egyptians at Rafah had been completely cut off from their homeland. It seemed to just be dawning on Meni that Pharaoh had not sent two full divisions merely to feed his small command. The man's eyes flicked anxiously to the four taciturn guards standing nearby. Ahmose sensed it was time to begin the interrogation.

"Why do you think I am here, Meni?"

"I assumed it was in response to my requests for re-supply, my Lord. I sent messages to Memphis after the last caravan was massacred by bandits."

"You think I came all this way to deliver your bread? No, Meni, we received no messages from you. Pharaoh was most disturbed. Do you know why?"

"He feared Rafah had been captured?"

"No, that it was betrayed."

"Surely you don't think that I..."

"I tell you what Pharaoh thinks, Meni. Whoever holds Rafah also controls the Mediterranean trade routes. The rebels in Thebes covet Rafah. You could turn it over to them. Become a wealthy man in the process."

"But now that you are here, My Lord, you see the truth."

"I see a nervous commander. I see his garrison safe and sound. I see hundreds of foreign troops as his guests."

"I never invited the Philistines here."

"Then why didn't you drive them away? Or notify Pharaoh of their presence?"

"I sent messengers..."

"Are we back to that again, Meni? Don't you understand? Incompetence or treason, it makes no difference. The headsman's axe is just as sharp."

66

"How can I prove my loyalty?"

"Tell me everything."

Ahmose said nothing as the torrent of words flowed from a frightened tongue. It did not take him long to determine that the cringing Meni was no traitor. Ahmose knew treason required more backbone than the young officer exhibited. The fool had doubtless achieved his rank through family connections, proof of the declining quality of leaders in Pharaoh's ranks. Still, Meni provided some valuable clues. Ahmose held up his hand when the jabbering man began to repeat himself.

"Enough, Meni. Turn command over to your subordinate. Your men will have ten days to recover before returning to Memphis."

"What about me?"

"You will come with me, Meni, while I investigate these so-called Philistine kings. Your eye-witness testimony may be useful. If they plot treason, they will lie about Rafah."

"I will not disappoint you, my Lord."

"Who's that Philistine officer you mentioned?"

"Phicol, my Lord."

"Fetch him."

Ahmose mulled over Meni's story while he waited. A single Philistine city, Gath, seemed to be the culprit. New questions arose in Ahmose's mind. Was Gath's king, Maoch, acting in concert with the rebels? Or was the man simply after the caravan revenues? Ahmose looked up when his tent flaps parted and a burly soldier entered. He wore armor typical of a high ranking Philistine officer, although the sentries outside had taken his sword. Ahmose judged Phicol to be about thirty years of age and would have described him as ruggedly handsome, if not for several deep facial scars. The Philistine's eyes bespoke cunning and intelligence. The Egyptian noble immediately perceived the man represented a greater challenge than Meni.

"Why are you here, Phicol?"

"You summoned me, Lord Ahmose."

"I don't like men to be clever with me, Philistine."

"I meant no offense, Sir."

"Then we will begin again. You brought infantry and chariots to Rafah. Why?"

"Arabu bandits raided Gath villages. King Maoch charged me with their destruction. The pursuit led me here."

"Much of your command seems ill-suited for that purpose, Phicol. Egyptians use chariots to chase bandits. We use infantry to occupy territory."

"Philistine infantry is quite mobile, my Lord. I use chariots to trap the enemy and infantry to crush them."

"But there are no bandits in Rafah, Phicol. So why do you remain?"

"Only Rafah has water sufficient for my men."

"Meni thinks you mean to starve his soldiers."

"Really? Meni asked for food for his men and I provided it."

"But not enough to meet their needs, Phicol."

"With respect, Sir, I am a warrior, not a quartermaster. I was surprised to find Meni's men so poorly prepared."

"Back to those bandits. You claim there are hordes of them, yet my men have seen not a single one."

"Egyptian tracking skills are not my problem."

"Do you mean to tell me these desert scum can ambush an Egyptian caravan without leaving a trace?"

"They're like that."

"Let me tell you what I am like, Phicol. I behead people who mock me."

"If that is your pleasure, Ahmose, then do it."

Ahmose was taken aback by Phicol's bold use of his name without any honorific. The Philistine's message was clear: he would not waste time being polite to someone threatening to kill him. The man was incredibly brazen. Up to that point, Phicol had played the role of loyal vassal to perfection, claiming to have simply provided food to a hungry ally. They both knew it to be a lie...and that Ahmose's men outnumbered Phicol's by twenty to one. Yet Phicol stuck to his flimsy tale without shedding a single drop of sweat. Ahmose carefully composed his thoughts before dismissing the brash Philistine.

"Fortunately for you, Phicol, that is not my pleasure today. Be assured; I will learn the truth. We will talk again before my return to Egypt."

"I'll be waiting, Lord Ahmose."

Ahmose felt a grudging admiration as he watched the departing Philistine officer. Ahmose seriously considered taking this audacious man into his personal service. Sipping his wine, Ahmose pondered the predicament he faced. Not long ago, a mere handful of Egyptian soldiers could have held Rafah. If anyone dared what Maoch had done, a horde of Egyptian chariots would have laid waste to his lands. However, those chariots were now needed to intimidate rebels in Upper Egypt. Thus Pharaoh's strategy was to gain the upper hand at home while saving face in the outlying regions. Ironically, Ahmose had advised his brother-in-law to temporarily abandon Rafah during the current crisis. Pharaoh had instead risked a gradual reduction of Rafah's garrison going unnoticed. Well, Maoch of Gath had noticed. Though extremely profitable, Rafah sat at the end of a tenuous supply line stretching across the Sinai wilderness. Maoch had gambled he could take Rafah while Egypt was in turmoil. Now Ahmose had to repair the damage as best he could.

Despite the size of his army, Ahmose was himself subject to some powerful constraints. Any solution Ahmose selected would have to be implemented quickly. Pharaoh ran a great risk by sending so many loyal soldiers outside Egypt proper, and Ahmose had explicit orders to be back in Memphis within six weeks. Neither could Ahmose afford heavy losses in battle. Pharaoh might as well hand the crown over to his subversive nephew if Ahmose returned with a battered army. If

70

one or more of the Philistine kings was in league with the Theban rebels, Ahmose had no choice but to fight. Hopefully, the Philistines were driven by greed rather than treason. In that case, compromise would be preferable to battle.

As he prepared for bed, Ahmose decided on his course of action. He would leave one regiment as a temporary garrison at Rafah to counter the troops from Gath. He would then take the rest of his army to call on each of the five Philistine kings. As to whether Maoch was acting alone, Ahmose had no doubt he could uncover the truth. What to do with that truth was another matter. Regardless, Ahmose knew that Canaan was unimportant in the grand scheme. Egypt was everything. These petty rulers had no comprehension of the vast wealth and power that existed along the Nile. Ahmose was comforted by his last thoughts before falling asleep that night. *Let these five pirate kings fight over the scraps of the Empire for now. One day, Pharaoh will take it all back.*

The Royal Palace of the Philistine Kingdom of Gaza

Kaftor, King of Gaza, fiddled nervously with the scraps on his plate and silently cursed Maoch for the hundredth time. His aggressive neighbor was the reason that Pharaoh's plenipotentiary, Ahmose, now sat across the banquet table. Maoch alone was responsible for the thousands of Egyptian soldiers now camped around his capital city. The clumsy timing of Maoch's naked grab for power had placed all of Philistia at risk. The King of Gath might consider himself a gifted tactician, but Kaftor thought the man's actions at Rafah were insane. The decline of Egypt's ancient Empire was a poorly kept secret. The current Dynasty had grown lethargic, concerned with little beyond the lush lands along the Nile River. The last few generations of inbred rulers paid scant attention to the growing strength of their Empire's outlying provinces. Even Egypt's traditional enemy, the Hittite Empire, was pulling back to their northern homelands. Kaftor saw the approaching power void in the region as clearly as Maoch did, and how Philistia was in an excellent position to fill it.

But a declining Egypt was not necessarily a weak Egypt.

Kaftor rearranged his ample bulk in his chair and grumbled once more about Maoch's folly. Kaftor believed the last Egyptian soldier would have marched away from Rafah of his own accord, given another few years. The coastal trade route would fall into Philistine hands, not through conquest, but because of Egyptian feebleness. By moving too soon, Maoch had incurred the wrath of a wounded, but still dangerous, Egypt. A fortnight ago, Ahmose had suddenly emerged from the Sinai Desert with an army greater than any Philistine king could match. The man had neutralized Maoch's soldiers at Rafah before commencing an intimidating trek around Philistia. One by one, the Philistine kings were forced to pay homage to Pharaoh. Gaza was the last city to host the Egyptian horde.

"Your hospitality is indeed exceptional, Kaftor, but it is time for business. Just the two of us. Here will be fine."

The servants, guards and dinner guests fled at a brusque signal from Kaftor. The King of Gaza surreptitiously wiped the sweat from his balding pate as a pair of Ahmose's attendants placed a wooden chest on the table next to their lord before departing. Despite the box's modest size, the table wobbled briefly under its weight. Ahmose waited until the doors to the hall were closed before speaking.

"Kaftor, you know why I am here."

"Rafah."

"Then you also know what Maoch is up to."

"I am more interested in what you know, Ahmose."

"As you should be. I have concluded that Maoch destroyed an Egyptian supply caravan to Rafah. Next, he sent Gath soldiers to starve out our garrison. Maoch would then control the coastal trade route."

"A most reckless action on Maoch's part."

"Yet none of this appears to surprise you, Kaftor."

"Actually, I'm a little ashamed that I didn't think of it myself. However, I assure you that Gath has acted alone in this matter."

"We would not be having this pleasant conversation if I thought otherwise, Kaftor."

"So...have you decided Maoch's fate?"

"For violating his oath, Maoch should be dragged before Pharaoh in chains, his lands laid waste and his cities burned."

"Betrayal demands a harsh penalty."

"But these are not normal times, Kaftor. Unfortunately, I cannot afford to lose a few hundred men to subdue Gath.

Pharaoh has higher priorities. Maoch's punishment must be delayed."

Kaftor maintained a neutral expression to mask his true thoughts. *You mean the loss of a few thousand men, Ahmose. You would undoubtedly conquer Gath, but Maoch would make you pay dearly. A substantial occupation force would also need to be left behind. You would be fortunate to limp back to Egypt with half your men.* Although Gaza appeared absolved of guilt, Kaftor did not like where this discussion was heading.

"If Maoch's punishment is in the future, Ahmose, what happens in the present?"

"I negotiated a new treaty with Maoch. Egyptian troops will be withdrawn from Rafah. Maoch will hold it in Pharaoh's name. Half the trade revenues will be sent to Egypt and half will go to Gath."

Kaftor felt his face grow warm with indignation. *That whore's son Maoch is not only escaping punishment, but he's getting wealthy in the process. This will make Gath the most powerful of the five kingdoms. Pharaoh's position must be more precarious than anyone here dreamed.*

"Rewarding disloyalty sets a bad precedent, Ahmose. Others may follow Maoch's example."

"Allow me to finish, Kaftor. You fear that Gaza will fall under Gath's shadow. However, Maoch will not profit from his deceit. Egypt has much experience in these matters. While the military solution must be delayed, political action can begin now."

"Meaning what, Ahmose?"

"I will set unseen forces in motion against Gath. I require a special man to bring down Maoch: someone talented, ambitious, devious, and without conscience. A man who could play the faithful friend until it is time to stick a blade between his victim's ribs and twist it. You were recommended, Kaftor."

"Coming from an Egyptian, I'm flattered. Military support from Egypt seems out of the question. What do you offer instead, Ahmose? "

Ahmose loosened the wooden chest's latch and raised the lid. Kaftor felt his heart quicken as his eyes beheld its glittering contents.

"One of these, Kaftor, every year."

A horde of ideas instantly invaded Kaftor's mind. Gaza's army could be expanded. Mercenaries, spies and even assassins hired. Maoch's officers and officials bribed behind his back. Kaftor estimated the chest contained more wealth than Maoch would collect in a year from Rafah. *Or did it?* Kaftor looked inquiringly at his guest and Ahmose answered the unspoken question.

"Yes, Kaftor, the contents are the same from top to bottom."

"Since this is too generous for a gift, there must be conditions."

"There are three. The first concerns Gezer, our last stronghold in the east. We have decided to reinforce Gezer, but the same tactics used at Rafah could be applied against it. You will not allow that to happen."

"Agreed."

"Secondly, you will keep Pharaoh informed weekly of everything happening in the region. Philistine, Hittite, Canaanite, Israelite...it does not matter. I'll leave scribes who can write the details in a language understood only at the Court in Memphis."

"Also acceptable, Ahmose."

"Finally, Gaza will supply iron weapons only to Pharaoh."

"We will gladly sell Pharaoh all he requires."

Ahmose's response was to close the lid on the chest of gold and lean back silently in his chair. The King of Gaza cursed himself. Kaftor's indiscreet excitement at seeing the open chest had ruined his ability to bargain with the Egyptian.

"Very well then, Ahmose. Supply."

"Since we are in agreement, there is one last detail. It is not one of my conditions, but I will leave it up to your discretion, Kaftor."

"And that is?"

"If something should befall Maoch, Pharaoh will be...grateful."

"How grateful, Ahmose?"

"You may keep anything that falls your way."

"Anything?"

Kaftor felt a sudden surge of pleasure at the Egyptian's hesitation. Now it was Ahmose's turn to be in the weaker bargaining position, for the man had gone too far to become stingy now. Kaftor thought that Egyptian arrogance might actually work in his favor. Ahmose would undoubtedly believe that any concession he regretted could be taken back later.

"All right, Kaftor. Keep *everything* that falls your way. But always remember where your allegiance lies."

"Naturally."

Delight filled Kaftor's heart as he stood on his balcony watching the Egyptian delegation return to their encampment. Obtaining both wealth and the means to bring down a hated rival would be enough for most men. However, it was the day's final negotiating point which provided him the greatest satisfaction. Egypt had effectively given Kaftor a free hand in Canaan.

Canaan had been at the mercy of the great powers along its borders for centuries, but a new day was dawning. The Hittites were exhausted, the Egyptians were distracted and the ancient Mesopotamian empires were crumbling. A unique opportunity existed for a new state to arise in Canaan, absorb its smaller neighbors and humble its former overlords. Kaftor knew it could be Philistia. Not an unwieldy coalition of five cities, but a single united Philistine Empire. Maoch also recognized the possibilities, but the aggressive fool had moved too soon. Gath's impatience would allow Gaza to surge ahead. Ahmose's gold and overblown promises were helpful, but not essential. What Kaftor required most was for the Egyptians to stay out of his way. He doubted another Egyptian army would be sent this far to the east in his lifetime. Kaftor thought it an appropriate metaphor to watch from his balcony as the sun set upon Egypt.

Chapter 6 - The Spies

Then Moses sent men to spy out the land of Canaan, and said to them, "Go up this way into the South, and go up to the mountains, and see what the land is like: whether the people who dwell in it are strong or weak, few or many.

From the Book of Numbers, Chapter 13, verses 17 and 18

Saul's home outside the town of Gibeah

War was no stranger in the land of Canaan. It was a frequent guest among the many strongholds dotting the crescent of fertile land which stretched between the River Euphrates and the Nile Delta. For Canaan was indeed a most obliging host to war. Its broad highways provided easy access for armies. The bountiful crops kept invaders well fed. The cool rivers and springs quenched soldiers' thirst. Its broad plains readily converted to spacious battlefields where generals maneuvered their regiments with ease. Yet Canaan was more than a crossroads. The land itself lured many a would-be conqueror seeking to add its richness to his domain. Although questions of possession might be settled through treaty or marriage, war had long been the preferred solution.

Canaan's longest running competition existed between the five kingdoms of Philistia and tribal Israel. Considering Israel's habitation of Canaan had been interrupted by a lengthy sojourn in Egypt, both powers were relative newcomers to the region. The two peoples were opposites in many ways, exhibiting all the commensurate strengths and weaknesses. Religiously, Israel's single God was defined by holiness while

Philistine deities were served by temple prostitutes. Militarily, Israel had quantity while Philistia had quality. Geographically, Israelite light infantry dominated the mountainous interior while Philistine chariots ruled the coastal plains. Naturally, the rolling hills between the two domains where Nathan lived, the *Shephelah*, were a constant point of contention. Dominance there had alternated between Israel and Philistia since the time of Samson. The most recent shift in Israel's favor had occurred nearly a generation before. A Philistine army foolishly invaded the highlands where it was crushed by the judge Samuel and his Israelite militia. The Philistine survivors crawled home to lick their wounds and learn from the experience. Since then, Philistia had cautiously encroached on Israel's borders by means of economic monopolies backed by military power. During Nathan's lifetime, the balance of power had largely shifted back to Philistia.

The Benjamite League sought to rally their fellow tribesmen against the growing Philistine hegemony. Kish, grandfather of Nathan's friend Jonathan, was the local commander in Gibeah. However, the same disunity which afflicted the rest of Israel was also prevalent in the tribe of Benjamin. The recruitment of thirteen year-old boys like Nathan showed how desperate the League was for manpower. Kish, by necessity, focused his limited resources around the border town of Gibeon, a strategic gateway into Benjamin's heartland. Although one of Benjamin's larger communities, Gibeon possessed no walls. Its fortifications had been razed during the Israelite civil war many generations before and never rebuilt. Yet merchants and craftsmen still congregated at this crossroads to create a vibrant marketplace.

Gibeon also represented the deepest Philistine penetration into Benjamite territory. Ten years before, soldiers from Gath had constructed a cluster of barracks on the town's eastern side. These structures were eventually enclosed by a ten-foot high stone wall complete with watch towers and ramparts. Counting its infantry, officers and auxiliaries, the Philistine garrison numbered over one hundred and fifty men. Gibeon provided a secure base from which Gath's commercial ventures could infest the local economy. Once the Gibeonites grew financially dependent on Gath, the Philistines could establish another outpost farther east and repeat the cycle. The Philistine strategy was both simple and effective. If the Benjamite League entertained any hopes of containing Philistine expansion, it would be at Gibeon. For that reason the League had tasked Kish with forcing out its Philistine garrison. Recent history had not favored the League.

Several years had passed since Kish's last military success. Maoch, King of Gath, had planted a fifty-man garrison outside a small village named Geba as a test of Benjamin's resolve. This incursion extended the Philistine presence ten miles deeper into Benjamite territory, but Maoch was eyeing a much bigger prize. Nearby was the strategic mountain stronghold of Michmash where Israel's two major road systems intersected. If the Philistines used Geba as a base to seize Michmash, they could cut off Judah, Simeon and Benjamin from the other tribes. This provocation had proved too much for even the pacifists in Benjamin to ignore. Over three hundred local men joined Kish to besiege Geba, forcing the King of Gath to withdraw his soldiers. Unfortunately, this was also the high water mark for the League's resistance efforts in the region. After the Philistines departed, the local Benjamites promptly went home and ignored any further requests for assistance from Kish. The Benjamite League's ambitions for Gibeon were still unfulfilled when Saul approached Nathan on his sixteenth birthday.

"Nathan, the League needs men for a special mission, one requiring boldness and discretion."

"When do I begin?"

"At least hear what I have to say."

"Doesn't matter. I want in."

"Well, you have the boldness. Discretion? Not so sure."

"Fine, Saul. First I listen. Then I volunteer."

"One mistake could kill you."

"I just want to kill Philistines."

"And there will be no fighting."

"What? I thought you said I might die."

"If we fail, Nathan, death is very likely."

"Just answer me this, Saul: will our success hurt the Philistines?"

"I guarantee it."

Nathan then strode silently in the older man's shadow while Saul laid out the clandestine mission. The Benjamite League leadership hoped spies might compensate for their military deficiencies. Past efforts to spy out Philistine intentions had been marginal at best, based mostly on gossip and chance encounters. The League's twofold solution was to insert full-time spies among the Philistines and create a system to distribute their information. By anticipating where the enemy was vulnerable, the League hoped to concentrate its limited resources more effectively. Saul then posed to Nathan the question the leaders had hotly debated.

"So Nathan, where would you send our spies?"

"A place with many Philistines, especially soldiers. And it must be accessible to Israelites."

"Not bad. Have any place in mind?"

"Gibeon."

"Why Gibeon?"

"It's close and accessible. Gibeon has a modest Philistine garrison, but its commander would be privy to Gath's plans. There's also a great deal of traffic between Gibeon and Gibeah. Our spies could slip in and out unnoticed."

"Those are all good reasons, Nathan."

"And one more. The League has already chosen Gibeon."

"Oh?"

"If it were anywhere else, Saul, the League would not have chosen you."

"I thought you would make a good spy, Nathan. You showed promise by catching the man who betrayed your father."

"That was mostly Jonathan."

"I know. He is coming as well."

"Where are we going?"

"Gibeon, of course. We will go there and seek out opportunities."

On the road from Gibeah to Gibeon

The next morning Nathan was riding donkeys with Saul and Jonathan to Gibeon. Saul had picked the three best animals from Kish's extensive herd, and Nathan's feet appreciated the luxury. As their mounts swayed down the dusty highway, Saul explained why both young men were the only practical candidates to train as spies. Men skilled in reading, writing and numbers were rare among their fellow tribesmen. Such tools were essential for espionage. Nathan now understood why his education had begun from almost his first day under Saul's roof.

The first glimpse of Gibeon's rooftops a few hours later reduced all three men to silence. The sun was nearly at its highest point when Nathan and his companions rode past the enemy outpost. They were soon watering their thirsty animals at Gibeon's public well. Saul cautioned Nathan and Jonathan not to stare at the Philistine sentries.

"Jonathan, your donkey has gone lame."

"She stumbled when some rocks gave way on the last hill."

"She must be replaced. I cannot have her ruined."

"Sorry, Father, I should have paid closer attention."

"Actually, this mishap provides me an excuse to explore the town. Stay here, Jonathan. Tend the animals. Note the traffic in and out of the garrison's gates."

"What about me, Saul?"

"Look around, Nathan. See if there is a vantage point which overlooks the outpost's walls. Avoid attracting attention. Act like a bored teenager."

"You mean like Jonathan?"

Ignoring Jonathan's rude gesture, Nathan set off on his task. His initial survey of the Philistine stronghold showed the original engineers had chosen its location well. No rooftop in Gibeon appeared to be high enough and close enough to look down into the garrison compound. A besieging enemy could rain a variety of missiles down on the defenders from such a position. As he rounded the back corner of the outpost, Nathan spotted a ramshackle structure about twenty yards from the garrison walls. Closer examination showed the decrepit building had once been a barn with a rundown stone corral on one side. Nathan entered its musty walls and spotted a rotting ladder beneath a skylight. He climbed out on the barn roof to stand in bright sunshine. Nathan found himself nearly level with the Philistines patrolling the outpost's wall. His pulse raced as he reckoned a mere two feet of elevation would allow him an unobstructed view of the compound. Then a sentry spotted

Nathan, shouted angrily and waved him off. Nathan hurriedly departed in frustration. The old barn would have made the perfect observation post, except for being so exposed. Nathan returned to the well and made small talk with Jonathan until Saul returned. The older man appeared puzzled.

"I am afraid you are walking home, Jonathan. I found a farmer willing to buy your donkey in the hope she will recover, but there is not another for sale in the entire town."

"Strange...grandfather has plenty to sell in Gibeah."

"There seems to be a shortage of draft animals in Philistia. The Philistines here are buying anything with four legs and sending it back to Gath. Even the local garrison has trouble meeting its own needs."

"Why does Gath need so many donkeys now, Saul?"

"Whatever the reason, Nathan, it cannot be good for us. Did you find a good lookout spot?"

"Yes and no."

"Explain."

"There's an old barn on the far side of the outpost. It has a great view, but it's too close to the walls. The Philistines chased me away."

"A *barn*, you say? Show me."

To Nathan's surprise, Saul made no attempt at stealth as they walked to the barn. Nathan could feel the eyes of the sentries on his back while Saul made a great show of examining the crumbling stone fence and the exterior of the old building.

The first thing Saul did upon climbing out on its roof was to smile and give the nearest sentry a friendly wave. The Philistine soldier appeared perplexed, but waved back. Saul then ignored the man while completing his survey of the property. Saul finally sent Nathan back to wait with Jonathan and reentered Gibeon. It was nearly dark before Saul returned.

"Gather up your things, Boys. Tonight we camp in Nathan's barn."

"What will the owner think about that, Father?"

"He does not mind. I promised to mend the fence, repair the barn and give him half the profits."

"What profits?"

"From the sale of donkeys."

"We have only two donkeys."

"Your grandfather has plenty."

"Grandfather never does business outside Gibeah."

"He will after I explain how it gets us the best spy post in Gibeon."

"So, Saul, how will the Philistines feel about the Benjamite League moving in next door?"

"They'll never know, Nathan. Our new partner is a local merchant named Ashbel. He will deal with the Philistines, not me."

"Does Ashbel know donkeys are not our only business?"

"Why should he? "

"Well, it's your decision, Saul."

"Something eats at you, Nathan. Out with it."

"The Philistines aren't fools. Anyone on top of that barn will arouse suspicion."

"That is *literally* covered by our business arrangement, Nathan. The pen and the barn will be used for the donkeys, fodder, tools and supplies. Our herdsmen will live on the roof. Naturally, they require shelter. We will erect a tent up there for them."

"Erect a *blind* is what you mean, Saul."

"A tent has many uses."

"The Philistines obviously evicted the barn's owners years ago. Why should they do us any favors?"

"It has already been a long day. We will come up with an idea tomorrow."

It was their wily business partner, Ashbel, who furnished the necessary idea. The merchant revealed the garrison commander had been recalled to Gath and his replacement was not due for a fortnight. Ashbel shrewdly suggested taking advantage of the transition to refurbish the barn and move in the donkeys. Most likely, the junior officer left in charge would be reluctant to take any action. Ashbel confidently predicted the new commander would not bother to undo what had already been done. Saul readily agreed with this proposal before departing with his son to make the necessary arrangements in Gibeah. Nathan would remain behind to repair the breaches in the animal pen. He gladly gave up his donkey to Jonathan. Getting Kish to approve the proposed deal would be neither easy nor pleasant. Nathan preferred to stay with the Philistines.

Entirely on his own now, Nathan decided boldness afforded him the greatest security. He borrowed some tools from Ashbel and set to work on the stone wall under the hot sun in full view of the garrison's sentries. At first, most of his sweat came from fear rather than the large stones he lugged around. At any moment a javelin or arrow might pierce his flesh, yet he kept his back to the Philistines. After an hour, Nathan risked a surreptitious glance at the enemy ramparts and counted twice the normal number of soldiers. An officer eventually appeared and initiated an animated discussion. Nathan could not understand any of the words, but at its conclusion, the officer and most of the soldiers disappeared down into the compound. More tense moments passed as Nathan waited for a detail to come around the corner and arrest him. However, the morning passed uneventfully, and he continued to work undisturbed. Ten days later, Jonathan arrived with thirty-four donkeys from Gibeah for the barn's newly rebuilt pen. His friend also brought five members of Kish's *eleph* to repair the barn and tend the animals.

The barn's restoration was nearly complete when the new Philistine commander entered Gibeon. Nathan had not witnessed the man's arrival, but word spread rapidly among the nervous townspeople. With Saul back in Gibeah, Jonathan had taken charge. Nathan was pleased to see his friend exhibit exceptional leadership skills for a teenager. When the some of the men in their band grew apprehensive, Jonathan calmed them. He reassured everyone that their best protection lay in the appearance of normality. As long as everyone did their daily work, Jonathan promised the Philistines would leave them in peace. Two days later, Jonathan's words were put to the test.

Nathan was the first to spot the small Philistine detachment approaching the donkey corral. The figure in front was unfamiliar, but the man's gilded armor left no doubt Nathan was getting first look at the new garrison commander. He immediately called for Jonathan and watched as the officer halted his eight soldiers about ten paces from the corral. By the time Jonathan arrived, the commander was leaning against the fence gazing intently at the animals within.

"What is it, Nathan?"

"Visitors."

"Well, we knew they would eventually come calling. Let's get it over with."

"What do you think the new commander wants?"

"Maybe the man needs a donkey."

Jonathan's cheery optimism failed to relieve Nathan's nervousness as they walked along the stone fence. He felt the eyes of the Philistine soldiers follow them until they stopped a few paces behind the commander. Jonathan silently indicated that Nathan should allow him to do the talking. Nathan felt the Philistine must be aware of their presence, yet the man still showed them his back. Apparently, the officer felt that speaking first was a sign of lower status. Jonathan finally shrugged and plunged ahead.

"Greetings, My Lord. How may I be of service?"

When the mysterious stranger turned around, Nathan's jaw dropped slightly. The Philistine commander was a teenager, barely older than himself.

"You can explain something to me, Hebrew. This property is dangerously close to the garrison's walls. My predecessor told me it was empty when he left. Now it is filled with men and animals. Why?"

"The land belongs to Ashbel, a respected merchant of Gibeon. My family raises donkeys in Gibeah. When my father learned of the need for donkeys here, he made an arrangement with Ashbel."

"And you are?"

"I am Jonathan, the eldest son of Saul."

"Who authorized your venture?"

"The officer in charge didn't object to our actions."

"That's not the same as getting permission. Your presence poses a threat."

"Does that mean you will send us away?"

"I might. Tell me more about your business."

Nathan was impressed by how calmly his friend explained their operation without giving away its connection with the Benjamite League. He recognized that part of the Philistine's purpose was to confirm that Jonathan was indeed what he claimed to be. Any hesitation or contradiction on

Jonathan's part would be seen as deception. The youthful commander listened quietly until Jonathan began quoting prices. Nathan was startled when the Philistine snorted with obvious disgust.

"Outrageous! Donkeys can be had in Gath for half that cost!"

This ludicrous assertion astonished Nathan. A shortage of donkeys in Philistia would drive their price up, not down. Then it dawned on Nathan that the Philistine had just initiated a business negotiation. He saw a gleeful glint in Jonathan's eye. His friend immediately assumed the persona of a merchant humoring his customer.

"If I may be so bold, My Lord, those animals must belong to a breed that is inferior to our own. My family sells donkeys by the score at the prices I mentioned."

"Yet those cheaper animals would be quite satisfactory for my purposes, Hebrew. And the purchase price is only one issue. There is also their care and feeding. Your countrymen robbed my predecessor blind in the purchase of grain and fodder. I will not repeat his mistakes."

"I may have a solution, My Lord."

"Explain."

"Don't *buy* my donkeys. *Hire* them instead."

"Why should I do that?"

"To save money. Pay for only the animals you use, and only when you need them. We will handle their shelter, feeding and watering for you. We will deliver the exact number of animals to your gate, whenever you desire, and take them back when you no longer require them."

"Your idea has merit, Hebrew, provided the price is low enough."

Nathan leaned against the stone fence as the haggling began in earnest. He detected that Jonathan was carefully allowing himself to be beaten down by the young Philistine. Typically, if the buyer set an extremely low price, the seller chose the animals to be provided. Instead, Jonathan granted the Philistine both privileges. Nathan suspected any savings would end up in the youthful commander's own purse. And by the time Jonathan was finished, that amount was quite substantial. Nathan was almost embarrassed for his friend at the end.

"Under what name should I place the contract, My Lord?"

"Use my name... Achish. This new arrangement should allow me to serve out my term in Gibeon in luxury."

"That is entirely your affair, My Lord. However, I would be careful about whom I told, lest word gets back to the King of Gath."

"Oh, I doubt Maoch will much care. He's my father."

Nathan released a long held breath as he and Jonathan watched the Philistine contingent depart.

"I thought you were going to end up paying Achish to use our animals."

"That would have been bribery, Nathan."

"Bribery might have been cheaper. Jonathan, your grandfather will flog you for those prices. Then your father will disown you."

"Considering we might have been executed, I believe we came out ahead."

"At least you tricked the young *Lord of Luxury* into sanctioning our operation."

"Nathan, please. Don't call him that again."

"He won't care. Achish is only interested in cheating his father."

"No, he isn't, Nathan. Remember how Achish kept peering over his shoulder? He was trying harder to impress his soldiers than intimidate me. Achish might be a king's son, but I wager this is his first command, and he's still insecure. So I made him look good in front of his men. Now he owes me."

"Your present was rather expensive. I hope Achish appreciates it."

"A real bastard would have seized our herd, imprisoned us and demanded a ransom. Achish may be audacious enough to do that in the future, but not today."

"At least we have an excuse to get inside the garrison."

"And that's only the beginning! What does Achish need donkeys for? Patrols and supply caravans! He'll have to give us their schedules well in advance so we can supply the pack animals."

"Then we pass the information on to Gibeah. Kish raids their caravans. Our people hide from Philistine foraging parties. It's brilliant, Jonathan!"

"That alone should make up for the loss of income. Agreed?"

"As long as you do all the explaining at home, Donkey Boy. Me? I don't want to be anywhere around when Kish hears about it."

Nathan later learned that Saul was extremely pleased with Jonathan's initiative. Even Kish eventually endorsed his grandson's arrangement with Achish; although Nathan heard the old man had been aghast when he first heard the terms. Fortunately, the Philistine garrison was not their only customer, and Jonathan was a born negotiator. Nathan was impressed by how quickly their losses with Achish were recouped in other contracts. He was not surprised to learn that offering bribes to a Philistine commander through unprofitable business deals was a time-honored practice. The majority of merchants in Gibeon had been operating that way for years.

Achish's first requisition for a weekly patrol came a few days later. Nathan entered the outpost's foreboding walls the following morning and delivered twelve donkeys to the sergeant on duty. No one seemed to mind that he lingered in the center of the compound while the Philistine soldiers loaded their supplies and equipment. Nathan was careful to note from which buildings the food, weapons, tents, soldiers and officers came. He deliberately stayed behind for a few minutes after the twenty-man patrol departed. His unobtrusive presence attracted not one bit of attention from the busy residents. Deciding he had depended on *Providence* enough for one day, Nathan padded out the main gate. He gave the sentry a broad smile in passing and received a friendly nod in return.

The lessons from Nathan's initial foray into the Philistine garrison helped them plan future visits. Saul wished to send his people inside so often that the enemy soldiers would take no thought of their presence. Therefore, every business activity generated a separate trip. For each patrol, an Israelite would come one day to schedule the donkeys, another day to deliver them, another to retrieve them and a separate day to collect payment. Jonathan even came up with the idea of *friendly* visits. An Israelite might show up at the garrison's gate unannounced with a small gift for the commander or special delicacies for the officers' mess or wine for the sergeants. The stated purpose of each visit was to show appreciation for the Philistines' business. By the third month, Nathan found he could enter the compound anytime during the day even when carrying nothing at all. The guards simply assumed he had a good reason for being there. Nathan thought it a delicious irony that the Philistines were not only financing the cost of their own surveillance, but were also providing a substantial income to the Benjamite League.

Chapter 7 - The Highlanders

When all that generation had been gathered to their fathers, another generation arose after them who did not know the LORD or the work which He had done for Israel.

From the Book of Judges, Chapter 2, verse 10

And you will cry out to the LORD for relief because of the king you chose for yourselves, and the LORD will not hear you in that day.

From the Book of I Samuel, Chapter 8, verse 18

Shechem, chief city of the tribe of Ephraim

The lean, willowy man with piercing grey eyes paused momentarily at the town square to consider which street to take next. Beker, an Elder of the tribe of Ephraim, was well acquainted with the streets and alleys of Shechem, his tribe's largest city. He decided on the long route to his midday rendezvous in a secluded quarter of the city. Beker required extra time this morning to compose his thoughts, and walking helped clear his mind. He stroked his reddish beard as he tried to visualize the people he must sway. He wanted to alarm his listeners enough to spur them to action, but not so much as to reduce them to despair. Striking the proper balance would indeed be a challenge, especially since Beker was dealing with a very temperamental audience. Yet, the possibility of failure never entered his thoughts. One did not rise as far as Beker had in only thirty-eight years by being pessimistic. As a young boy lacking any physical prowess, Beker learned to hone his mind as a weapon. His first life lesson had been how to survive by being inconspicuous. Observing safely from the shadows, he identified ways to pit the stronger boys against each other. He then befriended and recruited a few of these sturdy youths to serve as his cadre. By fomenting disunity among the other children, Beker leveraged the power and influence of his little band. Eventually, other children offered him allegiance in return for his protection. Since adults behaved essentially the same way, Beker continued to use his same tactics.

The group of Hebrew nobles waiting for Beker was collectively known as the *Highlanders*. As the name suggested, its members dwelt in the relative safety of Israel's mountainous interior. The Highlanders had no official duties, held no public office and answered to no one. Membership was by invitation only. Some, like Beker, were tribal elders, but all were men of wealth and influence. There were even a few Levite priests. First and foremost, they were pragmatists. The Highlanders had little loyalty to Israel as a nation. Their priorities were family, clan, and tribe, in that order. They viewed the inefficiencies of Israel's judges and national militia as a blessing. From their perspective, the current Israelite system provided the Highlanders with adequate protection at minimum cost.

Although there were a few exceptions, Beker's associates tended to be from one of the six *Mountain Tribes*: Ephraim, Manasseh, Issachar, Zebulon, Asher and Naphtali. The Highlanders' isolated northern possessions were less vulnerable to raids and invasion, allowing them to accumulate great wealth over successive generations. These prosperous clans were content to let their lowland brethren serve as buffers against Israel's predatory neighbors. Not surprisingly, those tribes occupying the border regions gradually grew weaker and less able to defend themselves. Many were forced to collaborate with their oppressors just to survive. Whenever their cousins' cries of suffering grew loud, the Highlanders could safely turn a deaf ear. Men like Beker were satisfied with the current state of affairs and saw little reason to place their own prosperity at risk.

Fundamental to the Highlanders' hegemony was the lack of unity among other tribes. Beker was amazed by how little effort was required to keep his foes divided. Only a few of the Lowland tribes ever joined together in a common cause against the six Mountain Tribes. Frequent crises gave rise to small rival coalitions, which sometimes included even part of Manasseh. The *TransJordan Tribes* of Rueben, Gad and the eastern half of Manasseh shared a vulnerability to desert raiders. The *Southern Tribes* of Judah, Simeon, Dan and Benjamin faced a common threat from the Philistines. The Highlanders usually ignored the tribe of Levi because its people possessed no separate homeland of their own. The Levites served as Israel's priests and lived among the other tribes. Levites might exert great religious influence, but politically they were weaklings. Beker and his Highland predecessors had skillfully played these groups off against each other for years.

But all that might now change.

Two men stood guard at the entrance of the imposing mansion which hosted Beker's meeting. Both bowed as the Highlander Elder walked past. Beker spied his two closest allies waiting in the courtyard: Helek of Manasseh and Elon of Zebulon. Muffled sounds of shouting and laughter confirmed the other Highlander representatives were already in the main hall. Beker had dispatched his invitations six days ago when he first became aware of the new threat. Some Highlanders might require a full week for travel, but Beker dared wait no longer. He asked Helek his most urgent question.

"How many are here?"

"Enough."

When he saw Elon nodding in agreement, Beker relaxed slightly. Helek's answer meant there was at least one influential Elder from each of the six mountain tribes. These men could not only carry the news back home, but also persuade the absent Highlanders to follow any plan which might be adopted today. Leading the debate would be Beker's responsibility. The three men were suddenly distracted when echoes of laughter reached the courtyard. Beker smiled as he addressed his companions.

"Sounds like they've had sufficient wine. They should be sober enough to listen, but too drunk to argue. Shall we begin?"

Helek and Elon matched Beker's grin with their own and followed him into the spacious chamber. The morning light streaming through large windows provided enough illumination that interior lamps were not required. Beker counted several dozen men lounging on the various couches and benches while partaking of the refreshments. Heads turned and conversations faded away as Beker advanced through the crowd to the front of the chamber. The more boisterous attendees began shouting before he could say a word.

"Beker! Why *are* we here?"

"This better be important! I left my fields because of you!"

"I left my herds!"

"I left my mistress!"

Beker allowed the raucous laughter from the last remark to wash over him. The pause gave him time to gauge the prevailing mood. He recognized the need to throw some cold water on this crowd. Beker quickly decided to abandon his introductory remarks and jump straight into the fray.

"The Patriarchs will meet in a fortnight."

All traces of levity evaporated. Beker had just announced a gathering of all the Elders in Israel. This body was the nearest thing Israel had to a government since the Exodus. It met only during times of emergency and observed few rules. One useful custom had evolved to avoid complete chaos. Each tribe designated one Elder as their spokesman on the *High Council of Elders*. Over time, these twelve representatives became known simply as the *Patriarchs*. The other Elders expressed their opinions, but the final decision for each tribe rested with its Patriarch. The Council's decisions were not necessarily based on the will of the majority, for the Patriarchs were by no means equals. One notorious example involved a border disagreement between the tribes of Dan and Ephraim over the ownership of three towns. Seven of twelve Patriarchs had sided with Dan, but Ephraim still ended up with the disputed towns.

The Highlanders had good reason to be alarmed. Once in session, there were no limits on what changes the Patriarchs might impose upon Israel. As his audience began to recover from its initial shock, questions were directed to Beker from many different quarters.

"Why, Beker?"

"The Elders of Gad fear the growth of Ammonite power."

"Gad has always been afraid of the Ammonites. Who's *really* prodding them, Beker?"

"The Monarchists, of course."

An angry rumble spread through Beker's audience. *Monarchist* elements had been promoting a king for Israel since Joshua's time. However, the few ambitious Israelites attempting to wear a crown had all come to bad ends. Each failed to garner enough support to establish a dynasty. The resulting instability was the antithesis of everything the Highlanders stood for. Support for a king was strongest among the border tribes who had less to lose. The Ammonites had a young ruler, Nahash, who hungered for new lands. Nahash's ambition provided the perfect opportunity for the Monarchists to panic Israel into establishing its own kingdom.

"Beker, can we prevent the Patriarchs from assembling?"

"Unlikely. Five other tribes support Gad's request. The rest dare not be absent."

"Can't just we buy off some of these Monarchist leaders? It's worked before."

"When we needed to bribe only one or two tribes, yes, it worked. However, threats from the Philistines in the west *and* the Ammonites in the east could drive *all* the border tribes into the Monarchist camp. If that happens, most Mountain Tribes won't risk being left out. That would push even the Levites to back a king."

One man who had obviously consumed more than his share of wine wobbled to his feet. Beker recognized him as Ishvi, from the tribe of Asher.

"Listen...all of you...this crisis will blow over just as it always has. Why? Because people only want a king *if he is from their tribe*! That is where the Monarchists fail every time. They will *never* find one king who will be accepted by all tribes! Beker...quit trying to scare everyone."

"So, Ishvi, do you propose we take no action? That we just enjoy our wine...and our mistresses...and pray that the Monarchists are as apathetic as we are?"

"What's so bad about a king anyway, Beker? He's only one man. He still needs us to rule."

A dozen other Highlanders, some still reasonably sober, voiced their agreement with this last remark. Beker viewed his associates with a mixture of sympathy and contempt. A few, like him, were shrewd politicians. The majority had wealth, but little idea of how to use it effectively. Some were cowards concerned only with protecting their inheritances. Beker masked his innermost feelings as he responded with a steady voice.

"Unless we are prepared, the Monarchists will convince the Patriarchs to select a king. If that king is a failure, we become the slaves of our neighbors. If that king is a success, we become his slaves."

"All right, Beker. I'll give you the benefit of the doubt, for now. What's your plan?"

"First, we shore up our most vulnerable area: the tribe of Manasseh. Half their people are east of the Jordan River and exposed to the Ammonites. They are your cousins, Helek. What would scratch their itch for a king?"

"Offer the usual inducements to their Elders. Titles to secure lands in the west...gold...promises of military support. It's stiffened their spines before."

"Excellent. Second, we propose replacing the judges with something more stable...perhaps make the office of Patriarch a permanent position."

His audacious suggestion immediately sobered the entire audience, just as Beker expected. Even Ishvi seemed to shake off the effects of the wine as he protested.

"You can't get away with abolishing the judges, Beker! The priests will say we are defying God!"

"Calm yourself, Ishvi... I just said we would *propose* it. My intent is to splinter the Elders into factions supporting either judges or patriarchs or kings. A stalemate means victory for us... and doom for the Monarchists."

Beker then poured himself some wine and sat back while his allies went to work. Helek, Elon and others moved about the chamber seeking out the most prominent Highlanders. They answered questions, offered reassurance and obtained commitments to promote Beker's strategy after they returned home. Once he sensed his friends had completed their mission, Beker signaled for more food and wine to be brought in. The remainder of the day was devoted to boosting his guests' morale during a sumptuous banquet. Everyone left in fine spirits, swearing to perform their assigned tasks before the Patriarchs' meeting. Beker asked Helek and Elon to remain after the other Highlanders departed. Alone with his two confidants, Beker felt secure enough to divulge his true feelings.

"We are in deep trouble, my Friends."

"How? The session could not have gone better, Beker. You handled that crowd masterfully, as usual."

"I didn't share everything I know, Elon. The Monarchists may already have six of the twelve Patriarchs under their influence...perhaps even under their control. "

"So? We have six Patriarchs under our control."

"Not true...we have only five firmly in hand, with one wavering. Much of eastern Manasseh is exposed to the Ammonites. Despite Helek's blandishments to his brethren, their Patriarch may be tempted by a king."

"I've swayed my Manasseh Elders away from the Monarchists before. Beker, I can do it again."

"The situation may already be beyond what you can do, Helek. Remember this... our brotherhood is powerful...not popular. If the Monarchists can rouse the common people, even some of *our* Patriarchs will switch sides."

"It's not like you to think all is lost, Beker."

"Nothing is lost, Elon. However, the three of us may require an alternate strategy. We must be prepared to look beyond the Highlanders in order to secure our futures."

Chapter 8 - The Monarchists

And the children of Israel grieved for Benjamin their brother, and said, "One tribe is cut off from Israel today. What shall we do for wives for those who remain, seeing we have sworn by the LORD not to give them our daughters as wives?" Then it was discovered that no one had come from Jabesh Gilead. So the congregation sent there twelve thousand valiant men, saying, "Go and strike the inhabitants of Jabesh Gilead with the edge of the sword. Destroy the children, every man, and every woman who is not a virgin." So the men found among the inhabitants of Jabesh Gilead four hundred young virgins and brought them back to the camp at Shiloh. Then the whole congregation sent word to the men of Benjamin hiding at the Rock of Rimmon, and announced peace to them.

From the Book of Judges, Chapter 21, verses 6 to 13

When you saw that Nahash king of the Ammonites was moving against you, you said, 'We want a king over us!' – even though the LORD your God was your king.

From the Book of I Samuel, Chapter 12, verse 12

The Philistine garrisoned town of Gibeon

Nathan and his five companions had spent the entire morning scrubbing down the barn in Gibeon. Kish was due that afternoon from Gibeah to inspect this extension of his donkey business. Even though their main task was spying on the adjacent Philistine garrison, Nathan and his fellow herdsmen still took pride in their cover work. They wanted to demonstrate how faithfully they looked after all their employer's interests. Nathan was not surprised to see that Saul and Jonathan accompanied Kish, along with twenty-three donkeys to be added to their corral stock. However, Nathan was concerned when Jonathan cut short any greetings. His friend took him by the elbow and led the way to a secluded corner of the building.

"Prepare for visitors after dark, Nathan."

"How many?"

"Three or four."

"Friendly?"

"Kish doesn't expect any trouble, but tell the lads to be alert."

"Who are they, Jonathan?"

"Even Kish doesn't know their names. He's meeting with them only as a favor to an old friend. They carry a message for the Benjamite League. This barn seemed a safe place."

"In the shadow of a Philistine garrison?"

"It's the last place the Philistines would look, Nathan."

That evening Nathan waited for the anonymous visitors in the shadows outside the barn. He carried no weapon, but felt quite secure. Two of his men, and their bows, were watching over him from places of concealment. These men would also ensure that the night's meeting was not disturbed by unexpected arrivals. Nathan heard the faint crunch of footsteps well before he spotted their owners. Several oil lamps gave the interior of the barn a warm glow while revealing four men on the path to the door. Nathan called out from his hideaway.

"Greetings, Gentlemen! What is your business?"

The first man in line appeared briefly startled by Nathan's disembodied voice, but quickly recovered his composure.

"We are here to meet Kish of Gibeah."

Nathan slipped into the light and beckoned the men to follow him through the door to the brightest part of the barn. Here Kish awaited them on a crude wooden bench. Saul sat on a slightly lower stool at his father's right hand, with Jonathan on Kish's left side, seated on a saddle which raised him a few inches from the floor. The other three herdsmen, and their concealed daggers, were perched behind Kish on grain sacks. Nathan knew the seating arrangement was intended to demonstrate the relative importance of those present. Nathan took his place on another saddle beside Jonathan. He gestured to the four strangers to be seated directly in front of Kish.

The visitors gazed upon an old blanket laid directly on the packed dirt floor.

Nathan hid his amusement at Kish's blatant indicator of the strangers' status as mere supplicants. The shrewd old man also thought the discomfort would help the men get to the point faster. If the visitors were offended, they gave no sign of it as they sat down. According to custom, the host would normally open the discussion, but Kish spoke not a word. It dawned on Nathan that Kish was not particularly pleased to see them. One of the guests finally broke the awkward silence.

"The message we bring is extremely sensitive, Kish. We had hoped to share it only with you and your most trusted men."

Nathan felt his face redden at the stranger's implication that he and Jonathan were not men. Both of them were in their seventeenth year and had repeatedly justified the trust of their fellow League members. Fortunately, Kish came to the boys' defense.

"Then speak. Only our most trusted men are here."

The speaker bit his lip at the social blunder. He inclined his head respectfully to both Nathan and Jonathan before resuming his conversation with Kish.

"I am Naaman, of Benjamin. My companions are Onan of Judah, Zerah of Simeon and Gemalli of Dan."

"You are also *Monarchists* recruiting the Southern Tribes to your cause."

"You are indeed well informed, Kish Ben-Abiel."

"Yet not well enough informed to know why you are here."

"To tell you the Patriarchs will meet at Shiloh before the end of the month."

"That is most kind of you. Why should I care?"

"Nahash, King of the Ammonites, is threatening our lands east of the Jordan River. The Patriarchs must respond."

"I own no land east of the Jordan. I have no quarrel with Nahash. The Transjordan Tribes have never done me any favors. This doesn't concern me."

"The Patriarchs will use this assembly to establish a kingdom in Israel."

"Oh, I have heard this story, Naaman. How does it go? A king requires the support of at least seven tribes to have any hope of success. The most you Monarchists have ever pulled together is five. The six Mountain Tribes will simply close ranks and block your efforts...as they always have...end of story."

"This time will be different. We have new allies."

"So, Naaman, have you finally convinced one of the Mountain Tribes to defect?"

"I can say no more."

"No, but you will *ask* more. You will ask me to persuade the Elders of Benjamin to demand a king."

"Kish, Israel is threatened by enemies from both east and west. No tribe has suffered more than Benjamin. You should be among the first to welcome a king."

"You mean no one has suffered more at the hands of its brother tribes than Benjamin. You baffle me, Naaman. No true son of Benjamin would ever place the interests of outsiders ahead of his own tribe."

"Do you question my honor, Kish?"

"I question your memory, Naaman. Have you forgotten the other tribes once banded together against us? How they exterminated all of Benjamin except for six hundred men?"

"That was long ago... and Benjamin was not totally innocent. Israel needs all its sons to stand together."

"Then let Israel follow Benjamin's example. Our men don't hide in the mountains. We kill Philistines... and those traitors who serve them."

Nathan was both surprised and relieved when the increasingly heated exchange was unexpectedly interrupted by a calm new voice.

"By the way, Kish...how is that working out for you?"

Nathan turned to find himself looking into the self-assured eyes of Onan the Judean. His innocent sounding inquiry monetarily caught Kish off guard. Nathan understood the cause for the flushed look that now came over on Kish's face. The resistance effort in Benjamin had been stalled for quite some time. None of the Benjamite League's recent activities had resulted in any long lasting benefit. Onan's next words confirmed for Nathan that the man already knew this.

"No answer? Then allow me to speculate. Your League has undoubtedly discovered that executing traitors has hurt your movement more than it has helped."

"Don't presume to judge us, Judean."

"No need to defend yourself...I'm sure they were all swine. However, your actions have created a dilemma for you. Many otherwise loyal Benjamites can't avoid collaborating with the Philistines at one time or another. They avoid you for fear your Benjamite League might burn *their* houses down...with *them* in it."

"The Benjamite League doesn't need traitors!"

"True, but your Benjamite League needs *these* people, Kish. It can't win unless your own tribe is united behind you. Oh...you'll kill a few Philistines. You'll feel heroic. But the people of Benjamin will never be free."

"I spit on defeatists. You believe our struggle hopeless because it soothes your cowardly conscience."

"You struggle is not hopeless, Kish, just your methods. You can't save Benjamin by ignoring the rest of Israel. Your League must begin by acknowledging the truth."

"And what truth might that be, Onan of Judah?"

"The Benjamite League can't obtain weapons on its own... can't field an army...can't drive the Philistines from its lands. Your League can't do a score of things required for victory...but a KING might!"

Onan's last statement seemed to echo in Nathan's ears. He looked out the corners of his eyes to gauge the reaction of his comrades. Kish was obviously displeased with Onan's words, but seemed unable to refute them. The expressions of the other League members ranged between anger and distress. Nathan could almost feel the frustration oozing out of Jonathan. Surprisingly, Saul seemed serene, as if relieved someone had finally brought painful facts out into the open. Nathan was unsure of his own feelings, but was intrigued by the possibilities Onan presented. He longed to ask questions, but knew he must defer to Kish. Nathan studied Onan as the man patiently waited for the others to digest his proposal. He finally heard Kish clear his throat.

"Benjamin is the smallest of the tribes, Onan. Do you Monarchists really *need* us? Or do you think us too weak to refuse? No empty flattery, Judean...just the truth."

"Earlier you referred to the civil war between Benjamin and the other tribes. Israel mustered more than ten soldiers for each of your warriors, yet Benjamin defeated them *twice*. Kish...we don't seek Benjamin because you lost. Israel needs Benjamin *because you nearly won*."

Nathan noted that Naaman and the other Monarchists appeared content with Onan serving as their spokesman, thus revealing the meeting strategy. Naaman, a fellow Benjamite, was merely a figurehead to get the delegation inside the Benjamite League. The ensuing confrontation revealed Onan as its true leader. Nathan wondered if the Monarchists were really a tool of the Judeans... and whether Kish was now considering that same possibility. A *king of Israel* and a *Judean king over Israel* were two entirely different matters. Nathan pushed aside these thoughts when Kish started to speak.

"Very well, Onan, I will speak with the Elders of Benjamin on your behalf. However, I hope the Highlanders give you a good fight before the Patriarchs. For if this *king* of yours cannot overcome their arguments, what chance has he against the Philistines?"

Chapter 9 - The Patriarchs

So, Samuel grew, and the LORD was with him and He let none of Samuel's words be false. And all Israel from Dan to Beersheba knew that Samuel had been established as a prophet of the Lord. Then the LORD began to appear again in Shiloh, for the LORD revealed Himself to Samuel in Shiloh through His Word.

From the Book of I Samuel, Chapter 3, verses 19 to 21

And Samuel said, "This is what the king who will reign over you will do: He will take your sons and make them serve as horsemen for his chariots, or as infantry running before his chariots. He will appoint your best men to be commanders over his thousands and captains over his fifties. He will conscript others to plow his ground and reap his harvest, and to make his weapons of war and equipment for his chariots. He will take your daughters to be his confectioners, cooks, and bakers. And he will take the best of your fields, your vineyards, and your olive groves, and give them to his officials. He will take a tenth of your grain and your grapes, and give it to his officers. And he will take your male servants, your female servants, your finest young men, and your donkeys, and put them to work on his projects. He will take a tenth of your sheep. And you will be his slaves."

From the Book of I Samuel, Chapter 8, verses 11 to 17

The town of Shiloh in the mountains of Ephraim

Beker regretted ever agreeing to Shiloh as the venue for this crucial meeting of the Patriarchs. It did have the benefit of being in Beker's homeland of Ephraim, but it was still a second rate town. The site held great religious significance for Israelites as a former home of the Tabernacle with its Ark of the Covenant, in which the Spirit of God dwelt among His people. However, a generation had passed since God and the Ark last resided in Shiloh. After being lost to, and then recovered from, the Philistines, the Ark now rested in the town of Kiriath-jearim. The faithful of Israel no longer trekked to Shiloh for their sacrifices and the town had declined as a result. Beker now joined some seventy other men as they all crowded into what was purportedly the largest room in Shiloh. Burning oil lamps and tiny windows combined to create an atmosphere of hot, stale air. Beker at least managed to secure a seat at the front where there was a small space between the audience and a long wooden table. There the twelve Patriarchs sat facing the other Elders.

Truth be told, there simply were higher priorities than comfortable accommodations on the Highlanders' agenda. Beker knew it was essential his faction's political capital be spent shrewdly. The Highlanders had concentrated their efforts on the selection of like-minded Elders as Patriarchs, with rather disappointing results. Beker considered only five Patriarchs from the Mountain Tribes to be completely reliable. The Patriarch from the sixth mountain tribe, Manasseh, was nominally in the Highlander camp, but the man came from eastern Manasseh where a strong Monarchist element existed. Beker was forced to assume the other six Patriarchs were all Monarchists. Beker's disappointment was compensated somewhat by the appointment of Ephraim's Patriarch, Hoshea, to preside over the session. Subtle signals to Hoshea should allow Beker to influence the proceedings.

A commotion at the rear of the hall caused a hush to fall over the tightly packed congregation. The sickly-sweet aroma of incense told Beker that the opening ceremony had begun. He turned to see a pair of Levites bearing smoking censers make their way down the narrow center aisle, followed by Gershon, the current High Priest of Israel. Four other priests followed close behind Gershon, one carrying a bleating lamb. A trailing pair of incense-burning Levites completed the white-clad procession. An outbreak of coughing told Beker he was not the only one having trouble breathing in the congested room. When Beker noticed a small brazier with hot coals a few feet away, he realized his respiratory troubles were just starting.

Gershon stopped next to the brazier and, competing for attention with the wailing lamb, offered a prayer requesting God's guidance and blessing for the proceedings. When Gershon finished, the other priests hastened into action. A knife flashed across the lamb's throat and silenced its cries. The spraying blood splattered on snow white garments as the practiced hands of the priests deftly carved the lamb into the prescribed pieces for a burnt offering. After one priest stacked wood on smoldering coals, the others arranged each portion of the lamb in its proper position on the altar. Within moments, a blazing fire consumed the sacrifice and sent it heavenward...or at least to the ceiling. Here the smoke collected and thickened. For a few moments, Beker feared suffocation. Complaints flowed from the crowd as the Levites departed with their incense. No one objected when Hoshea announced that deliberations would be delayed one hour to allow the air to clear. Beker paused to avoid the initial stampede to the entrance before following the others outside. Helek of Manasseh and Elon of Zebulon, his chief lieutenants, were waiting for him.

"Not a very auspicious start to the day, was it, Beker?"

"Could have been worse, Helek. They might have tried to sacrifice a bull in there."

"It was a waste of time, but someone feared the pious would complain unless they saw God being appeased."

"The Patriarchs can afford to waste time, but we cannot...especially you, Helek. What is the name of that Patriarch from Manasseh?"

"Shemida."

"He should be hearing your voice until it becomes his own."

"I know what to do."

"Have you won Shemida over yet? No?"

"Be fair, Beker. I've done everything except marry his ugly sister."

"Listen to me, Helek. We cannot allow Manasseh to side with the Monarchists. I do not care if you have to marry his donkey! You have done worse."

Beker watched as anger spread over Helek's flushed face. He prided himself on knowing how far to push an ally without making him an enemy. Beker locked eyes with the trembling man and found only hesitation and apprehension there. Beker smiled, please that he was still able to impose his will on the weaker man. Now was the time for soothing.

"What I really meant, Helek, was that you have endured much for our cause. We cannot succeed without you."

The color slowly left Helek's face, and the familiar expression of a faithful subordinate returned. Helek immediately put on his natural charm like a garment as he left to seek out Shemida. Beker heard a gruff chuckle from close behind and turned to view Elon's feral grin.

"Beker, I've never understood why you trust that mealy-mouthed rodent."

"I do not trust him. He uses others and I use him. Besides, Elon, I cannot do everything."

"You have me."

"Your talents lie in different areas, my Friend. Helek is the epitome of warm and friendly. But you are more like a sharpened blade."

"I *am* your blade, Beker. There's never been a problem that can't be solved by slipping a knife between the right person's ribs."

"That may be true for *any single problem*, but not *all problems*. No, Elon, your skills are best when used sparingly. I fear killing a few Monarchists now would only make them stronger in the future."

"I don't have as much faith in Helek as you do, Beker. Perhaps you are the one who should be making sacrifices."

"I believe in handling my own affairs. Anyway, God probably has better things to do."

"Want me to talk some of the undecided? My reputation can be very persuasive."

"Merely visit with our allies instead, Elon. Your hand upon their shoulders should stiffen their spines. Meanwhile, I will spy out our competition."

Beker thought his best use of the impromptu recess was to observe known Monarchists as they moved among the loitering crowd. He expertly detected the Monarchists' new allies and gauged their overall strength. He was even able to identify his counterpart among the Monarchists...Onan of Judah. The Monarchists circled the man like bees around a hive. Of course, Beker realized that his own role must be just as obvious to Onan. A short time later, Beker caught Onan's eye on his way back inside the hall. Onan nodded respectfully toward him and Beker returned the compliment. He felt a thrill knowing the actual battle was about to commence.

By the time Beker reached his seat, he had decided on a course of action. He would wait patiently for the Monarchists to expose their strategy. Beker was confident his underlings could respond adequately to the Monarchists' arguments during any debates. He knew the Highlanders had an inherent advantage by being on the defensive. Onan and his followers had the burden of proving to the Patriarchs that a king was superior to Israel's current circumstances.

Hoshea opened the session by calling on Shuni, the Elder from Gad, to explain his reason for requesting that the Council meet. Shuni began detailing at length the supposed threat from the new Ammonite king, Nahash. One of the Highlander Patriarchs interrupted this monologue to ask very bluntly what Shuni expected the Council to do. Shuni appeared slightly bewildered at being cut off so abruptly during his prepared remarks. After a few seconds of indecision, he finally blurted out his answer.

"Give us a king."

After that, the verbal blows and counterblows began in earnest while the Patriarchs listened impassively. The Highlanders in the assembly argued Israel had faced similar threats many times before and had always overcome them without a king. The Monarchists contended that the Ammonites and the Philistines together posed a unique challenge which demanded a strong king. An Elder from Asher retorted that Israel already had the *LORD* as its king, and *He* would always provide *a Judge* at the proper time to lead His people. Onan then argued the judges may have served well enough in the past, but Israel had grown from a collection of tribes into a nation...and a nation required a king. This remark infuriated many Elders. One even shouted that without the tribes, there *was* no Israel!

Beker was quite pleased by the intense debate's lack of direction. He assumed that the disunity of the Elders in the audience reflected the leanings of the Patriarchs. A stalemate between the Patriarchs meant no king, which suited the Highlanders' needs perfectly. Beker then noticed Shemida, the Patriarch from Manasseh, the least reliable Mountain Tribe, asking to address the assembly. To Beker's horror, the supposed Highlander ally began speaking in favor of the Monarchists. Beker gritted his teeth while watching Helek's pathetic attempts to get the rogue Patriarch's attention. Beker's eyes sought out Onan and observed the Monarchist leader smiling broadly. Beker realized then his prior estimations had been fatally flawed. Instead of twelve equally divided Patriarchs, the Monarchists actually enjoyed a seven to five advantage. Feeling control of the situation slipping away, he decided to wield his most potent weapon. Beker might have been outmaneuvered, but he was far from being defeated.

For the first time that day, Beker stood to speak. Even before Hoshea called for silence, the arguments began to subside. Every man present knew who Beker was, and even the hecklers wanted to listen. Beker could feel Onan's eyes on him from across the room.

"Honored Patriarchs, it has occurred to me that some of the Elders present may have made a false assumption about this day's proceedings. Apparently, they may believe that a simple majority of the Patriarchs is sufficient to create a kingdom. That would be a *false* assumption."

Beker's ears detect anxious whispering spreading out among the Elders behind him. He saw several of the Patriarchs seated across from him glaring in anger. Beker brushed aside this feeble attempt at intimidation and presented his challenge directly to the assembly as a whole.

"The truth is that a kingdom can be established in Israel only by a *unanimous* decision of the Patriarchs."

A breathless stillness briefly settled upon the packed hall only to be swiftly swept away by a flood of hysteria. Beker allowed the chaos to flow around him like a rock in troubled seas as he continued to stare calmly at the Patriarchs. Even many of the Highlanders apparently believed he had lost his wits. When the noise finally slackened, Beker knew the final battle was about to commence. He turned to find Onan standing and facing him.

"Beker, on behalf of this august assembly, I must ask how you came to such a remarkable conclusion."

"By simple, undeniable logic, Onan. I know for a fact that the six Mountain Tribes could never be *forced* to accept a king."

"Six?"

"Have it your way. Five tribes and the western half of Manasseh will not tolerate a king being forced on them."

"I still can't follow your reasoning, Beker. How will a minority of Mountain Tribes prevent Israel from having a king? Will they go to war against their brethren?"

"No need to be so bloodthirsty, Onan. Let's first think through the results of *only seven* Patriarchs favoring a king. Your new monarch would discover that he ruled only half a kingdom... and the *poor half* at that. He would also find that his half-kingdom was itself divided in half. The territory of the Mountain Tribes would separate his TransJordan Tribes from his Southern Tribes. How could your king protect all his subjects...if he can't move across the lands of the Mountain Tribes?"

"A king would fight anyone threatening the safety of his people...even you Highlanders."

"And what will this king use for an army? Can the Monarchists give one to him? No, I suspect the TransJordan Tribes would not be long in returning to the fold. First, eastern Manasseh will reconcile with their western cousins. Gad and

Rueben will follow once they understand how truly isolated they will be. That would leave only the Southern Tribes for your king. Then it's just a question of whether Dan or Benjamin abandons your faltering kingdom first... forcing even Simeon to withdraw. Tell me, Onan... does Judah think it can stand alone?"

"Your words are those of a desperate man, Beker. You think to intimidate the Patriarchs by threatening civil war. You Highlanders would destroy Israel if you can't have your way."

"You distort my meaning. The Mountain Tribes intend to remain just as they are. If Israel is broken asunder, it will be the Monarchists who are to blame."

"Beker...you are willfully blind to Israel's peril. You may delay the coming of a king...but you cannot prevent it."

"Is that the Monarchists' final word on the matter?"

"Yes."

"Thank you, Onan, for making clear that continuing this meeting is pointless."

At what should have been the moment of his triumph, Beker suddenly lost his audience. It was the last thing he expected. Every eye in the chamber was drawn away from Beker and Onan by a polite, but firm voice.

"Then no one should mind if I speak."

Gershon, the High Priest, faced the Patriarchs with his arms folded. Beker mistakenly assumed the man had departed earlier with the Levites. Beker knew Gershon's presence was no accident. The High Priest had obviously been waiting for the right moment to intervene. But why? Beker's glance toward Onan showed the Monarchist leader's unmistakable approval of Gershon's action. This implied Onan already knew what the High Priest would say, which could not be good for the Highlanders' cause. Beker now understood why the burnt offering had not been made outdoors, as was customary. The entire ceremony had been staged to allow Gershon to surreptitiously attend a meeting normally restricted to Elders. Beker saw Hoshea struggling for a proper response to Gershon's unprecedented request to speak.

"Unlike the other tribes, Levi was never given a specific territory by Joshua. Therefore, it is not entitled to name a Patriarch. I'm sorry, Gershon of Levi. You may be Israel's High Priest, but you have no standing here."

"I may not have any here, Hoshea of Ephraim, but I have great standing among the people of Israel. And I tell you as their High Priest that the LORD would not be pleased by His people making war on each other. Furthermore, I am certain that the people of Israel would not be pleased that their Patriarchs reached such a momentous decision regarding a king *without first seeking guidance from the LORD, the God of Israel!*"

Gershon had not yet said anything to indicate whether he favored a king or not. Still, Beker sensed an avalanche was building, one that would sweep either the Monarchists or the Highlanders from power. Beker knew his options were rapidly fading away; however, the wrong move could result in disaster. He had already been far more aggressive this day than he had any right to be; his bellicose words undoubtedly frightened even many of his allies. Yet Beker's instincts screamed that the

High Priest would ultimately favor the Monarchists. He decided to act on the first desperate idea that came to mind. At the very least, it would give him time to think of a better one.

"Gershon, are you taking it upon yourself to seek this guidance from the LORD?"

"Of course, that is the traditional role of the High Priest."

"How will you know the mind of God?"

"Well...the exact use of the Holy Ephod, the Urim and the Thummim is known only to the priesthood. However, I assure you, God's answer will be quite clear to me."

"And you think this method will reassure the people of Israel."

"Why shouldn't it?"

"I mean no disrespect to you, Gershon, but the people have had good reason to distrust their High Priests in the past. I give you the example of Eli and his sons. They abused the trust of their holy office to enrich themselves at the expense of the people and were punished by God."

"True, but I have never, and would never, act in such a manner."

"Certainly, certainly...but doubt may exist in the minds of the people. After all, you and the LORD will be the only ones present."

Beker could hear indignant shouts protesting his last words, probably from both Monarchists and Highlanders.

125

Casting doubt on the integrity of the High Priest was dangerous, but Beker saw no other options. A few voices even called for Beker to be stoned...but Gershon was not one of them. Instead, Beker saw a deeply troubled look on the High Priest's face. The noise subsided as Gershon began to speak.

"What if someone else approaches the LORD about a king? Someone the people trust completely?"

"Is there such a man? One who has *both* the trust of Israel *and* the ear of God?"

"Samuel."

"Samuel?"

"As a judge, Samuel is God's representative to Israel. Who better to settle this dispute?"

For many heartbeats, no one seemed to know how to respond to the High Priest's suggestion. Beker had prevented Gershon from taking control, but he was not sure if his situation had been made better or worse. Finally, a man in the very back of the hall spoke up.

"Is he still alive?"

This simple question generated some nervous laughter, but Beker could tell many did not know the answer. He was not sure himself whether this notable man still lived. Samuel began serving in the Tabernacle as a child. He later acquired a reputation for spiritual wisdom and was recognized throughout Israel as a prophet. After the disastrous defeat by the Philistines at Aphek, the resulting loss of the Ark of the Covenant and the death of the High Priest, Samuel filled the leadership void by assuming the duties of a priest. When the Philistines next threatened the Israelites again, Samuel assumed the third role of Israel's spiritual triumvirate and became a judge. His subsequent victory at Mizpah cemented his position in the hearts of Israel. A nervous Gershon began answering questions as they were shouted out by the audience.

"Yes, Samuel lives in Ramah. Old age limits him to traveling a yearly circuit between Ramah, Bethel, Gilgal and Mizpah."

"Haven't his sons replaced him as judge?"

"Samuel appointed them to be judges in Beersheba when he could no longer journey that far south. However, a judge holds his office for life."

"I've heard of them. They sell their justice to the highest bidder. Will the people still trust Samuel in spite of them?"

"Yes. Samuel has an impeccable reputation."

Beker quickly concluded that while Gershon might be an adequate priest, the man knew little about running a meeting. The assembly dissolved into small clusters of debate. Blessed with a welcomed breathing space, Beker sat down to consider the new dynamics. Onan did not seem as smug as when Gershon first spoke. Beker inferred that Samuel had not been part of any discussions between the Levites and the Monarchists. The leanings of this Prophet/Priest/Judge must be as much a mystery to Onan as it was to him. Beker sighed in frustration at his path still being as uncertain as ever. He closed his eyes to focus on making sense of this confusing array of observations, words, clues and instincts. Beker caught his breath as several fragments of thought suddenly came together to form a complete idea.

Of course...it was all so simple!

Beker immediately caught the eye of his fellow Ephraimite, Hoshea, and signaled his desire to speak. Once the Head Patriarch restored order, Beker put his scheme to work.

"Gershon...I accept your recommendation. I feel certain that Samuel will also be acceptable to the six Mountain Tribes. Let the Patriarchs and Elders journey next month to Ramah and ask Samuel to intercede with the LORD on this question of a king."

Protests immediately erupted from the Highlander delegation, along with a few painful cries. The Monarchists seemed perplexed, as if uncertain as to whether they had cause for celebration. Onan in particular bore an enigmatic expression as he stood to speak.

"Our brother Beker has spoken well. I too urge the Patriarchs and Elders, from *all* tribes, to refer this issue of a king to Samuel."

One reason Hoshea presided over the Council was that he did know how to run a meeting. Within moments, Hoshea had polled the other Patriarchs and announced that everyone should reconvene in four weeks in Ramah. The Patriarchs' decision was unanimous. As soon as he stepped out into the fresh air, Beker was mobbed by incensed Highlanders. They gave him no chance to soothe them with his usual beguiling eloquence.

"You have betrayed us, Beker!"

"Why did you not trust us with your real strategy?"

"I told *everyone*, exactly what *you* told me to say, Beker. Now I look like a fool!"

"Couldn't you tell that the Levites are in league with the Monarchists? Now you've asked a Levite to choose a king for us!"

Fortunately, Helek and Elon rounded up some servants and hastened to Beker's rescue by forming a protective ring around him. They made promises to explain everything later, but claimed now was not the time. After the last hothead had been steered away, Elon looked at his patron and sighed.

"Beker, have you lost your mind?"

"Elon. Elon. Couldn't you sense how the sand was shifting under our feet?"

"Yes, but I did not think you would simply surrender to the Monarchists."

"No one surrendered! I gave the Highlanders their best chance for victory!"

"You have a strange idea of victory, Beker. The pious sounding Gershon has sold out to the Monarchists. Do you really think Samuel to be any better? He's just another Levite. Samuel will hear God say exactly what his High Priest tells him to hear. It's all over except for the coronation."

"I pray the Monarchists are just that naïve, Elon. Stop and take a close look at this Samuel. Consider his record. In over thirty years as a judge, Samuel has *never* said a single word

129

about a king. Once Samuel obtains power, he *never* gives it up; in fact, he is passing it on to his sons. Trust me...Samuel does not want a king any more than you!"

"I had no idea you understood Samuel that well, Beker."

"I do not claim to, but I understand *power*... and what it does to a man."

Chapter 10 - The Judge

Then all the elders of Israel gathered together and came to Samuel at Ramah, and said to him, "Look, you are old, and your sons do not walk in your ways. Now make us a king to judge us like all the nations."

From the Book of I Samuel, Chapter 8, verses 4 and 5

And the LORD said to Samuel, "Understand what the people are saying; for they have not rejected you, but they have rejected Me as their King. As they have done since I brought them up out of Egypt, even to this day—forsaking Me and serving other gods—so they are now doing to you."

From the Book of I Samuel, Chapter 8, verses 7 and 8

The town of Ramah on the border between Benjamin and Ephraim

It had been ages since Beker slept in a tent. His back ached that morning despite the best efforts of his servants to create a soft pallet for him on the uneven ground. Yet some sacrifice of personal comfort was unavoidable since the small town of Ramah boasted even fewer amenities than Shiloh. Several hundred Patriarchs, Elders and servants seeking an audience with Samuel rapidly overwhelmed the limited housing. Tents at least offered a respectable amount of personal space and privacy compared to the rough huts clustered together within Ramah. Beker had the foresight to arrive a day early with his party and obtain a shaded campsite near water. Later arrivals fared much worse. The sight of his fellow dignitaries squatting at crude latrines like so many goat herders amused Beker to no end.

Helek and Elon joined Beker in his tent an hour after sunrise. They shared a simple breakfast prepared by Beker's servants before heading into town. As they neared Ramah, Beker saw most of the Patriarchs and Elders milling about the road in obvious distress. Samuel was not at his home, and no one knew where to find him. Beker ground his teeth in annoyance while Elon whispered bitterly in his ear.

"Incredible! We entrust the future of Israel to one man, only to find he has something better to do?"

"I should have met with Samuel myself, Elon. Apparently arranging a simple appointment is beyond the abilities of our illustrious High Priest."

"I would be the last to defend a priest, Beker, but this mishap may not be Gershon's fault."

"Meaning?"

"The old judge might be deliberating avoiding us."

"That is just what a man unwilling to relinquish his power would do. Elon, your mind is as sharp as your blade."

"It is as you surmised, Beker. Samuel does indeed oppose a king."

"Gather our people. We can shatter this Monarchist scheme once and for all."

Beker tried to gauge the crowd's reaction as his followers stirred the pot of their boiling emotions. Leaders of both factions were hotly debating how to proceed. Several Highlander Patriarchs proposed returning home in light of Samuel's absence. The Monarchists vehemently protested and prepared to bodily prevent any Elder from departing. Beker could not be more pleased at this turn of events. Either a cancellation or a riot would cripple the Monarchist cause, without any blame being attached to him personally. However, the timely appearance of a Levite dressed in white linen kept anyone from coming to blows. The young man announced that Samuel was awaiting them on a hill just north of Ramah. Beker sighed in mild disappointment. It would have been nice to wrap things up early. Still, Beker was more confident than ever that he held the upper hand.

Shemida, the presiding Patriarch this day, called the assembly to order and bade them to follow the young Levite. As he joined the procession, Beker reflected on how the power balance within the Patriarchs had shifted ever so slightly in favor of the Monarchists since the last session in Shiloh. His ally Hoshea was still Ephraim's Patriarch, but no longer enjoyed enough support to lead the Council. The appointment of Shemida of Manasseh as Hoshea's replacement was the best deal that Beker could broker for this crucial meeting. An Elder from Manasseh was a natural compromise candidate since western Manasseh was firmly in the Highlander camp while eastern Manasseh was sympathetic to the Monarchist cause. Helek had gone to great lengths to win over his fellow tribesman, but Shemida had proved immune to the blandishments of Beker's man. Shemida also vexed Beker for another reason...the man was not a leader. The other Elders from Manasseh had selected Shemida as their Patriarch *precisely* because he would not overshadow them. Beker wondered how well the man would stand up to a living legend like Samuel.

Beker was halfway up the hill before he spotted a lone figure at the summit. The judge was seated on a large rock strategically placed at the top of the slope, as confident as a general who had carefully chosen his battleground. The contour of the hillcrest required the Elders to stand directly in front of Samuel, as if they were wrongdoers awaiting his judgment. Beker and his supporters slithered between the bystanders to take up a position near the Patriarchs. The morning sun shone directly behind Samuel, making it impossible for Beker to read the old man's expression. Even seated, Samuel's head was at least three feet higher than those nearest him. Samuel cut such an imposing figure that Beker had to fight the urge to kneel. Beker found yet another reason to respect the venerable judge.

The old man had style.

Shemida stepped forward until he was within three paces of Samuel and initiated a staring contest. As the silence dragged on, Beker sighed in frustration at Shemida's futile tactic. Speaking first during negotiations was often seen as a sign of weakness. However, the Patriarchs and Elders had traveled all this way to ask the judge *for something*. Samuel knew he was the one dealing from a position of strength and could simply wait Shemida out. Impatient murmuring at his back finally compelled a flustered Shemida to speak.

"Samuel, you are old. Your sons Joel and Abijah do not walk in your ways. They pervert justice, they take bribes, they..."

Beker cringed as Shemida froze under Samuel's baleful stare. The Patriarch had botched what should have been a straightforward task. He was supposed to respectfully request that Samuel ask the LORD whether Israel should have a king. Speak up, step back, shut up. Nothing could be simpler. Instead, the fool had tried to sway the judge to the Monarchist side, only to end up insulting a national hero. Samuel finally spoke when it became painfully obvious that Shemida could not.

"Then before this old man dies, I hope you get around to why you're really here."

Shemida licked his lips, opened his mouth...and shut it just as quickly. This brief hesitation emboldened the anxious Monarchists to seize the initiative. Onan of Judah shoved his way through the crowd and stepped in front of Shemida. Beker thought Onan's bellowing could be heard by every resident of Ramah.

"Appoint a king to lead us, such as all the other nations have!"

The only sound on the hillside was the wind rustling in some nearby bushes. Both the words and their tone left the listeners completely stunned for a long moment. Beker was about to protest both Onan's inexcusable breach of protocol when a small cloud blocked the sun. He now had a clear view of Samuel's face, and the old judge was absolutely *livid*. Beker bit his lip and considered how to use this unexpected insight. He simultaneously seized Helek and Elon by their tunics and pulled them close enough that he could whisper in both men's ears.

"Tell our people to remain absolutely quiet! Not a single word!"

"But Beker, the Monarchists are..."

"Tell them to watch as the Monarchists slice their own throats. Now go!"

As his two friends pushed off through the throng, Beker grinned wickedly. It would be the greatest of ironies if the Monarchists were doomed by their own leader's abrasive tongue. As he turned, Beker was shocked that he could no longer see Samuel. It would have been beyond his wildest hopes for the old man to simply leave over Onan's rudeness. However, a second look showed the judge on his knees, facing the rock on which he had been sitting. Beker could hear faint sounds from Samuel, but no words. He realized the judge was *praying*. The Patriarchs and Elders looked at each other, but none knew what to do, other than wait. After a while, men began sitting down to whisper while impatiently watching Samuel. Beker observed his minions scurrying about delivering his instructions. Both Helek and Elon sat down with Beker a few minutes later.

"Well?"

"Our people know what to do, Beker. They're confused, but they'll obey."

"Helek, that's why we are the shepherds and they are the sheep."

Nearly an hour passed before Samuel resumed his seat on the rock. The assembly rose as one man and pressed forward to hear God's Word from His judge. Beker was puzzled by Samuel's first words, but he soon grasped the gist of the old man's message. Samuel was trying to talk the Elders out of requesting a king! Beker became almost giddy as he heard the dire warnings bursting forth from the judge's lips. Samuel declared that a king would enslave their sons and daughters, seize their best lands, take their prized herds, impose heavy taxes, and drag the country into war. Beker himself could not have composed a speech more favorable to the Highlander cause. He would carry the day if only his Highlander allies had the discipline to keep their mouths shut. When Samuel finished, he asked the Elders to repent of their presumption. A hundred Monarchists joined in a common shout.

"No!"

Onan then waved his compatriots to silence so he could address Samuel directly.

"We want a king over us. Then we will be like all the other nations...with a king to lead us... to go out before us and fight our battles."

Samuel appeared more distressed than ever as he knelt again in prayer. Beker contained his growing excitement with great difficulty. The congregation sat down once more and resumed their vigil. They did not have long to wait until Samuel rose and uttered a single command.

"Go home."

Then heeding his own words, Samuel turned his back on the befuddled assembly and shuffled off toward Ramah. A few men tried to initiate a debate over what the judge meant, but the attempt was futile. Beker now beheld a crestfallen Onan. The Monarchist leader had orchestrated a Council of the Patriarchs when he thought the time finally right to crown a king. He and his associates had hung all their hopes on this one meeting with Samuel. Expecting a definitive yes or no, they were sent home with nothing. All of the Monarchists' labors had come to naught. Onan and a handful of his followers watched glumly as the exuberant Highlanders descended the hill. One by one, even the die-hard Monarchists reluctantly accepted their defeat and departed.

On the other hand, Beker was thrilled by the day's events. Samuel's non-answer had vindicated Beker's strategy and restored his reputation among the Highlanders. Men who had publicly rebuked Beker now lined up to pay their respects. Overall, the experience left Beker with a grudging admiration for Samuel's shrewdness. The crafty judge knew how to say *NO* without actually saying *NO*. Samuel had deftly avoided taking sides in an impossible situation and still managed to preserve his prestige as judge. Samuel even kept God firmly on his side. Beker chuckled to himself about how badly he had underestimated this old man.

He should have sought out Samuel as a partner years ago.

Chapter 11 - The Seer

Now the donkeys of Kish, Saul's father, were lost. And Kish said to his son Saul, "Please take one of the servants and go look for the donkeys." So they passed through the mountains of Ephraim and through the land of Shalisha, but they did not find them. Then they passed through the land of Shaalim, and they were not there. Then he passed through the land of the Benjamites, but they did not find them. When they had come to the land of Zuph, Saul said to his servant, "Come, let us return, before my father stops caring about the donkeys and becomes worried about us."

From the Book of I Samuel, Chapter 9, verses 3 to 5

The hill country of Ephraim

Donkeys were the dumbest animals that God had ever created.

During the past three days, this had been one of Nathan's more pleasant thoughts regarding the smelly little beasts. How could anything that valuable, be so stupid? True, nothing else could match these nimble animals for transportation across Israel's rugged terrain, but Nathan sometimes doubted they were worth all the trouble they caused. Like today. He had recently come home from Gibeon where he worked with donkeys, donkeys and more donkeys. His intent was to spend time with his mother and sister. Instead, he was forced to waste three days on donkeys.

Nathan's travails in Gibeah had begun when an early morning count of the donkey herd turned up four missing jacks.

A dusty trail of hoof prints showed some of Kish's best breeding males headed northward toward the hills of Ephraim. A frantic Kish demanded the strays be recovered before someone else claimed them. With Jonathan tending the business in Gibeon, Saul and Nathan were the only reliable men available. Nathan followed Saul toward the main house to gather a day's worth of provisions. He filled a water skin at the well while Saul went inside to collect some bread and silver. As he approached the house, Nathan overheard Saul's wife, Ahinoam, laughing and declaring that the donkeys were just typical males. Saul did not respond to his wife's jibe, but left the family compound wearing a scowl.

"Nathan, I hate taking you away from your family, but it cannot be helped. Hopefully, we will be back tonight."

"Then why take silver?"

"We might need to buy more food. And if someone else finds the beasts, they will expect a reward."

"Kish will pitch a fit."

"He will get over it. Those animals are his best studs."

"Saul, what did Ahinoam mean about typical males?"

"She was just guessing why those jacks ran off."

"I was wondering about that. They have plenty of water and grazing here."

"They probably smelled a wild she-ass in heat. Sometimes the wild herds come down from the mountains after a long dry spell. It happens every few years."

"What if there is only one female?"

"The jacks will establish dominance in their usual way."

Nathan shuddered as he pictured this disgusting donkey behavior. He had thought it a joke before witnessing it for himself. Whenever a group of male donkeys formed a herd, they established dominance by *defecating*. Each jack would then sniff the dung of the others. Nathan assumed that somehow the animal's strength came through in its aroma. Once the ritual was completed, each animal assumed his place in the newly established hierarchy of the herd. Nathan found the entire process revolting, but Jonathan thought it superior to the way most people settled their disputes. After the first day of fruitless searching, Nathan decided that, if he had been Noah, those last two donkeys would never have been allowed on the Ark.

Nathan and Saul pursued the fugitive animals in a large arc north of Gibeah. The original trail had petered out on the first day, forcing them to rely on the dubious guidance of strangers. By the third day their food was gone, the silver spent and even the rumors about donkeys had dried up. He sensed Saul was ready to admit failure and return home. Part of Nathan was relieved, but an even greater part of him hated to be defeated...especially by some mangy, oversexed animals. While Saul rested at a small village's well, Nathan determined to query the locals one final time. His best efforts had managed to turn up only the slimmest of possibilities when Saul called him back.

"Nathan, our animals are either stolen or gone wild. No point in worrying our families any more. Time to go home."

"Saul, I found someone who can help us."

"Yet another donkey sighting?"

"Not exactly...a Seer lives in the next town. He's a highly respected man of God. They say all his prophecies come true."

"Nathan...we need donkeys, not prophets."

"He may be able to tell us how to find them."

"Look...a Seer will expect a gift for his assistance; it is how they eat. Our last silver bought breakfast. Is anything even left in the bag?"

Nathan sighed. He had overlooked the need for payment. He took the sack from his shoulder and shook it over his outstretched right hand. Out fell a rusty iron blade, a piece of flint and assorted food crumbs. Taking a final peek inside, Nathan spotted something shiny wedged in the bottom corner of the sack. He extracted a bit of silver weighing a quarter of a shekel, more or less. Saul laughed at the small metal fragment Nathan held between his thumb and forefinger.

"How many donkeys do you expect the Seer to find for *that*, Nathan?"

"He just needs to find one...the others will be nearby."

"Clever boy. All right, Nathan, we will try your Seer before we go home."

Upon reaching the next town, Nathan asked some girls carrying water pots for directions. He learned the Seer would soon to preside over a sacrifice in the nearby hills. They suggested waiting by the town gate for the Seer to come out. Lacking a description of the Seer, Nathan and Saul split up to question the townspeople. Nathan had barely started his inquiries when Saul frantically waved at him. Saul was speaking to a weathered old man with lively eyes and a beguiling smile. Nathan waited patiently while the men finished their discussion. He sensed something unexpected had occurred, as Saul seemed satisfied, but confused. Saul concluded his business by pressing their last piece of silver into the stranger's palm. The man accepted it with obvious reluctance. Nathan restrained his curiosity until Saul came within whispering distance.

"Was that the Seer?"

"Yes, Nathan, it was."

"Did he find our donkeys?"

"Well, sort of. He claims our donkeys returned home the day after we left. That is why your Seer initially refused any payment. I told him my peace of mind was worth the price."

"So why do you seem troubled?"

"He invited me to a banquet tonight...as his honored guest. You are too."

"That doesn't seem so bad."

"No, it is what else he said...strange things."

"What things?"

"Look, Nathan, I am fatigued. Ignore my ramblings. Our meal is waiting."

Nathan and Saul followed the Seer up a high hill where the man sacrificed a lamb before a large assembly. Afterwards,

143

the Seer led them to a banquet hall where thirty local dignitaries awaited. Nathan had never before dined amid such opulence, but his treatment was nothing compared to the hospitality extended to Saul. The Seer not only seated Saul in the place of honor at the table's head, but arranged for him to have the choicest cut of meat. Nathan grew lethargic as his stomach filled with tasty delicacies. He was grateful for the Seer's invitation to spend the night in his home. Nathan headed straight to bed while the two older men went up on the roof to talk. He slumbered peacefully until awakened by Saul's entry into their room just before sunrise. As he drifted off to sleep again, Nathan was struck by an odd thought. The Seer had found their donkeys, fed them well and provided cozy beds.

What would the Seer have done for an entire shekel of silver?

The following morning the Seer escorted his guests as far as the city gate before whispering something to Saul. Both men nodded in agreement before Saul addressed Nathan.

"I need to tarry here a while longer, Nathan. However, you go on ahead and wait for me in Gibeah."

"Can't I wait for you at home, Saul?"

"It would be best to arrive home together. One final thing... say nothing *to anyone* about my time with the Seer."

Somewhat bewildered, Nathan set off down the dusty trail. He reached Gibeah by midday and found a shady spot overlooking the road. As he waited, Nathan mulled over Saul's curious behavior. The man appeared to be in no hurry to confirm the Seer's assurances about his lost donkeys. Not only

144

was Saul lagging behind, but he wanted to delay Nathan as well. The admonition not to discuss the Seer was even more puzzling. Nathan had no idea what had passed between the two men, so what did Saul fear he might say? The whole experience with the Seer was exceedingly strange. Nathan still had no satisfactory explanation when he spotted Saul's towering figure silhouetted against the setting sun. The man appeared deep in thought, so Nathan quietly fell into step with him. Soon they were crossing the property of Saul's family. The first house they came to belonged to Saul's uncle, Ner. Saul stopped by when Ner called him over. Nathan was happily trotting to home when he crossed paths with Kish.

"So, Nathan, finally found your way back. Where's Saul?"

"He's at your brother's house."

"Good. I have big news. The Patriarchs asked Samuel for a king ten days ago."

"Are we getting one?"

"Hardly. Samuel sent those scheming vipers home with a harsh rebuke."

"Somehow, Kish, I feel disappointed."

"Don't worry, Lad, it's for the best. Now we can forget this king foolishness and get back to driving out the Philistines."

Chapter 12 - The Reluctant King

Then Samuel called the people together to the LORD at Mizpah. And he said to the children of Israel, "Thus says the LORD, the God of Israel: 'I brought up Israel out of Egypt, and delivered you from the hand of the Egyptians and from the hand of all kingdoms and from those who oppressed you.' But you have today rejected your God, who Himself saved you from all your adversities and your tribulations; and you have said to Him, 'No, set a king over us!' Now therefore, present yourselves before the Lord by your tribes and by your clans."

From the Book of I Samuel, Chapter 10, verses 17 to 19

And Saul answered, "Am I not a Benjamite, of the smallest of the tribes of Israel, and my family the least of all the families of the tribe of Benjamin?"

From the Book of I Samuel, Chapter 9, verse 21

Beker thought some days it simply did not pay to be the most intelligent man in a group.

The Highlander leader had predicted there would be repercussions following the Patriarchs' recent confrontation with Samuel. True, the judge's failure to appoint a king at Ramah demoralized the Monarchists and ensured that Israel's political situation remained unchanged. Yet, Beker knew better than to consider the issue of a king to be settled for all time. His Highlander faction could not afford to grow complacent after a single triumph. Beker warned his cohorts to remain vigilant for any clandestine efforts by the Monarchists. However, not one of his allies sent a single shred of useful information his way. The upshot was Beker being caught wrong-footed a few weeks later when Samuel issued a summons for the twelve tribes to assemble at Mizpah. This unforeseen event immediately threw all Israel into turmoil although Beker felt its impact sooner than most. Droves of Highlander zealots descended on his house in Ephraim demanding an explanation. Somehow it was Beker's fault they had not heeded his warnings. Projecting an air of confidence, Beker calmed the fearful, reassured the wavering and sent them all home with the same message.

Nothing had changed.

Beker portrayed Samuel's action as a natural response to Monarchist harassment. They must have exhausted the old judge's patience, compelling Samuel to quell this foolish demand for a king once and for all. Onan and his Monarchist minions were thus reduced to spreading rumors of an impending kingdom in an act of desperation. Beker guaranteed that as long as the Highlanders kept their heads, there would be no king. As he expected, his interpretation of the scanty evidence was well received by the Highlander faithful. Beker just wished he were really as confident as he pretended.

The truth was Beker had no idea what Samuel intended. The old judge had disappeared during the weeks prior to his earthshaking summons. Beker's hastily dispatched informants could discover only what Samuel *had not* been doing. Hoshea, the Patriarch for Ephraim, assured Beker that Samuel was not conspiring with any of the other Patriarchs. His Levite contacts confirmed the judge had not been with any of the other priests. Beker's spies in the Monarchist camp indicated that even their leadership was in the dark regarding the old man's intentions. Beker concluded Samuel had to be meeting with someone, but whom? Somehow this old recluse had emerged from the hills to single-handedly seize the initiative from Israel's most powerful leaders.

Samuel's appointed day at Mizpah dawned with Beker once again sleeping in a tent like some vagabond. The tiny village was adjacent to a series of ridges forming a broad basin with sufficient room for several hundred thousand spectators. The countless tents dotting the surrounding slopes supposedly contained at least one representative from every family in Israel. Samuel was expected to address the nation at midday from a rocky outcropping that served as a natural watchtower over the eastern approaches. Here the judge would be visible to everyone in attendance, if not actually heard by most. Those closest to the speaker would be expected to relay his words to the masses standing in the rear. When Mizpah began filling up before dawn, Beker was not concerned. His servants had already secured a prime spot from which he and his favored Highlander cronies could witness the proceedings.

Helek and Elon came to Beker's tent an hour before Samuel's scheduled appearance. Preceded by a dozen brawny servants, the trio began picking their way through the thickening crowd. Their progress was slow as Beker made frequent stops to greet and reassure numerous Highlander dignitaries along the way. They reached their viewing area mere minutes before Samuel ascended his stony pulpit. Beker felt an unanticipated sense of relief at the sound of Samuel's voice. One way or another, all his questions were about to be answered.

After a few minutes of listening to the solemn oratory, Beker began to smile. This message appeared to be merely a repeat performance of Samuel's speech at Shiloh. The sermon began with a moving history of God's protection of Israel since the Exodus. It concluded with Samuel's stinging accusation that an ungrateful nation had rejected their God by demanding a king in His place. The old judge still possessed an impressive voice and the vast throng stood meekly as his harsh rebuke echoed off the hills.

Then Beker's world fell apart.

Samuel ordered the Patriarchs of the twelve tribes to present themselves. Only a few thousand men near the front could actually see what was taking place, but others began buzzing with excitement as descriptions were passed through the crowd. Beker saw one of Samuel's Levite attendants hand each Patriarch a small fragment of pottery. His stomach churned anxiously as he watched each man scratch something onto his piece. The Levite then collected all twelve pottery fragments in an earthen jar, before delivering it to Samuel. Beker felt Helek tightly grip his elbow and heard Elon gasp while the nearest Highlander nobles turned worried eyes his way. Beker now perceived that he had been led into a well laid trap and the time for escape had passed. He watched helplessly as Samuel reached into the jar held by the Levite and extracted a single piece of pottery.

"Benjamin! Have your clan Elders present themselves before the LORD your God!"

Nathan squeezed forward in the crowd, but still could not hear Samuel's voice. He hoped Jonathan and Kish were close enough to be able to explain later what was happening.

Nathan blamed Saul for his predicament. His friend's father had been uncharacteristically sluggish in preparing their campsite, so Kish ordered Nathan to remain behind and help him secure the baggage. Once they were alone, Saul explained his real reason for dawdling. All anyone wanted to talk about that day was why Samuel had called the assembly. For some unknown reason, Saul wanted no part of that discussion. Eventually Saul told the impatient Nathan to run along, promising to follow at the proper time. Saul also asked Nathan not to tell anyone where he was. Bewildered, Nathan joined some other latecomers and pressed on to his present location.

This was but one more example of Saul's odd behavior since their search for Kish's lost donkeys. After three days of fruitless wandering in the mountains, Nathan and Saul had sought the aid of an old Seer. The man earned his fee by revealing that the donkeys had already returned home, but that helpful act somehow marked the beginning of Saul's strange conduct. It led to Saul being the unexpected guest of honor at a lavish banquet and spending an entire night talking to the mysterious old Seer. Even back home in Gibeah, Saul had been extremely reticent, as if afraid to begin a conversation with anyone.

A sudden change in the crowd drew Nathan's thoughts away from Saul. He marveled as an impromptu relay system slowly evolved once Samuel began to speak. Men with the loudest voices were asked to call out whatever they heard. The crowd shouted down the least effective volunteers and encouraged the best. Eventually, Samuel's message began flowing through the audience. The stern sermon could not have made a more powerful impact on the huddled listeners if it had come directly from Samuel's own lips. The flow of information momentarily dried up after Samuel called the twelve Patriarchs forward. Several other curious bystanders agreed to lift Nathan up on their shoulders to learn the reason behind this sudden lull. He described aloud how Samuel was taking something out of a jar. One of the men under Nathan began whooping excitedly.

"He's drawing lots! Samuel's drawing lots!"

A few others began rejoicing, but most, including Nathan, remained confused. He dropped to the ground and asked the excited man for an explanation.

"Foolish boy...it's how the priests seek God's guidance. Samuel expects God to direct his hand to the lot with the name of the new king!"

"So... will one of the Patriarchs be king?"

"Well...uh...good question, Lad. We'll soon know."

The crowd noise gradually increased as thousands of similar conversations took place, and then quickly faded away. Soon, Nathan's ears detected a rhythmic sound spreading across the valley. He likened it to the ripples caused by a stone thrown into a lake. Nathan realized it was the same word repeated over and over.

"Benjamin! Benjamin!"

The expectant silence around Nathan instantly gave way to pandemonium. There was some disappointment mixed in with the general excitement, but Nathan thought that was inevitable. The king could belong to only one tribe. Nathan nearly stumbled as the multitude suddenly began to shift.

Hundreds of exuberant Benjamites surged forward through the packed ranks. The other tribes parted to allow the joyous stampede to pass. Nathan spent many minutes eagerly pushing and shoving forward through the horde of excited Benjamites until progress became impossible.

"Make way! Make way!"

Nathan strained to see the source of the raucous commands. A determined group was forcing its way in the opposite direction through the advancing throng. Dozens of strong warriors strained to force a passage through the jubilant Benjamites. Nathan tried to squeeze out of the way, but ended up facing Onan of Judah. An old man walking with Onan suddenly locked eyes with Nathan. Both their jaws dropped. It was the Seer who had found their donkeys. He then seized Nathan by the arms.

"You are Saul's servant! Where is Saul?"

"Uh...well..."

"Find Saul...bring him to me *immediately!*"

Nathan hesitated because of Saul's request for privacy. Then Onan loomed so close that Nathan felt the spray of the man's spittle.

"Do as Samuel commands *NOW!*"

Events were moving too swiftly for Nathan's confused mind to comprehend. The mysterious Seer ... the lost donkeys...the great banquet...a new king...Samuel...find Saul. The judge instantly grasped Nathan's predicament. Samuel released his grip and placed a gentle hand on Nathan's shoulder.

"Fear not, Lad. Bring Saul here. These men will help you."

The gaping spectators became a blur to Nathan as his new escorts broke a path for him. The crowd gradually thinned until Nathan found himself on open ground with the other men. They trotted to the place Nathan remembered as Saul's campsite. The men waited patiently while Nathan frantically rushed from one mound of bundles to another. He began to fear Saul had disappeared into the wilderness when the back of a familiar head jutted out over a dark pile. He circled round and found Saul seated on the ground, leaning against a stack of grain sacks. When Saul lifted his head, Nathan saw the look of a cornered animal in the man's eyes.

"Saul...are you the new king?"

Saul shoulders sagged. The man seemed to age years in an instant.

"Yes."

"Well...they're waiting."

"I know. But, Nathan, do you understand what this means?"

Nathan blurted out his first thought.

"That my best friend is now a prince?"

Saul threw back his head and let loose a hearty laugh. He stood, draped his right arm over Nathan's shoulder and turned them both toward the sounds of celebration.

"Yes, Nathan...among other things."

The Highlander elite began surrounding Beker as soon as Benjamin's lot was drawn. Both their number and their ire grew as succeeding lots were drawn by Samuel for clan, then family and, finally, the king himself. Beker's servants had prevented any violence so far, but Helek and Elon both advised slipping away. His friends were correct, but Beker wished to tarry long enough to see the cause of his downfall. Beker tracked the new king's forward progress by how the crowd swirled and parted, much like the bow wave preceding a sailboat. He assumed the tall man at the center of this vortex to be his new monarch. Even at a distance Beker could discern that Saul, son of Kish, from the clan of Matri, in the tribe of Benjamin, possessed at least one useful attribute for a king.

Good looks.

The approach of Saul momentarily distracted the enraged Highlanders away from Beker. The more agitated among them began loudly heaping abuse on Saul. Beker marveled at the fools' lack of discretion. Such things may be thought, but *never* spoken aloud. Both his friends and his servants were visibly relieved when Beker finally agreed to a discreet retreat. Helek kept silent until they were at a safe distance.

"Samuel was dead set against any king a month ago, Beker. What made the old man change his mind?"

"Samuel never changed his mind, Helek."

"Been keeping something from the rest of us, Beker?"

"Only the fact that I was a fool. I totally misread that old man. His display of pious indignation at Ramah was meant to throw off everyone. A brilliant ploy...better than anything I have ever pulled off. Its success allowed Samuel to roam the countryside unmolested by any faction, interviewing potential kings and listening to their offers. From the very first, Samuel plotted to select a king...all by himself."

"Still, who is this Saul fellow? Did his family even belong to the Monarchists?"

"Not until today."

"So then... this King Saul...is he just some bumpkin?"

"He managed to cut a better deal with Samuel than we could. There has to be *something* to the man."

"Perhaps that is why God selected him."

"Oh, I suspect God had some help there. Do you really think Samuel *even looked* at what was written on those lots today? No, Samuel knew the outcome long before coming to Mizpah. The most galling thing is that Saul is such an *ingenious* choice for king."

"Seriously? Beker, the man is *a nobody*."

"True, Helek...but also irrelevant. Consider Samuel's viewpoint. Saul is from Benjamin, the *smallest* tribe. None of the other tribes will fear being dominated by it. Benjamin also has a reputation for the fiercest warriors in Israel. Everyone wants a king who can win battles. But here is the *most important* thing to Samuel: a novice like Saul will rely heavily on advice, allowing the old judge to be the power behind the throne."

"So a judge gives up power *and* keeps it at the same time."

"Helek, it is absolutely brilliant."

"But where does that leave us, Beker?"

"In need of a strategy to harness that power."

"Agreed. You better lay low for now, Beker. Elon and I can intercede for you with the other Highlanders, once they cool down. We can explain..."

"You will do no such thing!"

"What would you have us do?"

"You and Elon will immediately denounce me to anyone, and everyone. You have just this day learned that I have been in league with the Monarchists all along. Distance yourself from me, Helek, and assume leadership over our allies."

"But...but...why destroy yourself, Beker?"

"It's better to be seen as a cunning traitor than a gullible fool. Besides, I intend to make good use of my disgrace."

"How?"

"By becoming Saul's chief advisor."

"That's pretty arrogant, Beker...even for you."

"Not really, Helek. Saul *will* appoint me. He just doesn't know it yet. Once you spread the word that I, an Elder from Ephraim, am really a Monarchist, our new king will welcome me into his court. Saul cannot form a government from nothing, but I can. Saul needs me; the man *doesn't even have a crown*!"

"Onan and his Monarchists may think otherwise."

"Onan may not trust me, but he must accept me. His precious kingdom cannot survive without the Mountain Tribes' support, which I will deliver. When it suits me."

"So what will we be, Beker: Highlanders or Monarchists?"

"Stop thinking that way, Helek. A new day brings a new way."

"Still, it seems strange to support someone else's king."

"Don't be so short sighted, Helek. Who says the crown must stay with the tribe of Benjamin?"

Elon was close enough to hear every word spoken to Helek, just as Beker intended. Beker observed Elon containing his displeasure with great difficulty. He discreetly shouldered Helek to one side and pulled Elon over by the elbow.

"Very well, Elon...out with it."

"How can you put that *lackey* in charge, instead of me?"

"It is how the game must be played. Helek is a figurehead. He is good at that. I do the thinking. I am best at that. You scare people. You enjoy that."

"You are giving power to a snake, Beker. Helek could get ideas. He could bite you."

"That is why I will send his instructions through you. Stay one step ahead of him. How you keep him in line, I leave to your discretion."

"That's more like it, Beker."

Their conversation was interrupted by a distant chant echoing off the mountains around Mizpah.

"Long live the King! Long live the King!"

Beker smirked as he walked away. He would wait a month or two, until the shine wore off the new kingdom. Then he would apply for his new job.

Chapter 13 - The Right Hand

When you enter the land which the LORD your God is giving you, and possess it and dwell in it, you will say, "I will set a king over me like all the nations that are around me." Be sure to appoint over you the king whom the LORD your God chooses. He must be from among your brethren. Do not set a foreigner over you, someone who is not a brother Israelite. The king must not acquire great numbers of horses for himself, nor cause his people to return to Egypt to get more of them. For the LORD has told you, "You shall not go back there again." He must not take many wives for himself, lest his heart be led astray. He must not accumulate large amounts of gold and silver. When he takes the throne of his kingdom, he is to write for himself a copy of this law, taken from the book that is before the priests. He is to keep it with him and read from it all the days of his life, so that he may learn to fear the LORD his God and carefully follow all the words of this law. He is not to consider himself better than his brethren. He may not turn away from the law, not to the right nor to the left. Then he and his descendants will reign a long time over his kingdom in Israel.

From the Book of Deuteronomy, Chapter 17, verses 14 to 20

Saul's home outside the town of Gibeah

Nathan had never observed how a proper kingdom operated, but he suspected the Nation of Israel's new one was not off to a promising start. Clearly, there was much more to it than choosing a king. Having witnessed the chaos of recent days, Nathan understood why Saul had initially been so reluctant to accept the job.

Things had seemed so different four weeks ago at Mizpah when Samuel first introduced Saul. Enthusiastic multitudes cheered their new monarch then, despite the opposition of a small, but influential, minority. After hours of rejoicing, Samuel called the assembly back to order. The raucous celebration quickly subsided as the crowd strained to hear the words of their judge. With Saul standing at his side beneath the setting sun, Samuel produced a scroll and read aloud God's regulations for the new kingdom.

Samuel began with the People's responsibilities. They were to provide the Crown with one tenth of their crops and animals, plow the royal fields and reap the king's harvest. Israel's men would fight as Saul's soldiers. Its women would serve in the royal household. Anyone could be summoned as labor for public projects. The king could seize their best land and award it to his officials. Nathan sensed the crowd growing more and more subdued as each additional obligation was announced. The Kingdom of Israel was no longer a dream. The King of Israel was now a living, breathing person, to whom they were bound for life.

The remainder of Samuel's text was for Saul's ears. The king was not to greatly multiply silver and gold for himself, accumulate a large number of horses, or maintain a harem of wives. He was not to exalt himself above his people. The king was to read from the Book of the Law every day. Most importantly, the king was responsible to God for obeying every, single word of that law. Nathan could see the gravity of this final requirement etched in Saul's face. Samuel concluded by holding up the scroll and declaring these *Regulations of the Kingdom* would be deposited next to the Ark of the Covenant, as a testimony to Israel's future generations. After dismissing the people, the old judge disappeared without fanfare.

Nathan now felt pity for Saul. Samuel's instructions had dealt with *what* a king should do rather than *how* he should do it. As king, Saul possessed little more than a title: neither crown, nor throne, nor palace, nor army, nor money. Nathan wondered how any man could build so much from nothing. He sensed that many others were wondering the same thing. No one knew what was going to happen next.

Nathan initially took heart watching Saul warm to his new role. The new king spent hours greeting hundreds of well-wishers. Saul graciously accepted countless pledges of loyalty and offers of assistance, but Nathan cynically wondered how many would actually come to fruition. He was more impressed by those backing up their words with actions. When Saul departed the following day for Gibeah, he was accompanied by over a hundred men who had sworn themselves to his service. Of course, Nathan had no clue what this support would really cost.

The birth pangs of the new kingdom commenced once Saul arrived home with his burgeoning entourage. The first royal challenge was providing shelter for so many. Kish's estate, located on a hill a mile outside of Gibeah, had always seemed so spacious to Nathan. Saul's house was only one of five. The other four houses were occupied by the families of Kish, Kish's brother Ner, Ner's son Abner and Nathan. There were also several barracks housing the servant families. Yet these roomy buildings were overwhelmed by the new residents. Even with the barns pressed into service, over thirty men slept under the stars that first night.

The next complication for the king appeared a few hours later at breakfast. The number of mouths to be fed had more than doubled since the previous day, although Nathan recognized that fact was misleading. In truth, the food requirements had almost tripled since the new arrivals, all fit men, consumed much more than the women and children already in residence. Kish met the immediate dietary needs with an early slaughter of his lambs, securing enough time for additional foodstuffs to be purchased. However, Kish confided to Nathan that his silver and flocks would be exhausted in a few months unless things improved. Naturally, the situation worsened.

Saul had barely brought the needs of his enlarged household under control when the first supplicants began to trickle into Gibeah. Nathan sat in on their sessions with Saul whenever he could get a break from his own duties. While most visitors brought a gift, it was clear each expected to eventually receive something *more* valuable in return. For example, a delegation from the Elders of Benjamin presented Saul with his first crown. However, these delegates bluntly stated that the tribe of Benjamin expected to benefit from Saul's good fortune. Nathan admired how Saul handled even the most selfish guests with tact and grace, but he soon noticed the strain etching itself on the king's face. In the coming weeks, Nathan witnessed the situation get increasingly out of hand as the stream of petitioners to Gibeah became a flood. The donkey business in Gibeon languished with both Nathan and Jonathan needed in Gibeah. The gifts to Saul grew smaller while the demands made on the king increased. The discontented clamored for Saul to resolve long-standing feuds, avenge ancient wrongs and settle petty disputes. The ambitious solicited the king for commissions in a non-existent army, the right to collect taxes, and appointments as governors. The merchants offered their wares to the new kingdom while demanding monopolies in return. Nathan feared Saul would collapse without some relief from these scavengers. Yet the hordes continued to come. Squatter camps sprang up on Kish's land, crowds loitered outside Saul's house and strangers wandered his halls at will. Nathan watched in frustration as Saul struggled with how to balance what his people wanted against what they should receive.

Beker's arrival at Gibeah could not have been better timed, at least as far as he was concerned. Leaving servants to unpack his personal caravan, Beker wandered alone to the king's modest residence where the situation appeared to be exactly as he had anticipated. Whenever a crisis arose, would-be saviors always rushed forward to offer their services. It was Beker's experience that most of them were either madmen or fools. A cunning man always waited before committing himself to a cause. Saul's amateurish volunteers were floundering badly in their attempts to found a dynasty. Beker had deliberately delayed his journey to allow the new kingdom to descend to a level which was chaotic, but still recoverable. He spent his first morning in Gibeah studying the bedlam centered on Saul's house. Beker observed a veritable mob roaming the premises, engaging in shoving matches, striving to be the next to enter Saul's inner chamber. Beker smiled at the golden opportunity lying before him. All he need do now was recruit a suitable accomplice.

A big man moving smoothly through the crowd caught Beker's eye. When he discerned a strong resemblance to Saul, Beker knew he had found the perfect partner. It required only a few minutes to sidle up to his quarry, fawn over the man and extend an invitation for refreshments. Back in his tent, Beker learned over wine and assorted delicacies that his guest was none other than Abner, the king's cousin. Concealing his delight, he got Abner talking about himself, his royal cousin and the difficulties of the past few weeks. Beker listened sympathetically before casually explaining how his skills might be of benefit to Saul...and to Abner. The big man's eager eyes told Beker that he had netted his fish. Abner was ready for the good things of life, and Beker was quite willing to provide them, for a price.

When Beker and Abner entered Saul's house later that afternoon, they were accompanied by a few of Beker's scribes. Abner's brawny arms swept aside all in his path and Beker followed in the big man's wake. They reached the door to Saul's chamber just as one man was leaving and another was preparing to enter for his audience. Abner held back the man with his right hand and shoved Beker into the room with his left. The indignant protests behind Abner were cut short when he slammed the door shut and leaned back against it. Saul studied Beker with weary eyes, but the corners of his mouth gave a hint of amusement.

"And what does this one want, Abner?"

"To make life easier for you, Cousin."

Pandemonium spread through the royal residence an hour later when Abner and a score of armed men evicted every single visitor. Over a hundred angry men milled outside denouncing their rough treatment. A hush fell over the unruly group as Beker followed Abner out onto the front steps. Beker's three scribes took station beneath him while Abner's men pushed the crowd back. Raising his arms for silence, Beker addressed the restless assembly.

"The king will see no one else today!"

An ugly murmuring began, only to be silenced by a roar from Abner. Seeing order restored, Abner beckoned Beker to continue.

"Henceforth, the king will hold Court for three hours each morning, except for the Sabbath, of course. If you have any matter to bring before the king, give your name and purpose to one of these royal scribes. The most important requests will be granted royal audiences first. Return tomorrow morning to learn whom the king will hear."

One man ignored Abner's fierce countenance to challenge Beker.

"Who the hell are you?"

"I am the king's *Yameen*."

As expected, Beker's self-bestowed title confused his audience. *Yameen* literally meant *right hand* in their language. Beker had thought long and hard before selecting his title. He anticipated the competition over leadership positions within the new kingdom would be intense. Beker sought a distinctive rank which would both set him apart from and above the current crop of Elders, Patriarchs, Priests and Princes. Anything generic, such as "minister" or "advisor", would immediately be considered inferior to the long established titles. Not so with *Yameen*. Even the lowliest peasant would understand the king could only have one *right hand*. Nothing else could be closer to the king, or more useful to him. Beker intended for the office of

Yameen to become both respected and feared in the future. However, today the title carried no weight with the indignant man confronting Beker.

"Well, *Yameen*, I've waited a week to see the king. I was next in line when you barged in. I'm not going anywhere until..."

The man's words died on his lips when he spied Abner lunging forward. Beker was impressed by the big man's speed. Abner seized the hapless man and heaved him up on his shoulder. The others watched slack jawed as Abner lugged his squirming victim to where the road began to slope gently downward from the house. With a mighty grunt, Abner tossed the poor wretch down the hill. Abner turned toward the shaken spectators and grinned wickedly. Beker swiftly took advantage of the stunned silence.

"That man will be the *last* to see the king! Does anyone wish to be the *next to last*?"

The next morning Nathan wondered if his trembling knees were noticeable as he left Saul's house. He gawked at the massive crowd gathering near the bottom of the hill, one of several new customs being implemented that day. A body of Saul's men now forced all petitioners to wait where the main road crossed Kish's land. Another new policy was for an emissary to announce the names of those being granted an audience with the king. A fortunate few would then be allowed to ascend the hill to meet with their sovereign. The disappointed majority could either return to their tents to sulk or vent their frustration on the unfortunate emissary. This latter possibility mattered a great deal to Nathan since he *was* the aforementioned emissary. Saul's new adviser, Beker, had settled on Nathan as the logical choice out of many possible candidates. The *Yameen* explained to Nathan that the ideal person needed to be intelligent, trustworthy, willing to tolerate abuse and able to read. Nathan knew that final qualification probably eliminated most contenders. Beker even bestowed a new title on him: *Shoeyr*. When Nathan pointed out that *gatekeeper* was a lowly job, Beker politely disagreed. He explained Nathan would do much more than merely tend a door, for the *Shoeyr* controlled access to the king himself. Beker insisted *Shoeyr* would be an inferior post only if Nathan made it such.

Nathan found the *Yameen* to be incredibly persuasive. Beker could probably tell someone to go to hell and make the man look forward to the journey. With Beker's assurances ringing in his ears, Nathan trudged down the hill to meet his fate. The small scroll of names tucked under his arm grew heavier with each step. He was just seventeen years old and already burdened with misery. Apparently thankless jobs were an unavoidable consequence of education.

Neither the petitioners nor Saul's guards took any notice of Nathan's arrival. Not surprising; he had never warranted much attention before. Nathan silently glided between a few men to a large stone resting a few paces from the edge of the crowd, and then leaped up on it. From this vantage point, his head was nearly two feet higher than anyone else's. Nathan beheld over one hundred men growing more impatient by the minute. He looked at the short list in his hand and sighed. No matter what he said, at least nine men out of ten would be angry. One thought finally spurred him into action: *Waiting won't make this any easier.* However, Nathan was stumped as to how to begin. Acting purely on impulse, he startled everyone within earshot by roaring a Benjamite battle cry. Nathan was immediately rewarded with the full attention of his bewildered audience. This small victory gave him the courage to proceed.

"I am Nathan, the *Shoeyr*. My duty is to announce those selected for this morning's audience with King Saul. After I call..."

"You're the what?"

"*Shoeyr.* It means *gatekeeper.*

"We know what it means, Boy. But there ain't no gate here."

"Shut up and let the lad do his job. How many names on your list, *Shoeyr*?"

The blunt question momentarily threw Nathan off stride. He licked his lips and decided on a simple response.

"Eight."

"*Eight?* Are you daft? Don't you see how many of us there are?"

An outbreak of ugly murmuring signaled a change in the crowd's mood. Nathan nervously looked at Saul's guards, but no help seemed to be forthcoming. He would have to weather this storm alone.

"Please, Sir. If there is any extra time, others will be summoned."

"And how many will that be?"

Nathan's hesitation only encouraged more catcalls and complaints. An expensively dressed, heavyset man pushed his way to the front and waved for silence. Nathan gauged the man's importance by how quickly the others acquiesced to his command. It appeared the morning's troubles were just starting.

"I'm Tola of Issachar. I didn't come all this way to take orders from some *stable boy*. Now just trot back up that hill and send down *a man* who knows what he's doing."

This condescending remark changed everything for Nathan. His apprehension was instantly replaced by anger. With that anger came clear thinking. Nathan refused to give in to his tormentors. He had just struck bottom which meant things could only improve. Now was the time for cold-blooded boldness, perhaps even a well-chosen bluff. Nathan glanced at his scroll and saw Tola's name at the very top of the list. He decided to gamble on a hunch.

"And what was your name again?"

It seemed as if the entire assembly all inhaled in astonishment.

"Tola! An Elder of Issachar!"

Nathan calmly crossed his arms and gazed skyward. He rubbed his chin, as if struggling to recall some insignificant fact. He finally looked at Tola and slowly shook his head.

"Should I know you?"

The indignant Tola could only sputter in response. Faint laughter began spreading throughout the crowd. Nathan noticed grins break out on the faces of the guards. His hunch was proving correct; Tola might be important, but he was not popular. Nathan pretended to study his list of names intently. His next words were full of sympathy.

"I am most sorry, Tola. You are not on this morning's list. Not only that..."

After the brief pause, Nathan's voice took on a harsh edge.

"Even if the king holds additional audiences today, he *won't* be seeing you. Return tomorrow. Perhaps your luck will improve."

Nathan then quickly read the other seven names from the appointment list. He then picked out a grinning face at random and announced that its owner would receive the final audience. Nathan smiled broadly as it dawned on Tola that his spot had just been given away. Most of the crowded cheered Nathan's audacity; seeing a bully humbled was always good entertainment. Tola pushed forward as if to pull Nathan from the stone, but found his path blocked. One of the guards, a stocky man of middle age and medium height, gently tapped Tola on the chest with a stout wooden cudgel.

"You heard the lad...I mean, the *Shoeyr*. Come back tomorrow."

"Get out of my way! Do you know who I am?"

"Do you really want to go through all *that* again?"

The guard's sly question left Tola speechless and everyone else roaring with laughter. The heavyset man waddled off with as much dignity as he could salvage. Nathan nodded to his new-found ally and made a polite request.

"Captain, please escort the others up to the king's residence."

Pleased at his unexpected promotion, the guard bowed from the waist and rounded up Nathan's selections. Most of the crowd drifted away, although a few remained nearby in the hope of being summoned later. When no one was left to watch him, Nathan hopped down to the ground and staggered over to the nearest tree. He hid his face against its trunk and began crying softly. He had performed his new job miserably. He had lied. He had made a powerful enemy. Nathan's wit had earned a cheap laugh, but at what cost?

After a while, Nathan noticed Beker coming down from Saul's house. The *Yameen* spoke briefly with one of the guards, and then looked around. Beker's eyes finally settled on Nathan. The two men simply stared at each other for a moment before Beker marched back up the hill. Nathan tried to piece together a meaning from this wordless encounter. Beker must have noticed Tola's absence and come down to learn the cause. The *Yameen* was apparently so angered by the *Shoeyr's* incompetence that he did not even want to discuss it. Nathan made his way back to the stone and sat down. He closed his eyes and grimaced. He was in the deep dung now.

"Sir...Sir, where do you wish us to set up?"

Nathan shook off his melancholy mood and found himself facing a dozen of Beker's servants. The men were carrying an assortment of fabric, wooden poles, rope, tools and furniture. It dawned on him that they were all waiting patiently for his response.

"Set up what?"

"Your canopy, Sir."

"What's it for?"

"Why... for your shade."

"My shade?"

"As the *Yameen* instructed. We also have a table and benches for you."

"Oh, of course...uh, set it up behind that stone."

The man bowed to Nathan and set the others to work. A ten-foot square canopy quickly rose on the specified site. The servants anchored it firmly in place with ropes and tent pegs. Nathan sat down on the padded bench and rested his elbows on the smooth wooden table. The morning sun was beginning to burn hotly, and the shade was a great blessing. The canopy's exposed sides allowed a cool breeze to enhance the effect. Nathan glanced around to see his new shelter had attracted a fair amount of attention from the waiting petitioners, as well as some jealous looks. Nathan ignored the spectators and acted as if he was used to this level of comfort. Footsteps crunching on gravel caught Nathan's attention. He turned to see three young women carrying platters of food and a pitcher. They silently laid out an assortment of bread, fruits and cheeses before Nathan. After pouring a goblet of wine, the women departed as quietly as they had arrived. Thinking this the most confusing day of his entire life, Nathan began to eat. The cool shade and his full stomach soon made him feel drowsy.

"Comfortable?"

The unseen voice startled Nathan out of his reverie. He tried to hide his embarrassment as Beker plopped down on the other bench and poured himself some wine.

"Yes, I'm, uh, quite comfortable. Confused, but comfortable."

"Why confused, Nathan?"

"I bungled my first day as *Shoeyr*. To be rewarded is confusing."

"You mean *Tola*? Young man, you handled that pompous ass *magnificently*."

"Truly?"

"Nathan... in our roles, we speak with the voice of the king. When Tola insulted you, he insulted Saul. You have to put such fools in their place right away or they will spread like weeds. Trust me...Tola, and the others, will respect you now...even better, they will fear you."

"Why?"

"You've demonstrated your power over them."

"But I don't want to be feared."

"I hate to disillusion you, but being feared will get you farther in this life than being loved. Look...Tola was my fault,

Nathan. I should have provided more guidance on your first day. That is why I set up this little station for you. It shows that I, and ultimately the king, approve your treatment of Tola. You may not need to be feared, but *we do*."

"I'm beginning to understand, Beker...I mean *Yameen*."

"Save my title for our public performances. Otherwise, I am simply Beker. May I give you some advice?"

"Certainly!"

"Next time, read only one name at a time. Keep the rest of the petitioners in suspense. They will be on their best behavior for fear of being passed over. Oh... your battle cry is most impressive, but a trumpet is more dignified. Several of the guards carry *shofars*. Have them summon the people for you with their trumpets."

"Thank you, Beker. I appreciate your wisdom in these matters."

"I can still learn new things, myself. For example...you surprised me, Nathan. You displayed a talent I had no idea that you possessed."

"What?"

"The ability to handle pressure. Most men panic and give into either fear or anger. You have a rare gift. Well, here is the list of the king's additional appointments for the day. Make any changes that you see fit."

The trumpeting of shofars a few minutes later brought the petitioners running like pigs to a feed trough. Things unfolded exactly as Beker predicted. There were no questions or complaints when Nathan announced the appointments, one name at a time. Many used the interlude between announcements to ingratiate themselves with Nathan. He found Tola of Issachar to be exceptionally polite, even though the man knew he must wait until tomorrow. Nathan was extremely impressed by Beker's ability to create order from chaos.

Beker periodically looked out a window and noted the improved performance of the young *Shoeyr*. He had kept from Nathan the real reasons for his selection. Beker knew these first days of audiences would be messy. By controlling access to Saul, Beker could wield significant power as the king's true *Gatekeeper*. However until his position at Court was secure, Beker could not afford to risk humiliation. Neither could he share his precarious hold on power with someone who might eclipse him. Enter Nathan... an unassuming boy who could serve as proxy for Beker. Nathan was sent out as a sacrificial lamb. Instead, the boy proved to be a lion cub. Beker resolved to keep this promising young man close at hand. He hated to underestimate anyone. It usually proved costly later. Yet the cultivation of the youthful Nathan would have to wait...for now.

Greater issues required Becker's attention. The fledgling kingdom of Israel had no capital, no palace, no treasury, no revenue, no army, no laws and no government to speak of. Truth be told, it was a stretch to even call Saul the King of Israel. The man was barely the King of Benjamin, the smallest of the twelve tribes. His Monarchy would end before it began if its numerous deficiencies were not addressed in short order. In many ways, Saul suffered from too much help. Beker found the original men entering the new king's service to be an odd mix of patriots, zealots, wealth seekers and fools, often working at

175

cross purposes. The result was a morass of competing, often contradictory, demands on an overstretched Monarch. Each tribe had also sent a representative to Gibeah, but these men usually spent their time trying to control the king, rather than assisting him. Beker knew Saul's bureaucracy needed to be brought into line... much like the unruly petitioners. Actually, he found the whole situation quite pleasing. In chaos, there is opportunity and Beker was truly in his element here.

Beker's first task would be to subdue his true competitors in the rapidly expanding Royal Court. Fortunately for his purposes, most of Saul's followers seemed to have sincere, if rather naïve, motives. The young Nathan was a prime example. Beker could easily manipulate such well-intentioned men into benefiting both Saul and himself. That left a greedy and ambitious minority to be dealt with. They would have to be bought off, driven off, neutralized, made into allies...or simply made to disappear. Onan of Judah presented Beker with his greatest challenge. The man's strong Monarchist credentials initially made him the dominant figure at Saul's fledgling Court. However, Beker perceived Onan to be more skilled at rallying the masses than at governing them. Beker assumed this limitation was why the man had not tried to seize the Throne for himself. That being the case, Onan's strategy would have been to create a kingdom first, and then turn it over to someone else to run, most likely from his own tribe of Judah. Beker assumed that condition would have been part of any secret bargain struck between Onan and Gershon, the High Priest. In any event, Onan's plan had fallen apart when Gershon unexpectedly delegated the choice of a king to Judge Samuel. Now Onan, the Judean, was stuck supporting Saul, a Benjamite king. Beker saw a great opportunity for himself here. He would use Saul as a counterweight against Judean ambitions, and *vice versa.* In the process, Beker would slowly marginalize Onan, remove the other Monarchists from favor and make Saul dependent on his *Yameen.*

Circumstances forced Beker to move cautiously in the following weeks. Onan and his Monarchists still wielded great influence, and he could not afford to arouse their suspicions prematurely. In addition, each tribe was extremely protective of its own interests. They were jealous of each other and suspicious of their unproven king. Ironically, the Highlander Tribes, originally the staunchest opponents of a king, provided the most reliable support to the Crown, thanks to Beker's connections. As for the opposing factions, he decided the best course for the present would be to go *around* them rather than go *through* them. After Beker had subtly established his powerbase, they would all come begging to him. He simply needed to make the proper plans.

Something new was needed to further Becker's ambitions...an organization that did not encroach on anyone else's existing political domain. Beker slipped a proposal into one of the weekly meetings of the Royal Court that men be appointed to *minister* to the needs of the king. As he expected, no one objected to such a harmless sounding idea. The Elders envisioned a collection of butlers, cooks and bodyguards, but Beker had a grander scheme in mind. Each minister would actually be responsible for an entire government function: collecting taxes...building an army...writing laws...growing crops...public works. Even as the true duties of each minister became known, most at Court would probably react with understandable indifference. If the tribes still held all Israel's wealth, what could these ministers do without Tribal approval? Beker knew the answer: a great deal. Anyone seeking royal favors would eventually find it necessary to go through the *appropriate* minister first. Those who refused would see their requests languish and die. Over time, each minister would appoint additional ministers to serve under him. Beker's government would start small, but through superior organization it would eventually surpass all of Israel's squabbling factions.

Naturally, all this added complexity would require the king to lean heavily on his *Yameen* for counsel. Beker would truly become Saul's "right hand".

The success of this endeavor depended on Beker finding the proper men at Court to serve as ministers. He began by weeding out the true parasites and threats to his authority, while recruiting those who could be of value, either to the kingdom or to him personally. Beker's ideal minster possessed both a useful strength *and* an exploitable weakness. Examples were men who were honest, but politically naïve...wise, but greedy...hard working, but vain...wealthy, but lazy. Such men would make effective ministers, yet remain under Beker's thumb. Still, Beker knew there was a limit to what could be accomplished under the present circumstances. All his schemes, deals, and intrigues could buy only a little more time for the newborn kingdom to toddle forward. Beker's experiences with the darker side of human behavior had made him skeptical of Providence. However, there was no question in his mind that Saul needed a miracle to last out the year...or, at the very least, exceptionally good luck.

Chapter 14 - The Mercenary

And Saul also went home to Gibeah; and valiant men went with him, whose hearts God had touched. But some troublemakers said, "How can this man save us?" So they despised him, and brought him no presents. But Saul kept silent.

From the Book of I Samuel, Chapter 10, verses 26 and 27

Along the Gibeah-Gibeon road

Nathan discovered that the prestige of being a *Shoeyr* was indeed fleeting. At first, scores of influential men vied for his attention, pleading with the young *gatekeeper* to grant them a royal audience. That changed by the third month of Saul's reign as the number of visitors to Gibeah began slacking off. No one gave a second thought to the *Shoeyr* if everyone was assured of seeing the king the same day. The daily audiences were gradually cut back from three hours to one. The truth was that *Yameen* Beker made the actual selections, and Nathan had grown bored serving as the man's mouthpiece.

Nathan was not overly disappointed at his diminished role since there was much to do in the new kingdom. He quickly became aware of a hierarchy in the conduct of royal business. The most important tasks went to Saul's relatives, such as Jonathan and Abner. Beker's cronies seemed to get less critical, but still prestigious jobs. Boring, low priority work was given to servants. That left tasks which were critical *but* boring, projects requiring an equal measure of intelligence and patience. When offered one of these thankless jobs, Nathan had naively accepted and, even worse, performed well. His reward was to be assigned more of the same. Nathan had inadvertently learned a valuable life lesson. Good work was often its own punishment. This day was an excellent example.

Nathan had spent the past five hours watching an empty, dusty road. At least he was fairly comfortable under a scrubby shade tree on the hillside with a clear view of the terrain. On the good side, Nathan had food and water to last the whole day. On the bad side, he might need it. For Nathan was waiting for someone. He had no idea when the man would arrive or what he looked like. The need for secrecy was so great that nobody in Gibeah did either. Yet Nathan was to somehow identify the correct traveler and guide him safely to Saul. It was just the latest in a long line of important grunt jobs. Actually, Nathan looked forward to meeting Saul's mysterious guest. He did not know the man's name, but Nathan knew his reputation.

Nathan's limited information had come from Judge Samuel. The anonymous stranger was a soldier, formerly a high ranking Hittite officer, a scourge of the Philistines and now a mercenary seeking employment. Samuel thought such a man might train an army for Saul. At the king's request, the old judge had arranged for the Hittite to come to Gibeah this day. For fear of Philistine spies, the Hittite was not told Saul's exact location, thus the secret roadside meeting.

Lacking any physical description, Nathan decided to look for a man of war. Unfortunately, most of the traffic that day had four legs and the rest bore little resemblance to a soldier. In midafternoon, Nathan spotted a lone figure cresting a nearby ridge. As the traveler drew closer, Nathan discerned he was a foreigner, and a poorly dressed one at that. He immediately discounted the man because of an obvious limp.

Yet another disappointment. Nathan was enjoying a swig from his water skin, when a booming voice interrupted him in mid-gulp.

"You! Boy!"

Looking up in bewilderment, Nathan realized that he had been hailed by the limping man. He started to answer, but caught himself. Indeed, Nathan felt miffed at being called a boy by some scruffy stranger. He decided to ignore the man until shown some respect. However, the loud stranger was not to be put off so easily.

"Are you Saul's man?"

Startled, Nathan's eyes darted around, but thankfully saw no one else within earshot. Nathan stormed down the hill before the man could draw anyone else's attention. Nathan stopped a few paces from the stranger and whispered his own question.

"Why do you ask?"

"So, you're not deaf after all."

"Answer my question."

"Saul is expecting me."

Nathan stared at the man in wide-eyed surprise at the unimpressive stranger. Nathan was no giant, but he still stood nearly two inches taller than the stranger. The man was stout, although Nathan detected solid muscle beneath the patched garments. He judged the balding stranger to be about 40 years old, based on the amount of gray in the otherwise dark brown hair. Nathan counted a number of scars on both face and limb. The man also sported a nose which appeared to have been broken more than once. Most striking were the man's piercing green eyes. Confused, Nathan blurted out exactly what was on his mind.

"You can't be Samuel's man!"

"And why not?"

"Because you don't look like a, a..."

"Look like what I really am? That's the whole point, Lad. I could hardly wear Hittite armor through Philistine controlled territory to a secret meeting with their sworn enemies."

The Hittite tilted his head as he made a quick appraisal of Nathan.

"Samuel said Saul has an intelligent son. I hope you are not him."

"No, I'm Nathan."

This innocent and sincere answer evoked a deep belly laugh from the Hittite. Belatedly recognizing the unflattering light in which he had just cast himself, Nathan blushed. The older man smiled and patted him on the back.

"Don't feel bad, Nathan. Most men have much to learn from me. My name is Karaz. Let's go find this king of yours."

Later at Saul's home, Nathan led Karaz toward the immense tree where Saul preferred to hold afternoon meetings. They watched as servants placed a large chair beneath the leafy shade, along with a small bench. An afternoon breeze cooled the assembly as the principals of the Royal Court assumed their places. Saul naturally occupied the lone chair with Jonathan taking the bench at the king's right hand. Abner loomed imposingly behind his royal cousin while Beker, the *Yameen,* stood on Saul's left. Nathan was amused when a brief look of annoyance flashed across Beker's face. The *Yameen*'s title literally meant the *right hand*, but the man could hardly expect Jonathan, the Prince and Heir, to take a lesser position on the left. *Or was Beker really that vain?* Nathan pushed the distracting thought aside as he escorted Karaz to an open area before Saul.

With all eyes focused on the Hittite, Nathan slipped in behind Jonathan and held his breath. Protocol was one of many things the Royal Court still lacked. Nathan normally stood in the audience, but if no one objected, this day would set a favorable precedent for him. Beker caught Nathan's eye and gave him an approving nod. Abner greeted him with an indignant snort but said nothing. Nathan suppressed a grin over his small triumph. Saul and Beker exchanged a few whispers before the *Yameen* addressed the Hittite directly.

"We know little about you."

The Hittite strode forward until he was three paces from Beker. After looking the man up and down, Karaz spoke in a calm, but firm voice.

"And you are...?"

"I am Beker, the king's *Yameen*."

"Then he must be Saul, King of Israel...my new employer. "

"That remains to be seen, Hittite."

"Relax, Beker. I probably won't turn him down."

Nathan had never before seen the *Yameen* at a loss for words. Karaz had deftly turned Beker's condescending manner to his own advantage. Beker was accustomed to controlling conversations and his face turned scarlet at losing the initiative. Seizing the moment, Karaz spoke directly to Saul.

"My name is Karaz. Until last autumn, I served as a general of the Hittite Empire. The king chose me to train his heir in the art of war. At first, border clashes with the Philistines provided ample opportunity for the boy's instruction."

When Beker tried to interrupt, Saul held up a restraining hand and spoke for himself.

"What do you mean by *at first*?"

"One year ago, the Philistines attacked the border city of Kadesh. I directed my prince in preparing an ambush which captured hundreds of Philistines. We impaled their officers, castrated their soldiers and sent the survivors home in tears. The border has been quiet ever since."

There was low murmuring as the audience absorbed this information. Nathan turned toward the sound of laughter from his left. It came from Abner. Not a surprise. Nathan suspected Abner had his own military aspirations and they probably did not include serving under a foreign commander. Saul granted his cynical cousin permission to speak.

"Tell us, Karaz: is your wardrobe the current fashion in the Hittite Empire?"

"Actually, it's not much of an empire anymore. More like a collection of warlords who fight for the king when it suits them. But I doubt your interest is in clothing, Friend. You are skeptical. Would a successful general be as poorly dressed as I am? Unfortunately, there are many contenders and pretenders for the Hittite throne. One of them assassinated the Crown Prince and put me out of work."

"So, Hittite, you are not invincible."

"Alas, I do confess to a major weakness. I tend to side with losers."

A sharp laugh from Jonathan indicated he was the first to appreciate the sly manner in which Karaz had just insulted them all. Expressions of indignation and outrage abounded as others caught the Hittite's underlying meaning. Abner raised his voice over the tumult.

"We don't need some vagabond outcast to rescue us."

Karaz was in no hurry to defend himself. Instead he crossed his arms and exuded confidence. The assembly quieted as they waited for the foreigner's response. After what seemed to Nathan like an age, Karaz spoke softly.

"Then why did you invite me here?"

Nathan was amazed by how easily Karaz humbled his critics, especially Abner. He tried to gauge the mood of the other Israelite leaders. Saul appeared impressed. Jonathan displayed admiration. Beker's face was inscrutable. It finally fell to Saul to respond.

"Samuel recommended you."

Karaz bowed his head respectfully. But now Abner was ready for another assault.

"I'm curious, Karaz. *Why* did you come?"

"I was seduced by your vast wealth."

"You dare mock us?"

"I dare make this truth painfully clear: *we need each other*. That you need my military skills is beyond question. Here's why I need you."

As Karaz shifted his weight from one leg to the other, a brief look of pain came over his face. Saul immediately called for a stool to be brought forward. Karaz gratefully sat down.

"A recent wound. Walking long distances still aggravates it. It is part of my story which began seven months ago."

Karaz then described the recent Hittite conspiracy. Simultaneous assassination attempts were made on the Crown Prince and Karaz. The general arrived home to find his family dead and his assassins waiting. Karaz killed all of them, but sustained a serious wound to his thigh. A servant girl cared for him during an escape to the coast, where they had taken a ship to Joppa. Fearing retribution from the Philistines, Karaz and the girl sought refuge in the highlands of Israel. Here Karaz crossed paths with Samuel and learned about a king without an army. When others tried to raise questions, Saul waved them all to silence.

"Very well, Karaz. You need me. I need someone *like you*. But why should I trust *you*?"

"Because of a detail I left out until now. Those assassins? They were Philistines."

"Why would the Philistines involve themselves in Hittite politics?"

"With the remnants of the Hittite Empire embroiled in civil war, Philistia can expand northward. Through your lands, Saul."

"Valuable information, Karaz, but I must ask you again. Why should I trust you?"

"Those bastards killed my wife and children. I can hurt them the most by helping you."

"Can you indeed?"

"Just watch me."

Chapter 15 - The Trainer

So, the LORD was with the men of Judah. They took possession of the hill country, but they could not drive out the inhabitants of the plains, because these people had chariots of iron.

From the Book of Judges, Chapter 1, verse 19

Again, the children of Israel did evil in the sight of the Lord. They served the Baals and the Ashtoreths, the gods of Syria, the gods of Sidon, the gods of Moab, the gods of the Ammonites, and the gods of the Philistines. They forsook the LORD and did not serve Him. So, the anger of the LORD was hot against Israel. He sold them into the hands of the Philistines and into the hands of the Ammonites. They oppressed the Israelites for eighteen years, even the children of Israel living on the east side of the Jordan in Gilead. Moreover, the Ammonites came west over the Jordan to fight against Judah, against Benjamin, and against Ephraim, so that Israel was in great distress.

From the Book of Judges, Chapter 10, verses 6 to 9

Praise be to the LORD my Rock, Who trains my hands for war, and my fingers for battle.

From Psalm 144, verse 1

Saul's home outside of Gibeah

As King Saul's newly appointed *Aluf*, or high commander, Karaz devoted his first month in office to analyzing the kingdom's military plight. Naturally, someone needed to accompany the Hittite until he learned his way round Saul's Court. Another boring job requiring intelligence and patience. Another perfect fit for Nathan. Still, he might finagle a military career from his humble role as Karaz's aide.

Nathan's typical day with Karaz consisted of mostly standing around and waiting to run errands. He did pick up a few interesting tidbits, though. Karaz's annual income was the princely sum of twelve talents of gold, payable at the end of the year. Provided there still was a Monarchy, of course. For the present, the mercenary's compensation was limited to room and board. Karaz claimed not to mind this arrangement, for it supposedly gave him even greater incentive to succeed. Nathan also learned Karaz's time was consumed by two principle endeavors. The first was interviewing the available experts for every last detail about Israel's current militia system. The second was enduring lectures from those selfsame experts on why Israel's militia system could never be changed.

It was during this transition that Nathan met Weena, the servant girl who had saved Karaz's life. She arrived in Gibeah with the Hittite's meager possessions ten days after Karaz's meeting with Saul. Nathan embarrassed himself by gaping when Karaz introduced her. Weena was very young, rather pretty...and extremely pregnant. Karaz waited until after the girl was settled in his quarters before commenting on Nathan's unguarded reaction.

"Is something bothering you, Nathan?"

"Yes...I mean no...I mean...who is the father?"

189

"I've taken Weena as my wife, so I better be."

"She's younger than I am."

"I assume that is your awkward way of saying that I am too old for her."

"I'm sorry, Karaz. I don't mean to..."

"It's all right, Lad. Life can be complicated, especially mine. Weena is an exceptional woman. We will have fine children. And I did not force myself on her. Satisfied?"

"Yes."

"Now if that's all settled, we can keep our appointment with yet another of your people's military geniuses."

The day finally came for Karaz to present his findings to the Royal Court. Nathan was grateful to be seated safely behind Karaz once the veteran mercenary began to assail his captive audience. He thought the Hittite could be no more merciless on a battlefield than he was in his criticisms of Israel's military capabilities. Disunity. Tribal pride. Lack of chariots. Primitive weapons. Courage without discipline. Tactics without strategy. Too many generals. Too few leaders. Part-time militia instead of trained soldiers.

Nathan watched as each exposed weakness struck the assembled warriors as hard as any blow to the face. Karaz concluded that it was no wonder Israel had been victimized by its smaller neighbors. The Hittite took no prisoners during his vigorous assault on Israel's military heritage. Nathan feared some hothead might even draw a blade, but decided Karaz had left his listeners too shocked to retaliate. While no one challenged the Hittite's accusations, Nathan could practically smell the smoldering resentment in the room.

Then Karaz masterfully switched tactics and carefully drew fresh hope from his words of despair. Nathan was entranced as Karaz conveyed his vision for a future Royal Army of Israel. Studying the crowd, he suspected there were many secret converts to Karaz's dream. However, a handful of incensed militia leaders wasted little time in tearing the meticulously prepared plan to shreds. The excuses given for rejecting Karaz's proposals ranged from the vast expense to honoring the traditions of Joshua. Unable to assail the mercenary's military competence, a few instead raised questions about Karaz's loyalty.

Nathan recognized that these hollow arguments actually concealed a deep-seated fear of a Royal Army. The tribes preferred a dependent king. Their Elders were loath to give Saul a tool with which he could dominate them. Ironically, they seemed to be taking Samuel's dire warnings about a Monarchy to heart, albeit rather late.

After the session was adjourned, Karaz stayed behind for a lengthy discussion with Saul. When the king waved Nathan away, he waited impatiently at a discreet distance from the whispered exchange. After Karaz took his leave of the king, Nathan fell into step with him.

"I guess you're not getting your army."

"Would you be surprised that I didn't expect to?"

"Then why bother, Karaz?"

"Several reasons. There always has to be a first time...and I have gleaned much from the effort."

"Such as?"

"The Court can no longer simply ignore Israel's military shortcomings, not after today. I've also brought all their objections to a Royal Army out into the open. It's a significant start. I'll do better the next time."

"But there was so much opposition."

"True...but did you notice how few actually spoke out? Most men present said nothing. That means they want to be convinced. Persuade them and Saul will have his army."

"How will we do that?"

"We?"

"Sorry, Karaz, I didn't mean to..."

"Don't apologize, Lad; I'll take all the support I can get. As to your question: a miracle would be nice. I understand that is a specialty of your God."

"Yes, when it's in His will."

"Well then, if a miracle isn't convenient, a small war will also do nicely. Either way, I have some time on my hands."

"Saul didn't dismiss you, did he?"

"Oh no, Saul understands. He just thinks it best if the *foreign mercenary dog* disappears for a while until everyone calms down."

"That was pretty rude, even for Abner. So, what will you do?"

"Saul thought I might begin some military training for Jonathan."

"What about me?"

"I'd be extremely disappointed, Nathan, if you didn't ask."

The following morning, Karaz led Nathan and Jonathan to a crossroads outside of Gibeah. The Hittite found some shade under a rocky outcropping with a clear view of the countryside. After making himself comfortable, Karaz closed his eyes. Nathan turned to Jonathan and saw a bewilderment that mirrored his own. After standing quietly beside the snoozing man for several minutes, Nathan was overcome by curiosity.

"Karaz, when's our lesson start?"

Karaz never opened his eyes.

"It's already begun."

"What do we do?"

"Make yourselves comfortable. Then impress me."

Nathan looked to Jonathan, counting on his friend's princely status. Jonathan's voice was full of indignation.

"That's our lesson today? How to sit in the dirt?"

"Have something better to do?"

Jonathan's face grew dark, but he remained silent. Karaz was correct. There was nothing else for either young man that day. When Jonathan sat down in a huff, Nathan did likewise. He thought Karaz might be sleeping, but the man looked up briefly every time someone or something passed by. Nathan had to admit, the man possessed keen senses. Otherwise, the vaunted mercenary was proving to be a serious disappointment. The hours passed slowly and noiselessly, interrupted only when the three would drink water and eat their provisions. Finally, Karaz shaded his eyes and gauged the sun's position in the sky.

"That should be long enough. Well, Lads...impress me."

Jonathan exchanged a disbelieving look with Nathan before responding.

"How?"

"You could start by telling me what happened here today."

"What happened? Nothing happened!"

"Really? Nathan, do you have anything to add to that astute observation?"

"Only that we wasted an entire day watching nothing happen. Impressed yet, Karaz?"

"No, I'm not. What a shame. It seems you both expect a teacher to earn your respect first. So be it."

Nathan listened with Jonathan in amazement as Karaz described every single person, beast and cart traveling the road that day, even down to how long ago they had passed and in which direction. His frustration over the boring day vanished as Nathan found himself unexpectedly jealous. It was a truly an impressive mental performance. Karaz raised an eyebrow in amusement before he continued.

"You were expecting to engage in some swordplay or learn battlefield strategy, weren't you? Well, my ardent young warriors, you're not even remotely ready."

"That may be true, Karaz...but I don't see how counting sheep and wagons will prepare us."

Karaz rolled his eyes at Nathan's indignant retort.

"Then listen to this little tale...and learn."

The two boys settled back to hear Karaz describe his first mission as a young soldier. The Philistines had taken two towns from the Hittites' Aramean vassals. Karaz's regiment was sent to get them back. The Hittite force was thought sufficient... provided the two newly established Philistine garrisons did not support each other. Karaz's ten man squad was sent to watch one town while the remainder of their regiment assaulted the other. His squad was to immediately report the movement of any Philistine soldiers out of the town. Karaz and his companions lay peacefully in the shade for three days, until an angry Hittite captain showed up. Karaz's regiment had been ambushed by an unexpected Philistine force. The furious captain led Karaz's squad into the town they had been watching. Not a single Philistine soldier was to be found.

"Care to guess where those missing Philistines were? Jonathan?"

"Ambushing your regiment?"

"Exactly."

"But you didn't see them leave."

"Oh, but we did, Nathan, we certainly did. The Philistines expected us to be watching. So they disguised themselves and divided into small groups. My companions and I totally missed the fact three hundred more men *left* town than *entered* it that day. Then the captain gave us a lesson we would never forget."

"He lectured you on vigilance?"

"No, he beheaded our sergeant. Much more effective than a lecture. Learn from it. Carelessness such as you both displayed today could get you killed. Worse, it could get me killed."

"That's just a road, Karaz, not a battlefield."

"Wrong! Wrong! Wrong! Get this through your skulls: you are *always* on a battlefield!"

Nathan and Jonathan both went pale at Karaz's sudden vehemence. The older man held their gazes to ensure his words were sinking in.

"Lads, most wars are won or lost *between* the battles. Your best weapons are your eyes, your ears and your mind. Most people look without seeing and listen without hearing. *That* was today's lesson. Questions?"

Both young men dropped their eyes and mumbled their understanding. Karaz seemed satisfied by their new-found humility.

"Then understand this: Saul has plenty of spear carriers. What he lacks are men with the vision to lead them. Jonathan...a king needs a prince who can succeed him one day. Nathan...that prince needs a man to watch his back. Therefore, I will expect more of you with each day."

Karaz proved as good as his word during the rest of the week. Nathan and Jonathan were subjected to increasingly intense physical and mental exercises. Nathan grudgingly grew to appreciate what an exceptional teacher the Hittite was. Karaz believed in breaking difficult skills into smaller tasks that could be mastered in succession. Each lesson logically built upon the previous ones. Consistent with their preparation for leadership, Karaz treated the boys' mental mistakes more seriously than their physical failings. Yet even the additional drills taught Nathan more than they punished him. There was never any malice in Karaz's methods. It was simply hard, honest work. Each night in bed, Nathan found his muscles sore, his mind aching, but his confidence growing. When they broke for the Sabbath, Karaz announced weapons training would begin the next week. Of course Karaz being Karaz, his idea of weapons training was to begin without any weapons.

The first morning after the Sabbath was devoted to what Karaz called the "dance of death". The Hittite first explained how proper footwork laid the foundation for victory in personal combat. Mastery allowed a savvy veteran to literally dance circles around a fatigued opponent until an opening appeared for a death blow. Karaz then introduced Nathan and

Jonathan to a simple drill by drawing a large circle in the sand. There were only three rules. Stay in the circle. Touch your opponent's chest or head with your right hand. Use only your left hand to deflect his touch. Nathan immediately grasped the game's underlying meaning. The right hand was a sword and the left was a shield. A touch was a mortal wound.

Nathan watched as Karaz engaged Jonathan in the first round and was amazed by the older man's graceful movement, despite a bad leg. Nathan barely had a chance to blink before Karaz scored a touch on Jonathan, and it was his turn in the circle. He lasted only slightly longer than his friend. After a few humiliating rounds, Karaz began to hold back. He would still lunge at his pupils, but stopped short of touching them. As a result, Nathan and his friend repeatedly stumbled to the ground without Karaz even laying a hand upon them. The experience was both humbling and instructive. The boys worked to near exhaustion without gaining a single touch on their teacher.

Karaz decided to break for water and a lecture. Nathan drank deeply as he listened to Karaz explain how footwork had contributed to his easy success against them. Karaz then demonstrated a basic stance to the boys. They were allowed some practice time before the game was resumed. Breaks became more frequent as Karaz added variations of the basic stance whenever he felt his students were ready. Victory still eluded both young men for a while, but they were holding out for longer periods and stumbling less. Nathan had the first breakthrough. He crowed in triumph after finally scoring a touch against Karaz. After Jonathan quickly followed in the next round, Karaz called for another water break.

"This drill has become too simple. I can't have you getting bored. Let's switch hands!"

"Why switch? I'd always hold a sword in my right hand."

"Tell me, Jonathan. Do right hands ever get injured during a battle?"

It was frustrating to begin afresh, but Nathan found himself learning the reverse moves more rapidly than the first set. He scored his next touch on Karaz in only half the time. When Karaz halted for the midday meal, both Nathan and Jonathan were achieving victory against their instructor nearly one time out of every three. Karaz laid out his future expectations for them while eating.

"We will begin each day with similar, but increasingly more complex, drills. Soon you will begin competing against each other, rather than me."

"How long must we perform these drills?"

"Until you die...and I mean that literally. Your combat footwork must become as natural as walking. Slack off...and your next battle will probably be your last."

"We could just stop being warriors."

"Trust me. That would be worse than dying."

"I just don't think we need to practice *every* day."

"So, Nathan... you've mastered the art of footwork?"

"I could do it with my eyes closed."

"Funny you should mention that. Here's something for the afternoon."

Karaz handed each boy a long strip of heavy cloth.

"What's this, Karaz?"

"A blindfold."

"Wait...you don't mean..."

"Do you Boys think all battles are fought in bright sunshine?"

Nathan found Karaz to be a true genius at devising merciless training exercises, ones which the Hittite always performed flawlessly. Nathan thought nothing could be worse than repeating their earlier drills while blindfolded. He should have known better. The next morning, Nathan and Jonathan both stared in disbelief at their training area. Karaz had arrived early and arrayed it with logs, rocks, thorn bushes and shallow pits. Karaz took in the boys' dismay and grinned.

"Take heart, Lads. A warrior rarely fights on smooth, flat ground."

The next week Karaz began each morning with drills, but only for the first few hours. The bulk of the day was given over to various running and lifting exercises. Both young men grew excited on the fourth afternoon when Karaz produced a pair of axes. However, the purpose for the axes turned out to be rather mundane. Each boy was taken to a tree, given an axe and told to begin chopping using only the right arm. When fatigued, they were instructed to chop with the left arm. Near exhaustion, they switched to both arms, chopping first from the right and then from the left. Rest. Repeat. Rest. Repeat.

The third week of training brought the first step toward real weapons: wooden swords. Karaz taught Nathan and Jonathan how to combine swordsmanship with their newly acquired agility and strength. The now familiar drills and exercises remained a part of the daily schedule, but were greatly reduced in duration. Karaz began leaving the two young men alone for hours at a time. He explained that Saul would soon require more of his time. During the fourth week Karaz's presence was gradually reduced to one hour a day. He would evaluate his pupils' progress and then assign them new skills to master. Evening lessons were added during the fifth week. After supper, Nathan would join Jonathan in Karaz's quarters for their introduction to battlefield strategy and tactics.

During the second month of training, Karaz familiarized his two pupils with every imaginable type of fighting implement. Nathan learned how to use a shield for attack, as well as for protection. Spear drills against Jonathan using wooden cattle prods came next. Succeeding weeks saw Karaz bringing in specialists to instruct Nathan and Jonathan in the mastery of javelins, bows, slings, clubs and daggers. Where the boys already had some familiarity, Karaz improved their technique. Even the most unorthodox weapons were not overlooked. An entire week was devoted to fighting with farm implements such as axes, sickles, hoes, and threshing tools. Nathan protested on the day that the finer points of fighting with rocks were covered.

"Seriously, Karaz, rocks? In a real battle?"

"Sometimes, Lad, your weapons are where you find them."

Even after a strenuous day's work, Nathan looked forward to the evening sessions in Karaz's quarters. The Hittite reviewed his campaigns against the Egyptians and the Philistines. Karaz explained the circumstances and tactics of each battle in a way that was both understandable and entertaining. Nathan especially liked when Karaz used a *sand table* to represent the battlefield. The Hittite would begin those lectures by pouring a bucket of sand on a large table. The experienced veteran would then meticulously shape the gritty surface from memory to recreate hills, valleys, and rivers. Small stones were added to represent towns, and pieces of wood used to track the movement of armies. Karaz would have his pupils kneel so their eyes were level with the table top to appreciate a soldier's view of the battlefield. Nathan was then instructed to slowly stand, as if ascending a tower, so he could appreciate what was unseen from ground level. Karaz concluded one evening's lecture by using a term which was unfamiliar to Nathan.

"So, Lads, capturing this one town was the key to controlling the entire river valley."

"What's a key?"

Jonathan's giggle was cut short by Karaz's frown.

"Have you ever used a key, Nathan?"

"No."

"Wait here."

Karaz disappeared momentarily into his bedroom before returning with a wooden chest. He dumped the heavy box on the sand table with a thud that shook the flickering oil lamp. The lid had an ordinary metal hinge in the back, but a strange square of iron on the front caught Nathan's eye.

"Open it, Nathan."

Despite his best efforts, Nathan could not budge the lid. Karaz then placed a bent piece of iron in Nathan's hand and pointed to the iron square on the chest.

"That is a lock. It prevents you from opening the chest. This is a key. Use it to open the lock."

"How?"

"See the hole here? Place the key in it."

Nathan required several attempts before discovering the proper angle which allowed the key to be inserted. He then tried to open the lid again, but to no avail. Karaz allowed Nathan to struggle briefly before offering advice.

"Once inserted in the lock, the key must be turned."

Nathan was frustrated in his initial attempt to twist the key to the left. However, turning it to the right proved to be more fruitful. Feeling some resistance at first, Nathan continued to rotate the key until his efforts resulted in a loud, metallic snap. Nathan feared he had broken something until he saw Karaz's reassuring smile. This time, the lid yielded to his touch.

"Let's apply your experience to tonight's lesson, Nathan. The town I mentioned was like the lock. Defeating its garrison had the same result as turning the key. The valley, like the box, was then open to us."

Nathan and Jonathan had lost interest in both keys and locks by this time. Both were focused on a pile of leather scrolls within the open chest. Karaz smiled at his students' curiosity.

"I was going to save these until later, but now is as good a time as any."

"What are they, Karaz?"

"The only treasure I could bring with me: my maps."

As Nathan watched expectantly, Karaz brushed the sand off the table and lovingly unfurled one of the supple pieces of leather on its wooden surface. Nathan's initial impression was of vibrant colors and obscure markings.

"It's pretty, Karaz. What good is it?"

"A map works like the sand table, Nathan, except it never changes."

Try as he might, Nathan failed to see any connection. He could not relate the map's seemingly random scratches and paint splotches to anything familiar. Jonathan struggled with the concept as well. Even when Karaz patiently explained which marks were mountains or rivers or valleys, they were still incomprehensible to Nathan. Then Jonathan asked the breakthrough question.

"Karaz, where are we on this map?"

"See this black mark, Jonathan? That is Gibeah. The name is written next to it."

"I can't read that."

"Sorry, I forgot. It's in Hittite script."

Nathan was still disoriented, but now he had a point from which to begin. He scanned the nearby markings until a harp-shaped bit of blue paint caught his attention. He pointed to it excitedly.

"What is that, Karaz?"

"That would be your Sea of Galilee."

"And the blue line connected to it?"

"The Jordan River, which leads into..."

"The Dead Sea! That's the Dead Sea, isn't it, Karaz?"

Karaz leaned back on his bench and nodded in satisfaction. Nathan eagerly leaned over the map to study the markings around the now familiar blue paint splotch. Nathan fondly remembered walking with his father along the shores of a huge lake before heading down the west bank of the Jordan to a deep, arid depression containing the great salt sea. In his mind's eye, Nathan related the map markings with the actual mountains, plateaus and valleys visible during his journey. Jonathan soon caught up with Nathan and both boys began guessing the identity of each terrain feature. Karaz patiently confirmed or corrected their guesses, but otherwise allowed his pupils to make their own discoveries. After covering everything visible on the map, Nathan made another intuitive leap.

"Where did you come from, Karaz?"

"It's not on this map. This edge would need to extend for another fifty miles to reach the Hittite border lands. Would you like to see where I lived?"

"How?"

Karaz smiled and carefully rolled up the map before replacing it in the chest. He removed another leather scroll of similar dimensions and laid it out before the two young men. Nathan was immediately confused. The colors and the symbols were familiar, but none were in the same place as the first map. When Nathan saw Jonathan was equally lost, his eyes turned to Karaz for guidance.

"Use the same key to unlock this map, Nathan, which you used for the other one."

Nathan mulled over his mentor's cryptic clue. Acting on sudden inspiration, he began searching for a harp-shaped bit of blue paint. He found it in less than a minute.

"This is the Sea of Galilee isn't it, Karaz? That is the Jordan River. That is the Dead Sea."

"Yes...yes...and yes, Nathan."

"But everything is so tiny."

"This map shows a larger portion of the world. To fit more land on the same size piece of leather, everything must be smaller."

It all fell into place for Nathan. The Sea of Galilee had become his *key* to *unlocking* the mystery of maps. Karaz then led them on a tabletop tour of the Hittite Empire, the lands of

Egypt, Israel's neighbors and even a few islands in the Mediterranean Sea. Their session lasted until the oil in the lamp burned out. Karaz bade them sleep well, for tomorrow's exercises would be as demanding as ever. Nathan knew that he would rest well this night.

For now he understood the entire world.

Chapter 16 - The King's Call

Do not pervert justice or show partiality. Do not take a bribe, for a bribe blinds the eyes of the wise and twists the words of the righteous.

From the Book of Deuteronomy, Chapter 16, verse 19

Then Nahash the Ammonite came up and besieged Jabesh-Gilead. And all the men of Jabesh-Gilead said to Nahash, "Make a treaty with us, and we will serve you." But Nahash the Ammonite replied, "I will make a treaty with you on the condition that I gouge out the right eye of every one of you and so disgrace all Israel." The elders of Jabesh-Gilead said to him, "Give us seven days, so we can send messengers throughout all Israel. If no one comes to rescue us, we will surrender you."

From the Book of I Samuel, Chapter 11, verses 1 to 3

The town of Gibeah

It was like watching a wadi drying up after a thunderstorm.

Beker could no longer hide the dreadful truth: Saul's kingdom was withering away. The man was a pauper king with diminishing prospects. The *Yameen* had labored mightily to mask the Monarchy's many shortcomings through his deal making. Yet the king had been appalled at Beker's aggressive efforts to garner support for his Crown. The *Yameen* in turn was miffed by his naïve king's inability to understand how the world really worked. The powerful and the wealthy would invest in a risky proposition only if great profits were possible. Therefore, Beker must promise rewards of gold in the future in exchange for contributions of silver in the present. Besides, Saul had no real reason for concern. If the kingdom prospered, Beker could renegotiate these arrangements from a position of strength. If the kingdom failed, what did they matter?

Unfortunately, even greed had its limits. Beker's thinly veiled attempts at bribery eventually were perceived as desperate, even hopeless. Those few who still journeyed to Gibeah tended to be poor and needy. Saul held court so infrequently that he returned to plowing his own fields. Saul claimed physical labor helped him think, but Beker recognized despair when he saw it. The evidence indicated a growing number of Israelites felt they might not need a king after all. Saul might hide from this unpleasant truth behind a yoke of oxen, but Beker was too heavily vested in the new kingdom to give up. He was willing to employ extraordinary means to remain in power.

Earlier in the year, Nahash, King of Ammon, had frightened Israel's Elders by blatantly preparing to occupy the Jordan River Valley. Such a move would cut off Rueben, Gad and half the tribe of Manasseh from the rest of Israel. After absorbing these Israelite territories, the Ammonites could easily drive through the Jezreel Valley to the coast. This move would isolate the northern tribes of Asher, Naphtali, Issachar, and Zebulon, leaving them ripe for conquest. Nahash could then slice off additional portions of the remaining tribes at his pleasure. Israel's response was to unite behind a king and wait for war. However, as often happens in such affairs, the enemy had failed to behave as desired. While Nahash's sanity might be debated, Beker knew the man had excellent advisors. As soon as the news spread about Israel's king, the Ammonites' aggressive movements ground to a halt. There was little doubt in Beker's mind about the reason. Nahash expected Saul's reign to be short. The Ammonites could afford to be patient and allow the new kingdom to collapse before striking. Beker privately admired such an efficient and economical strategy. He respected a man who waited and watched before committing himself.

Confronted with a shrewd adversary, the Royal Court floundered, and Israel lost heart. All agreed the king needed to quickly regain the Nation's confidence. Exactly how eluded everyone, except Beker. He used his contacts within the borders of Ammon to find an exploitable weakness. Knowing the other advisors would panic at his scheme, Beker chose to execute his plan in secret. That was the reason his long-time ally Elon had come to Gibeah. His other chief supporter, Helek, might be the better politician, but Elon excelled at the skullduggery Beker had in mind. Once they were secure in his chambers, Beker wasted no time on pleasantries.

"Elon, I need you to arrange an *incident* inside Ammonite territory within a fortnight."

"What did you have in mind, Beker?"

"Remember that problem you handled in Gezer?"

"Who's the target?"

"One of Nahash's sons."

"If you mean the Crown Prince, Beker, the answer is NO. I arrange the death of others, not my own."

210

"This one is merely a concubine's son. However, his death should get Nahash's attention. Can you do it?"

"If I knew where to find him, yes, it's possible. It'll be messy. And it'll be difficult covering our tracks."

"I want a clear trail leading back to Israel."

"That's insane, Beker. Nahash will hit us with his entire army!"

"Precisely, my Friend. We must goad Nahash into attacking before Saul's flimsy kingdom collapses. The Ammonites will come eventually. Better for us sooner than later."

"So what do I tell my men? Leave clues, but don't get caught?"

"Leaving a few Israelite bodies for the Ammonites to find should do the trick."

"They're assassins, Beker, not fools."

"Then take some fools along. Slit their throats on your return."

"That's better. Where should the trail lead?"

"Jabesh-Gilead."

Saul's home outside the town of Gibeah

The most significant day in the Kingdom of Israel's brief history began normally enough for Nathan. With no audiences that day, Saul had yoked a pair of oxen and headed off to the fields where his plow awaited. The king was not expected back until midday when the oxen were to be fed, watered and rested before the afternoon's plowing. Nathan was busy in the barn when a pair of strangers trotted past. He continued working until the clamor of voices caught his attention. The sight of an agitated crowd gathering around Saul's house drew Nathan out of the barn. The mass of men was so tightly packed that Nathan could not get close to learn the reason for the commotion.

"Follow me, Lad."

Nathan turned to see Karaz wielding a short wooden cudgel he was in the habit of carrying. He watched in amusement as his mentor began lightly rapping people on the knees with it. The startled men gave ground to allow Karaz to pass with Nathan close on his heels. Nathan quickly reached the entrance to the house to look up at five men standing on the steps. Two were the strangers Nathan had noticed. Beside them, Beker and Abner were engaged in a heated discussion with Jonathan. Karaz expressed displeasure with the course the conversation was taking.

"They should heed what the boy says."

"Who should, Karaz?"

"Abner and that whatever-he-calls-himself...Beker. Our two visitors carry important news. Judging from their expressions, it's not good. Jonathan advises waiting until the king returns. Beker wants to hear their report now, in public, and Abner is siding with him against your friend."

'What's the harm? Everyone will learn of it eventually."

"Here? Now? Lad, that's a sure recipe for panic. Saul has problems enough without a mob letting its fears run wild. No, a good leader prepares his people for bad news. Beker just wants to take control of the situation. The man promotes himself too much for my taste."

"You think him a threat to Saul?"

"I'll wager he tries on Saul's crown when no one is looking."

"Then why don't you stop him?"

"A wise general chooses his battles carefully, Nathan. I'm the new face here in Gibeah. I don't have the clout to make Beker back down. Not yet, anyway."

Their whispered conversation was interrupted by a shout from Beker. Jonathan's frustrated expression indicated his friend had lost the argument. The two visitors were introduced by Beker as messengers from the city of Jabesh-Gilead, now under siege by the Ammonite forces of King Nahash. This shocking news threw the entire assembly into an uproar. Thanks to Karaz's maps, Nathan understood the magnitude of the threat now facing Israel. The fertile Jordan River Valley was protected on all sides by rugged mountains and plateaus with limited means of access. One of the few eastern approaches lay through Jabesh-Gilead. If this strategic city fell to Nahash, the entire valley from the Sea of Galilee to the Dead Sea would be open to conquest. The Ammonites could swallow up the tribes of Gad and Rueben as easily as a snake would a couple of mice.

The crowd grew so raucous that only the most severe threats from Abner allowed the Jabesh-Gilead messengers to be heard. Nathan learned how their offer of immediate surrender was met by incredibly harsh terms from Nahash. The Ammonite king would spare the city only after the right eye of every single inhabitant was gouged out. The stunned city Elders requested seven days to seek help from their Israelite brethren. If no assistance came, Jabesh-Gilead would accept its bitter fate. Surprisingly, King Nahash had agreed. That was two days ago. Nathan's thoughts were interrupted by Karaz's iron grip on his elbow.

"Well, this is a bloody shambles. Come, Lad. We must find Saul before Beker helps him right out of his kingdom."

"I understand what you mean. Bad news must be handled in better ways."

"THAT...was the worst possible way."

"Gouging out an eye. Nahash must hope to frighten us into surrender."

"Actually, it's a clever tactic."

"How so, Karaz?"

"Most men hold a sword in their right hand and a shield in their left. Put out a man's right eye and he is blind on his weapon side. When he raises his shield, the left eye is covered, and he is completely blind. He also has trouble gauging distance, making it worse for an archer or slinger."

"Why not gouge out both eyes?"

"One eye leaves a man ineffective as a soldier, but still useful as a slave."

"I intend to keep both of mine."

"Then use them to watch Beker."

"What did you see?"

"Actually, it was something I didn't see...surprise. Beker was worried, even fearful, but he *wasn't surprised*."

"You can read a man's face that well?"

"Those who cannot, die young in my profession."

"You just don't like Beker, do you, Karaz?"

"You have me there, Lad."

Nathan spotted Saul on the road prodding his yoke of oxen along with a wooden goad. Both men jogged as rapidly as Karaz's bad leg allowed. Saul's cheerful greeting was cut short by Karaz. Only the lowing of the thirsty oxen broke the heavy silence hanging in the air after Karaz delivered the distressing news. Nathan witnessed an ominous mood come over Saul. The man seemed to transform from a simple farmer into a vengeful monarch before his eyes. Even though the king spoke calmly, Nathan sensed the white-hot anger behind the words.

"Nathan, tell Beker to assemble my Court. Then find a dozen reliable men and have them meet me in the barn. Karaz, we have much to discuss. Walk with me."

Within the hour Nathan stood in his usual spot behind Jonathan and gazed upon the various Tribal representatives seated cross-legged in the shade of Saul's great tree. He studied Beker surreptitiously. His initial observations were most intriguing. For example, Beker normally displayed a cool demeanor, but he had a tendency to briefly exhibit strong emotions after turning away from a person. And there was something else. Nathan was not sure, but he had the impression that Beker was *pleased* by the day's events. He then noted Karaz leaving the barn where Saul had taken the oxen. The sounds of chopping from the barn indicated Saul had his men busy on some project. Nathan was shocked once he got a close look at Karaz. The Hittite was as pale as a new lamb's wool.

A knot of men bearing bulky objects exited the barn with Saul before Nathan could inquire about Karaz's abnormal pallor. Since the barn was behind the seated dignitaries, only Nathan, Jonathan, Karaz, Abner and Beker were aware of their approach. Nathan was startled when a stream of profanity exploded from Abner's lips. A scowling king strode to the front of the assembly, followed by twelve men bearing large hunks of meat dripping blood. Nathan felt his stomach turn as he recognized a pair of heads belonging to Saul's oxen, but that was not the worst of it. Saul was splattered with blood from hair to foot.

The Tribal delegates were horrified at the gruesome specter of their king. Nathan waited anxiously as Saul made eye contact with each and every man present. Most were too shaken to utter a sound. Nathan spotted a puddle of urine seeping out from under one man's robes. Satisfied he had made the desired impression, Saul nodded to his twelve gory attendants. The air filled with howls of protest as a bloody hunk of meat was dumped in the lap of each Tribal representative.

Then the audience cringed in silence as Saul stormed among them.

"Go! Take this meat back to your tribe. *THIS* is what will be done to the oxen of anyone who does not follow Saul and Samuel. As Jabesh-Gilead was once destroyed for not heeding such a warning, so that city will be saved by your obedience to it."

Every eye followed the king as he stalked among them. Nathan had never heard Saul speak with such intensity before. Even Abner and Beker appeared by intimidated by their newly energized Monarch.

"Four days. In four days, the fighting men of your tribes will muster at Bezek."

A few Elders pleaded for more time. Saul responded softly, which made his words even more menacing.

"Get your people to Bezek in four days...or I swear their lands will be as bloody as this meat. You should leave. Now."

The delegates tripped over each other in their haste to depart. Nathan would have been amused had not the circumstances been so dire. He thought Saul appeared suddenly fatigued as the man headed home. Nathan then heard a familiar voice over his shoulder.

"Well, Lad, that was different."

"I didn't think the sight of blood would affect you so much, Karaz."

"Oh, I've seen worse slaughters involving men. No, it was Saul's behavior that threw me. He chopped up those poor beasts like a man possessed. What's all this about Jabesh-Gilead and a warning?"

"A similar method was used many generations ago to summon Israel to war."

"So, you Hebrews have a history of cutting up cows as a call to arms."

"Actually, it was a woman. Each tribe received a piece of her."

"Seriously? Even the Philistines aren't that crude, and they sacrifice their children."

"She was already dead. Her murder was the reason for the war. Anyway, Jabesh-Gilead was the one city that didn't send men to fight. After the war, they were almost completely wiped out as punishment."

"I'm surprised no one mentioned it before."

"It's a sensitive topic to us Benjamites."

"Why?"

"Jabesh-Gilead was called to join the other eleven tribes in a war against *us*."

"So now a king from Benjamin issues the same threat to those tribes. You Hebrews do love your little ironies. What got Saul all worked up to save this particular town?"

"Most Benjamites have a great-great-great-grandmother from Jabesh-Gilead."

"How did that come about?"

"Our great-great-great-grandfathers kidnapped them."

"You Benjamites are some pretty nasty bastards."

"Does that bother you, Karaz?"

"Not at all. Saul will need all the nasty bastards he can get if he wants to keep his crown."

Chapter 17 - The First Battle

When the messengers from Jabesh-Gilead came to Gibeah of Saul and told the news to the people, everyone wept aloud. Just then Saul was returning from the fields behind his oxen and he asked, "What is wrong with the people? Why are they weeping?" Then they repeated what the men of Jabesh-Gilead had said. When Saul heard these words, the Spirit of God came upon him in power, and he burned with anger. He took a pair of oxen, cut them into pieces, and sent the pieces by messengers throughout Israel, saying, "This is what will be done to the oxen of anyone who does not follow Saul and Samuel to battle." Then the fear of the LORD fell on the people, and they turned out as one. When Saul mustered them at Bezek, the men of Israel numbered three hundred thousand, and the men of Judah thirty thousand. They told the messengers who had come, "Say to the men of Jabesh-Gilead: 'Tomorrow, by the time the sun is hot, you shall have help.'"

From the Book of I Samuel, Chapter 11, verses 4 to 9

Five miles from the Ammonite camp at Jabesh-Gilead

Pausing beside the royal pavilion at Bezek, Nathan beheld what Saul had accomplished with a few hundred pounds of raw meat. Thousands of armed men arrived hourly in response to the king's bloody summons. Tomorrow was the last day of the grace period Nahash had granted the city of Jabesh-Gilead to consider his harsh surrender terms. Each passing minute increased the chances of Ammonite scouts discovering Saul's scattered forces prematurely. However, the Israelite militia gathered at of Bezek for two reasons. The unremarkable little village lay just over five miles from Jabesh-Gilead, and a nearby mountain sheltered it from Ammonite eyes.

Nathan was hurrying to a council of war which Saul had just called. He joined over a hundred men crowded into a secluded ravine, a mixture of tribal Elders and clan commanders. Abner had stationed a score of men nearby to turn away the curious. Lacking an invitation, Nathan cunningly attached himself to Jonathan. They slipped in beside Saul, Samuel, Beker, Abner and Karaz as the council was called to order. First up was the latest scouting report by an Elder from Gad.

"My scouts have observed the enemy for the past three days. Over forty thousand Ammonites are encamped around the city. Furthermore, they..."

"Stop."

"What?"

"Stop talking. You're confusing everyone."

The Gadite Elder's eyes bulged as Karaz strode forward. Many gasped at the Hittite's lack of courtesy, but Nathan was certain he heard a few snickers as well. Karaz turned his back on the indignant man and addressed Saul directly.

"My King, please summon the men who have actually laid eyes on the enemy."

Saul whispered something to Abner, who immediately departed. Meanwhile, the Gadite seemed ready to have another go at Karaz. Nathan was curious what his mentor would do.

"What gives you the right to interrupt me?"

"The truth. There are no forty thousand Ammonites here."

"You call me a liar?"

"I'm not questioning your honesty, Friend. You just don't know what you are talking about."

"You have no proof, Hittite."

"Then I'll find some. What is the population of Jabesh-Gilead?"

"I'm not sure."

"Guess."

"Perhaps two thousand, if you count women and children."

"Then consider this, Gadite. Forty thousand Ammonites *wouldn't spend an entire week pissing around* waiting for a city that small to surrender. Nahash would leave a single regiment behind to starve out the inhabitants and already be across the Jordan River."

"That is only your speculation!"

"Oh, I'm not finished. How much will forty thousand soldiers *eat* in one day?"

"I have no idea."

"Until you find out, you should *keep quiet*."

Karaz's bickering with the Gadite was interrupted by the return of Abner with five men in tow. Nathan assumed the rough looking warriors were the scouts Karaz wished to interrogate. However, he was bewildered by Karaz's questions.

"Have you men seen the Ammonites? Don't be shy. Any of you may answer."

"Yes, Sir. We all have."

"Excellent. Anyone know what horse dung smells like?"

"Horse dung?"

"It's not a trick question."

"I do."

"Good. Did you smell any during the past few days?"

"No."

"Smell any camel dung?"

"Actually, I did."

"Now we're getting somewhere. Did you hear any men using tools? Things like axes, hammers, shovels."

"The Ammonites cut firewood."

"But no other use of tools?"

"That's right."

"What did you see on the roads?"

"An endless stream of ox carts."

"Going in full and coming out empty?"

"Yes."

"Were any wagons carrying strange wooden structures?"

"No, nothing like that."

"Did you see any infantry on the road?"

"Just those escorting the wagons."

"That's everything I need to know. Thank you. You men may go now."

Nathan beheld puzzled looks on the faces of every man present, including the king. The self-assured Gadite launched his attack before Karaz could add a word.

"That is what you consider important, Hittite? Dung, tools and wagons?"

"Sometimes noses and ears see more than eyes."

"You waste our time!"

"Really? Since you seem fascinated by dung, I'll start with it. No horse dung means *no horses*, which means *no chariots*."

"Any fool knows the Ammonites possess no chariots."

"They've hired chariots from the Arameans in the past. Or didn't you know that?"

Nathan felt the prevailing mood turn deadly serious at this unexpected insight. This frightening possibility had been overlooked by everyone except Karaz. Having their Tribal militia caught in open ground by chariots would be a disaster. Karaz allowed the others a moment to digest this particular tidbit before continuing.

"We now know the Ammonites have no chariots at Jabesh-Gilead. But they do have camels for their scouts."

Nathan sensed the Gadite's support was waning, but the pompous man refused to give up.

"So what if the Ammonites scouts have camels? They are still only desert scum."

"Nahash will place them on high ground with good visibility and access to a road. The Ammonites will have ample warning if we attack in daylight. That means a night assault."

"That decision is not yours to make, Hittite."

"You are correct. That is a decision for a king."

The Gadite finally had no retort for Karaz. Nathan perceived all eyes turning toward their Monarch. He recognized the heavy burden being placed on Saul. The king stared hard at his military chief while cautiously choosing his next words.

"What else have you gleaned, Karaz, which others have overlooked?"

"The absence of large wagons and lack of construction is significant. They explain why Nahash gave the city a week to surrender. The Ammonites brought no siege equipment and

225

have built none on site. Neither have they have fortified their camp."

"So Nahash has been idle?"

"I doubt it, My King. The nearest Ammonite supply depot is a two day journey. The heavy road traffic indicates Nahash is moving his supplies up closer to where he expects to fight."

"How many men do you think Nahash has?"

"Something made Nahash rush his preparations. Therefore, I believe he is short of soldiers and Jabesh-Gilead's reluctance to surrender has created problems for him. An assault on the city walls would probably kill more Ammonites than he can afford to lose. Also, there are limits on how many men can been fed by a supply train that is two days long."

"I need a number, Karaz."

"Perhaps ten thousand soldiers, with an additional five thousand camp followers."

"Why we must have twenty times that number with us!"

"Except that Nahash has soldiers, *real* soldiers. Better armed, better trained, better led."

"Are you suggesting we wait for more men? Jabesh-Gilead's week runs out tomorrow."

"Not at all...although that deadline no longer matters. The city could hold out on its own for weeks, perhaps months. However, there is a greater reason not to wait."

"Being?"

"You can't hide your warriors at Bezek indefinitely. They lack the necessary food and water. More likely, the Ammonites will become aware of your militia and slip away."

"But Jabesh-Gilead would be saved."

"Not really. Nahash would simply withdraw his forces to a safe distance until you left."

"Then I would pursue him."

"The pursuit of an intact army is more complex than you might think. Your people lack the experience to pull it off. It's not a matter of bravery, but coordination. The Ammonites will simply find a good place to ambush your warriors. I've done the same thing many times myself. This enemy must be defeated decisively, my King...tonight."

"Very well, I approve. Karaz, I appoint you as my *Aluf*. When will my army leave for Jabesh-Gilead?"

"Never, my Lord."

Nathan saw Saul's expression go blank at the abrupt answer. A wave of confused murmuring spread throughout the crowd.

"Listen. Everyone. What you have out there is *an unruly mob*...not an army."

Karaz's bluntness ignited a firestorm among the war council's attendees. Nathan trembled as men stood and shook their fists at Karaz. Only Saul's repeated shouts for order allowed Karaz to continue.

"You have twelve tribes. Your fighting units belong to separate clans. How many generals are here who have never met before? Much less fought together? Send your supposed army out on a night assault, and come dawn, they'll be found wandering in *twelve* different directions."

The crowd settled down somewhat, but Nathan still detected much resentment, albeit mostly from the older, softer men. The warriors seemed to content to hear Karaz out.

"A night assault. One tribe. Its best men. That's your only hope."

An ear-shattering chorus of "NO" echoed off the surrounding hills. Nathan could make no sense of the bedlam that followed. Finally, a grizzled warrior stood. He apparently commanded great respect, for a score of voices demanded silence so he might be heard.

"Which tribe gets this honor, Hittite? The rest will look like cowards!"

An anonymous voice in the rear of the assembly interrupted before Karaz could respond.

"Damn the honor! Who gets the plunder?"

A mixture of laughter and grumbling told Nathan that this second question was of greater concern than the first. He looked on as Karaz engaged Saul in a brief whispered conference. Soon both men were nodding. The crowd hushed as Saul stood to face them.

"Tonight, every tribe, save one, will cross the Jordan River tonight and lay in wait. They will ambush the Ammonites as they flee to their homeland. Regarding the plunder..."

It seemed to Nathan everyone stopped breathing while Saul paused.

"*No man*, on pain of death, will take *any* plunder from the Ammonites this night. It will be collected after the battle and divided between the tribes."

Although some satisfied murmuring greeted the king's decree, Nathan felt the tension increase. But Saul had not finished.

"However, the tribe assaulting the enemy's camp tonight will face greater risks than the rest. Therefore, that tribe will receive a double portion of the plunder. As for which tribe..."

Saul eyes swept the audience. Nathan thought the king was attempting to look into their hearts and find the proper leader. After a moment of contemplation, Saul appeared to have made his decision.

"It will be the tribe volunteering first."

Nathan was as stunned as anyone at this unprecedented decision. He expected to see men leaping to their feet to demand the privilege of being first to fight, but he was wrong. Instead, each tribe huddled separately and engaged in heated debates. Nathan was astonished by the topic being argued. Each group was arguing about whether the potential casualties were worth the additional plunder! These dubious discussions came to a sudden halt when the same grizzled warrior called out again.

"Judah will go!"

"What is your name?"

"I am Jephunneh, commander of Judah's clans."

The shocked expressions of the other Judeans told Nathan that Jephunneh had not waited for a consensus. One of their Elders even grabbed the commander's tunic hem and tried to pull him back down. A swift kick in the man's ribs from Jephunneh dissuaded further attempts to interfere. His authority now established, Jephunneh turned back to Saul.

"We'll let the scribes work out our share later."

Hearty shouts of approval indicated admiration from the other warriors. Most Elders sat in sullen silence while the king smiled broadly at Jephunneh. Nathan tried to read the mood of the other men seated around Saul. A thoughtful Karaz quietly inspected the Judean commander. Excitement radiated from Jonathan. Abner had exhibited a sour look ever since Karaz was appointed *Aluf*. Beker's feelings were inscrutable, as always, although Nathan detected a hint of amusement. The war council hushed as Saul stood to his feet.

"Very well, Jephunneh of Judah, I accept."

"My King, I have an idea."

"Yes, Karaz?"

"Send the messengers back to Jabesh-Gilead to deceive the Ammonites."

"How?"

"By agreeing to surrender tomorrow. The Ammonites will have cause to celebrate tonight, and what is a celebration without wine?"

"An excellent suggestion. *Aluf* Karaz, I leave you to work out your tactics with Jephunneh. The rest of you will cross the Jordan tonight. Samuel will make sacrifices at sunset. Depart after that. Take up positions east of the city before dawn."

As the men filed out of the rocky hollow, Nathan hung back in the shadows. He was overcome with curiosity about how Karaz and Jephunneh would carry out their attack. One of the Hittite's lessons had concerned knowing when to be bold. Nathan took a deep breath, assumed a business-like air and marched into Karaz's tent after the other two men. Both leaders sat down at a table containing Karaz's maps. When Nathan pulled up a stool to join them, Karaz raised an eyebrow but continued his discussion with Jephunneh. Nathan savored his small victory, but knew not to press his luck. Unless asked something, he would keep his mouth shut.

"Here is the route I propose, Jephunneh."

"Your path will take the most time, but it's the easiest to traverse in darkness."

"Now this is where things get messy. How many warriors do you have?"

"Judah sent three hundred *elephs*."

"So at full strength, you would muster thirty thousand men."

"More or less."

"Which means *fewer than half* of them actually showed up. And *only half* of those are any good."

Nathan felt a shiver run down his spine at the menacing look in Jephunneh's eyes.

"Tough talk, Hittite."

"I can back it up, Jephunneh. None of your *elephs* has more than seventy men. Many have fewer than fifty. That includes men, boys, and grandfathers."

"Let's not quibble, Karaz. Assume I have fifteen thousand Judeans. What do you propose?"

"Leave behind anyone younger than twenty or older than thirty."

"There'll be a riot if you try to send them home."

"They can hold Bezek so we have a stronghold to fall back on."

"They might go for that, Karaz. Which leaves six or seven thousand men for your attack."

"Split them into three divisions. Saul will lead one, Abner another, and I'll take the third."

"Judeans don't like taking orders from a foreigner."

"That's why you'll be my field commander, Jephunneh. And Nathan here will be my aide."

Nathan felt his pulse race at the prospect of his first battle. He noticed Jephunneh giving him a skeptical, but friendly, look.

"This boy doesn't look twenty."

"Benjamites appear younger than their actual age."

"Well, he's your problem, Karaz. I better get started. You've given me a real mess to sort out."

"Have your Hebrews assemble on the plain north of Bezek. We'll meet you there."

"By the way, Hittite, we prefer *Israelites*. The uncircumcised call us *Hebrews*."

"And just what do you think I am?"

The five-mile night march to Jabesh-Gilead reminded Nathan there was no such thing as a simple battle. The assault force got off to an agonizingly slow start. Organizing six thousand Judeans from dozens of different clans into three new divisions proved an immense effort. Karaz's demand that men older than thirty be left behind had completely disrupted the normal chains of command. Nathan could barely hear Karaz shouting over the pandemonium.

"Jephunneh, gather your top commanders around that fire. We need to discuss tactics."

"Define *top* commander."

"Your best leaders. Ten would be ideal, but no more than twenty."

"I doubt you understand how our militia works, Karaz. Judeans are born leaders. I'll do my best, but no promises."

Nathan heard Karaz cursing in Hittite a short while later as they neared the gathering of *top leaders*. Peering over his mentor's shoulder, Nathan saw over a hundred men crowded around the fire. Jephunneh awaited with a bemused look on his face. Seeing the angry glare of Karaz, the Judean leader simply shrugged. *Welcome to the world of Israelite militia, Hittite!* Undaunted, Karaz muttered climbed into the back of an oxcart and bellowed for attention.

"Since you are all *top commanders*, I can keep my orders simple."

Karaz's blatant sarcasm instantly subdued the crowd.

"When I tell you to stand...STAND! When I tell you to charge...CHARGE! And when I tell you to retreat...you better run like hell!"

The Hittite then hopped to the ground and stomped off into the darkness. Karaz's curt orders elicited some laughter, but Nathan noticed many veteran warriors nodding their heads in agreement. Karaz maintained simplicity and clarity were the best attributes of a good battle plan.

Nathan saw the other Israelites were long gone when the Judean divisions finally departed after midnight. The rugged terrain between Bezek and Jabesh-Gilead could be covered in two hours during daylight. Nathan judged his companions were making half that speed in the darkness. Everyone shivered miserably in the bitter chill of the desert night.

Nathan was dissatisfied with the crude club and plain wooden shield he carried. He had hoped for something more deadly than a stout piece of wood embedded with a sharp stone and attached to his wrist by a leather thong. Karaz had pulled it from his personal arsenal, claiming this *old friend* had saved his skin on many occasions. His mentor assured him that it would be more useful than a sword for close combat. Still, Nathan felt secure as he hefted its weight. He had little cause for complaint; many of the men around him carried little more than sharpened sticks.

The three divisions quietly crossed the Jordan River together at a shallow ford. Nathan had his first view of the enemy in the foothills leading up to Jabesh-Gilead. The bodies of Ammonite lookouts lined the top of a ridge, victims of Israelite advance scouts. Even the camels were killed, lest the Ammonite camp be roused by animals returning without riders. The assault force split up just over a mile from their destination, Saul taking the northern route, Karaz continuing due east, and Abner looping around to the south. The plan was for the Saul's division to have the honor of leading the attack. The others were to wait until they heard the blare of the king's *shofar*. Nathan moved out at the head of his column beside Karaz and Jephunneh, barely able to discern the long line of militia marching beneath the stars. Their formation inevitably stretched out while the men negotiated the narrow path into the mountains. Treacherous footing caused dozens to fall behind with sprained ankles and broken bones, but this was the least of the Israelites' concerns. Karaz was becoming agitated over the noises emanating from the column. None of the sounds were exceptional: coughing, sneezing, low talking, sliding gravel, yelps of pain, cursing and the like. However,

Nathan knew what was acceptable for an individual was disastrous when multiplied two thousand times.

"Damnation, Jephunneh! Didn't you explain the need for stealth to your Judeans?"

"Men grow weary. They forget."

"Then start sending them back. Shaming a few will quiet the rest."

"The Ammonites already outnumber us, Karaz."

"It'll be worse if they hear us coming."

Jephunneh glared at Karaz for a few seconds, before dropping back. Indignant voices from the rear told Nathan the harsh order was being implemented. The noise level rapidly diminished until the division advanced in near silence. Nathan soon discerned the glow of campfires against the blackened sky. Unexpected movement ahead caused Nathan and those around him to freeze in place. Karaz darted forwarded and returned a moment later with one of the lead scouts. The man led the way to a shallow ravine where Karaz directed the arriving Judean warriors to sit down. The place provide a convenient refuge where their scattered formation could assemble. The Israelites were concealed from view, but close enough to hear faint conversations between the Ammonite sentries. Nathan felt his heart beating so strongly that he feared the enemy would hear it. After several hundred Judeans had entered the ravine, Karaz called a hasty officers' meeting, which surprisingly now included Nathan.

"Spread the word. As soon as everyone is in position, *we go*. Listen for a *shofar*. But if the Ammonites raise an alarm, don't wait. Attack with however many men you have."

"But the king's division must lead the assault!"

Nathan was shocked to realize that he had blurted out those insolent words. No one else reacted when Karaz leaned into his face. The other officers seemed content to let Nathan to clean up his own mess.

"Lad, if your God grants us the gift of surprise, I'm *not* going to waste it. Got any objections, Jephunneh?"

"Oh, I'm with you on this, Karaz. I suspected as much when you gave our division the shortest route."

"Consider this your first battlefield lesson, Nathan. There are some things a king is better off not knowing."

Muffled laughter around Nathan showed the others were in agreement. As the meeting broke up, Jephunneh whispered in Nathan's ear.

"Don't tell your Hittite this, Lad, but I begin to like him."

Nearly a thousand warriors were idling in the secluded ravine when the Israelites' luck ran out. The steady flow of militia slowed to a trickle before stopping completely. Half their division had vanished. Nathan peered fearfully down the dark path while Karaz and Jephunneh had a heated discussion. Jephunneh collected a score of men and headed back in search of the missing warriors. Karaz encouraged Nathan to maintain a confident appearance lest fear break out in the ranks. After a while, Karaz pulled Nathan aside.

"I'm going to check on Jephunneh. Take charge, Lad. I won't be long."

As Karaz melted into the darkness, Nathan had a horrifying revelation: the fate of Israel rested on his shoulders! True, he was surrounded by dozens of veteran leaders, but none knew both Karaz and Jephunneh were absent. Nathan wondered if he should ask one of the older men to take over, but decided against it. His very request might sow the seeds of panic. However, the question became moot moments later. A shout from an Ammonite sentry was answered by voices from the encampment. Nathan could see the shadows of men beginning to stir around the enemy campfires. He could feel the Israelites' courage wavering as nervous militia sought direction from their startled officers. Anxious voices calling for Jephunneh received no answer. The smell of fear was spreading when Nathan allowed his instincts to take over.

Nathan grabbed a *shofar* from the hands of its protesting owner. Placing his lips to the ram's horn, Nathan blew long and hard. The somber notes energized the men behind Nathan. Hundreds streamed from the ravine and raced toward the Ammonite camp bellowing the battle cries of their clans. Nathan tossed aside the *shofar* to take up his own arms. At that moment, he was much less afraid of the Ammonites than he was of facing Karaz. Nathan reached the front ranks of the charging Judeans by the time they reached the perimeter of the enemy camp. The Ammonites were still forming a battle line as Nathan and the militia crashed into them. When an enemy soldier lunged out of the darkness, Nathan instantly assumed the correct defensive posture with shield on his left arm and war club poised in his right hand. He held this position for two heartbeats before sliding a step to his left and spinning to his

238

right. The Ammonite's sickle sword glanced off Nathan's shield and sliced through empty air. With his foe now off balance and vulnerable, Nathan completed his pivot to the right while drawing his war club back across his chest. He then whipped his right arm around to chop at the base of his opponent's neck. Nathan felt the stone head bite deeply into the man's spine. He wiggled the handle a few times until the club worked itself free. In his heart, Nathan exulted. *"My first victory! My first kill! When I see Jonathan..."*

The sound of crunching sand pulled Nathan from his reverie. Karaz's training took over as Nathan crouched in the darkness and raised his shield. A heavy blow splintered the upper half of his shield just where his head would have been. Based on his practice with blindfolds, Nathan knew where his attacker must be. He drew back his right leg and kicked towards an unseen knee. Nathan's ears registered the crunch of bone, a pain-filled shriek and the sound of a body hitting the ground. Nathan discarded his shattered shield, raised his club with both hands and chopped down on a shadowy head. He heard a mushy sound and felt a warm spray on his face and arms. He repeated the action for good measure. One of Karaz's maxims immediately came to mind. *Never make the same mistake twice*. After checking his victim, Nathan carefully searched the nearby shadows. He had almost been decapitated for ignoring another of Karaz's most basic lessons: *celebrate at home*. The Hittite's pithy little rules took on a whole new relevance during combat.

Seeing the battle had moved on, Nathan trotted over a small rise to find out what lay ahead. Numerous fires outlined the immense enemy encampment. His division's assault had swept to the heart of the Ammonite position before stalling.

Nathan feared the Israelites' initial advantage was fading before the Ammonites' superior numbers. His head snapped to the left at the sound of an invisible *shofar* from the north. Saul's division was making a timely appearance. The flicking fires revealed the enemy withdrawing to avoid being surrounded. A more distant *shofar* then blared to Nathan's right, undoubtedly Abner's southern division making its presence felt. The prospect of a three-sided fight apparently unnerved the Ammonites. The enemy's disciplined retreat degenerated before Nathan's eyes into a full-fledged rout.

Unexpected noises from behind caused Nathan to spin around and grip his club tightly with both hands. He relaxed when the murky darkness revealed Israelite militia instead of Ammonite reinforcements. The lost half of his division had finally found its way to the fight. As the fresh men poured past, Nathan called out to two familiar figures.

"Karaz! Jephunneh! I was about to go looking for you two."

"Half of our people took the wrong path. Jephunneh had just rounded them up when I found him."

"It appears Karaz and I have missed the fun."

"Speaking of which, Nathan, do you have any idea why my division *was not where I left it*?"

"Yes, Karaz, I do."

"Well?"

"There are some things an *Aluf* is better off not knowing."

Jephunneh roared with laughter while Karaz glowered and gave his pupil that *We'll talk later* look. Nathan judged it a good time to change the course of conversation.

"The battle moves on, Karaz. Should we join in the pursuit?"

"No, Nathan. Our brains are needed more now than our weapons. We must secure the camp, care for the wounded and guard against a counterattack. Jephunneh, can you put your *lost lambs* to work?"

"Sure, Karaz. Just don't repeat that nickname where they can hear it."

The sun now crept over the eastern mountains and illuminated the newly captured camp. When the wind changed direction, Nathan was nearly overwhelmed by the stench from men's bowels having been sliced open. There was also a strange taste on his tongue which Jephunneh attributed to blood in the air. Karaz abruptly stopped and stared at Nathan with genuine concern.

"Is any of that yours?"

Nathan examined himself in the dim morning light. Dark stains were splattered all over his clothing, arms and legs...blood stains. Nathan imagined that his face must look absolutely frightful.

"I don't think so."

"Let me see, Son."

Jephunneh's hands ran swiftly over Nathan's limbs, worked his joints, poked his chest and carefully examined his head. Finding nothing more serious than bruises, the Judean pounded Nathan's shoulders with both fists, after the manner in which warriors congratulated each other. Nathan found this thumping both painful and satisfying at the same time.

"Nathan, you truly are a man. No matter how old you really are."

Chapter 18 - The Second Start

So Saul separated his men into three divisions; during the last watch of the night they broke into the camp of the Ammonites and slaughtered them until the heat of the day. Those who survived were scattered, so that no two of them were left together. Then the people said to Samuel, "Who is it that asked, 'Shall Saul reign over us?' Bring the men to us and we will put them to death." But Saul said, "No one shall be put to death this day, for today the LORD has rescued Israel." Then Samuel said to the people, "Come, let us go to Gilgal and there reaffirm the Kingship." So all the people went to Gilgal, and confirmed Saul as king in the presence of the Lord. There they sacrificed peace offerings before the Lord, and Saul and all the Israelites had a great celebration.

From the Book of I Samuel, Chapter 11, verses 11 to 15

The plains of Gilgal in the Jordan River Valley

A fortnight after his first battle, Nathan found himself at the heart of the grandest celebration in Israel's history. He gazed up at Saul seated regally on a hilltop near the town of Gilgal, flanked by Samuel the Judge and Prince Jonathan. The victorious *Aluf* Karaz and the *Yameen* Beker were stationed immediately below their king. Elders from every Israelite clan stood slightly farther down the hill. Nathan stood with the next group, the military commanders who defeated the Ammonites. He had been unsure of where to stand until the Judean commander, Jephunneh, took him in hand. Nathan's youthful presence raised a few eyebrows among the war chiefs, but none

243

questioned Jephunneh's judgment. Nathan was grateful to the older man, for the view was spectacular.

Gilgal was a natural assembly area, located on the broad plain of the Jordan River Valley and protected on nearly every side by imposing mountain ranges. Hundreds of thousands filled the great plain below, more than had attended Saul's selection as king at Mizpah. Many then had questioned Saul's fitness to rule and the Monarchy languished as a result. Samuel shrewdly recognized the best way to eliminate any lingering doubts was through a public inauguration of their new king after a great triumph. All Israel marveled at the magnitude of the Ammonite defeat. Saul's daring nighttime assault had driven the enemy from his camp and yielded a wealth of plunder. King Nahash had tried to rally his broken army a few miles east of Jabesh-Gilead, only to see his force crushed by the bulk of Israel's militia sweeping up from the south. Nathan heard the Ammonite king had deserted his doomed soldiers on the back of a camel.

Nathan turned his attention to Samuel when the judge began making the Peace offerings. This particular type of sacrifice was used to establish a covenant, such as now existed between the people of Israel, their king and their God. The new kingdom had a rocky beginning and Saul was not the only one who would benefit from a fresh start. Samuel saw the benefit of confirming the king's authority over his people and the LORD's authority over them both.

The old judge followed the sacrifices with a lengthy rebuke of the Nation for their lack of faith and obedience. Nathan felt the people grow tense as dark clouds rolled in from the mountains. Rain and thunder from the heavens provided a terrifying context for Samuel's words. Fear spread through the soaked congregation, for this was the dry season when rain drops were rare. As the storm blew past, Samuel's voice switched to a reassuring tone. He proclaimed that God forgave their weakness and would bless His people as long as both they and their king were obedient. Otherwise, He would sweep them all away. Then Samuel dismissed the people and departed for his own home. As Nathan left, he was uncertain how the judge's message affected his personal plans for vengeance against the Philistines.

That evening in his tent, Beker resolved to establish royal housing at key locations throughout Israel. He was sick of sleeping under musty wool on gritty sand. The project would be expensive, but as long as the right people benefited, he could manage the complaints. Of course, that was only the beginning. He still had a government to build. Laws must be enacted, ministers appointed, workers drafted and property acquired. Beker would see all this accomplished because his patron Saul was now a real king, thanks largely to the Ammonite king's rashness.

The ever lethal Elon and his assassins had executed their mission with cold-blooded efficiency. Nahash must have flown into a rage over the murder of one of his sons, even a bastard one. The vengeful king then followed Elon's trail of dead stooges all the way to Jabesh-Gilead. The botched Ammonite invasion was better than anything Beker dared hope for. It all reinforced his belief in the benefits of coolly waiting and watching. If Nahash had done nothing, the fledging Israelite kingdom would have collapsed in a matter of weeks. If the Ammonite king had taken the time to assemble a larger army and proper siege equipment, he could have stared down any

Israelite force sent against him. A part of Beker wanted to express his gratitude to Nahash with a gift. His mouth watered at the potential new revenues that could be extracted for the Monarchy. Samuel's warnings about the true cost of a Monarchy always made Beker smile. The king was actually a bargain; it was the ever-expanding royal government that was expensive, particularly at the top.

Countless opportunities for personal wealth were now open to Beker. As *Yameen*, Beker would have a host of new favors to sell in the Crown's name. Merchants would pay a handsome premium to have royal business directed their way. Those seeking a title or commission would gladly provide generous gifts. Beker could profit from renegotiating earlier agreements, made when the survival of the kingdom was in doubt. He felt it only just. At the time those applicants had paid for mere possibilities, now they were getting certainties. Which was why Beker had been expecting the Reubenite just now entering his tent. He had been dodging the man for days. The man appeared quite impatient, just as Beker had intended him to be.

"Greetings, Hezron. I apologize for my sparse accommodations. The only hospitality I can offer is a stool, and a rather crude one at that."

"You're a hard man to find, Beker."

"Yes, the ceremony, don't you know. Endless apologies. How may I be of assistance?"

"Two months ago, we discussed a government position for me. I would manage the king's lands for him."

"Of course I remember, Hezron. A most lucrative appointment...acquiring land, hiring labor, selling the crops and animals. A great deal of wealth would pass through your hands."

"Well, Beker, I haven't pressed the issue while there was nothing to manage. Saul's victory has changed all that now. It's time for me to receive my appointment."

"And that will be one of my top priorities. Just as soon as I receive the rest of your *donation*."

"The rest? *The rest!* It may have slipped your mind, Beker, but I already paid you *five* talents-weight of gold!"

"I forget nothing, Hezron. Please remember I also told you that the true value of this position could not be determined at that time. Now it can be."

"That was not our agreement, Beker, but I see where this is headed. How much are we talking about?"

"Ten talents of gold."

"So you're doubling the price on me from five talents to ten?"

"You misunderstand, Hezron. The total price is not ten talents of gold. It is ten *more* talents. Your original five was a down payment."

"No, Beker. Not another shekel more."

"Then watch as I open the position to bidding. Not everyone is as honest as you and I. A greedy man would find ways for some of the royal wealth to stick to his fingers. What I am offering you is a true bargain. Others will gladly pay double, even triple, that amount."

"You must return my five talents if you sell to another."

"A trifle taken out of my handsome profit. Decide what you really want, Hezron. Your five talents back? Or the posting of a lifetime?"

"We had an agreement, Beker. The king is also bound by it."

"By all means, Hezron, take it up with him."

Beker waited until Hezron had stomped out before breaking into laughter. *A wealthy sucker was more valuable than rubies.* The naïve oaf would soon learn that all paths to the Throne led through the *Yameen*. Beker's ambition required extending his political influence, and the victory at Jabesh-Gilead provided the opportunity. Now that Saul was a power to be reckoned with, many previously tepid supporters were desperate to redeem themselves in the eyes of their king. In the aftermath of the Israelite victory, they sought the royal favor by offering to kill anyone who had openly opposed Saul, which included many of Beker's former Highlander allies. Saul displayed excellent political instincts by extending mercy to his former critics. However, Beker saw no harm in convincing his old associates they owed their lives to his influence over Saul. After treating Beker as a traitor for joining the Monarchist camp, they had not expected his forgiveness. He found their profuse expressions of gratitude gratifying, but also pathetic.

These thoughts caused Beker to take stock of his chief competitors within Israel's Monarchy. First and foremost was

Saul. The neophyte king had surprised Beker during the Jabesh-Gilead crisis. The memory of the blood-stained Saul distributing pieces of oxen still made him shudder. Beker had witnessed a transformed man bend an entire nation to his will and drive it to an unlikely victory. Since then however, Saul seemed to revert to his former self. Beker concluded that while Saul was an amazing leader, his strong outward demeanor hid a host of insecurities. The king was not to be taken lightly, but Beker was confident Saul's inner man could be managed.

Surprisingly, the elderly Judge Samuel loomed as the greatest challenge to Beker's ambitions. Instead of slinking off into retirement, Samuel now stood at the pinnacle of his power. Saul owed his crown to the old man and depended heavily on Samuel for counsel. For the time being, Beker must accept the judge's authority in the new kingdom as greater than his own. Samuel was also the first man to ever intimidate him. Beker was accustomed to dealing with rivals who feared, or at least respected, him. Samuel was the exception. Contrary to others, the old judge showed *indifference* to Beker's schemes, as if they did not matter. Samuel was no fool, so Beker assumed the old man was holding something back. Regardless, Beker intended to drive a wedge between Saul and Samuel. The judge's performance today was particularly disturbing. On this day of jubilation, what did the old man do? He *scolded* the Nation for desiring a king! But of even greater significance, Samuel publicly laid the groundwork for *deposing* Saul. The Nation had been put on notice: a king could be *swept away* for any transgression. Beker had no trouble interpreting Samuel's underlying message. The judge had given Saul the crown and could take it away anytime he saw fit. Such power would keep Saul, or any king for that matter, under Samuel's thumb. Beker could not help but admire the old man's shrewdness.

The king's cousin Abner was not so much a competitor as a dangerous weapon to be handled with care. Beker discerned the man was secretly jealous of Saul and longed for his own place of honor. Abner would make a formidable leader one day, but this insatiable hunger for glory was his weakness. Beker foresaw the two of them forging an effective partnership; all that was necessary was the proper application of flattery. Abner could bask in the cheers of the Nation while Beker wielded real power from the shadows. The big man would not even feel the hook Beker would place through his nose to be led around like a gelded bull.

Beker judged that Jonathan might one day be a far greater king than his father. Jonathan had the makings of an effective ruler: handsome, popular, intelligent and courageous. Combined with training from the Hittite mercenary Karaz, the result was a very confident young leader. Yet confidence encouraged rash decisions in one so inexperienced. Jonathan would pose a definite challenge, but not for many years. Jonathan was a problem that could be ignored for the present. Beker's successors would deal with him.

Karaz, the outsider, was a true puzzle. Beker had yet to figure out what game the mercenary was playing. Karaz had so far rebuffed his overtures at an alliance. Beker was miffed when the Hittite's behavior made it clear that Karaz was merely tolerating the *Yameen*. By all appearances the man was a loyal and capable military advisor, but strong ambition was also an essential component of that profession. Through his training, Karaz was cultivating a strong allegiance from the young prince, which by itself roused Beker's suspicions. One thing was certain; Karaz's potential influence was limited. Israel would never accept a gentile as a leader in his own right.

As for the other members of the Royal Court, Beker saw little threat there. Onan's mission was completed with Saul installed as king, and the Judean's influence was on the wane. The rest of Onan's Monarchist faction had already fallen in line with the new order. The Highlander aristocracy would flock to Beker's side simply because they had nowhere else to go. Beker was confident that he could recruit, suborn or drive off any other aspirants for power. Besides, he always had Elon's blade as a last resort. While preparing for bed, Beker realized the affair at Jabesh-Gilead had revealed a new star rising on the horizon.

Beker's sources were rather vague, but somehow the youthful Nathan had recently earned great respect on the battlefield. Beker recalled being impressed during Nathan's brief tenure as the *Shoeyr*. He carefully considered the young man's attributes as sleep began to overtake him. Nathan lived in Saul's household and was virtually a member of the royal family. He was the best friend and confidant of Jonathan, the heir to the throne. The young man benefited from Karaz's intense training program. Yet Nathan was consumed with a bitter hatred for the Philistines, the result of witnessing his father's death at their hands. Beker smiled sleepily at his summation of Nathan: *talented, with an exploitable weakness*. This boy was definitely someone worth cultivating.

Hezron arrived at Beker's tent early the next morning. Eating his fireside breakfast, Beker noted with pleasure the bulky leather purse clutched by the defeated man. He lived for little moments like this. Beker made brief eye contact with Hezron before continuing to silently chew his food. He would force Hezron to speak first and thereby acknowledge his weaker position. After a moment the Reubenite sighed and tossed the purse at Beker's feet.

"There it is, Beker. Ten more talents of gold. Just as you asked."

Beker spoke between bites.

"Fifteen more talents, Hezron. Ten was yesterday's price."

Chapter 19 - The Trap is Planned

Now as Samuel was sacrificing the burnt offering, the Philistines drew near to battle against Israel. But the LORD thundered with a loud thunder upon the Philistines that day, and threw them into such a panic that they were routed by the Israelites. The men of Israel rushed out of Mizpah and pursued the Philistines, and slaughtered them along the way to a point below Beth Car. Then Samuel took a stone and set it up between Mizpah and Shen. He called its name Ebenezer, or Stone of Help, saying, "Thus far the LORD has helped us." So the Philistines were subdued, and they stopped their invasion of Israel. And the hand of the LORD was against the Philistines during the lifetime of Samuel.

From the Book of I Samuel, Chapter 7, verses 10 to 13

The Royal Palace in Philistine Gath

"So now the rabbits have a king."

Abimelek, *Archon* of the Philistine Kingdom of Gath, saw others were also perplexed by their sovereign's peculiar statement. King Maoch had summoned the eight members of Gath's war council to his palace to learn how Israel had defeated Ammon. Everyone now stood around a massive stone table covered by an enormous map of Canaan. Three were army commanders. Three were ministers responsible for the logistics of Gath's military campaigns. The newest member of this select circle was also its youngest: Achish, the nineteen-year-old heir to the throne. Abimelek, Maoch's master of internal politics and diplomacy, rounded out the group. He was also the best informed since espionage was his specialty. Seeing several other council members sheepishly looking his way, Abimelek reluctantly assumed the role of spokesman.

"Rabbits, my King?"

"You're not usually so slow, Abimelek. I mean the Hebrews. They multiply like rabbits. They hide in their holes when threatened. They have the imagination of rabbits."

The king's explanation of the royal witticism naturally elicited laughter from his officers, especially since it came at Abimelek's expense. The *Archon* took no offense, but felt the need to respond.

"It is my duty to remind the king that these same *rabbits* rose up under their Judge Samuel to deliver a crushing defeat to Philistia during your father's reign. More recently, they came out of their holes to slaughter an entire Ammonite field army."

"Don't give the Hebrews too much credit. Nahash is a swaggering fool."

"True, the Ammonite king's judgment is questionable, but there is nothing wrong with his generals."

"Then perhaps their ruler's stupidity is contagious. Those great military minds let Nahash delay his invasion for a week so his victims could send for help. Only to be later surprised in their beds by some vagabond king and his peasant militia!"

"Thus proving this Hebrew king is a dangerous adversary."

"Nahash's army was not that large, Abimelek."

"He fielded more men than Gath can muster. If it weren't for our chariots..."

Maoch abruptly raised his hand to cut off any more arguments from his *Archon*, but Abimelek had made his point. The other commanders and ministers waited tensely while the king composed his thoughts. Abimelek glanced at the thoughtful looking Achish. The Heir had spent a term in Hebrew territory commanding the garrison at Gibeon. A simple training assignment, but Abimelek was interested in any insights the future ruler of Gath might have. Abimelek's attention snapped back to Maoch as the king began speaking.

"I have a simple question. I want a simple answer. Is there an opportunity here for Gath?"

Abimelek already had an answer, but waited while the others whispered among themselves. His eyes fell on Phicol, hero of Gath's seizure of Rafah. The man had been promoted swiftly after his expedition forced the Egyptians to turn over that profitable outpost to Maoch. Phicol appeared to be waiting for an opportune moment to present his views. The others fidgeted uncomfortably, except for the king's son. Abimelek perceived a barely contained excitement in Achish. Sensing his king was growing impatient, Abimelek once more took the lead.

"There is an opportunity for us, my King. However, we will need help."

"From one of the other Philistine kingdoms?"

"From all of them."

"Explain."

"If there is one thing more dangerous to Gath than a Hebrew king, it is another Philistine king."

"You're thinking of Kaftor of Gaza."

"They all pose substantial threats. Kaftor is just the most blatant."

"Make your point, Abimelek."

"If you go against Israel alone, and fail, the other Philistine kings would pounce on a weakened Gath. On the other hand, conquering Israel would make Gath the greatest power in Philistia. The other four kings might feel compelled to move against us before we could harness our newfound strength."

Maoch gave his *Archon* a sour look, but said nothing. Abimelek knew Maoch dreamed of the day when his four peers would bow before him. However, today was not that day.

"I know you, Abimelek. You already have something in mind."

"We need to determine the capabilities of this Hebrew king. In the past, the Hebrew judges would produce a great victory and then fade away. Even the dreaded Samuel has retired. Question: Will a Hebrew king outlast a Hebrew judge? Find a way to test this man, my King...one with little risk."

"We could burn some Hebrew villages, Abimelek, and see what happens."

"Gath cannot act alone. The Philistine Council of Kings must consent to a joint expedition."

"My brother kings would first demand proof that this Hebrew king poses a threat to us all."

"Therein lays your challenge, Sire."

"How do I start a war, without going to war?"

"Precisely, my King. We must provoke this Hebrew king into some aggressive action. Our provocation must be simple, yet something which cannot be ignored. It must tempt the Hebrews to attack a place of our choosing, but also keep our losses to a minimum."

"Your ideas then, Counselors. Find me a place. Give me a plan."

The council members gazed intently at the map on the table. It had been presented to Maoch's great-great-grandfather by the reigning Pharaoh to mark the territory Gath would govern in Egypt's name. Abimelek knew better than to take the lead in this discussion. It was safer to let the military members propose a strategy for the others to refine. So the *Archon* was startled when Achish broke the silence by uttering a single word.

"Geba."

Abimelek remembered Geba as an abandoned Gath outpost some ten miles east of their garrison at Gibeon, the site of Achish's first command. He was intrigued to hear Achish's reasoning since the young man was the only person present to have possibly seen Geba. The *Archon* noted only two others, besides himself, not visibly annoyed by the prince's disregard of protocol. The first, Phicol, ran his eyes over the map, obviously searching for possibilities. The second, Maoch, displayed a mixture of amusement and pride as he indulged his heir.

"Why Geba, Son?"

"Control of Geba is vital to the Hebrews. It is the gateway to their mountain strongholds. Hundreds rose up when you tried to post fifty soldiers there. Think what they would do if you sent a few hundred."

"Very well, Achish, you've given me a place. Do you have a plan?"

"Reinforce Gibeon. Then transfer its entire garrison to Geba."

"Abandon Gibeon? That's insane!"

Abimelek looked up after Phicol blurted out his objection. The officer's face reddened at the realization he had just rebuked his future king. Maoch remained silent, but appeared more curious about the outburst than offended. Phicol quickly bowed his head and apologized.

"Forgive me, my King. It was not my place to speak."

"Actually, Phicol, I had the same thought. Feel free to probe my son's strategy."

Abimelek saw confidence swiftly flow back into Phicol's eyes, which were then focused on the prince. Achish coolly returned the veteran commander's withering stare.

"We can support and supply soldiers in Gibeon, Achish. Why leave them dangerously exposed in Geba?"

"Bait is supposed to appear helpless, Phicol."

"But our bait should not actually be helpless. Those old fortifications in Geba must be in shambles."

"We can repair them in a day. It will take much longer for the Hebrew king to rally his army."

"Why not hold both Gibeon and Geba? We have enough soldiers."

"An abandoned Gibeon is more of an enticement, Phicol."

"True, the Hebrews couldn't resist occupying Gibeon. But what does that gain us, Achish?"

"The Hebrew king can either take Gibeon or besiege Geba. He might even attempt to do both. Regardless, his forces must come out into the open. Then we tie down his army and bring in reinforcements from Gath."

"He might choose to ignore us."

"Abimelek says this king is a Benjamite. Geba is deep in his homeland. He can't disregard our challenge without appearing weak to his people."

Abimelek found merit in the young prince's arguments. Achish's plan showed a keen eye for both tactics and politics. Occupying Geba was one of several moves Abimelek had considered himself, but Achish's use of the Gibeon garrison was a nice touch. Even more impressive was how well the prince had anticipated his father's thinking. After a moment Phicol turned to Maoch and nodded approvingly. However, Abimelek saw the king was not completely convinced.

"Not bad, Achish, but it's still a war without the consent of the Council of Kings. We could end up fighting both outraged Hebrews and jealous Philistines."

"Which is why Geba would be perfect, father. The outpost there may have been temporarily abandoned, but it is still ours. We are merely reclaiming our property."

"So you would argue we are just moving a few of our soldiers from one part of Gath to another. Your evidence is extremely thin, Son."

"The other kings have done worse, Father."

"Yes, they have indeed."

The king's broad grin announced his approval of Achish's scheme. However, Abimelek expected one final issue to be raised. The *Archon* did not need to be a prophet to foresee that the prince hoped to lead this expedition. Obviously, the young man was ready for greater responsibilities, but this mission required more experience than the teenager possessed. Maoch firmly met his son's eager gaze while announcing his decision.

"Phicol, would you accept a commission to hold Geba, as my son has described?"

The *Archon* noted Achish manfully attempting to mask his disappointment by staring at the map. The young man could not dispute that his father had selected a suitable commander.

Both boldness and cunning were required for this endeavor, and Phicol possessed them in abundance. The officer replied without hesitation.

"Provided I have a suitable force, my King."

"You'll have the garrison from Gibeon, nearly one hundred and fifty men. What else?"

"A company of heavy infantry and a company of foot archers."

"No chariots?"

"It's poor terrain for horses. Besides, I don't want to scare off your rabbits."

"Agreed. Phicol, I appoint you as my governor for Gibeon and Geba. Of course, you 'll need a reliable second-in-command."

The speed with which Achish's head popped up almost caused Abimelek to chuckle.

"Since this was all Achish's idea, Phicol, take him with you. That is, Son, if you are available."

"I'll need a suitable rank, Father. Say promotion to Regimental Commander?"

"A bit excessive, Achish, but consider it done. Abimelek!"

"My King?"

"Make the necessary arrangements. The Council members are at your disposal. Notify the garrison in Gibeon. Detach the companies of infantry and archers for Phicol from my personal regiment. I want them at Gibeon in a fortnight and everyone at Geba in a month."

"I can also schedule the next meeting of the Council of Kings shortly after that."

"Excellent suggestion, Abimelek. A Hebrew attack on Geba should convince the other kings to mobilize their armies. Who do you like as supreme commander?"

"You would be the logical choice, Sire. It would allow the other kings to blame any problems on you."

"Then it is settled. We will draw this Hebrew king out and see what he is made of."

Chapter 20 - The Royal Army

But the people refused to listen to Samuel. "No!" they said. "We want a king over us. Then we will be like the other nations, with a king to lead us and to go out before us and fight our battles."

From the Book of I Samuel, Chapter 8, verses 19 and 20

No king is saved by the size of his army. No warrior escapes by his great strength.

From Psalm 33, verse 16

Saul's home outside the town of Gibeah

      Walking in Jonathan's shadow, Nathan slunk into the room where the Royal Council met. He was accustomed to entering his friend's home anytime he pleased, but the place was becoming a palace rather than a mere residence. Today's meeting was emblematic of this change. Beker, functioning as the king's *right hand*, felt Saul needed protection from the self-seeking hordes trying to influence every royal decision. The *Yameen* reasoned that the Royal Court might excel as a social institution, but it floundered badly at administration. Thus, Beker inaugurated the Royal Council, a smaller body with a more exclusive membership than the Royal Court. This elite group would help the king make faster and better decisions. The requirements for a seat on the Royal Council seemed rather vague, but Nathan suspected friendship with the *Yameen* to be the most important prerequisite. The evolving royal protocols left Nathan in a quandary about his role in the kingdom. His mentor Karaz had come to Nathan's rescue by appointing him as *Naar to the Prince*. Officially, his job was to serve as Jonathan's armor bearer, but *Naar* was a title which allowed Nathan access to Court functions. However, attendance at Royal Council sessions was more restricted. None of the members would object to Jonathan's presence, but they might question why he required an armor bearer. And Nathan desperately wanted to be here today, for Karaz was again requesting the creation of a Royal Army of Israel. The discussion would definitely be more interesting than the usual petty bickering.

Two dozen men of various ages and backgrounds squeezed into what was normally the house's dining area. Rough wooden benches provided seating for most. Saul occupied a chair on a small platform along the far wall, making the king visible to the attendees. Beker and Abner stood on the platform behind the king. When the crowd parted slightly to allow Jonathan to take his customary seat at the king's right hand, Nathan remained inconspicuously at the back of the crowd. Nathan released a long held breath when Abner finally ordered the room sealed and Beker called the Council to order. Saul beckoned Karaz to come forward as the first order of business. Nathan knew from Karaz that approval of an army was not a foregone conclusion. Many Tribal commanders felt the Israelite militia's recent victory over the Ammonites proved a national army was unnecessary. Karaz had barely begun his presentation before he was interrupted by a single word from the audience.

"Why?"

Karaz closed his eyes for several seconds before responding, but Nathan doubted the Hittite was surprised. Most likely, his mentor was fighting the urge to strangle the impertinent ass. Karaz had taught Nathan that you must humor fools in order to get something from them.

"Your kingdom has enemies. Someone will need to defend it."

Before Karaz could resume his discourse, Helek of Manasseh stood to object. Nathan recognized the man as Beker's longtime associate and frequent spokesman. The *Yameen* had remained silent regarding creation of a royal army, but Helek never went against his patron. Nathan suspected this exchange of question and answer was part of a planned performance.

"For three hundred years, Hittite, the tribal militias have fought our wars."

"Have they won all of them?"

"They have faithfully served every Israelite commander since Joshua."

"Again...has your militia won all those wars?"

"History is irrelevant. Our militia just destroyed a mighty Ammonite army!"

"How many times can you do something for the first time?"

Karaz's seemingly random question caught Helek and the rest of the Council off guard. The Hittite allowed the confused silence to briefly hang in the air before answering himself.

"The answer is…only once. Your neighbors now know your militia can overwhelm an unprepared army in the dark. Don't expect any of them to make that same mistake again."

Helek appeared totally unprepared for this argument. However, when the nobleman faltered, Elon of Zebulon entered the fray. Nathan immediately glanced toward Beker, for Elon was another staunch supporter of the *Yameen*. Beker's expression remained impassive as Elon spoke, but the conspiracy was now clear to Nathan.

"The militias just go home after a war, Hittite. Soldiers must be paid. We have no wealth to waste on an army. Comeback when we can afford your dream. At least wait until our scribes can draft tax laws."

Nathan wondered how many others were waiting to gang up on Karaz. He feared that Beker's minions might yet again quash a Royal Army. Yet, Karaz's cool response showed no trace of concern.

"Elon, your enemies will come against you with soldiers, not scribes. You Hebrews need an army, a very good one, and it will be expensive. Your Judge Samuel told you as much when you decided to get into the king business."

"A standing army has never been our way. Joshua himself established our system. Each tribe raises its own militia whenever necessary. It is both efficient and effective."

"Really? Some three hundred years have passed since this Joshua died. Today your people control less than half the land that you claim your God gave you. I have to wonder where the problem lies. Is it your God or your militia?"

Nathan was alarmed by violent reaction ignited by Karaz's calm rebuke; even Saul grew pale. The king slowly resorted order, but Elon still shook his fist at Karaz.

"Our people have produced great warriors since the time of Abraham. Do not presume to teach us how to fight, Hittite! Do not belittle our God!"

"Calm down, Friend. I have respect for both your God and your militia. I wouldn't be here otherwise. My point is that you face a different situation than Joshua did. Your God doesn't need to change, but your military strategy does."

"Warriors are warriors, whether they fight for the tribes or the king."

"Ah, but there is a great difference between one thousand *fighters* and one thousand *soldiers*. The training and discipline of an army multiply the effectiveness of each individual. This allows a regiment of soldiers to defeat a far greater number of fighters."

"How so?"

"With fighters, you have only one chance to get everything right. Once the battle commences, their commander's job is finished. He has no more influence on the outcome than an archer has over an arrow in flight."

"Such is the nature of war."

"But war doesn't have to be that way! Soldiers learn to take advantage of their opponent's mistakes. The Philistines make up for their smaller population by producing very good soldiers. They are the masters of your coastal plains and your hill country. That is why your fighters must wait until the Philistines venture into your mountains where their formations and chariots are less effective. If your militia are so damn effective, why hire a broken-down mercenary like me?"

Elon seethed in silence at Karaz's plain speaking. The man looked to the other Council members for support, but no one rose to challenge Karaz. Nathan noticed even Beker turn away from his ally. Elon glared at Karaz one final time before sitting down. The situation was still extremely volatile and Nathan feared some hotheads might physically attack Karaz. However, the Hittite calmly concluded his remarks.

"I want the best for Israel. I want to build you an army. I want to make your fighters into soldiers."

It required a full day of wrangling, but Karaz and his army emerged victorious. Nathan was slightly deflated later to learn it was at best a partial victory. Only the idea of a Royal Army had been approved. The fight over what kind of army Israel would have still lay ahead. As always, Karaz took it all in stride. The Hittite permitted Nathan to come along that evening for a very exclusive meeting with Saul. Upon entering the room, Nathan saw that only Karaz, Saul, Jonathan and he were present. Beker and Abner were noticeably absent. Saul asked Karaz to begin.

"Whenever I helped someone set up his own army, I had to decide whether numbers or quality had the greater priority. The answer always depended on when the next war was expected. So, Saul, can you avoid making war for the next year?"

"Possibly."

268

"What about the next two years?"

"I doubt we can count on two years without war."

"Fair enough. I would prefer to build one regiment at a time, but you'll probably require greater numbers at the beginning. I recommend starting with three regiments, roughly three thousand men. It would be unrealistic to expect me to have more ready for battle in a year."

"We must also take politics into account, Karaz. Four powerful Tribal Elders approached me an hour ago. They can convince the rest of the Royal Council to approve an Army of twelve thousand men."

"Hebrews never fail to amaze me. First they resist any army at all, then they demand a large one."

"The Elders fear their influence will be diminished, Karaz."

"They asked for a king. It seems a little late to worry about that now."

"They fear each other. The concern is that a few of the larger tribes will dominate the army and, thereby, the kingdom. Therefore, each tribe will select one thousand of its men for the Royal Army."

"Should have expected this. I swear...nothing beats a good squabble between relatives. Look, Saul, you know the tribes will keep their best warriors at home. They'll send you the dregs. You need to recruit your own soldiers."

"Karaz, you could still pull three good regiments out of twelve thousand men."

"I'll spend the next year weeding out the rejects instead of training soldiers. No, I must start with three thousand good men."

"You'll receive little gold, unless you take twelve thousand."

"So, your army won't have uniforms, but they'll be better soldiers. Three thousand."

"Couldn't we have both?"

"Do you want an army or a parade? Three thousand."

Nathan's frustration grew as the argument flowed back and forth between the king and his *Aluf*. He glanced at Jonathan and received only a worried look from his friend. Eventually, Karaz built up an irresistible argument for a three thousand man army. At the end, Saul merely shook his head.

"Perhaps I should have Abner to speak to the Council members, Karaz. Most are afraid of him. Can I promise to make Abner a general?"

"NOW you're thinking like a king."

Chapter 21 - The Trap Is Laid

Keep me, O Lord, from the hands of the wicked. Protect me from violent men, who conspire to make me stumble. Proud men have hidden a snare for me. They have spread out their nets. They have set traps along my path.

From Psalm 140, verses 4 and 5

Village of Geba in central Benjamin

Achish groaned quietly as the Philistine column approached Gath's abandoned outpost outside the Benjamite village of Geba. He had assured King Maoch of Geba's suitability as a base from which to provoke the Hebrews. Yet even now, Achish recognized that the old fortifications were in ruins. He had never actually laid eyes on the place, relying instead on scouting reports submitted during his term at Gibeon. Achish scowled as his former garrison marched past. He would find the lazy scoundrels who had misled him. Their days were numbered.

Situated atop a gently sloping hill, the ramshackle fort looked down upon an intersection of two roads leading into the Israelite highlands. Some unimaginative engineer had laid out a simple square with sides roughly 150 feet long, surrounded by a wall of local rock six feet high. An inner dirt rampart provided an additional eighteen inches of elevation for the walls' defenders, greatly facilitating their delivery of arrows and javelins to the enemy. The extra height also allowed the defenders to clamber on top of the wall to strike down at attackers. The rudimentary barracks and crude supply sheds within the compound would have accommodated fifty men in minimal comfort. The fort had a single gate on its eastern side facing the road junction, allowing the Philistines to control all traffic.

However, Achish recognized that the ruins no longer deserved to be called a stronghold. The neglected outpost had suffered greatly from both the elements and scavenging locals. While three sides of the perimeter appeared to be at least partially intact, the south wall was almost non-existent. Deep wheel ruts leading down to Geba bore mute testimony to Hebrews extracting stones to improve their dwellings. The compound's buildings had fared even worse. Achish could not spot a single intact roof. The grumbling of the three hundred and fifty disgruntled soldiers might be unintelligible to Achish, but their feelings were clear. Even Phicol shot him a harsh look, but the new governor gave orders as if nothing were amiss. With sunset in less than two hours, the Philistines would bivouac in the open area outside the south wall. While the officers attended to their platoons, Phicol and Achish began an inspection of the dusty compound. The older man waited until both were out of earshot before speaking.

"So, Achish, are you a liar or a fool?"

"You may regret those words, Phicol."

"Perhaps. One day you *may* be king, but today I *can* execute you."

"You'd never get away with it."

"Don't count on it. Maoch might reward me for eliminating an incompetent heir. So answer my question, Achish. Liar or fool?"

"My scouts deceived me."

"So you're a liar. That's better than being a fool, though not by much."

"I'm sure you lie, Phicol."

"The trick is to never tell *stupid* lies. You won't last long on the throne, Achish, unless you learn the difference. You should've told me that you've never been here."

"I feared you'd think Geba was indefensible."

"Geba is indefensible. If the Hebrews laid siege to us here tomorrow, we wouldn't last a fortnight."

"Surely we can rebuild the walls in time."

"Forget the walls. What will we drink? That old cistern might be adequate for fifty men, but we'll drink it dry in a week."

"Running back to Gath, Phicol?"

"Certainly not! I promised Maoch to draw out the Hebrew king."

"If we can't defend Geba, we'll be slaughtered."

"We don't defend. We attack, using Geba as our base. Have scouts cover all the approaches. Once the Hebrews are on the move, we ambush them. Either Maoch will rescue us, or we cut our way out."

"Impressive, Phicol. The other Philistine kings will have no choice but to follow my father. I apologize for misleading you."

"You didn't, Achish. I knew this job couldn't be as easy as you described."

Three days later, Achish stood in the center of the decrepit outpost that was Geba. He watched a train of empty ox-carts wind its way down the road back towards Gath. The sun beat down on over two hundred sweating soldiers busily digging a ditch around the perimeter of their bivouac area outside the south wall. The rest of his battalion were either posted as sentries or patrolling the surrounding hills with Phicol. The veteran commander was studying as much of the surrounding landscape as possible before the Hebrew militia arrived. In the meantime, Phicol had tasked his nineteen-year-old subordinate with improving Geba's defenses. The raised wooden platform on which Achish stood was one of the few serviceable structures remaining in the old compound. Its floor was six feet higher than the outpost's walls, could easily accommodate eight soldiers in full armor and provided an excellent view of the surrounding terrain. A chest-high wooden stockade provided protection while still giving archers an excellent vantage point. So far, the only signs of Hebrews were some curious children who watched the toiling Philistines. Achish knew the absence of enemy warriors meant little, since competent scouts were nearly invisible.

Achish expected the Hebrews to arrive in force within a week. Phicol, on the other hand, felt their militia would require at least double that time to receive the information, devise a strategy, muster their forces, gather provisions and travel the required distance. True, the Hebrew militia had attacked the Ammonites in less than a week, but their battle plan lacked any military sophistication. The Hebrew king had simply turned loose a large mob in the dark and relied on Ammonite ineptitude. Achish actually hoped the Hebrew king would rush to battle again. He was confident the Philistines could break up any large, undisciplined force and destroy it piece by piece.

Per Phicol's instructions, Achish was refurbishing Geba to serve as a base camp, not a fortress. Its defenses would be sufficient to repel the type of night raiding so favored by the Hebrews, but little more. To that end, the badly damaged south wall was not being repaired. Its stones were instead being scavenged to fill in gaps in the other three walls. Phicol's idea of a deep ditch to protect the southern approaches made much more sense. The original compound was too small to accommodate over three hundred and fifty men anyway. Its rundown buildings now held the battalion's supplies, while most of the Philistines slept outside the ruins of the south wall, but behind the protective ditch. When completed, the five hundred foot long entrenchment would run along three exposed sides of the bivouac area and effectively double the size of the outpost. The ditch would be ten feet wide and five feet deep, with the excavated earth piled up on the inner side to form a dirt rampart rising nearly ten feet above the trench floor. A crude barrier indeed, but Achish doubted any attacker could scale it in the dark. His men's labors were hindered due to a lack of excavating equipment, and Achish felt a twinge of guilt over this. The Philistines would have brought better tools if he had been more honest with Phicol about Geba. Then again, the work might be backbreaking drudgery, but it had the benefit of keeping the idle men from mischief. Achish expected the digging would require at least a week, although they did have incentive for finishing sooner. After all, their lives might depend on it.

Satisfied with the day's progress, Achish exited the platform by means of a ladder protruding through a trap door in the floor. He mulled over various aspects of Phicol's strategy while inspecting the work of his troops. The outpost's hastily re-roofed sheds now held more than a month's worth of provisions. A supply train from Gath was scheduled weekly for two reasons. The first was to replenish the food consumed by the garrison during the previous week. The second was to sound an alarm if the enemy closed the road to Geba. This would allow Maoch time to rally the other Philistine kings, rescue Geba and crush the Hebrew king. Achish was amused when an ancient Hebrew legend came to mind. It concerned a similar group of three hundred Hebrews who had defeated thousands of Midianite raiders. What a delicious irony that would be if the tale was rewritten with the Philistines as the victors and the Hebrews as the vanquished. All that was necessary was for the rabbits to show themselves.

Chapter 22 - The First Field Command

It is useless to spread a net in full sight of all the birds.

From the Book of Proverbs, Chapter 1, verse 17

The plains of Gilgal in the Jordan River Valley

As the sun set at Gilgal, Nathan followed his friend Jonathan into the king's spacious tent...one of the few items of military equipment possessed by the Royal Army. Saul's three thousand recruits might sleep under the stars, but they would be disheartened to see their king doing the same. Nathan's eyes adjusted slowly to the dim light provided by oil lamps suspended from tent poles. The tent contained little in the way of furniture, requiring the score of officers and advisors in attendance to sit on blankets. A scribe knelt by a small table with writing instruments and his own lamp. Opposite the entrance, Saul occupied the only chair, with Jonathan taking a stool beside his father. The *Yameen*, Beker, and Abner, the king's cousin, occupied their usual places behind the king. The Royal Council members paid no attention to Nathan as he took his usual position standing behind them. After Beker called the assembly to order, Saul nodded toward one of his donkey herdsmen, newly arrived from Gibeon.

"Tell the others what you have told me."

"My Lords, the Philistines recently tripled the number of soldiers in Gibeon. Worse, these reinforcements appear to be hardened veterans, not the usual garrison troops. Three days ago, they all marched out of Gibeon."

A babble of anxious voices filled the tent until Abner loudly demanded silence. Saul proceeded to question the herdsman as the tension increased.

"Where did they go?"

"I followed them to Geba."

"How many?"

"Two companies of infantry and one of archers. Between three hundred and four hundred men."

"So there are no Philistines in Gibeon?"

"Yes, my King."

Nathan was now too stunned for words. A Philistine occupation of Geba was unexpected, but their abandonment of Gibeon was unbelievable. A grim looking Saul turned to his *Aluf*.

"Your thoughts, Karaz?"

The Hittite mercenary had been unusually quiet for such ill tidings. Karaz shrugged as he spoke.

"The Philistines have their reasons. I doubt any of them benefit you. "

"You suspect a trap then."

"This Philistine move to Geba stinks like old fish. Why does an abandoned outpost suddenly require more soldiers than it can hold? Why garrison it with elite troops instead of the usual conscripts? But the worst smell comes from Gibeon. Abandoning it makes no sense. Gibeon provides a better base for expanding into your lands, while isolating their men in Geba begs us to exterminate them!"

Several long minutes of frantic whispering followed Karaz's observations. Nathan took this as a sign that the others were as mystified as himself. Jonathan offered the only suggestion.

"If your enemy acts foolishly, search for what you have missed."

A smirk appeared on Karaz's face.

"So, Lad, you remembered a lesson. Now apply it for us."

Nathan sensed every eye focusing on the young prince. Jonathan calmly leaned forward until his elbows rested on his knees before speaking.

"The Philistines want us to attack Geba. It's bait."

"Then why abandon Gibeon, Jonathan?"

"More bait. An empty Gibeon makes Geba appear vulnerable."

"You suspect a trap?"

"An oversized garrison at Geba could tie down us for weeks. If a Philistine army is hidden nearby, it could surround our army and destroy it."

Nathan heard Karaz take in a deep breath while considering the words of his former pupil.

"That is a possibility, Jonathan, but we could easily escape such a trap. I can't see the Philistines going to so much trouble just for that."

Karaz turned back to Saul's herdsman.

"Gibeon is a Gath outpost. Have you seen troops from any of the other four Philistine cities?"

"No, only soldiers from Gath."

"Then this move from Gibeon to Geba is truly perplexing, my King. Gath would not attempt an invasion alone."

"Why not? We lack the strength to stop even a single Philistine city."

"Because it is not their way. No Philistine city ever fights alone. Their Council of Kings always sends a common force, with soldiers from each city's army. Everyone shares the risks and the benefits."

"That may be how the Philistines always fought you Hittites, Karaz, but Gath certainly has the strength to take more land from us."

"Yes, Gath has the strength to take your land, but not to hold it."

Karaz held up his hands as numerous voices tried to object.

"The Philistines have a proverb. If you put one crab in a pot, it will crawl out. But, if you put several crabs in a pot, none will escape. Why? As soon as one crab tries to crawl out of the pot, the others will pull it back in."

Seeing puzzled looks, Karaz continued.

"Gath must contend with the other Philistine kings. They see each other as a greater threat than all the Tribes of Israel combined. Their Council acts as counterweight against an overly ambitious Philistine king trying to *crawl out of the pot.* They would move against Gath before allowing it to grow stronger at their expense. Not unless Gath..."

Karaz stopped speaking when Saul cleared his throat.

"Then the answer is obvious, Karaz. We do not take their bait."

There was a murmur of agreement from many others, but Karaz gently shook his head.

"My King, ruling a kingdom requires taking risks. This move to Geba may be a Philistine way of testing the first King of Israel. Do nothing and you will seem weak while Gath appears strong. Your people's enthusiasm over the Ammonite victory will wane. But be bold, and this could strengthen your kingdom."

Nathan waited silently with the others while Saul considered his *Aluf's* words.

"Karaz, our soldiers here in Gilgal are enthusiastic, but untrained and poorly armed. One day they will be the core of our army. We cannot afford to waste them in a hopeless battle."

"That is not what I propose, my King. It is not enough to just react to every Philistine move. We must be a step ahead of them in our plans."

"How so?"

"By occupying not only Gibeon, but also the pass at Michmash. The Philistines in Geba will be squeezed between our forces. When their supplies run low, they will retreat without costing you a single man. If other Philistine forces move against you, burn their outpost at Gibeon and withdraw. The enemy will find the road blocked at Michmash and go home empty-handed. Make the Philistines dance to your music. You emerge as a strong king while gaining time to build your army."

A host of heated conversations immediately broke out in the tent. Saul allowed his officers and advisors time to debate Karaz's proposal before calling on his *Aluf*.

"Your plan requires dividing my army, Karaz."

"Yes, my King, I propose taking one thousand men with me to Gibeon. I could hold Gibeon and harass Geba. Leaving you two thousand men to occupy the pass at Michmash."

"Even if what you say is true, Karaz, would my gain...our gain be worth the risk?"

Nathan noticed the king change meaning in mid-sentence. Karaz chose to overlook it. Others, like Beker, might not.

"Yes, my King. Provided we respond strongly, but not too strongly. "

Confused muttering followed these words, but Karaz pressed on.

"Whenever the Philistines open with a small move, we respond with a slightly greater one. Suppose the Philistines don't withdraw from Geba, but put an army in the field. You would then summon Israel's militia to Michmash. The Philistines would then be confronted by your numerically superior force defending a strong position. The Philistines would be forced to either retreat or assume more risk, allowing you to choose an appropriate response."

"Moves and countermoves, but how will it end, Karaz?"

"Who knows? Ultimately, it will be our zeal against their experience. The military odds are heavily against you for the foreseeable future, but consider this. Being able to fight at a time and at a place of your own choosing is priceless."

Nathan thought Karaz had won the day until an arrogant challenge interrupted the proceedings.

"I know a cowardly plan when I hear it. Is this what we pay you for?"

Nathan stiffened when he recognized the voice as Abner's. While the king's cousin lacked Karaz's military expertise, Abner exerted great influence in the Royal Council. He shot a glance at Beker, but the *Yameen* seemed undisturbed by the outburst. Nathan knew Beker would intervene if any discussion was not going his way. Nathan inferred from the *Yameen's* silence that a trap had been laid for Karaz. However, the Hittite faced his fearsome heckler with confidence.

"Actually, Abner, I've not been paid anything yet. I assume you have an alternative plan?"

"The king should take all three of his regiments to Geba, smash these invaders, withdraw to Michmash and then wait to see what the Philistines do."

"Not all that different from what I suggested, Abner, except you take greater risks for fewer benefits."

"What risks, Hittite? We have surprise and numbers."

"Philistines have swords. Our men have stone-tipped spears. They wear armor. We don't. They fight in disciplined formations. We can't. I won't even mention their chariots. These little details make a great difference on the battlefield."

Surprisingly, Abner chose not to respond. This restraint puzzled Nathan until he caught Beker whispering in the king's ear. Saul considered his *Yameen's* words for a moment before speaking.

"If I agree to occupy Gibeon and Michmash, Karaz, I will make one change to your plan."

"And what would that be? "

"I cannot afford to waste your skills to watch a few Philistines in Geba. If Philistia invades, I will need your counsel immediately."

"Samuel is experienced at war. He could advise you in my stead."

"Samuel may not be available when I require him."

Nathan was surprised to observe Saul's jaw tighten slightly at Karaz's suggestion. *"Is a rift growing between Israel's last judge and its first king?"* If Karaz noticed Saul's discomfort, he gave no evidence of it. Instead, the mercenary folded his arms and gazed at the dirt floor. After a moment, he looked Saul in the eye.

"Then let your son take them."

Nathan felt a shiver go done his spine as all eyes turned toward Jonathan. The young prince briefly looked startled, but quickly assumed an air of quiet confidence. Beker tried to whisper to Saul once more, but the king waved him away. Since none dare risk insulting the king by doubting the ability of his heir, it fell to Saul to ask Karaz the obvious question.

"Is he ready?"

"For this task? More than ready. It's time for our brave prince to prove that he can lead men."

Nathan nearly jumped when Karaz abruptly turned and pointed at him.

"And send this lad as his second in command. He's almost as good as his prince. The two steady each other."

Nathan felt relief when many of the attendees nodded in approval. These were warriors who had witnessed both young men in battle against the Ammonites. His attention was drawn back to the front where Karaz now leaned into Jonathan's face.

"Remember, my Prince, all this will work if you simply *hold and harass*. We want hungry Philistines, not dead Hebrews. Understand?"

Jonathan held Karaz's gaze without flinching.

"I understand."

Next Karaz moved back to where Nathan stood sweating, the seated men moving slightly to clear a path. Karaz came close enough that when he extended his arm, his index finger nearly touched Nathan's nose.

"And I hold you responsible for what your prince does. Understand?"

"Yes."

While Nathan tried to regain his composure, Karaz's plan was adopted with only minor alterations. As the men began filing out of the tent at the end, Nathan slipped in behind Karaz and whispered in his ear.

"You might have prepared Jonathan and me first."

"When? I fully intended to take that regiment to Geba. I had no idea Beker would attempt to steal it away from me."

"How could Beker steal it? He can't command soldiers."

"He could through Abner. I'd wager my firstborn that's what Beker said to Saul; that a king should trust only a blood relative with his army, not some foreign pagan. So I outmaneuvered our crafty *Yameen* by nominating the king's son over a mere cousin. It worked, too. Saul couldn't risk publicly humiliating his own heir."

"Abner's older and more experienced than Jonathan. Perhaps he would be the better choice."

"He's also more ambitious, Nathan, and far too cozy with Beker. Together, those two could turn Saul into their tool. Abner may be a natural leader, but he's not the military wizard he thinks he is. Not yet, anyway. No, Jonathan is a much better risk."

"I'm confused, Karaz. Jonathan commands, yet I am the one who will be held accountable."

"Certainly gives you the incentive to help your friend make good decisions, doesn't it?"

"Tell me, Karaz. Did you kill the other crabs before you crawled out of your pot?"

"Careful, Lad. *YOU* are not a prince. I can trounce you anytime I wish."

Chapter 23 - The Bold Gamble

For waging war, you need guidance, and for victory, seek many advisors.

From the Book of Proverbs, Chapter 24, verse 6

The Israelite occupied town of Gibeon

Nathan never wanted ever again to be second-in-command of anything. The title came with too much responsibility and too little power. He reached this sobering conclusion while stretched out on a crude bed in the recently captured Philistine outpost at Gibeon. His friend Jonathan fared even worse as the regiment's commander. Nathan reflected on the staggering challenges which the young prince initially faced. Training had barely commenced for Saul's three thousand recruits. None of the three regiments envisioned by Karaz had yet been organized. Officers were non-existent. Their weapons consisted mostly of farm implements, handmade spears, clubs, and a few dozen bows. How these soldiers were to be supplied with food and water on the march was a mystery.

Even so, Jonathan and Nathan were given ten days to form a functioning regiment from virtually nothing. Strangers were randomly tossed together into companies, with even less thought applied to the lower level formations. Jonathan resorted to asking each virgin squad to elect a sergeant from among its members. The sergeants then elected one of their number as company captain. The resulting ten captains reported to Jonathan as their regimental commander. The danger was ending up with officers selected for popularity rather than leadership, but time permitted nothing better. The Royal Army of Israel, in truth, consisted not of soldiers, but of farmers, shepherds, craftsmen, merchants and a host of other occupations. One day they might develop a true military culture, but that day lay well in the future.

Relying heavily on Karaz's lessons in prioritization and delegation, the two novice commanders eventually settled into a manageable routine. In short, all the dirty jobs went to Nathan so Jonathan could focus on real leadership. Strategy was planned, companies reorganized, men demoted and promoted, duties assigned, weapons prepared and supplies gathered. Jonathan assured Nathan that what they had accomplished in ten days was no less than a miracle.

Then their regiment actually took the field.

A fit man could march the thirty miles from Gilgal to Gibeon in a single, though grueling, day. A regiment of one thousand soldiers could never hope to move that swiftly. Additional time was required to form up into units, load equipment, prepare meals and provide a continuous supply of water to overheated troops. Karaz had taught that average soldiers should be allowed two full days to cover that same distance. It took four days for only half their regiment to reach Gibeon.

Nathan found that keeping his companies intact during the march was a near impossibility. Few of the new officers had earned the respect necessary to bring their soldiers to heel. Men stopped when they were tired, ate when they were hungry and slept as long as they wanted. Nathan recognized it was foolish to expect otherwise. These budding soldiers of Israel had come to kill Philistines, not march in formation. Progress was so dreadful, Jonathan pushed ahead with a small vanguard, leaving Nathan to prod the rest along. It was most fortunate that Jonathan found Gibeon empty of Philistines. The strung-out Israelite column would have been easy prey for even a small enemy force. Nathan arrived in Gibeon just before sunset on the fourth day with their first five companies. He expected the others to straggle into town throughout the following day. Hearing that Jonathan was off gallivanting around the countryside, an exhausted Nathan had fallen into the first bed he could find. He was enjoying a hard-earned slumber when Jonathan barged into his room. The prince set a burning oil lamp on a rough table before sitting down on Nathan's sore feet. He growled at Jonathan and kicked his legs free. Nathan pulled his knees up to his chest in the dim light and gazed bleary eyed at his friend's excited face.

"You can sleep later, Nathan. The regiment is moving out tomorrow."

"I must be having a nightmare. You couldn't have said tomorrow."

"But I did."

"Half our men are still on the road, Donkey Boy."

"Then we'll leave the day after."

"We just got here."

"We're going to capture Geba!"

Nathan now found himself fully awake. He swung his legs out of bed, placed his feet on the cold, rough floor and sat

290

up next to Jonathan. Nathan was stunned to realize that his friend was completely serious.

"Refresh my memory, Jonathan. Which part of our orders to *hold and harass* allows us to capture Geba?"

"We can forget those orders."

"Forget *Karaz's* orders? Just like that?"

"I'm sure he would agree. Things have changed."

"What's changed?"

"Those orders assumed that Geba was bait to lure us into a Philistine ambush. Well, I've been off scouting. There are no Philistines within a three day march. No Philistines, no ambush! Nathan, we can take Geba!"

"Jonathan, Geba is a fortified position defended by veteran warriors."

"You heard Karaz tell my father that the military situation was heavily against us. For the first time, it's in our favor!"

"Taking Geba requires a lengthy siege or heavy losses. We can't afford either, and certainly not both."

"Nathan, I promise you this. There will be no siege. There will be no heavy losses. Otherwise, I'll turn around and come back to Gibeon. Then it will just be harassment."

"So, how do you take Geba *and* keep your promise?"

"I've roughed out a plan, but need your help with the details."

"This whole idea scares me, Jonathan."

"You've never been afraid of the Philistines before."

"Oh, I'm not afraid of them. I'm scared of Karaz. Remember, he holds me responsible for anything you do."

A grizzled Philistine scout named Uruk observed the Israelites' departure from Gibeon two days later. He saw barely a score of Hebrews remaining behind to hold the town. Uruk dispatched a runner to Geba with the news their enemy was on the march. He shadowed the irregular column's progress from the shelter of the surrounding hills. The Hebrew companies grew more disorderly with each succeeding mile. The undisciplined army seemed almost reluctant to advance, but the final confirmation of his foe's incompetence was yet to come. Instead of occupying a position from which they could dominate Geba, the Hebrews set up camp some two miles short of the Philistine outpost. Although Geba was not visible from the enemy encampment, only a pair of gently rolling ridges now separated the two forces. Uruk decided to deliver this vital intelligence to the Philistine governor personally.

The Philistine garrison outside the village of Geba

Seated in his tent at Geba as the sun set, Phicol shook his head in wry disbelief as he considered the report from his chief of scouts. This had to be the first military action for the

Hebrew commander. A seasoned leader would have better timed his advance on Geba and established his siege lines around the Philistine position before nightfall. Instead, the fool placed his entire force within easy striking distance of the Philistines. The enemy did heavily outnumber his soldiers, but the Philistine governor was unconcerned. The Hebrew officers seemed to have their hands full just keeping their rabble together. Uruk reported fewer than fifty enemy archers and that the rest of the Hebrews were poorly armed. Word had come earlier of the Hebrews also occupying the key crossroads at Michmash. That meant potentially half of Israel's field army now lay exposed before him. His mind rapidly sorted through various tactics in search of a practical plan. Within minutes, Phicol assembled his officers.

"We're going to treat the Hebrews to a breakfast they will never forget."

Phicol's jest was greeted with the predatory grins from everyone except Achish. He assumed the prince was fretting over his own role in the coming battle. Most likely, it would disappoint the young man, but Phicol had greater worries. Visibly impatient, Achish spoke.

"What do you plan to serve them, Phicol?"

"A pre-dawn ambush. An infantry platoon will guard the camp. Two hours before sunrise, I'll take everything else against the Hebrews. Uruk has men watching every road and trail. They'll warn us if our guests attempt to leave early."

"Will I lead your infantry or archers?"

"Neither. You will defend the camp."

"I'm no watchdog."

"Achish, you are whatever I say you are. I need a secure base to fall back on. Such responsibility falls to my second-in-command. That's you, unless you're not up to it."

"I never said that."

"Good. You'll have fifty heavy infantry, my best men. Questions from anyone? Then get busy."

Phicol remembered his first battle and felt some sympathy for the young man. However, his king had made it abundantly clear that Phicol was not to return to Gath without Achish. As his officers departed, the governor signaled one to stay behind. Once alone, Phicol whispered to Davon, the platoon leader being left with Achish.

"If our future king falters, take over. I'll square things with his father later."

"Understood, Phicol, but I think he just needs some seasoning."

"Then see that he gets it."

Two miles from the Philistine garrison at Geba

Jonathan met with his company commanders as soon as the moon set. Nathan stood quietly behind his friend where he could feel the warmth of a campfire. The strength of Jonathan's strategy was its simplicity, but everything still depended on how the Philistines reacted. At the conclusion of this meeting, the prince must decide whether or not to gamble the lives of his men. Jonathan had every ear when he spoke.

"We needed to convince the Philistines that our men are a disorganized mob. I think we succeeded."

Rueful laughter came from the assembled captains. Nathan envied Jonathan's skill at relieving tension in the face of danger. The prince set about collecting final bits of information.

"What are the Philistines up to?"

"Our scouts report activity in their camp, just as you expected."

"Good. Have we located their scouts?"

"Hiding in all the obvious places. Should we kill them?"

"Only the ones I point out. Has everyone been fed?"

"Most were too nervous, but they had the chance to eat."

"This is your last chance, my Friends. Does anyone have a reason not to proceed? I'll only be angry if I find later that you held something back."

Nathan peered over Jonathan's shoulder to study the ten faces illuminated by the nearby flames. He saw anxiety; he saw nervousness, but not a trace of fear. After a lengthy silence, the prince announced his decision.

"Then God's will be done. See to your companies."

Nathan headed toward his tent when he felt Jonathan's hand on his shoulder.

"Nathan, I'm sorry, but I can entrust your task to no one else."

"We've been over this, Jonathan. I can handle it."

"You'll be in the position of greatest danger."

"Yes, but I get to sleep longer."

Chapter 24 - The Trap Is Sprung

Look! The wicked bend their bows. They make ready their arrows on the strings that they may shoot from the shadows at the upright in heart.

From Psalm 11, verse 2

On the road from Geba to the Israelite camp

Covered by the early morning darkness, a hushed Philistine column sallied forth from Geba. Two companies of infantry and another of archers, some three hundred men in total, followed Governor Phicol westward over the first ridge. He could barely make out his chief scout, Uruk, leading the way through the murky night. Fifty heavy infantrymen still guarded their basecamp, meaning the assault force consisted mostly of lightly armed garrison troops, but Phicol had no misgivings. Tonight's action would be an ambush rather than a toe-to-toe fight. However, Phicol could not help feeling apprehensive while descending into the valley separating the Philistine and Hebrew positions. It was an ideal place for the enemy to stage his own ambush. But the Philistines navigated the valley without incident, and Phicol relaxed as the second ridge came into view.

The Philistine column halted while Phicol and Uruk ascended the ridge for a peek at the Hebrew camp. A crouching Uruk directed Phicol along the ridge crest to where a well-concealed Philistine scout monitored the shadowy Hebrew encampment. He surveyed the scene while Uruk quietly interrogated the lookout. Remnants of scattered campfires provided Phicol with a view of sleeping men and strolling sentries. Phicol heard the typical night sounds of a large camp: hobbled oxen lowing restlessly, men coughing in their sleep and the occasional soldier relieving himself. There were few shelters of any kind and little evidence of equipment or supplies. Phicol turned slightly when Uruk hissed at him for attention.

"Camp's been quiet since sundown. They've no idea we're here."

"Unfortunately, Uruk, Hebrews are notorious for their stealth."

"So am I, Phicol. I've had eyes on their camp from the start. Every goat trail between Geba and Gibeon has a scout with a trumpet watching it. If the bastards get tricky, we'll hear something."

"Unless the Hebrews have killed your men."

"I asked for time to check on my scouts, but you were in a hurry. It's your call, Governor."

Phicol knew the blunt-speaking Uruk was correct. There was nothing to be gained by delaying his decision. Surprise had been achieved. His troops were in position. Uruk's scouts had done everything possible. The faintly glowing horizon meant Phicol had mere minutes to set his men in motion. But in which direction? Toward the Hebrews or back to Geba? After a final look at his slumbering enemies, Phicol summoned his officers.

Minutes later, two hundred Philistine infantry armed with sword and shield crested the ridge, advanced twenty paces and halted. Phicol had ordered their javelins left stacked on the reverse slope. He knew missiles hurled in the night could be as dangerous to his men as to the Hebrews. Darkness necessitated close combat where blades worked best. Phicol now signaled his archers to take positions at the top of the ridge. He winced slightly as their captain loudly barked out commands, and then relaxed. It was too late for the Hebrews to escape the trap. The archers notched their arrows and used the campfires below to mark their targets. As one man, a hundred bows were bent and held for a breath before their arrows were loosed. Four flights of arrows raced toward the sleeping camp in quick succession. Phicol marveled at the deadly skill of his professionals as the agonized sounds of wounded men rose up from the darkness below. Phicol visualized confusion and panic spreading among the Hebrews as they attempted to flee an invisible killer. The archers paused as concealed torches were brought forward to light arrows for a final volley. A hundred tiny flames soon dotted the ridge. On command, the burning arrows were pointed heavenward and released. As the flames streaked across the still black sky, Phicol had a brief glimpse of an enemy in chaos. He saw the Hebrew camp clearly outlined where the flaming arrows had struck. His archers then slung their bows and drew swords. Hundreds Philistine voices joined in a blood-curdling cry before charging down the ridge in search of slaughter.

In the Israelite camp two miles from Geba

Nathan had not anticipated the Philistines beginning their attack with archers. It was an ominous start for Jonathan's strategy. He had been so hopeful a few hours before when the prince slipped away with seven hundred men. The prospect of battle galvanized the neophyte Israelite regiment. Most of their men still considered drilling and training as things to be shirked, if not ignored outright. Now, even the worst delinquents obeyed with eagerness. Nathan recalled another of Karaz's maxims. *Nothing focuses a man's mind like death.* However, this first contact with the Philistines was going badly, and it was up to Nathan alone to salvage the situation. The soldiers remaining under his command had spent the night preparing for the anticipated enemy assault. Nathan's three companies were arrayed in groups of fifty, all facing the nearby ridge. Understanding they would bear the brunt of the coming attack, a few brave souls stood guard near the ridge, tended campfires and made the small noises expected from a sleeping army. Three Israelite campfires burned brighter than the rest: one was near base of the ridge, another was in camp's center and the third marked the outer edge of the campsite. These marked rally points for Nathan and his men. Depending on how the battle went, he could signal his soldiers to advance towards, or retreat to, one of these fires.

Nathan was initially puzzled by the whistling sounds overhead until he heard first cries of pain. He froze seconds later as a line of flaming arrows on the ridge revealed the enemy arrayed against him. Nathan felt a brief surge of satisfaction in seeing they had succeeded in drawing the bulk of the Philistine garrison away from Geba. *Good for Jonathan. Not so good for me.* The enemy force was similar in size to his, but likely better trained and equipped. Nathan's first responsibility was to get his men out of bow range. He ordered a retreat to the last fire, a cry picked up by his officers. Hopefully, most of his soldiers would halt as instructed and not keep on running into the night. The next step would be to form his infantry into a battle line, fronting their forty-two archers. If the Israelites rallied quickly enough, they might hold the camp, although that was not their primary mission. Nathan's band needed to keep the Philistines occupied long enough for Jonathan's seven companies to capture Geba. With the first hints of sunrise over the eastern hills, the Philistines would soon comprehend the true size of Nathan's command. *Would they still take the bait?* The enemy must attack, or Nathan's soldiers would be forced to go on the offensive. Neither prospect appeared promising.

On the ridge overlooking the Israelite camp

Phicol first sensed trouble when the battle was only moments old. His men were advancing too quickly through the Israelite camp. There were far too few Israelite bodies littering the ground. Phicol's attack faltered as many Philistines fell to plundering, despite the threats of their officers. Worse yet, the rapidly spreading dawn revealed a large cluster of men at the extreme end of the Hebrew camp. Phicol yelled for his chief scout.

"Uruk! How many Hebrews camped here last night?"

"Nearly a thousand."

"And how many do you see over there?"

"Two, maybe three hundred."

"So where are the rest?"

"Either retreating to Gibeon or attacking Geba."

"I need your best guess, Uruk."

"Geba."

"Why Geba?"

"We heard no warning trumpets, meaning the Hebrews slit the throats of my scouts. They wouldn't have bothered for a retreat."

"Then Geba it is. Sound the recall. We'll see if there's a lion among these Hebrew rabbits."

On the outskirts of the Israelite camp

Nathan was frantically preparing a defensive position when he heard the sound of Philistine horns. If they heralded an attack, his poorly armed men were doomed. Nathan studied his adversaries in the morning light. The Israelites had survived so far by the narrowest of margins. Only the opportunity for plunder had prevented the Philistines from overrunning his beleaguered force. Now the Philistine officers were reforming their scattered soldiers with impressive speed. Nathan wondered why they did not advance, for his shabby defense posed little threat. A second blaring of Philistine horns brought every Israelite to instant attention. Thanks to Karaz's training, Nathan recognized the first trumpet signal as a recall. The second trumpet call was for advancing in company formation. Nathan shared the silent tension of his men waiting for the enemy ranks to move. Many Israelites began praying aloud for a miracle that few really expected. Then the prayers ceased, almost as quickly as they had begun. The Israelites began rejoicing as the Philistines marched back up the ridge, but Nathan simply clenched his jaw. The Philistine commander had recognized his men as a decoy; something both he and Jonathan knew was inevitable. Hopefully, the prince and his seven hundred men were now at Geba. Before launching his own assault, Jonathan was to detach two of his companies to block the road. Those two hundred Israelites might delay the returning Philistine force, but they could not stop it. That was where Nathan came in.

Shortly after the Philistine rearguard disappeared, Nathan set off in pursuit with the remnants of his three companies. From the top of the first ridge, he spied both the Philistine column crossing the valley and the Israelite blocking force on the next ridge. A delicate balancing act would soon commence. If the Philistines tried to penetrate the blocking force, Nathan would attack their rear. If the Philistines turned to face Nathan, the blocking force would move to his assistance. The Israelites did not have to win this skirmish. They just had to keep the Philistines occupied until a victorious Jonathan came to their rescue from Geba. There were other less favorable outcomes, but Nathan had no time to dwell on them.

Chapter 25 - The Reversal of Fortune

Saul chose for himself three thousand men from Israel. Two thousand were with Saul at Michmash and in the mountains of Bethel, and a thousand were with Jonathan in Gibeon of Benjamin. The rest of the men he sent back to their homes. Jonathan attacked the garrison of the Philistines that was in Geba, and the Philistines heard of it.

From the Book of I Samuel, Chapter 13, verses 2 and 3

The Philistine garrison outside the village of Geba

A shout from the Geba watchtower provided Achish with the first indication of danger. One moment, the prince was listening for clues to Governor Phicol's progress against the Hebrew camp. Seconds later, he was bounding up a crude ladder and peering toward the southwestern hills beside his lookout. The rising sun revealed hundreds of armed men milling about on the slopes barely half a mile away. Achish's mouth went dry as various possibilities raced through his mind. Had the Hebrews camped to the east defeated Phicol? Or had their king brought two armies to Geba?

Achish looked down from the watchtower when his platoon's lieutenant, a man in his mid-twenties named Davon, requested orders ...Achish's orders. In that instant, his predicament became clear. The enemy had pulled off a tactical surprise; exactly how was unimportant. Achish and his fifty-three men simply had to deal with it. He nearly ordered Davon to man the walls, but immediately rejected this as a feeble gesture. Geba's shabby defenses could never withstand an attacker with a ten to one advantage. The Hebrews would swarm over the walls and through its gaps to overwhelm his meager force. Given some archers, Achish might have held out for a considerable time. Several well placed volleys of arrows could decimate the front Hebrew ranks and give the other attackers second thoughts. But Phicol had taken every archer, leaving Achish only javelins, swords and shields. Yet, Achish's curiosity soon overcame his fear. *Why did the Hebrews hesitate?* Given the priceless gift of time, he had a flash of inspiration. Achish called down orders to Davon without any explanation. The lieutenant appeared puzzled, but obeyed, nonetheless. Having committed himself, an unexpected serenity came over Achish. He did not even care that others had been beheaded for what he had in mind.

On the road to Geba in hot pursuit of the Philistines

Nathan was desperate to slow the Philistines returning to Geba, but they seemed determined to ignore his efforts. If the enemy force arrived before Jonathan secured the enemy outpost, disaster loomed for the Israelites. Two of Jonathan's companies blocked the road ahead, but Nathan knew three hundred battle-hardened Philistines would brush them aside with ease. He must somehow convince them to turn and face his three companies. Glancing at the bow of the man trotting at his side, Nathan chose a new tactic.

"Archers! Advance and let fly! Advance and let fly!"

Two score men sprinted to the head of the Israelite column and unslung their bows. Nathan watched them cluster in two separate groups, notch arrows, draw and release. The result was a ragged volley which mostly fell short. However, the Israelite arrows did drop several of the Philistine rearguard. This minor success encouraged Nathan enough to try again.

"Archers, keep moving! Keep attacking!"

Nathan was gratified by the archers' response to his orders. While the first group of archers loosed another volley, the second ran twenty yards past them before releasing its own arrows. Wave after wave of Israelite arrows fell as the two groups alternated advancing and attacking. When the stinging Israelite archers could no longer be ignored, the enemy column slowed. Nathan swallowed hard as the Philistine infantry formed a shield wall in front of their own archers. His men skidded to a halt without being ordered. Now it was their turn to dodge arrows.

The Philistine garrison outside the village of Geba

Achish led fifty-three Philistines out the compound's eastern gate as the first Hebrews crawled over the walls on the opposite side. He listened to the clinking mail armor so characteristic of heavy infantry in motion. Sewn onto a tough linen tunic, the small bronze rectangles provided shoulder-to-thigh protection against swords or missiles. Provided, of course, that some sharp point did not find one of the armor's tiny, but numerous, gaps. A helmet, a pair of bronze greaves and a large iron rimmed wooden shield completed their uniforms. Heavy infantry advanced slowly, but they rolled over any lightly armed foe foolish enough to stand against them. Despite the armor, Achish knew his only viable option was to rejoin Phicol's assault force. Even so, he was not coming empty handed. While the

Hebrews inexplicably delayed their assault, Achish's soldiers gathered food sacks, water skins, arrows and javelins. These essentials had been tossed into a large wagon now being pushed and pulled by twenty burly Philistines. Achish could hear the Hebrews behind him howl as they began looting the garrison's baggage. He had little time to savor this additional stroke of luck, for his next challenge was just coming into view.

The Philistine platoon was ascending the nearby ridge when Achish spotted a large band of Hebrews lining its crest. Even though heavily outnumbered, Achish knew his men must advance or die. He halted his platoon and summoned their lieutenant, Davon.

"Form your men into double ranks with javelins, swords and shields. Leave everything else."

"Even the wagon, Sir?"

"If we survive, we'll come back for it."

"Sounds like you're planning to punch through that bunch up there."

"No other way around it, Davon. We'll hold formation until just before contact, and then give the Hebrews a surprise."

The Philistines soon were ascending the ridge in double ranks, twenty-five men abreast. Achish, the lieutenant and two sergeants followed just behind the second rank. Achish counted at least one hundred Hebrews ahead and suspected even more waited on the reverse slope. Whatever their enemy lacked in weaponry, Achish saw they made up for in aggression. The sound of crude spears banging on wooden shields and fierce war cries poured down on the advancing Philistines. He expected everything to come down to a contest between greater Hebrew numbers and superior Philistine tactics. Achish waited until the enemy was fifty paces away before giving orders.

"Javelins up!"

Each of Achish's soldiers carried a pair of javelins strapped to their backs. At his command, fifty javelins were held aloft.

"Let fly!"

The well synchronized javelin volley threw the Hebrews into disorder. Few were actually hit, but Achish sensed the enemy force degenerating into individual fighters. They were now vulnerable, provided Achish employed the proper tactics. It was time for his first trick.

"Wedge!"

With practiced precision, the Philistines along both flanks began sidestepping inward while their comrades in the center surged ahead until their formation resembled an arrowhead. Achish was positioned just behind the tip when his men began advancing again as a unit. By the time the maneuver was completed, the Hebrew captain had regained a measure of control over his rattled warriors. Now Achish's men suffered their first casualties as spears, arrows and rocks rained down on them. A wailing *shofar* prompted the Hebrews to charge downhill. Achish kept his voice calm while shouting his next commands.

"First rank, javelins! Second rank, draw swords!"

The leading edge of Philistine soldiers advanced with javelins held over their shields. They were rocked backwards at the point of impact as the screaming Hebrews slammed into them. Slowly, Achish's wedge of heavy infantry began shedding the enemy warriors like raindrops. Stepping over their fallen foes, the javelin wielding Philistines used overhand thrusts to force their way through the opposing mob. Most of the Hebrew weapons lacked the longer reach of the Philistine javelins. However, Achish recognized the tide was turning against him. The Philistines began to lose their javelins as they were either stuck in a dying man or pulled away during the close quarter fighting. Achish's front rank switched to swords as needed, but lost their greater killing range. More of his men went down, but stopping for fallen comrades meant death. As the Philistines pushed deeper into the mass of fanatical Hebrews, their flanks were overlapped. The veteran Philistines in the second rank then turned and stepped backwards while defending the formation's rear. Inevitably, the Philistines' progress ground to a halt as the Hebrews' greater numbers came into play. Achish waited as long as he dared before calling upon his final trick.

"Open!"

With a desperate surge forward, the tip of the Philistine wedge burst open to release Achish and the swordsmen who had been biding their time in the formation's center. Exhausted Hebrews swiftly fell to the hacking blades of the more rested Philistines. Achish was so intent on his personal combat that reaching open ground came as a surprise. Although his tired soldiers were still heavily outnumbered, Achish watched in amazement as the Hebrew survivors raced away toward Geba. At least fifty enemy bodies littered the slope. A quick count by Achish showed forty-two of his men still standing, though many bore wounds. Puzzled, Achish hurried to the top of the ridge, for his men had fought well, but not that well.

The lead elements of Governor Phicol's assault force stood only a hundred paces from Achish. His own foes had fled to avoid being crushed between the two Philistine formations. Phicol's troops advanced in good order, but their rearguard was fighting a running battle with another Hebrew force. Achish watched Phicol's infantry and archers form a skirmish line at the base of the ridge. The pursuing Hebrews halted, but their archers continued to harass the Philistines. Achish instructed Davon to rest the platoon while he reported to Phicol. The two leaders quickly exchanged accounts of their adventures that morning. Phicol cut off Achish's attempted apology with a sharp gesture.

"Any blame, Achish, is mine. I left you in an impossible position. Don't apologize for getting out of it."

"But Geba is lost, and with it, our shelter and supplies."

"Soldiers are more valuable than a pile of rocks. Even brought me a wagon full of supplies, didn't you? You've given me options, Achish. I intend to make good use of them."

"What's our next move?"

"Well...I see four possibilities."

"That's three more than I do."

"First, we draw the Hebrews into battle on the plain below. Once they commit to an attack, we'll outmaneuver them, divide them and cut them to pieces."

"And if they decline our invitation to battle, Phicol?"

"Then we retake Geba."

"Leaving us besieged in a ruined fort."

Warning shouts from the Philistine lookouts briefly distracted Phicol. Achish saw the Hebrews had advanced near enough to shower the entire ridgeline with arrows. Achish and Phicol raised their own shields to deflect the incoming missiles. Phicol ordered his skirmishers to push the enemy archers back before responding to Achish.

"I agree, Achish. Geba has served its purpose."

"What is our third possibility then?"

"We bypass Geba and return home to Gath. The question is whether the Hebrews have blocked our way."

"Even so, Phicol, we'd force our way through."

"However, Achish, I'm tempted by something else: retaking Gibeon. It'd give the Hebrew king a nasty shock. I'll wager it's lightly defended. A forced march would leave this lot far behind and get us to Gibeon by nightfall. Which do you..."

Phicol's sentence ended in a gurgling sound. Achish turned to see a bloody arrowhead jutting out from the side of the governor's neck. The wounded man dropped to his knees and then fell on his left side. Calling for help, Achish took firm hold on the protruding shaft from behind and broke it off. Grasping the arrowhead, he pulled the rest of the arrow forward and out of the dying man's neck. Bright red blood spurted out with every heartbeat. Phicol's eyes soon closed, and a moment later his breathing stopped. A stunned Achish ignored the nearby voices until a few words finally broke through his daze.

"What do we do now?"

Achish gazed numbly into the faces of Phicol's officers as the awful reality crashed down on him. Some Hebrew archer's blind luck had just promoted a teenager from apprentice to commander. Each of his three captains had served longer than Achish had been alive. He considered asking one of them to take over, but promptly rejected this cowardly thought. Unless he assumed the burden of command, Achish could never expect these men, or any others, to accept him as their future king. The officers would bicker, the soldiers would lose heart, and their force would fall apart deep in enemy territory. More than anything, Achish needed time alone to think. He turned back toward Geba, in the pretense of studying it. Achish slowed his breathing and recalled Phicol's last words. The Philistines had to move either towards Philistia or Gibeon. Now was the time to establish his authority in everyone's eyes. Accordingly, Achish did not even face his three senior officers when he spoke.

"Get your men ready to march. Place the archers in the center of the column with the infantry on their flanks."

"March? March where?"

"I'll let you know when you're ready, Captain!"

Insecurity had made Achish's answer to the impertinent question sound harsh. However, it turned out to be the perfect response. Any commander worthy of respect would come down hard on a rude subordinate. His officers could not be allowed to view him as teenage boy. The offending captain swallowed hard when Achish turned blazing eyes upon him.

"Of course...Sir! Apologies."

"Distribute the weapons and provisions I brought from Geba."

"Yes, Sir!"

"All armor, save helmets, is to be left behind."

"You would make a gift of our armor to the Hebrews?"

Achish considered this last question to be a sign of progress. Coming from the captain of the heavy infantry, it was full of concern, yet still respectful. Those men would be loath to part with their mail armor. Naturally, their commander would speak up for them. The archers and garrison troops wore leather vests instead of armor for protection, so their officers said nothing. Achish responded politely, but firmly to the skeptical captain.

"We must march fast and far. Would you rather the Hebrews strip the armor off your exhausted soldiers before cutting their throats?"

"No, Sir. I would not. Neither would my men."

"Report back to me when all is ready."

Achish was relieved when the three captains bowed and trotted off. He had gained himself precious minutes to choose between Gibeon and home. Gath was the safer choice while occupying Gibeon had its own merits. The ubiquitous Hebrew militia could harass them to either destination. In the end, the decision was obvious. While Phicol might have inspired his soldiers to retake Gibeon, Achish had yet to earn their trust. So, it must be either home or death.

Reassurance now came to Achish from an unexpected quarter. He happened to be near the heavy infantry when they were ordered to strip off their armor. Achish pretended he was too busy to notice the grumbling of common soldiers, like any good officer. Strangely, the complaining began fading away far more quickly than he expected. Achish then heard one of the sergeants he had led out of Geba dressing down a disgruntled soldier.

"Shut your mouth. The boy knows his business."

When his captains returned, Achish felt prepared. He noticed the chief scout, Uruk, accompanied them. As the senior officer, the garrison captain was now Achish's second in command, and thereby spokesman for the others.

"Sir, all companies stand ready to march."

"We head west to Gath. Can you guide us there, Uruk?"

"Sure, but I can't guarantee we'll get there, Achish."

"That's Lord Achish."

"I'll try to remember that... Lord Achish."

"Captain, prepare a litter for the governor's body."

"Sir, we have wounded who cannot walk."

"We must outrace the Hebrews. We don't have the luxury of carrying wounded."

"There is the wagon, Sir."

"A wagon will slow us down. Men will exhaust themselves pushing it. We must go to places it can't."

"But the Hebrews will mistreat our wounded."

"I don't intend to leave any wounded behind, Captain. Permit men to leave the ranks to... say farewell to their wounded friends. If a man has no friends, his sergeant must take care of him."

Achish could tell from their somber expressions that his captains understood what he meant by *saying farewell*. No Philistine expected mercy if he fell into the hands of the Hebrews. A wounded soldier would prefer a less painful death from a comrade. While his officers seemed appalled, the brusque Uruk gave Achish an approving nod. Still, the garrison captain persisted.

"That could be trouble, Sir. The soldiers will not like it."

"If you can't control your men, Captain, I'll find someone who can."

"That will not be necessary, Sir."

"Good. We leave in ten minutes."

After his captains departed, Achish released a long, slow breath. Achish had little doubt his second-in-command would depose him at the first sign of weakness. He strode toward to the front of the formation without looking to either side.

However, once Achish reached the head of the Philistine column, he noticed familiar faces. His platoon from Geba had placed itself in the vanguard. Having seen the heaviest fighting that morning, these men had every right to a less exposed position. As Achish walked past them, he received respectful nods and even a few smiles. He was thoroughly perplexed by the time he came upon their lieutenant.

"Haven't had enough of me for one day, Davon?"

"The boys thought you still needed looking after, Sir."

"Tell them I feel safer already. Send out your skirmishers, Lieutenant. It's time to get this parade moving."

Chapter 26 - The Partial Victory

Let God arise. Let His enemies be scattered. Let His foes flee before Him.

From Psalm 68, verse 1

Five hundred paces from the village of Geba

Nathan and a handful of his Israelite soldiers cautiously ascended the ridge overlooking Geba. Many minutes had passed since the Philistine rearguard vacated the ridge crest, but Nathan feared their entire formation lay in wait on the reverse slope. Ironically, Nathan considered a Philistine ambush here to be a good thing, for it delayed their return to Geba. Prince Jonathan's strategy had depended on tricking the enemy garrison there into a night attack on the Israelite regiment's camp. Nathan and three hundred men would then hold their camp against the Philistines while Jonathan captured Geba with the other seven hundred. The first part of the Israelite plan worked to perfection, but the Philistines attackers saw through the deception once the sun rose and rushed back to defend their base. Nathan immediately set his men to harassing the retreating enemy column in order to buy more time for Jonathan.

From the top of the ridge, Nathan spied the dust of several hundred Philistines marching away in orderly ranks. However, the enemy column was now headed westward instead of north toward Geba. Nathan was perplexed. The Philistines were still a potent fighting force, yet something induced them to abandon their outpost. It obviously was not

Nathan's band; the Philistines had repeatedly brushed them back with ease. He also doubted that they felt threatened by Jonathan, for the prince's men were still busy securing the enemy outpost. Nathan ordered his captains to bring up their companies and find the men some food and water. Meanwhile, he intended to get some answers from Jonathan.

Nathan soon discovered Geba to be in absolute chaos with hundreds of Israelites simply meandering through the outpost. These ill-disciplined men were busy scavenging enemy belongings, guzzling wine, or arguing over various baubles. He found a thoroughly frustrated Jonathan at the center of this maelstrom. Nathan pulled his friend by the elbow into a shed to escape most of the noise.

"Why are you still here, Jonathan? The Philistines are getting away!"

"Nathan, I've been trying to get out of Geba for the past hour!"

"What happened?"

"The night march went beautifully. We killed their scouts. Arrived undetected. Blocked the road. Surrounded the outpost. But..."

"But then your troubles began."

"My companies were too spread out. Took me forever organize an assault."

"Karaz would have handled things better, Donkey Boy."

318

"Well, Karaz wasn't there. Anyway, half my men got hung up in a ditch on the south side. By the time they got past it, their officers had lost control."

"Did the defenders give them a hard time?"

"There were no defenders, Nathan. Place was empty by the time I got over the wall."

"I fail to see your problem, Jonathan. You won."

"Except I now had a howling mob on my hands. With no one to fight, they fell to looting. Apparently, the Philistines pay better than we do."

"Meanwhile, there's a Philistine column headed who knows where."

"What shape are your men in, Nathan?"

"They're ready to fight."

"Then it's up to you. Chase down those Philistine bastards. Force them to stand and fight. Grind them down. I'll clean things up here and join you as soon as I can."

On the western road to Gath

Achish had heard that a general's job largely consisted of evaluating bad options and selecting the least worse one. This skill never guaranteed success, but it often made survival possible. Today, distasteful choices were forced on Achish even before the former governor's corpse was cold. The galling part was that Achish would recognize any mistake only after it was too late to recover. Ironically, the Hebrew strategy was of secondary importance to him. The greatest threat to Achish's troops came from a relentless predator known as time...thus his latest distasteful choice. Achish's men could spend the remaining daylight moving faster towards home or conserving their strength for a fight. Achish compromised by allowing the Philistine column to rest for ten minutes after every five thousand paces. The pursuing Hebrew army undoubtedly moved faster, but this was a pace the Philistines could maintain indefinitely and still put up a stiff fight.

Watching the sergeants goad stray soldiers back into their ranks reminded Achish of another danger. He must keep his men thinking of themselves as a unit and not as individuals. It was the common soldier's unpleasant lot in life to be sacrificed for the good of the army. Achish knew the Philistine formation would fly apart if enough men thought their odds of survival were better alone. The softer garrison troops concerned Achish the most. They made up half of his command and their panic might infect even the most stalwart veterans. For now, the Philistines' discipline held as their rhythmic strides chewed up the distance separating them from home.

One mile west of Geba

Nathan finally had the hated Philistines on the run; yet he felt only frustration. The long-awaited opportunity to punish the murderers of his father was slipping away. Nathan had pushed his men at a blistering pace for over an hour without catching a whiff of their fleeing foe. He clenched his teeth thinking of the wasted time at Geba. He regretted now the hour spent collecting two hundred of Jonathan's men to combine with the survivors of his original three companies. Many of these hastily recruited reinforcements now strayed so far ahead as to be effectively out of his control. Nathan wished courage and patriotism motivated their swiftness. It was more likely that their appetite for plunder had been whetted at Geba. Only the fact that his command now outnumbered the retreating Philistines gave any comfort to Nathan. It was not even necessary for him to defeat the enemy army. Jonathan would soon follow with an even larger force. Nathan merely had to slow the Philistines down and allow a vengeful Israelite host to corner them. Provided he could find his elusive quarry. A cloud of dust on the horizon quickly drove the gloomy thoughts from Nathan's mind. His body shivered with a predatory thrill.

Time was now Nathan's ally.

Chapter 27 - The Pursuit

I pursued my enemies and overtook them; I did not turn back till they were destroyed. I crushed them so that they could not rise; they fell under my feet. God armed me with strength for battle. He made my enemies bow at my feet. He made my enemies turn their backs in flight, and I destroyed my foes.

From Psalm 18, verses 37 to 40

Twelve miles from the Gath border

A shout from the Philistine rearguard caused Achish to look back from the hilltop he had just scaled. The lieutenant named Davon rushed to his side and pointed toward the horizon. The distant figures could barely be seen, but Achish had no doubt they were Hebrews. He was overcome by anger when he realized the entire Philistine column had halted because of the commotion.

"No one told you *bastards* to stop! Keep moving!"

Officers and sergeants sprang into action at Achish's harsh rebuke. Like a fat earthworm, the head of the Philistine formation began stretching forward, allowing each of its segments to advance in turn up the hill. Achish reckoned the pursuing Hebrews less than a mile away, meaning the gap was closing fast. And then what? Achish decided to consult Davon, since the diligent lieutenant seemed bent on serving as his *de facto* adjutant.

"How long do we have, Davon?"

"Perhaps an hour, Sir."

"We could outrun them."

"With respect, Sir, that works to their advantage. Sooner or later, we'll have to fight. Running will just exhaust us."

"Can't have that, Davon, can we?"

"No, Sir. A suggestion?"

"Please."

"This is as good a place as any."

"We can't allow the Hebrews to pin us down until their reinforcements arrive, Davon."

"Then something quick and bloody would seem to be in order."

"I like the way you think, Davon. Can you handle the garrison troops for me?"

"Their captain won't like taking orders from a lieutenant."

"Ask him if he wants to be demoted."

"I can't wait to see the look on his face. What'd you have in mind, Sir?"

Two hundred paces behind the Philistine rearguard

From deep within Nathan's memory, Karaz's voice seemed to shout a warning. The retreating Philistines were no longer in sight, but his instincts smelled danger. Accordingly, Nathan slowed to focus on what lay before him. At first, he only saw hot-blooded Israelites eager to close with their prey. Then Nathan's eyes widened as he comprehended the magnitude of this blunder. His scattered force was charging blindly up a hill toward an unseen enemy.

"Stop! Come back!"

The leading edge of Israelites halted at the crest of the hill, as if in response to his frantic orders. Nathan felt relieved until those men began streaming back down in panic. Assuming the pell-mell retreat was triggered by something on the other side, Nathan had mere seconds to prevent a slaughter. Ironically, the confusion of the moment began to work in his favor. The Israelites began to clump together at the bottom of the hill as the slower soldiers caught up with their retreating comrades. Nathan decided here was where the Israelites must make their stand.

"Captains, form a battle line! Archers in the second rank!"

A chorus of high-pitched whistling noises drew Nathan's attention back toward the hill. A volley of Philistine arrows from unseen archers now fell on the hundred or so Israelites still descending the slope. Their disorganization proved an unexpected blessing as most of the enemy shafts struck empty ground. Still, Nathan counted a score of his men writhing in the dirt. A full company of Philistine infantry began advancing over the hillcrest as a second volley of arrows flew towards the Israelites. Not only did more of his men go down, but many of the survivors continued running past Nathan's position and into the tree-covered hills beyond. A ragged volley from his own archers caused Nathan to scream in anger.

"Hold your arrows! Let them get closer! Wait for my command!"

The third Philistine volley hit some men in the Israelite battle line as the enemy infantry surged down the hillside. Nathan watched in dismay as the Philistine charge gained momentum with each passing second. He chose to put his limited number of arrows to use before it was too late.

"Let fly!"

The Israelite archers were accurate, but their impact on the enemy charge was negligible. Nathan sensed the courage seeping from his men as a second company Philistine infantry came over the hill. The battle had reached a critical junction. Nathan watched helplessly as a trickle of Israelites to the rear threatened to become a flood. His archers wavered between holding firm and fleeing. Nathan visualized his defense collapsing when the enemy infantry crashed into his lines. His best men would stand and be butchered while their comrades fled. Nathan now remembered one of Karaz's dictates: above all else, a commander must preserve his army. The front rank of Philistines was within fifty paces when Nathan made up his mind.

"Retreat! Run for the trees!"

The Israelite soldiers needed no further encouragement to take to their heels. Nathan joined them in flight while looking back over his shoulder. The Philistines came to a halt just past his men's original position. Nathan walked backwards while watching the Philistines reform their ranks and resume their march. Upon reaching the forest's edge where most of the Israelites clustered, Nathan called for his captains.

"I want ten men to scout the Philistines. One will drop out every hour and wait to guide Prince Jonathan. Gather up the rest of your companies and follow me."

"Follow you? Not a chance! You got our men killed for nothing!"

Nathan turned to face a rugged-looking man in his thirties. He assumed the troublemaker to be from one of the companies which accompanied Jonathan to Geba. Karaz said to expect men to challenge his right to lead, especially in light of his youth. Nathan knew his best tactic was to respond with calmness and confidence, even though he felt neither. Besides, if he could not stand up to a single malcontent, he did not deserve to command. The trick was to somehow discredit the man in the minds of his comrades. He decided to make some informed guesses. It was risky. Nathan might lose all respect if he were wrong; however, this was no time for caution.

"Our job was to delay the Philistines so Jonathan's men could catch up. Well, we succeeded. The ambush was unfortunate."

"And whose fault was that, Boy?"

"It was yours, you greedy fool."

"Mine?"

"You broke ranks. Encouraged others to follow you into a trap. And for what? More plunder? Their blood is on your head."

"I've killed over lesser insults."

"Truth is no insult. What's in that bundle you're carrying?"

"Nothing! Besides, I wasn't the only one."

Perspiration now streamed down the face of Nathan's adversary. The man's defensive manner bore witness to the accuracy of Nathan's accusations. He smiled at this small triumph, but knew it only mattered if it won over the rest of his soldiers. Nathan turned his eyes on the men standing nearby. Seeing looks of shame, Nathan decided to restore his soldiers' morale.

"We'll speak no more of this. The Philistines are the real enemy. And I know how to get more help."

Eleven miles from the Gath border

The Philistines were enjoying a brief respite when Hebrew *shofars* began wailing from the hills behind them. Achish hastily gulped water to wash down a few bites of bread before summoning his officers. Under his direction, the Philistine column swiftly reformed. The company of archers again made up its core, with the garrison troops guarding both flanks, and his heavy infantry, minus their armor, split between the front and the rear. Achish was about start his force in motion when distant *shofars* began to answer the original

Hebrew horns. He found these new sounds more ominous because they came from the road ahead. The noises merged to echo off the hills and create for Achish the illusion of being surrounded. He sensed the mournful noise had the same effect on his soldiers. Achish injected a confidence into his voice that he did not truly feel as he addressed the anxious ranks before him.

"What you hear are the Hebrews rallying their militia. Each horn ahead of us calls a company to gather in its town. However, the leader of their army is behind us. The militia must first find him before they can come against us. We'll make good use of that delay. Keep moving, stay strong and I promise you will see home again."

Achish's speech drew only blank stares from his troops. For a moment, he feared his bold words had sounded empty to the veteran warriors. Suddenly a harsh metallic clanging assaulted Achish's ears. A handful of men were banging their swords against iron-rimmed shields in unison. It was a ritual soldiers used to embolden themselves and intimidate their enemy. The rhythmic beat began at the front of the column with the platoon Achish had led out of Geba. It spread rapidly through the entire column until it was taken up by the rearguard. For a moment, Achish allowed wave after wave of the defiant clamor to wash over him. Its intensity grew until he finally raised his arms for silence.

"Meanwhile, it's most kind of the Hebrews to provide us with music as we march. Forward!"

Raucous laughter greeted Achish's wry humor as the column stepped off behind him. Achish managed to hide his relief at receiving this crucial vote of confidence. As the enemy

328

shofars continued to wail, he felt satisfaction over his hurried choice of words. Achish almost believed them himself.

Nine miles from the Gath border

Barely an hour had passed since the humiliating ambush, but Nathan was ready to strike his next blow against the retreating Philistines. These were the same hills where he fought mock battles with his boyhood friends in years past. Nathan remembered a location where the road passed through a narrow gap in the hills. He led his Israelite soldiers along familiar shortcuts until they were nearly a quarter mile ahead of their prey. Along the way, Nathan collected several *elephs* of local militia. With close to five hundred men, he now outnumbered the Philistines. However, since the enemy's superior weapons and discipline would crush his men in a toe-to-toe fight, Nathan had devised different tactics. The Israelites remained in concealment while a few Philistine skirmishers passed the ridge where they lay. Fearing some overzealous farmer might cost the Israelites the element of surprise, Nathan had interspersed his soldiers with the militia. When the enemy's main body appeared a few minutes later, Nathan nodded to his trumpeter. The man held a *shofar* to his lips and blew a long, shrill blast.

The Philistines were still in line-of-march when the howling Israelites broke cover, but the enemy infantry deployed with impressive speed. The Philistines on the near side of the column formed a battle line only seconds before the first Israelites made contact. For the next minute, even the poorly armed militia pushed the Philistine infantry back by sheer weight of numbers. Nathan was gratified to see how the

Philistine archers struggle to find clear targets without hitting their own men. Then foot soldiers from the far side of the Philistine column filtered through to stem the Israelite tide. When the Philistine vanguard and rearguard threatened to outflank his men, Nathan signaled his trumpeter to sound the retreat. Most of the Israelites made it safely behind the ridge. The Philistines pursued until called back by their own horns.

Nathan immediately herded his exuberant Israelites off to their next battleground. He lagged behind to survey the results of the recent skirmish. Nathan counted nearly twenty Israelite bodies on the field, but grudgingly accepted their loss. At least a dozen Philistines lay dead and many others had limped away wounded. Even better, the scattered enemy force required extra time to reassemble. As Nathan turned to follow his men, he estimated this particular action had purchased at least another half-hour for Jonathan to catch up.

Eight miles from the Gath border

The next Israelite attack employed the same tactics a mile later, but with less satisfactory results. Nathan was shocked when the Philistine column did not stop and deploy. Instead, a mixed platoon of infantry and archers split off from the Philistine column to face the onrushing Israelites. The enemy infantry formed a protective screen and then knelt, giving their archers a clear view for their first volley. Nathan was horrified to see a score of his men go down well short of the enemy position. This level of carnage was simply too much for the Israelite militia. Nathan cringed as his front rank panicked and collided with their comrades who were still advancing. This chaotic bunching merely provided the Philistine archers with even better targets. As the Israelites fled, the Philistines sprinted away to rejoin their column. This time Nathan had suffered dozens of casualties for no gain. There was no time for grieving though. Nathan must instead rally his disheartened command and find a response to this new Philistine tactic. A simple, but deadly, plan took shape in Nathan's mind as he continued the pursuit. There would be no ambush this time. They would attack the Philistines from the rear in open ground. He explained the details to his captains as they ran alongside.

Seven miles from the Gath border

When their enemy again came into view, the Israelites assumed a tightly packed formation and closed the distance. A mixed Philistine platoon of infantry and archers broke off, just as before, to act as a rearguard. As the first volley of enemy arrows was being readied, Nathan blew his *shofar*. The Israelite formation promptly split into three companies, each following one of Nathan's army captains. One company continued straight ahead, another broke to the left and the third wheeled to the right. Each company then spread out to form the broadest possible front. This unexpected maneuver caused most of the Philistine arrows to strike empty ground. Nathan's sprinting soldiers were now too widely dispersed for a concentrated volley. The startled enemy archers now faced a serious dilemma: wait for commands or pick their own targets. Most finally chose to aim at his center company, but their efforts were uncoordinated and ineffective. Meanwhile, Nathan's right and left companies threatened to surround the Philistine rearguard. Whether at a command or by mutual agreement, the entire enemy platoon broke and ran for the receding Philistine column. Nathan was ecstatic when the entire enemy formation turned to rescue their beleaguered comrades. One by one, he beheld the fleeing Philistine infantry and archers being dragged down. Nathan wished to bag them all, but Karaz had warned him about commanders who grew too greedy in the heat of battle. At least a score of the Philistine rearguard had fallen, the enemy formation was exhausting itself running to and fro, and invaluable time had been gained for Jonathan. Satisfied, Nathan recalled his men. This time the cost was only eleven Israelite dead. Nathan felt a twinge of guilt, as he recognized it was becoming easier to accept the death of his men.

As the afternoon shadows began to lengthen, the two armies had settled into a murderous routine. The Philistines would lead while the Israelites followed just out of bow range. Every half mile or so, Nathan would order a charge against the rear of the enemy column. The Philistines would then halt and turn, but remain in their marching ranks. The Israelites would advance until driven off by enemy archers. Nathan's men would retire to a safe distance until the Philistines resumed their trek. This bloody cycle was repeated multiple times over the next two hours. Nathan estimated one Philistine went down for every two Israelite casualties. This imbalance was partially offset by the possibility for many injured Israelites to recover. None of the Philistine wounded would enjoy such good fortune. Although distasteful, the odds were sufficient for Nathan's immediate purpose. More importantly, the enemy column's forward progress had slowed dramatically. Nathan also noticed that with each succeeding skirmish, the Israelites were allowed to draw closer before the enemy archers responded. At first, he suspected another trick, but soon realized his foes must be running short of arrows. If nightfall caught the Philistine outside the safety of their walled city, their discipline would collapse in the darkness, and a great slaughter could commence.

Four miles from the Gath border

Nathan was preparing another skirmish when the Philistines did the unexpected. Incredibly, the enemy column forded a shallow stream, broke ranks and settled down for a meal. It was tempting to send his men off in a wild charge, but Nathan recognized the dangers of attacking across even a small body of water. He brought his soldiers as close to the stream bank as he dared and ordered them to rest as well. One of his captains flopped down next to him and passed Nathan the leather bag from which he had been drinking. Expecting water, Nathan nearly choked at the taste of an extremely potent wine. Then he drank his fill.

"Will they make a stand here, Nathan?"

"Not with a Gath garrison only a few miles distant. The Philistines are gathering their strength for one final push."

"Seems like a good time to hit them."

"We want them to stop. If they're doing exactly what we want, why risk our men?"

This debate was abruptly interrupted by the blare of *shofars* from the direction of Geba. Nathan saw a vast horde pouring down the slopes onto the plain. All fatigue vanished as Nathan joined his soldiers in cheering the arrival of their fellow Israelites. All their running, fighting and dying would finally be rewarded. Now he and Jonathan would eradicate this invading vermin.

Chapter 28 - The Ruse

I have seen something else under the sun: The race is not to the swift, nor the battle to the strong, nor does food come to the wise, nor wealth to the brilliant, nor favor to the learned; but time and chance happen to them all.

From the Book of Ecclesiastes, Chapter 9, verse 11

West of the stream

Achish gulped several handfuls of cool water from the stream while studying several hundred Hebrew warriors milling around on the opposite bank. He had decided to risk one final rest stop for his exhausted troops. Achish pondered why the Hebrews were allowing his men this brief respite. The other commander was either very stupid or very cunning. The man had begun the chase badly by stumbling into an obvious ambush. Yet, this leader also proved capable of learning from his mistakes, adapting on the run and motivating raw militia. As a result, the two armies had engaged in a series of moves and countermoves throughout the afternoon. Achish shook his head at the irony of the situation. He had been teaching some unknown Hebrew opponent how to defeat Philistine tactics. So far, Achish managed to remain one step ahead of his pursuers. As the sun began to set over the western hills, Achish knew he needed to conjure up at least one more trick.

The unwelcome sound of Hebrew *shofars* to the east instantly changed everything for Achish. He squinted at a dark mass of men surging across the plain. His Philistines were already in dire straits, even without this new threat. The

335

Hebrews would soon have over a thousand men to throw against his three battered companies. Achish yelled for Davon to get their troops back into ranks. He had only two options now. Achish could make a stand at the stream, or he could run. Neither choice was appealing. Even though they might be poorly armed militia, the Hebrews would eventually overwhelm the tired Philistines in a straight up fight. Flight offered little more hope. The Philistines had been marching and fighting nonstop for over sixteen hours. Several miles still lay between them and the safety of their nearest garrison. Achish feared the better rested Hebrews would run down and slaughter most of his men.

There was a third option open to Achish: he could flee with a small bodyguard while the bulk of his force fought and died. Achish rejected this alternative, but not out of any loyalty to his soldiers. He would never again be entrusted with a military command after such a cowardly act. One of his brothers, even a bastard, could replace him as heir to the throne. For better or worse, his future would be settled on this dusty Benjamite plain. Most of his archers were down to three arrows, so the matter should be decided very quickly. He planned to fall on his own sword rather than be captured alive. It disgusted Achish to imagine how the Hebrews might abuse his body. Achish began fidgeting with the gold chain dangling from his neck, wondering if some goat herder would wear it tomorrow. Then a bold idea burst through Achish's dreary thoughts. He was almost trembling when Davon approached with his report.

"Two hundred and fifty-three ready for battle, Sir. I ordered seven men slain who could no longer stand."

"We're going to lose this game, Davon. It's time to play a different one. Collect every piece of gold or silver or copper our soldiers are carrying...chains, rings, bracelets, anything shiny. You have five minutes. Use the men from your platoon. Here's my contribution."

Achish handed over his gold chain and two silver bracelets to a mystified Davon. He kept back only the signet ring identifying him as a Prince of Gath.

"The men may resist, Sir."

"Ask the fools how they plan to spend it in hell."

"I wouldn't remind them of death, Sir. Not now."

"Then tell the men that I will repay them myself."

"Sir! Some will exaggerate how much they gave."

"I'll be very happy to haggle with them, Davon... tomorrow."

East of the stream

Jonathan was not yet visible to Nathan as the Philistines once again headed west at their fastest pace of the day. He was torn between waiting for his prince's arrival and taking immediate action to prevent the escape of their prey. Nathan compromised by ordering his men to cross the stream and wait for instructions. The retreating Philistines left a broad trail of shiny objects in their wake. Nathan could not identify the tiniest items, but he had no doubt about the largest ones. The Philistines were discarding their helmets and shields. Nathan's

337

skin tingled at the implications. The Philistines were abandoning any pretense of organized resistance. They now gambled their lives in a desperate race for survival, one which Nathan knew weighed heavily against them. His fresher militia would begin running down the most fatigued Philistines in a matter of minutes. Any heathen who turned to fight would die. The scattered Philistines would never find their way to safety after sunset. Vengeful Israelites would hunt them down tomorrow like wild dogs. Nathan was thinking how his father would be pleased when a familiar voice interrupted his musings.

"What's happening, Nathan?"

"They're making a run for it, Jonathan!"

"My men need water. Can yours give chase?"

"They're already across the stream."

"Then pursue and kill, Nathan! Drive them into the hills. I'll be right behind you."

Nathan flashed his friend a predatory grin and shouted orders ahead to his captains. His soldiers set off in pursuit while Nathan was still fording the stream. However, a nasty surprise awaited him on the far bank. Instead of running after the enemy, Nathan's troops were stumbling over each other and engaging in fistfights. Scores of men were on their hands and knees, scrambling through the dirt. Others ran ahead for a short distance before falling to the ground themselves. Nathan shoved his way through the seemingly deranged men until he spied the cause of their insanity. Helmets and shields were not all the Philistines had discarded. Nathan found himself looking at a well-sown field...seeded with silver pieces, gold jewelry and other valuable trinkets. The most disheartening sight was witnessing his officers joining in the frenzied scuffle for Philistine plunder. Tears poured down his face as he vainly attempted to push men forward. Nathan had already shouted himself hoarse when a powerful hand gripped his shoulder. He was dimly aware of Jonathan at his side, wearing an expression that was both frustrated and sympathetic.

"It's finished, Nathan. Recall your men. We're going back to Gibeon."

The Philistine garrison at Aijalon

Achish was starting on his second jar of wine when Davon walked through the door of his quarters at the Gath outpost. The rooms recently belonged to an officer who had been summarily evicted to accommodate the son of his king. A cool evening breeze flowed through the windows, causing the large oil lamps on Achish's table to flicker. His soldiers had become separated in the darkness, and Davon had been counting heads as the stragglers stumbled through the gate. The lieutenant stood to attention, but Achish waved him over to the table and shoved an enameled cup of wine into his hand. Davon gratefully slumped down on a stool and drained his beverage in a single swallow before speaking.

"Final count was two hundred and thirty-nine, Sir. Anyone who hasn't made it here by now, isn't coming."

"We'll rest the men here for two days and then leave for Gath. I've already sent a courier to my father. His war has begun."

"You have quite a story to tell him. Your final trick was especially clever."

"And costly. How much treasure did we leave in the dirt to distract the Hebrews?"

"No idea. I asked the sergeants tally it up first thing in the morning."

"Then I'll want to settle my debts with the men tomorrow afternoon. Best to get the haggling over with. Now I have a question for you, Davon."

"I'm at your service, Sir."

"Actually, that's what I want to discuss. It's time I had my own personal guard. Would your platoon have any objections to leaving my father's service and entering mine?"

"None that some extra silver in their purses won't solve."

"Don't you mean in your purse, Davon?"

"Please, Sir. My men trust me. They know they'll get most of it."

"Then I'll make the necessary arrangements. By the way, you're a captain now."

"Thank you, Sir."

"And you may call by my name from now on."

"An even better promotion ...Achish."

"Trust me, Davon; you'll earn every bit of it. Starting now."

"Meaning?"

"Did you notice those men being carried by their comrades?"

"Yes, Achish, there were about ten of them."

"Why was that?"

"They couldn't walk on their own."

"Yet I specifically ordered such men to be given a quick death and left behind."

"Common soldiers are more loyal are to each other than to us, Achish. And no harm was done by it."

"I disagree, Davon. Next time, they may choose to ignore a truly important order."

"Sometimes an officer must turn a blind eye. Popularity within the ranks can be worth more than gold. You gained great favor with the men today. Why waste it?"

"Because I intend to cultivate something better."

"What?"

"Fear."

"True. Fear often accomplishes more than love. But consider this, Achish. Once you go down that road, you can't go back. Neither of us can."

"Do you wish to back out, Davon?"

"Think you'll ever regret this choice?"

"I will *never* regret it."

"Then I'm your man. So, how do you want to handle the punishment?"

"Each wounded man will be given the quick death he should have had. Behead every soldier who carried them."

"Men usually take turns carrying the wounded. Half our survivors could be involved. That many executions might start a mutiny."

"Then do not search too hard, Davon, but I want at least one healthy man executed with each wounded man who dies. That should make the rest think twice about tempting fate again."

"Then it's best to get it over with quickly, Achish."

"I leave it to you, Captain."

The punishment demanded by Achish was meted out before sunrise. The twelve wounded men were all sleeping as their throats were quietly slit. Achish assumed they awoke painlessly in the afterlife, not that it really mattered to him. Davon discreetly arranged for the executions of twelve disobedient soldiers to be performed by strangers from the local garrison. The bodies were cold before any of their comrades from Geba could voice a single protest. After allowing time for gossip to circulate, Achish took an unescorted stroll among his troops. He saw this as a necessary risk. Either these common soldiers would bend to his will, or one would shove a blade in his back. Most avoided eye contact, so Achish spoke to them directly. Overall, he was satisfied by the results. Achish detected a respectful fear, but not broken spirits. The men would spread rumors throughout Gath about their ruthless, young commander, but Achish expected these would only enhance his reputation. Afterwards, he relished his midday meal and looked forward to the day's next challenge.

It was time for Achish to honor his pledge to repay the valuables donated by his men to ensure their mutual escape from the Hebrews. He passed nearly every survivor from Geba waiting in the afternoon sun outside the garrison commander's quarters. Achish entered and sat down behind a roughhewn table where Davon had already placed a stack of the soldiers' petitions for reimbursement. He glanced at Davon and gave a low whistle while mentally calculating the total. The captain could not know the actual cost meant nothing to Achish. The Geba expedition was a success, and his father would gladly open Gath's treasury to him. However, Achish was not interested in finances now. This afternoon's session was intended to lay the foundation for his future rule. Achish beckoned the sergeant stationed at the door to approach.

"Sergeant, do you know which soldiers are the least reliable?"

"Of course, Sir. That's my job."

"Good. Send them in first. One at a time."

Achish noticed Davon raising an eyebrow in surprise, but he decided to leave the officer in suspense. There was always a chance things would not go as Achish intended. The sergeant returned a moment later followed by two soldiers, one at least ten years older than the other. Both men immediately bowed to Achish.

"Sergeant, I said one at a time."

"I know, Sir. Only one has the claim. The other is his witness."

"So which of you is making the claim?"

The older man stepped forward.

"Me, Lord Achish. I gave you a golden medallion on a chain. Took it last year when we raided a Hittite town. Carried it ever since for luck."

"Must be quite valuable. Naturally, some might wonder how a common soldier would come to possess such a treasure. Bringing along a witness makes good sense."

Achish pulled Davon over and whispered in his ear. The captain smiled wickedly before leading the younger man to the next room. The claimant began sweating while Achish leaned back with crossed arms. Davon returned shortly with the younger man, whom he now stood with behind the older man. A quick nod from Davon signaled he was ready for Achish to proceed.

"Now all I need from you is a description."

"Description, Lord Achish?"

"It's not a trick question. Start with the length of the chain. Face me when I speak to you! Don't look at your friend."

"About two feet long, more or less."

"Was it gold as well?"

"Ah...yes. Yes, it was."

"Now for the medallion."

"What about it, my Lord?"

"It's image, Man! It's image! There's no point in making a blank medallion."

"Uh, well...it was the head of a man. A god or king, I never knew which."

Achish kept one eye on the younger man throughout the interrogation. He noticed a stream of urine trickling down the inside of the man's left leg to pool around his feet. Achish then looked over at a smirking Davon.

"Well, Davon?"

"Not even close, Achish. These two never bothered to get their lies straight."

The urine-stained man instantly fell to his knees while the other stood trembling.

"Forgive me, Lord Achish! It was his idea. He forced me to lie for him!"

"And for half his take, no doubt. Sergeant."

"Sir?"

"This man did the thinking, so behead him. Since the other only lied, cut out his tongue."

"Right away, Sir."

"Do it in the center of the compound. And send the next man in."

Six burly soldiers dragged both screaming miscreants out of the room. An ashen-faced soldier entered and took their place before Achish. The man seemed transfixed by the mournful howls echoing down the hall. He did not even bow until nudged by Davon. When screaming resumed afresh in the distance, Achish held up his hand to signal the man to wait. The late afternoon breeze carried every sound through the room's lone window. Achish heard one of the condemned men began whimpering while the other pleaded for mercy. The pitiful cries ended abruptly with the sound of iron slicing flesh, crunching bone and thudding into wood. Soon the whimpering man resumed his screams. These slowly became gurgling noises from a mouth which could no longer form words. Achish briefly scanned the list on his table and addressed the claimant trembling before him.

"It says here that you reported donating three gold pieces. Is that correct?"

"There's been a mistake, my Lord! It weren't no three gold pieces. I said three copper pieces."

"Are you sure? I want to be fair."

"Oh, yes! Quite sure!"

"Here is one...two, three pieces of copper. Are these satisfactory?"

"Oh yes, Sir. Most satisfactory!"

"Good. Send in the next man, Sergeant."

"There's no one else waiting, Sir."

"Not one?"

"They all skedaddled after the execution."

"See, Davon? I told you that I'd be happy to haggle with them."

Chapter 29 - The Repercussions

Jonathan attacked the Philistine outpost at Geba, and the Philistines heard about it. Then Saul had the trumpet blown throughout the land and said, "Let the Hebrews hear!" So all Israel heard the news: "Saul has attacked the Philistine outpost and now Israel has become a stench to the Philistines." And the people were summoned to join Saul at Gilgal.

From the Book of I Samuel, Chapter 13, verses 3 and 4

The Royal Palace of Philistine Gaza

Kaftor fidgeted on his throne while waiting for the Egyptian emissary at his Royal Palace in Gaza. He accepted the foreigner's tardiness as inevitable; after all, Egypt was the overlord, and Gaza was the vassal. However, Kaftor considered all such attempts at diplomatic dominance to be counterproductive. If one was indeed superior, why did he need to prove it? The Egyptian's posturing meant nothing to Kaftor, but the man's cargo was everything. The emissary bore the latest payment from Ahmose, the Pharaoh's brother-in-law. Beset by traitorous plots at home, Pharaoh had secretly hired Gaza to forestall rebellion along Egypt's eastern frontier. Kaftor had his own ambitions, of course, but for now it suited him to maintain the current balance of power in the region. After the chaos of the past week, a fresh infusion of wealth was essential to Kaftor's schemes. His chief rival, Maoch of Gath, had convinced the other three Philistine kings to go to war against the Hebrews. This left Kaftor no choice but to make the vote unanimous, even confirming Maoch as Philistia's supreme commander. Gaza's forces were committed to marching within the week and Kaftor was counting on Egyptian gold to fund his share of the expedition.

The sound of trumpets in the outer hall brought Kaftor's mind back to business. He gazed down imperiously on the exquisitely garbed dignitary approaching his throne. Kaftor recalled his ambassador's report on the man. The courier was a minor Egyptian functionary named Menes, whose influence was based solely on the few drops of royal blood flowing through his veins. Kaftor knew that while blood was often equated with loyalty, it was not foolproof. It did not even guarantee competence, as Menes' feigned tardiness seemed to indicate. However, surrounded by ambitious rivals as he was, Pharaoh was forced to rely on even his most distant relatives, regardless of their ineptitude. Diplomacy did not seem to be one of Menes' talents, judging by how brusquely he addressed Kaftor.

"Philistia goes to war. Why?"

The Egyptian's rudeness so unnerved one of Kaftor's attendants that the man spilled some goblets from his tray. The golden cups clattered noisily as they rolled across the stone floor while servants scrambled after them. Kaftor was actually grateful for this brief distraction. It was unseemly for a king to give in to a sudden rush of anger; that would make Menes appear to be an equal. Kaftor used the delay to decide how to put Menes in his place, diplomatically speaking. He answered as if indulging an impudent child.

"The Hebrews."

"That horde of vagabond shepherds? They don't even have a king!"

"They do now, Menes. Managed to rout a Philistine garrison. Also killed the governor."

"Are the rebels in Thebes behind this?"

"The Hebrews appear to have acted alone."

"Without an army? No, Kaftor, Pharaoh won't believe that tale. What's really behind it?"

"My guess? Maoch of Gath provoked this incident as an excuse to expand his territory."

"Ahmose pays you to bring down Maoch, not help him prosper!"

"Maoch won over the other three kings with promises of plunder. Philistia would have still gone to war over my objections. I'd have lost influence for nothing. Tell me, Menes, how that would help Egypt."

Kaftor grew bolder during the prolonged silence which showed that Menes had no better idea how to handle the current crisis. Kaftor had just verbally slipped a knife into the arrogant Egyptian. Now was the time to twist it.

"Remember, Menes. They used to be your slaves. A strong Hebrew nation would most likely favor Egypt's enemies."

"Very well, Kaftor, I will recommend that Pharaoh permit your war to take place. There is one condition, though."

"No disrespect to Pharaoh, but this war has already begun. However, Menes, what is your condition?"

"Maoch's power must be broken."

"When?"

"Before he grows stronger."

"Assassinating Maoch now will be difficult. He's the supreme commander after all."

"I did not say you had to kill him!"

"You give me very little time, Menes. Nothing else is feasible. It will also be expensive."

"Ahmose has already paid for your services, Kaftor."

"My agreement with Ahmose did not include *regicide*. Dealing with Maoch was specifically left to *my* discretion. But you already knew that, *didn't you*?"

Kaftor felt nothing but contempt for Menes. The Egyptian was proving to be as feeble a negotiator as he was a diplomat. *The man should have at least asked for a chair first!* Kaftor casually leaned back on his plush cushions while Menes stood below and fumed in frustration. The king was content to allow the emissary to consider his weak position. Ahmose had ten thousand soldiers at his back last year when he dictated terms to Kaftor. Menes, on the other hand, had come to Gaza without a single arrow in his quiver.

"How much is Maoch's life worth, Kaftor?"

"You mean *his death*, Menes, but we can discuss the details after we dine."

Kaftor used the evening meal to size up Menes. Kaftor detected a multitude of weaknesses within the self-important Egyptian. He had only to decide which ones to exploit for this occasion. He found emotions could be far more effective in bargaining than cold, hard facts. A feral smile came over Kaftor's face as a plan came together. He would soften up his opponent and have some fun at the same time. Kaftor selected a piece of pork from a platter and tossed it onto the floor beside Menes's chair. The Egyptian gave Kaftor a puzzled look while following the flight of the meat. Menes was startled by a flurry of movement in the dark corners of the great hall. A mangy creature scuttled out of the shadows on all fours to sniff the piece of pork near the emissary's feet. Menes's lip curled in disgust at the beast's foul odor.

"Why do you keep such a grotesque dog, Kaftor?"

"*I AM NOT A DOG!*"

The Egyptian chortled in amusement at the prospect of a talking animal. Kaftor began counting the seconds until he heard the anticipated shriek of dismay. Menes had just realized that he was actually staring into an upturned human face. The emissary's horrified expression was everything Kaftor could have hoped for. The man was distracted from his wine in mid-sip. The goblet halted short of Menes's lips, but continued to tip forward to spill wine down the front of his elegant robes. Meanwhile, the wretched creature on the floor gave Kaftor a look of both rage and despair before clenching the meat between his teeth and retreating into the shadows.

"He is quite good at cleaning up the scraps, is he not? I would introduce him to you, Menes, but I seem to have forgotten his name."

"He has no hands, no feet. Was he born that way?"

"No. He came to my Court three years ago posing as a merchant. I cut off his arms at the elbows and his legs at the knees after he was caught spying for the Hittites."

"You cut them off...yourself?"

"I take great pride in being to amputate a limb with a single stroke. He is the prize of my collection."

"Your collection?"

"Yes, quadruple amputation is my penalty for treachery. It is wondrously effective as a tool of diplomacy. I have enjoyed excellent relations with my neighbors since implementing it."

"I have never heard of such a thing in Egypt."

"Of course you have not. No Egyptian would be so perfidious."

The rest of the meal passed in dead silence. Kaftor feared for a while that he had succeeded too well. He intended to intimidate the Egyptian, not incapacitate him. Serious negotiating would be impossible if the man were scared witless. However, color soon returned to Menes's face and Kaftor felt the man was now suitably vulnerable. He was somewhat disappointed by how squeamish the Egyptian was. Kaftor sighed to himself. So few people appreciated effective diplomacy.

Later that evening Kaftor strolled under the stars on his private balcony and reviewed the day's events. After a brief bargaining session, Menes had retired to his quarters suitably drunk and was undoubtedly snoring in the arms of a beautiful courtesan. Kaftor had humbled a pretentious fool, enriched himself and deflected Egyptian attempts to interfere in his kingdom. All in all, it was a day to be proud of. There was still one matter for Kaftor to attend to before seeing to his own pleasures. He rang for his chamberlain.

"Yes, Sire?"

"Summon that so-called mercenary general from Crete. I have work for him."

Israelite occupied Gibeon

Nathan was relishing a short nap under a shade tree outside the old Philistine outpost at Gibeon. There had been little time to rest since Jonathan drove the Philistines from Geba. Granted, most of the Philistines returned safely to Gath, but their withdrawal had boosted the morale of Jonathan's regiment beyond measure. After returning to the regiment's stronghold in Gibeon, Nathan discovered just how much work a victory could generate. He and Jonathan suddenly found themselves responsible for the security of half Benjamin's territory. Requests for assistance and demands for protection poured in from the surrounding communities. Most of Nathan's waking hours were consumed in reassuring anxious dignitaries. Jonathan sent messengers to Michmash to alert King Saul to the situation, but no instructions were forthcoming. Until then, the young prince was forced to fend for himself. Jonathan stationed two Royal Army companies in the newly captured outpost at Geba. Naturally, all the work for provisioning these troops fell to Nathan. Now he was taking a break before tackling the multitude of tasks required to permanently settle Jonathan's other eight companies in Gibeon. Nathan had barely closed his eyes when his repose was interrupted by a voice both stern and familiar.

"You boys have created a real mess."

Nathan glanced up to see his mentor, Karaz, peering down at him. He hopped up and started to speak when Karaz waved him to silence.

"Take me to Jonathan. *Now.*"

The softness of Karaz's voice belied its intensity. Nathan led the way to Jonathan's room, but found it empty. They soon spotted the prince laughing with some of his officers in the street nearby. Jonathan's smile vanished when Karaz curtly beckoned to him. Once inside the prince's quarters, Karaz turned on his young protégés.

"Was the concept of *hold and harass* just a little too advanced for you?"

Although the question was directed to both of them, Nathan was relieved when Jonathan accepted the responsibility to answer.

"I found a different situation here than the Royal Council expected."

"Did you now?"

"The Council feared Geba was bait to lead us into a Philistine ambush. Instead, I discovered that we greatly outnumbered them. The chance for a great triumph had fallen into our hands. It would have been a sin to waste it."

"I'm still struggling with this Hebrew concept of sin. In this case, it appears to mean *NOT* doing something foolish. Did you remember anything we discussed that night? Particularly how we were going to *gradually* respond to the Philistines with greater force?"

"But my response was stronger than the Philistines' provocation."

"Yes, so strong that it united all of Philistia against Israel. But that may not be the worst thing you've done."

"I don't understand."

"Messengers arrived at Michmash with glorious accounts of your victory. I saw fear in Saul's eyes when his soldiers began praising the name of Jonathan. They believe you will be a great king one day. Saul wonders if today is that day."

"But I'm no traitor!"

"Oh, I tried to reassure Saul that you were merely an idiot. But your disobedience destroyed my credibility. Remember, I recommended you for this command. By the way, Saul is now claiming credit for your victory before the rest of Israel praises you too."

"Perhaps Samuel can intercede with my father."

"Samuel? *Samuel?* Have you any idea what's been going on?"

"We've heard nothing for over a fortnight."

"Then allow me, my Prince, to acquaint you with the disaster you've wrought. After you roused the Philistines,

Samuel left Michmash to rally the tribal militias. With me out of favor, Saul grew dependent on Beker and Abner. That's when things began falling apart."

"What do you mean?"

"Saul went to Gilgal to await the men recruited by Samuel. The plains of Gilgal are the best place to assemble an army, but only if the Philistines are denied the mountain pass at Michmash. So, the king left Abner in charge of the two thousand soldiers holding Michmash. Well, you know how Abner is. It didn't take him long to piss off everyone. The army officers began streaming to Gilgal to complain to Saul, taking their men with them. Eventually Abner felt the need to leave Michmash to defend himself. With each succeeding day, fewer men remained to guard the pass."

"How few, Karaz?"

"Three, maybe four hundred when I left this morning. That's why I came looking for you."

"What can I do?"

"Get your regiment to Michmash, Jonathan, before the Philistines learn what idiots we are. If they occupy the pass first, your father is finished."

"It will take a day to get my men ready. Meanwhile, Karaz, tell Michmash that reinforcements are on the way. As you pass through Geba, take both companies there with you. That will give you two hundred more men until I arrive."

"I can't go, Jonathan."

"But I need you at Michmash."

"I am no longer the *Aluf*. To the Royal Council, I'm a scheming foreigner using you to overthrow the king. No, Jonathan, you must solve this problem on your own."

"That's nonsense, Karaz."

"Political infighting is part of every royal court, Lad. Why should worshiping only one God make your people any different? I've been a target since the day I first swore loyalty to Saul. After what you did at Geba, Abner and Beker were finally able to oust me."

When these last words left Jonathan speechless, Nathan tried his best to be helpful.

"Can't you just explain everything to Saul?"

"We're long past that, Nathan. Jonathan must reconcile with his father without my help. Abner's cronies will scream *conspiracy* if they see me whispering into the prince's ear. However, you're an entirely different matter. They'll think nothing of his young friend standing by his side."

"Can I really help Jonathan overcome them?"

"Never underestimate the advantage of being underestimated, Lad."

Karaz looked wistfully at the ceiling.

"You know, I can see some definite advantages to that *Theocracy* your people used to have."

That evening, Nathan stood with Jonathan and Karaz watching the regiment prepare to leave the next day. Karaz's head suddenly jerked around as a group of men walked by with Philistine swords. The Hittite immediately called out to them.

"You! Where did you get those swords?"

The tallest man in the group turned in annoyance.

"From the Philistines we killed."

"How many do you have?"

"At least fifty. Enough for half of my company."

"Well, you and your friends can just stack them in that cart. I have plans for those swords."

Most of the men hesitated at Karaz's forceful tone, but the tall man never wavered.

"The hell we will."

"Don't make me hurt you, Boy."

"You want to try and take my sword, Old Man?"

Jonathan was about to intervene, but Nathan saw Karaz wave the prince off. The Hittite calmly examined a pile of firewood and selected a stick about three feet long with the same diameter as his wrist. He then confronted his sword-wielding challenger.

"You look more like a goat herder than a soldier. And you don't know the first thing about using that sword. I can tell by the way you grip it. The first Philistine you met would just take it away from you. Probably take your life as well. You're better off using a club. Give it to me before you hurt yourself."

A large crowd gathered to watch the unequal confrontation. Nathan heard them howl with laughter after each of Karaz's taunts. The tall man was obviously embarrassed to be shamed by a poorly armed cripple. The stranger finally lunged toward Karaz, trying to split the Hittite in half with an overhead swing. The mercenary seemed to effortlessly glide from side to side as he avoided the younger man's clumsy thrusts. Karaz used his crude stick to easily parry the heavier sword while moving ever closer. In what seemed to be one continuous move, Karaz feinted to throw his adversary off balance, whacked the man on the wrist to make the sword drop and then kicked his hapless foe's weight bearing leg from under him. Barely perspiring, Karaz thrust his stick under the prone man's chin as if he were ready to strike a killing blow. He then eyed the rest of the crowd.

"Swords in the cart. Now!"

Nathan chuckled later as Karaz counted fifty-seven Philistine swords. Jonathan put his hand on the shoulder of his mentor.

"Thank you, Karaz, for the best entertainment I've seen in a long time."

"Everything I said to that big goat herder was true. Men shouldn't have swords until they have been trained to use them. Why, those louts would need a week just to master the basic footwork."

"You mentioned having a plan."

"Jonathan, give me these swords and fifty handpicked men. In a month, they'll not only know how to use a sword, but will be able to train ten men each. Within a few months, the Royal Army of Israel will have its first regiment of trained swordsmen."

"You need to stay away from me for a while, Karaz. Geba is a convenient out-of-the-way place. Conduct your training there."

"Good. The first man I want is the big goat herder. If I can train that clumsy clod, I can teach any Hebrew."

"Where will you get the additional swords for this new regiment, Karaz?"

"I just train 'em, Jonathan. Equipping 'em is your job."

Chapter 30 - The Race

*Saul chose three thousand men from Israel. Two thousand were
with him at Michmash and in the hill country of Bethel. A
thousand were with Jonathan at Gibeon in Benjamin.*

From the Book of I Samuel, Chapter 13, verse 2

The Philistine capital of Gath

A groggy Achish trotted after the courier bearing the
emergency summons from his father, King Maoch. Commanders
were supposed to report to their king immediately upon
returning from a mission, but he had spent his first night back in
Gath enjoying a night of pleasure. Achish had assumed his
father would grant him some leeway after his hard fought, but
ultimately successful, expedition to Geba. That proved to be
wishful thinking. Worse, the king had been kept waiting for
hours while his couriers scoured Gath's taverns and brothels.
Even now, Achish was uncertain where he had ended up last
night. He vaguely remembered hours of gambling, a very
entertaining bath, some unbelievably agile women and a
drinking contest against an ugly brute from Crete. Perhaps he
could sooth his father's anger by offering to take him there.

The going became slower as the two men neared their
destination. The plaza adjacent to Gath's Royal Palace was
swarming with soldiers, merchants, slaves, donkeys, wagons; all
the paraphernalia required for a major military expedition.
Despite being heir to the throne, Achish still had to shove his
way through the pandemonium like a commoner.

As he ascended the Palace steps, Achish realized Maoch was too busy to scold a tardy son. Achish's curiosity was piqued when he realized the courier was heading toward his father's private quarters, rather than the council hall. Achish was ushered into a secluded chamber which he had not known even existed. The room felt cramped even though only three men were seated around a small table: King Maoch, his *Archon* Abimelek and the veteran scout Uruk. He suspected there must be some history between Uruk and Maoch. Achish slid into an empty chair and received a bemused smirk from his father.

"Got the whoring out of your system for now, Son?"

"For a few hours at least."

"Good enough. Uruk, tell Achish what you've learned."

"The Hebrew king musters an army on the plains of Gilgal. As long as his men hold the pass at Michmash, we can't touch them. Yet, his soldiers are abandoning Michmash."

"All of them?"

"A few hundred Hebrews still remain."

"That's an invitation to cross the mountains and destroy his army. No one is that stupid, Uruk."

"I have three Hebrew spies in Michmash, Lord Achish. Their reports all match."

"How reliable are your Hebrew traitors?"

"Their families will be butchered if they lie. Beyond that, who knows?"

"Then this Hebrew king is a most obliging enemy, Father."

"Uruk, my son's sarcasm indicates he suspects a trap. Could the Hebrew king really be that clever?"

"Hard to say, my King. His actions so far lack subtlety. However, subtlety won't be necessary if he catches us in the hill country west of Michmash."

"You've been unusually quiet, Abimelek."

"I prefer to let military men make their plans first, my King. That makes it easier for me to criticize them later."

"So you advise against moving on Michmash?"

"Not at all, my King. Seize the pass at Michmash if you can. That will effectively cut their southern tribes off from their northern ones. Once in possession of this high ground, your army can easily sweep the Hebrew army from the plains of Gilgal. Then occupy the land of Benjamin. The other tribes will abandon a king who cannot even protect his own home."

"Michmash is a gate that swings both ways, Abimelek. It might be bait for a Hebrew ambush."

"Then you must first close it, my King."

"Achish, can you close this gate for me?"

"Yes, but I'll need even greater authority to do it. What can you give me, Father?"

Achish could not resist staring at the ornate golden ring which had been on his right hand since leaving his father's secret chamber. It was a royal signet ring, one of several used by the King of Gath. He could not resist staring at the powerful object while waiting for Davon, captain of his bodyguard. Maoch had made it abundantly clear to his teenage son that the ring was being loaned, not given. But while he bore the royal signet, Achish was accountable only to the king. Every other inhabitant of Gath would be subject to his orders. He pushed his daydreams aside when a breathless Davon strode into the room.

"Your message said to run, Achish. Trouble?"

"The best kind of trouble, Davon. The king commands us to take the pass at Michmash from the Hebrews and hold it until the rest of our army arrives. My guards are to carry armor, weapons and provisions for one day. Nothing else. We leave within the hour."

"No disrespect to your father, but we have fewer than forty men."

"That's why my father gave me this."

"Nice ring. I'd rather have more soldiers."

"It's better than soldiers, Davon. By using the king's signet, I've acquired two companies of infantry and a company of chariots with archers."

"Then why not request an entire army?"

"No, Davon, I've thought this through carefully. We must get soldiers to Michmash before tomorrow night. That means a small force traveling swiftly."

"Infantry can't cross forty miles of rugged country in a day and a half, Achish."

"They won't have to. Our infantry and chariots come from our advance guard at Beth-horon. Two chariot squadrons are waiting to transport us there. Traveling through the night, we'll arrive at Beth-horon before midday."

"Still leaves fifteen miles and only half a day to reach Michmash. Assuming those men will be ready to start marching immediately, of course."

"Nobody walks, Davon. Two infantrymen will ride in each chariot, along with the driver and its archer. The horses should be able to bear the extra load for that far."

"Using two hundred horses to move four hundred men that far and that fast? It's never been done."

"You can do it, Davon."

"Me?"

"You're my new field commander. Take charge once we reach Beth-horon."

"That may not go over well with the charioteers. Those horsemen consider themselves nobility."

"Invoke my name, Davon. *Scare them*."

The predatory smile crossing Davon's face pleased Achish. Despite the royal signet ring, many soldiers would see Achish as a mere teenager. He needed to leverage Davon's talents to gain their respect more quickly. Achish had made inquiries about Davon since returning from Geba. Despite being only five years older than his prince, the young officer had already earned an enviable reputation. As Achish watched Davon depart, he thought of his father's favorite general, the late Phicol. Perhaps he had found his own Phicol.

On the road to Beth-horon

The thirty-mile journey from Gath to Beth-horon proved to be the most painful night Achish had ever endured. His previous experience in chariots was limited to short jaunts over relatively smooth terrain. However, provincial roads were an endless succession of ruts which rattled both teeth and bone. The seasoned charioteers simply bent their knees to cushion the bumps, a skill which Achish failed to master. He fretted over the condition of his infantry after such an arduous ride. Achish glanced sideways at Uruk, whom his father had sent along as a guide. He was annoyed to see the old scout dozing in his chariot while standing up.

Achish felt as if he had pulled a chariot himself by the time his group arrived at their destination. Beth-horon shimmering under the midday sun was a beautiful sight. The town itself was unremarkable, but reaching the Philistine's advance camp on schedule meant Achish's ambitious scheme was still achievable. The Philistine horses were played out by now. The lathered sides of the animals heaved as the chariots rolled into the encampment. While the exhausted horses could now rest, Achish's work was only beginning. Four hundred soldiers still needed to reach Michmash before sunset.

As they had feared, none of the Philistines at Beth-horon were prepared to depart. Davon immediately justified

Achish's faith in him. The veteran infantry officer knew the key to handling foot soldiers was their sergeants. After a vicious tongue lashing from Davon, each sergeant had his subordinates scrambling after their equipment. The chariot company proved more obstinate. When the indignant charioteers objected to overloading their precious vehicles with infantry, Davon took a different tack. The spectacle of their former commander being stripped and whipped worked wonders with the attitudes of the horsemen. Meanwhile, Achish consulted Uruk on how best to cover the remaining fifteen miles to Michmash.

"This leg of our journey is shorter, but more challenging, Lord Achish."

"Just call me Achish when we're alone. I'm sure you address my father in private by his name."

"Like father, like son. Anyway, Michmash is a natural fortress. The road there is bad enough, but you also want to cram four men and their equipment into each chariot. Traveling too fast will kill the horses."

"We must reach Michmash today, Uruk, and in daylight."

"Don't forget, Achish. Hebrews love ambushes."

"We must ignore that possibility."

"That's taking a big risk."

"If the Hebrews know we are coming, Uruk, we might as well turn around and go back to Gath."

"If that's your decision, Achish, I'll live with it. Or die with it."

"Just get me there, Uruk."

"Then I'll work out a plan. A moderate trot for the horses with two rest stops seems best. That should get us to Michmash one to two hours before sunset. Exhausted, but there."

"I'm expecting a fight, Uruk. Can you do better than *exhausted*?"

"Only if you want to fight in the dark."

"Then we must hope the advantage of surprise makes up for our fatigue."

"I've an idea to give us an edge, but you may have to bully someone."

"That's what royalty lives for, Uruk."

"There's another chariot company here at Beth-horon. Commandeer one of its squadrons, but use it to carry only the drivers. Those horses would be less fatigued when we arrive at Michmash. Twenty fresh chariots might prove decisive in a close battle. If you can you get them, of course."

"Let's see what my ring can do."

Twelve miles from the Michmash pass

369

Nathan studied the eight Israelite companies marching behind him toward Michmash. After the fighting at Geba, he estimated the regiment retained eight fit men out of every ten original volunteers. Jonathan was leaving behind a token force at Gibeon to discourage Philistine raids. Michmash was more vital at the moment. The prince reckoned his men were too few to hold both towns against determined Philistine attacks. Nathan spotted Karaz and his fifty aspiring swordsmen bringing up the rear of the formation. Where the road forked a few miles ahead, Karaz would lead his small band east to Geba and order the two garrison companies there to meet Jonathan at Michmash. Despite the immediate need for fighting men, Nathan knew trained swordsmen were vital to the Royal Army's future. Although their soldiers were not yet professionals, he appreciated how the regiment's marching discipline had improved. Men still slowed to whatever speed was most comfortable for them, but no one was dropping out of the column to nap or cook food. They should cover the twelve miles to Michmash in about six hours. Prodded along by their swearing officers, Nathan was confident the Israelite force would reach Michmash at least an hour before dark.

Two miles from the Michmash pass

Achish tensed as the two rugged cliffs flanking the pass up to Michmash came into view. He was holding his breath, even though no one could possibly hear the sound. The hundred and twenty Philistine chariots clattering behind him made a racket only a deaf sentry would miss. Achish had earlier proposed halting the column while Uruk probed ahead. The veteran scout had shrugged off the request, reasoning that either the Hebrews were ready, or they were not. Achish had reluctantly deferred to the older man's intuition. The lack of any enemy response as the Philistine chariots cantered only increased Achish's anxiety. *Were the Hebrews incompetent lookouts or cunning ambushers?* Achish's chariot was nearly at the foot of the pass when a frantic shout came from above. He beheld tiny figures swarming at the top of the southern cliff. A surge of excitement washed away all of Achish's fears. Ambush or not, his force was committed. Achish directed his charioteer toward the vehicles carrying Davon and Uruk.

"Davon! Call up the chariots with fresh horses. Mount them with archers from the First Squadron."

"Shall I lead them in, Achish?"

"No, I will. Dismount the infantry and then send the other chariot squadrons after me. Put Uruk in charge of them. I want you to bring up the infantry as soon as you can."

"Could be a trap."

"No choice, Davon. I must risk everything on one roll of the dice."

As his troops prepared for action, Achish found himself encompassed by raucous noise and choking dust. He dismounted and waited for his freshest chariot squadron to move up. Monetarily alone, he was nearly overwhelmed by the pandemonium he had unleashed. Achish briefly considered remaining to help Davon sort things out. He had to laugh the absurdity of the idea. *A nineteen year-old boy wondering if a savvy veteran like Davon required his assistance? Ridiculous!* Achish was still grinning when his twenty chariots rolled up with archers. Achish selected for his own use a chariot parked alongside that of the grizzled lieutenant who served as squadron commander.

As he approached his chariot, Achish admired the exquisite composite bow held by its archer. Unlike a solid wood bow carried by foot archers, he knew this composite bow had been made by meticulously gluing layers of sinew, wood and horn together. When drawn, the outer layers of sinew were stretched while the inner layers of horn were compressed, imparting far greater energy to an arrow than wood alone could provide. These magnificent weapons had near double the range of their solid wood competitors. In a moment of envy, Achish realized that he needed a bow fit for a prince. Achish motioned for the archer to hand over his weapon and dismount. The proud bowman was loath to give up his precious weapon to anyone, even a prince. However, the man reluctantly submitted to common sense, handed over his bow and hopped to the ground. As Achish raced away toward the top of the pass, he could see the forlorn archer scowling at him.

The vigorous horses of Achish's squadron required only a few minutes to reach the plateau where the city of Michmash lay. He guessed it would take at least twice that time for the weary horses of his other chariots to cover the same ground. His infantry would probably require five times as long. He feared the Hebrews would block the pass long before the bulk of the Philistine force could get through. Most likely, the coming battle would be decided by the thirty-nine men now galloping after Achish.

Achish was encouraged by his first view of the Michmash plateau. Hundreds of Hebrews rushed about like ants whose hill at just been kicked over. When Achish directed his driver toward the enemy camp, the other nineteen chariots automatically followed. Achish perceived the frenzied Hebrews to be more mob than army. Still, the enemy outnumbered his small band by better than ten to one. He needed to break up the opposing force before it found a leader.

Achish shouted instructions over the clattering chariots to their lieutenant, who translated them into signals. The Philistine vehicles seamlessly flowed around Achish to form a single rank, twenty chariots across, and charged directly at the center mass of the enemy foot soldiers. When Achish notched his bow, the other nineteen archers mirrored him. He pulled and released at extreme range. The volley from the other archers followed their prince's arrow into the front rank of the Hebrews. The Philistines spent the next few moments launching as many shafts as possible. Achish counted scores of fallen Hebrews, but knew merely inflicting casualties would not be enough. Unless the opposing multitude dispersed, his chariots would crash into a wall of bodies and be overwhelmed. Achish felt his driver pull back on the reigns to slow their horses and discerned other drivers doing the same. Achish pulled out his dagger and shoved it against his driver's ribs. The man responded by lashing his horses to full speed. Achish glanced back and saw the other chariots now straining to keep up. The Philistines' aggressiveness was rewarded with the Hebrew formation splitting down the middle. Individual enemy soldiers began fleeing in any direction which took them away from the death dealing machines. The Philistine archers kept up their volleys as the chariots passed through the chaotic mass. Achish ordered a halt one hundred yards later to regroup. Only two chariots had been lost in the wild skirmish, but Achish sensed the battle was about to turn against him.

Achish estimated over three hundred Hebrews still faced his chariots. Worse, competent leadership finally seemed to be asserting itself among his foes. The enemy soldiers were organizing into companies and spreading out to cut off the Philistines' line of retreat. Achish noticed for the first time dozens of archers among the Hebrew infantry. Achish realized the bold charge could not be repeated. His chariots would be forced to run a gauntlet which most would not survive.

Achish was mulling over his limited options when an unexpected commotion erupted at the rear of the Hebrew formation. The first of Achish's fatigued chariot squadrons had reached the plateau. He recognized Uruk in the lead chariot which stopped while the remainder of its squadron moved to cut off the Hebrews' best escape route. Achish grinned as Uruk directed the trailing squadrons to surround the panicking Hebrews. The enemy companies promptly disintegrated. Achish signaled his own squadron to stand down while their comrades pursued the fleeing foe eastward toward Gilgal.

As he leaped from his chariot, Achish found himself confronted by the archer whose bow he had appropriated. The stern-faced man stretched out his right hand and gave the young prince a determined look. Achish instantly handed over the magnificent bow. The fierce warrior carefully grasped his precious weapon like someone caressing a lover.

Achish turned to survey the battlefield and let out an anguished scream. His chariot squadrons were giving up their pursuit. Uruk's chariot rolled up while Achish was still seething. Uruk calmly pointed at the returning chariots, and Achish's wrath cooled as he examined them. The chariots were pulled by animals lathered in sweat, lungs heaving, unable to keep their heads up. Achish looked up at Uruk and nodded reluctantly. It might be days before these horses would again be fit for duty.

The only sign of Davon and his foot soldiers was a cloud of dust rising over the pass. The Hebrews would be long gone before the Philistine infantry could begin a pursuit. Yet, Achish was loath to let his prey escape so easily, not while he still had one asset left. Achish immediately searched for the officer in charge of his personal squadron. He found the man using the floor of a chariot for a seat while slowly pouring a helmet full of water over his head. Seeing Achish's shadow loom over him, the startled lieutenant instantly shook the droplets from his face and stood to rigid attention. Achish gently raised his hand to set the older man at ease.

"You did well today, Lieutenant. Think you can do even better?"

"The horses are ready. My men are eager. We await your orders, Sir."

"I don't want the enemy to regroup. Pursue them. Scatter them. Scare them."

"For how far, Sir?"

"As far as you can, Lieutenant."

"MOUNT UP, YOU MULE JOCKEYS AND ARROW SLINGERS! YOU'RE WITH ME!"

The look of pleasure in the gruff lieutenant's eyes reassured Achish that he had matched the right man with the right job. Eighteen chariots raced eastward as one toward Gilgal. The number of Hebrews which thirty-six Philistines could kill was limited. However, the number they could terrify was far greater. With luck, the frightened survivors would sow panic throughout the Hebrew camp at Gilgal. Achish felt triumphant as the enthusiastic charioteers pulled away. He even received a salute from the archer whose bow he had borrowed.

One mile from the Michmash pass

Nathan strode up a hill outside the small village of Migron to get his first look at the vital pass of Michmash, now barely a mile away. He had gone on ahead while Jonathan acquired water for their thirsty regiment. Nathan found a spot where he could view both the pass and the plateau on which the town of Michmash lay. It was a formidable position. Whoever held Micmash could control all travel through the heart of the Israelite highlands. Even the names of the two cliffs which shaped the pass were intimidating. The cliff to the north was called *Bozez* which meant *slippery,* and the southern cliff was called *Seneh* which meant *thorny*. God willing, their regiment would secure both the town and the pass before dark. However, Nathan's first impression was that God seemed to be otherwise inclined.

"Jonathan!"

"Coming!"

Jonathan was halfway up the hill when Nathan called. The prince sprinted the remaining distance and gave Nathan a reproachful look as he neared.

"Remember to keep your voice calm around the men, Nathan. Now, what is it?"

"Look west of the town."

Nathan winced as an especially profane oath escaped his friend's lips.

"Only one thing raises a dust cloud like that, Nathan."

"Chariots."

"Any idea how many?"

"Could be a hundred, Jonathan. Could be a thousand."

"No matter how many chariots those sons of whores have, we've got to get up there!"

On the Michmash plateau

The Philistine charioteers were about to unharness their horses for the night, when Achish heard Uruk's lookouts raise the alarm. He and Davon raced from the Philistines' temporary campsite to the cliff edge which offered a panoramic view of the countryside below. Slightly out of breath, Achish beheld company after company of armed men marching over a hill barely a mile distant. The Philistines were in dire straits. Achish's one fit chariot squadron was off to the east, chasing fugitive Hebrews through the brush. The remaining Philistine horses could not walk a mile before keeling over. His heavy infantry was fit enough, but vastly outnumbered. Even supported by the eighty chariot archers still left in camp, their battle line would eventually be overwhelmed. Achish attempted to project a confidence he did not feel while addressing his two senior subordinates.

"Gentlemen, it appears the Hebrews have seen the error of their ways."

"This is a fight you can't win, Achish."

"Agreed, Uruk. Therefore, we must win without fighting. Recommendations, Davon?"

"Convince the Hebrews not to attack. Trickery is about all we have left. Make ourselves appear larger than we are."

"I like that. We can start on the cliff summit here. Uruk, take my bodyguards. Move them around among the rocks and bushes."

"I'll make it look like a regiment is up here."

"Davon, you get the dangerous job. Deploy the rest of our men at the bottom of the pass. Make our position look as imposing as possible."

"I have a few ideas, but if it comes down to fighting toe-to-toe, we're finished."

"I'm open to alternatives, Davon."

"Abandon the chariots and save our men. We can flee on foot into the hills and then slip back to Gath."

"No retreat this time, Davon. My father needs this pass. Today it must be victory or death."

"You can't tell these men that, Achish. Discipline will collapse before the Hebrews ever get here."

"Then tell them reinforcements from my father will arrive within the hour."

"Truly?"

"No. But in an hour it won't matter."

Eight hundred paces from the Michmash pass

Nathan marched beside Jonathan at the forefront of ten Israelite companies advancing across the valley floor toward Michmash. He pitied those in the rear eating the dust kicked up by seven hundred pairs of feet. Besides, Nathan preferred to see what he was fighting. Even now, he could tell the Philistines held at least one of the two flanking cliffs, although the pass itself appeared empty. However, that changed a few minutes later. A single company of Philistine heavy infantry came down the road and smartly deployed in a single rank to block the bottom of the pass. There was something unnerving about how efficiently the Philistines moved into position. Their confidence in the face of the more numerous Israelites implied these men were not alone. As Nathan anticipated, a second company of heavy infantry appeared and meticulously formed a second rank behind their comrades. The men following Nathan grew silent at this first sight of the enemy, but maintained their steady advance against the smaller force.

The first appearance of chariots in the pass sent a ripple of tension through the Israelite ranks. A foot soldier's great nightmare was to be chased across the open plain by a chariot and then skewered by an arrow or a spear. Nathan glanced sideways at Jonathan, but the only visible sign of distress was a slight tightening of the prince's jaw. Personally, he was appalled by how a single squadron of twenty chariots, each carrying only a driver and an archer, was enough to intimidate an entire regiment of Israelites. The fearsome vehicles moved slowly and deliberately down the pass to take position behind the protection of their infantry. They were joined by a second squadron. Then a third squadron. Then a fourth. And finally a fifth. Nathan could almost feel the companies at his back faltering as the Philistine squadrons majestically paraded through the pass. Nathan counted fewer than one hundred chariots, but their slow, methodical deployment created an illusion of far greater numbers. The enemy was now only a few hundred yards away and still Jonathan made no effort to address the regiment's rapidly declining morale. Nathan thought perhaps his friend's own courage made him unaware that his soldiers' fear was growing with each step forward. Regardless, it was Nathan's duty as second-in-command to broach this unpleasant subject with his prince.

"Most of our men have never seen a chariot before, Jonathan."

"As long as they stay together, Nathan, there's little to fear."

"A little fear can grow into a large one."

"Another of Karaz's pithy proverbs. It's all the more reason for us to close with the Philistines as quickly as possible."

"Jonathan, their archers can concentrate on a single company until it breaks."

"Leaving our other companies free to advance."

"Or flee in panic."

"We must recover this pass. My father's army at Gilgal depends on it. Unless you intend to munity, Nathan, back off."

"A battle begun now will end after nightfall. The advantage then shifts from numbers to experience. Who will that favor?"

"You think I don't know these things?"

"Then you know what must be done, Jonathan."

"Spit it out, Nathan. What are you trying to do?"

"I'm following Karaz's orders. I'm to help you mature into a great commander...and an even better king."

In the Michmash pass

Fewer than four hundred Philistines surrounded Achish in the pass leading up to the Michmash plateau. Standing there, on foot, sword drawn, Achish sent a powerful message to his infantry. If the prince faced the same fate as his foot soldiers, victory must be possible. The charioteers also drew courage from Achish's example. Understandable, since their weary horses provided only slightly greater mobility than a man on foot. The Hebrew advance had wavered noticeably at the appearance of Philistine chariots, but the effect seemed to be short-lived. The enemy regiment continued its relentless approach. Still, Achish thought Davon's efforts at intimidation were quite praiseworthy.

"My congratulations, Davon. A truly magnificent performance. The men will be rewarded. The survivors, anyway."

"We're lucky none of the horses collapsed limping down the slope. It would have spoiled the entire effect."

"Those Hebrews have no idea how exhausted our animals are. If they have the stones for a fight, Davon, send out all five squadrons. The mere sight of chariots in motion terrifies them."

"Maybe. I'll wager that's the same lot we faced at Geba. Raw, but tough."

"Well, it's too late to retreat."

"It's not too late for you, Achish."

"To what purpose?"

"You're heir to the throne. You must survive."

"No, Davon. Crowns never follow failure. Better to die here."

Achish's debate with Davon ceased when the Hebrew column unexpectedly ground to a halt. He assumed the Hebrews were preparing for a final charge, although they had chosen an odd location for it. The distance was still too great to Achish's thinking, and the ground ahead offered better footing. He saw runners heading out from the lead company, undoubtedly to pass on their commander's orders. Achish would have used trumpet calls. Their amateurish waste of precious daylight could only benefit the Philistines. Yet, what happened next made Achish's jaw drop.

"Davon! Are they turning around?"

"Doing it rather clumsily. But they're definitely retreating!"

"A trick?"

"I doubt it, Achish. It will be dark before they could regroup and attack."

"Somehow, defeat has spawned a victory."

"I believe that's what the Hebrews call a miracle."

"Perhaps, Davon, I owe their god a favor."

Chapter 31 - Sins of the Father and the Son

"What have you done?" asked Samuel.

Saul replied, "When I saw the men scattering and that you did not come at the appointed time, and that the Philistines were assembling at Michmash, I thought, 'I have not sought the LORD's favor.' So I felt compelled to offer the burnt offering."

"You have acted foolishly," Samuel said, "You have not kept the command the LORD your God gave you. If you had, He would have established your kingdom over Israel for all time. But now your kingdom will not endure. The LORD has sought out a man after his own heart and appointed him leader of His people, because you have not kept the LORD's command."

From the Book of I Samuel, Chapter 13, verses 11 to 14

On the Michmash Plateau

Achish pulled the woolen cloak tightly around his shoulders as he toured the camp with Davon. He hated how the oppressive heat of day gave way to the deep chill of night. His shivering soldiers were burning wood scraps, scrub brush and horse dung for warmth. Forced to leave their personal belongings behind, all lacked the comfort of Achish's luxurious cloak. He thought it good for common soldiers to see that their prince was a step above them. Achish observed one notable exception to the pervasive discomfort. Uruk lay bundled in thick blankets while snoring contentedly, unimpressed by Achish or anyone else. The flickering lamps of nearby Michmash beckoned seductively, but Achish chose not to quarter his troops there. The Hebrews were well known for their sneak attacks. It was imperative that his soldiers remain in the pass, enduring the night's cold, the day's heat and short rations until his father's vanguard arrived. So far, his men were holding up reasonably well, although the sergeants took roll every hour as a precaution against desertion. However, at the last campfire Achish overheard the words he dreaded most.

"Where are the gods-cursed reinforcements that *little bastard* promised?"

The question could have come from any of twenty men huddled together around the softly glowing flames. Achish sensed an outraged Davon preparing to surge forward, but he put out a hand to stay his commander. Instead, Achish stepped alone into the light where he could be seen clearly by every man present. Jaws dropped all around at the sight of the *little bastard*. Achish took stock of the upturned faces and recognized fear, not mutiny. He patiently allowed the tension around the fire to build, before pitching his voice low, as if sharing a great secret. Each soldier involuntarily leaned forward in anticipation.

"You know how kings are. They only move when it suits them."

A brawny sergeant cut loose a hearty belly laugh and, within seconds, his mirth infected the other shivering men. As Achish and Davon headed to their own sparse accommodations, they could hear the laughter spreading from campfire to campfire as the prince's jest was passed on. Davon shook his head at the commotion.

"You're a real piece of work, Achish."

"But am I a good commander?"

"Better than good. You're lucky."

"Even so, Davon; find out who made that *little bastard* remark. I want the insubordinate maggot squirming on a short stake by dawn."

One mile from the Michmash pass

Nathan was guided only by starlight as he trod up the hill from Migron with food for Jonathan. His prince was still gazing across the valley where the sky above Michmash reflected the glow from Philistine campfires. His friend had not stirred from that same patch of ground since calling off the Israelite attack a few hours before. Nathan eased down beside him and extended a wooden bowl of bread and dried meat until it touched Jonathan's elbow.

"You had no other choice, Jonathan."

"That still doesn't change the taste in my mouth."

"Then eat this. Probably won't taste any better, but at least it'll be different."

Nathan was relieved to hear a slight chuckle as his friend began chewing a few morsels from the offered bowl. Still, Jonathan never took his eyes off Michmash.

"Michmash is only a place, Jonathan."

"But it is a rather important place, Nathan."

"Karaz taught us that a commander must preserve his army."

"A better commander would have found a way to have both his army and the pass."

"And a worse commander would've lost both."

"I've been reliving the day, Nathan, trying to find where I went wrong."

"And here I was afraid you were drowning in self-pity. Well, I've made a few observations myself. Care to hear them?"

"As if saying no would stop you."

"The truth, Jonathan? Retaking Michmash was always a mirage. Our soldiers are unprepared to face chariots."

"If we got there first, the chariots wouldn't have mattered."

"You couldn't know that Michmash was being abandoned."

"I should've known something was amiss there."

"Saul made Abner the *Aluf*. He lost Michmash, Jonathan, not you."

"However, Karaz was deposed as *Aluf* because of me. And that, my Friend, is where your well-intentioned attempt to comfort me falls short."

Nathan found little comfort himself that night, and sunrise only brought more bad news from the west. A Philistine chariot corps had left Beth-horon. Its lead elements were expected at Michmash sometime in the afternoon. Yet these six hundred chariots were but the tide preceding a far greater flood. Each passing hour brought a new report of additional enemy columns on the road to Michmash. The Philistine Kingdoms of Gath, Gaza, Ashdod, Ashkelon and Ekron were on the march. Within a few days, the enemy presence in Michmash would number in the thousands. Given a week, it would be tens of thousands.

The news from the east proved to be even more disheartening to Nathan. It arrived that afternoon in the form of Judge Samuel. Only Samuel. No one else. Nathan and Jonathan strode out to meet the elderly judge, but their greetings were ignored as the man trudged past, his eyes fixed on the ground before him. Nathan observed many Israelite soldiers anxiously awaiting a word of encouragement as the solitary figure drifted through their rough encampment. Nervous murmuring arose in the wake of Samuel's silent passage into the village. Nathan could actually hear the apprehension spreading throughout the camp. A judge was the face of God to Israelites. If Samuel was displeased, then God was displeased. Nathan thought nothing could damage the morale of the regiment more. Unfortunately, Nathan soon discovered he was mistaken.

Saul, Abner and six hundred soldiers arrived from Gilgal three hours after Samuel. Nathan's suspicions were aroused when the newcomers camped a further two miles away, near Saul's home outside Gibeah. Nathan recognized this as a deliberate attempt to keep Abner's men from talking to Jonathan's regiment. Nathan sought out his friend for some answers but learned that Jonathan was in a meeting with his father. He quickly found Saul's hastily erected tent, but two soldiers barred his entrance. Nathan was about to inflict some serious bruises when he felt a strong grip on his shoulder. He turned to face a smirking Abner.

"Special council meeting, Nathan. Royal family only."

"I attended Saul's councils before you ever did, Abner."

"The rules have changed."

"Is Jonathan in there?"

"Yes."

"Then he needs me. I'm his second-in command."

"And I am the *Aluf*, Boy. That makes me your superior."

"Abner, you will never be my superior."

"Mocking me gets you nowhere, Nathan. Things are different now. So unless you plan to defy the king's orders, behave yourself."

The determined expressions of the guards finally convinced Nathan to back down. Still, he knew it looked bad to submit to a bully. Out of the corner of his eye, Nathan spotted a padded stool just to the right of the closed tent flaps. His intuition said it belonged to Abner, since no common soldier would dare sit in the presence of the *Aluf*. Nathan casually stepped between the guards and picked the stool up, never taking his eyes from Abner's. The sudden curl of the older man's lip indicated Abner was indeed its owner. Planting the stool just five paces in front of the royal tent, Nathan settled down to wait for Jonathan to emerge. He noticed a guard glaring at him with undisguised contempt. Nathan tilted his head to one side and locked onto the man's eyes with a menacing stare. The impudent guard dropped his gaze to the ground after only a few seconds.

"You seem distressed, Nathan. Can I be of service?"

The unexpected voice caused Nathan to twist around on his stool. He stared up into the benign and smiling face of Beker, the *Yameen*. Something about Beker's solicitous inquiry reminded Nathan of a shepherd trying to keep his sheep in line.

"Abner and his henchmen won't let me inside."

"Some sort of misunderstanding, I'm sure. The past few days have been most stressful for the king. He's merely trying to handle one problem at a time."

"And Jonathan is one of those problems?"

"A poor choice of words. The king is consulting with the prince."

"Saul used to value my advice too, Beker."

"The king is now responsible for an entire nation, not just his own household. However, Nathan, it is possible for you to have even more influence with Saul than before."

"Is that so?"

"A well-placed patron at Court can provide you with unlimited access to the king. You have great potential, Nathan. I would be honored to sponsor you."

"Is there a cost associated with your patronage, Beker?"

"Only to repay a favor with a favor."

Nathan masked his unease with a smile which matched Beker's own. Their conversation was quickly forgotten when sounds of angry shouting filtered out through the tent walls. Beker immediately rushed inside. Nathan was annoyed to see how the guards obligingly stepped aside for the *Yameen*. Apparently, Beker was now part of the *Royal Family* and he was not. The tent flaps abruptly parted, and Jonathan stalked out. Nathan fell in step with his friend, barely able to contain his curiosity until they were out of earshot.

"Trouble?"

"I have set events in motion that I never anticipated."

"Such as?"

"Samuel has turned against my father. Claims God has rejected him as king."

"Disturbing, but how can that be your fault?"

"Two days ago, some Philistine chariots appeared on the Plains of Gilgal. Probably that same lot we faced at Michmash. Thousands of my father's militia panicked and fled across the Jordan River. Some of the Royal Army went with them."

"I'm surprised Samuel didn't stop them, Jonathan."

"Samuel wasn't at Gilgal yet. Hundreds of men were fleeing by the hour, so my father decided to act. He offered sacrifices so his troops wouldn't think God had deserted them."

"Certainly Samuel would be the best choice, but one priest is as good as another."

"Nathan, there was no priest. My father made those offerings, even though it's specifically forbidden. A man usurps God's authority by acting as both king and priest."

"So who will replace Saul? You?"

"Not a chance according to Samuel. Apparently the LORD plans to start a new dynasty with someone else."

"Who? When?"

"Samuel didn't say."

"What will we tell your regiment?"

"I no longer have a regiment, Nathan. All soldiers are now under Abner."

"Abner can't handle that many men. Saul must give you another command out of necessity. When's the rest of the army due from Gilgal?"

"Those six hundred men my father brought today? That's all there is."

"But Saul had two thousand soldiers!"

"Not any more, Nathan. It's another addition to my list of sins."

"Quit whining, Jonathan. You can't take the blame for everything!"

"Who better? I lost an army, cost my father his crown and opened the front gate for the Philistines. For what? An insignificant little dung heap called Geba. No one else has caused so much damage, with so little effort."

"Bet you had some help."

"Meaning?"

"Our illustrious *Yameen*. Have you noticed how Beker prospers after each succeeding crisis? He now controls access to Saul, employs Abner as his lackey and isolates you from everyone."

"That would explain much, Nathan."

"There's more. Beker wants to be my friend."

"A friendly Beker is as absurd as a tame viper. It seems our good *Yameen* has won this particular battle. I can count on no one except you, Nathan, unless you've decided to accept Beker's offer."

"I wouldn't have told you about it if I had. Besides, we still have Karaz. Anyone here know what he's doing at Geba?"

"No one asked. For now, let them believe Karaz deserted us."

"Good thinking. A body of trained swordsmen could be quite useful later."

"Nathan, I want this clearly understood. There'll be no civil war. My goal is to save my father from those who would destroy him, be they Philistine or Israelite."

"Or even a judge?"

"Samuel is different. Openly defying a judge will tear the Nation apart. Trust me on this, Nathan. We must accept what Samuel says for now, even if it denies me a crown. Besides, God is merciful. Perhaps Samuel can intercede for my father."

"Fine, Jonathan, be an optimist. But in the meantime, what *will* we do?"

"Rather, what *can* we do? For now, the answer is *nothing*. So do whatever you wish tonight, my Friend. Worry for the both of us if you like. Me? I intend to find some wine and a bed."

"But it's not even dark yet."

"More time for the wine then."

Watching his disheartened prince stroll off, Nathan felt no desire for either wine or sleep. His ambitions depended on Jonathan's family retaining the throne. If their dynasty collapsed, so would his chance to punish the Philistines for his father's murder. He searched for a viable way out of his predicament without alienating Jonathan. Rebellion was not acceptable. Samuel was not to be challenged. Jonathan was powerless. Saul was inaccessible. Karaz was unavailable. Abner was Beker's tool. Nathan even considered feigning allegiance to Beker, but doubted he could fool the wily *Yameen*. Killing Philistines seemed easy in comparison. Whatever leadership arose from the ashes of Saul's dynasty would likely seek an accommodation with the Philistines. And Nathan would never be in an accommodating mood toward his mortal enemy.

The sound of men preparing their evening meals made Nathan aware of the lateness of the hour. His fruitless deliberations had left him with a rumbling belly. Nathan gathered bread and water from his tent and went in search of solitude. He found a cleft in a nearby ridge and contemplated the crimson and purple sunset. Nathan let his mind drift as he chewed the dry bread while softening it with sips of water. As his mind slowly went numb in the gathering twilight, a radical thought began to take shape.

The first oil lamps were being lit in the humble houses of Migron as Nathan went in search of the obstinate judge. He first sought directions from people heading home in the growing darkness. After several false leads, Nathan finally risked a few copper pieces to hire a scruffy beggar claiming to know where Samuel resided. Payment in advance, of course. His guide meandered through a few alleys before stopping at a dwelling so shabby that it lacked a door for its entrance. The interior was unlit and Nathan saw no signs of life within. He grabbed his so-called guide by the sleeve and vented his displeasure on the unfortunate soul.

"I paid you to take me to Samuel. Well, I don't see him! Do you see him?"

"Begging your pardon, young Master, but you asked where the judge stayed, not where he was."

"All right then, where *is* Samuel?"

"Don't know, Sir. He wanders about, but this is where he's been sleeping. At least it was last night."

Nathan grudgingly relaxed his grip. The beggar pulled free and scuttled off into the shadows, leaving Nathan to ponder his next move while gently fingering his dagger. In the dying light, he decided his best course was to wait inside the crumbling structure and hope for Samuel's return. Nathan halted at the entrance, allowing his eyes to adjust to the inner darkness. After a few steps, he stumbled over something. Nathan froze when his clatter was followed by faint sounds from the back of the house. He jerked the dagger from his belt when a disembodied voice reverberated off the walls.

"What do you want?"

"I seek Judge Samuel."

The ensuing silence was more unnerving to Nathan than any spoken threat. His ears strained to catch the sounds of an assailant creeping closer, but heard nothing. It dawned on Nathan that the stranger might be as unprepared for this encounter as he. The sound of metal striking flint helped Nathan gauge the other man's position. After several unsuccessful attempts, a lamp wick finally caught fire and dimly illuminated the entire room. A shadowy figure shuffled forward to set the oil lamp down on a battered table in the center of the room. Nathan instantly recognized a venerable voice.

"Well, young man, you've found me. Now what happens?"

"You're a difficult man to track down, your Judgeship."

"It'll be easier on us both if you simply call me Samuel, especially since you seem familiar to my eyes."

"I spent a night in your home at Ramah. With Saul."

"Ahhh! I remember now. You were the servant."

"And we spoke again at Mizpah. You asked me to help find Saul."

"Of course. Nathan, isn't it?"

"I'm honored you remember. You lit no lamps. Are you in hiding?"

"I thought it best not to alert people to my location. Especially Saul's men."

"Only Philistines and traitors should fear the king's men, Samuel."

"Fearing the LORD has cured me of fearing any man, my Son. You hold that blade like an expert. Is it for me?"

"That depends how our conversation goes."

"Then you have my full attention, Nathan."

"First, I'm here to ask...no, to demand you support Saul as king."

"Is that all? That's easy enough."

"Don't treat me as a fool."

"I always respect men with weapons, Nathan. The truth is I've loved Saul since God first brought him to me."

"Then prove it. Tell our people that Saul still enjoys God's favor."

"I can't do that. Not even to save myself."

"At least tell Saul privately that God has not rejected him."

"No, Nathan. That lie would be a more damaging than the other."

"You've already done worse than lie, Samuel. Because of you, our warriors flee before the Philistines."

"And how exactly did I accomplish this?"

"You made our king and our people lose heart."

"You haven't thought this through very well, have you, Nathan? Our soldiers didn't desert at Gilgal because they saw a few Philistine chariots. They fled because they saw Saul was afraid of them."

"You lie! Saul is the bravest man I know."

"You've been away from Court for a while. When Saul's rule was shaky, he eagerly sought God's guidance. But as his kingdom flourished, Saul turned to the counsel of men. Now, power substitutes for prayer. Leadership gives way to posturing. Desperation replaces courage. Saul has become a king who no longer trusts God."

"But you told Saul that another king would take his place."

"I merely reminded the king of what he already knew."

"Just who is this new king anyway?"

"I haven't the foggiest idea."

"I don't believe you, Samuel."

"Nathan, I'm not doing the one doing the choosing. I can't pull Saul off his throne because I never put him there in the first place. The LORD did. He will announce the new king when it suits Him."

"Granted, Saul overstepped his authority by offering sacrifices, but his punishment seems too great."

"Look at the other nations around Israel. It is only a small step from priest-king to god-king. One day Israel will have such a king. He could have been a descendent of Saul. But not anymore."

"Saul faced an emergency."

"Nathan, there will always be emergencies for a king. Understand; this is about much more than a burnt lamb carcass. It's about Saul's true character."

"But doesn't Saul deserves the opportunity to make things right?"

"The LORD *gave* Saul a chance to repent. Instead, Saul justified his rebellious behavior with excuses. He blamed me. He blamed the people. He even blamed the Philistines, as if those pagans are responsible for his behavior."

"What about Jonathan? He could replace Saul."

"There are many reasons why Jonathan cannot be king: pride... ambition...disobedience..."

"You're confusing him with his father, Samuel."

"I think not. Take his little adventure at Geba, for example. Once Jonathan was off on his own, he arrogantly disobeyed his orders. Disaster followed. No different than Saul at Gilgal."

"You're wrong, Samuel. Jonathan will take his father's mistakes to heart."

"No, Nathan, he would forget."

"So how long will Saul remain king?

"Could be days. Might be years. So, how is our discussion going, Nathan? I notice you haven't put away your blade."

"Not as I expected."

"Then allow me a question. Nathan, do you serve the LORD?"

"Of course! Everyone does."

"Then I find your interpretation of the sixth commandment to be most unusual."

"We're at war. *Thou shalt not kill* doesn't apply."

"Well before you slit my throat, Nathan, I ask two things of you. First, decide if you truly do serve the LORD."

"I already answered that."

"I mean to the point of setting aside your own desires in favor of God's."

"And the other?"

"Once you have settled the first issue, then decide if I am a traitor. If the answer is *yes*, then come back with your blade. I won't be hard to find."

"You might change your mind later."

"Nathan, you are either God's chosen instrument for my death, or you aren't. Running would be pointless."

"I'll agree, Samuel, provided you answer, I mean really answer, one final question. Why would the LORD take the kingdom away from Saul, and then allow him to keep it?"

"Oh that's an easy one. God's not being merciful to Saul. He's punishing Israel."

On the Michmash Plateau

Achish smiled broadly while surveying the burgeoning Philistine encampment at Michmash. The recent transformation of the plateau was truly amazing. Only a few days before, he and a few hundred exhausted soldiers had won the race to Michmash, driven off its defenders and stared down a much larger Hebrew relief force. At stake was mastery of Israel's central highlands, upon which the fate of his father's entire campaign depended. Achish had intimidated the Hebrew army by shuffling his meager forces around to create the illusion of an immense Philistine presence. Achish had run out of tricks when Gath's chariot corps finally appeared, vanguard of the largest Philistine military expedition ever assembled. The road from Beth-horon became a Philistine river of chariots, infantry, supply wagons and camp followers. Units from Gath were followed by Philistine regiments from Gaza, Ashdod, Ashkelon and Ekron. Blood was nearly shed after some men from Ekron urinated in a well claimed by Ashdod. Of course, Achish managed to stake out the best sites for his father's troops. More importantly, he ensured Gath's soldiers were camped astride the road leading off the plateau and back to Philistia. This subtle tactic ensured no one went home without King Maoch's permission. For now, an uneasy truce existed between the rival Philistine armies. Achish knew the best way to divert soldiers from mischief was to keep them busy and well-fed. He listened to the sound of hundreds of bakers and butchers preparing breakfast for their comrades who would spend the day digging and building. Some other distraction would be required once their encampment was finished. Fortunately, the time for battle was near.

The presence of bodyguards from each of the Philistine cities indicated a meeting was taking place in King Maoch's tent. The gathering was likely restricted to the five kings and their top generals. Achish ached to be part of this obvious strategy session, until he realized how to turn the situation to his advantage. Achish might not have been invited, but then again, he had not been told to stay away either. The prince would simply show up at his father's tent. It would be instructive to see if anyone had the stones to ask the son of the Supreme Commander to leave.

Achish ignored the bodyguards as he confidently strolled toward the closed entrance until one of his father's guards intercepted him. The prince raised a quizzical eyebrow and stared evenly into the Gath soldier's eyes. The guard's jaw opened and closed twice before the man quietly stepped aside. The tent fell silent when Achish pulled open the flap. He moved a chair to his father's side and sat before any of the bewildered audience could utter a word. As he anticipated, all five Philistine kings were present, accompanied by a military aide. Achish was not at all surprised to see his father was attended by Uruk. This merely confirmed his suspicion that the commoner was much more than a mere scout. The kings from Ashdod, Ashkelon and Ekron seemed inclined to allow the Supreme Commander's Heir to participate. Only Kaftor of Gaza appeared annoyed, but voiced no objection. Achish thought he detected a glint of pride in his father's eye as Maoch resumed speaking.

"As I was saying, we can field a vast horde of infantry and chariots by the thousands. But they are useless unless we find the Hebrew army!"

"So how did you manage *to lose them*, Maoch?"

"Uruk, please *enlighten* Kaftor."

"Certainly, my King. We haven't lost anything. The original Hebrew regiment is still south of us. However, the rest of their army has yet to make an appearance."

"You mean the Hebrew king has eluded you."

"I mean there are two possibilities, King Kaftor. One is that the Hebrew king has cleverly dispersed his soldiers to lure us into an ambush."

"And the other?"

"That he has no army."

"You are merely informing us of your ignorance, Uruk!"

"I am not finished. The next step is to determine which one is correct."

"Do you have a plan, Uruk? Apart from walking into an ambush or hiding from a non-existent army."

"I have hired a company of Judean mercenaries. They'll have a better chance of finding the Hebrews than any of us."

"And betray us to their brethren."

"They've served me well before. While my Judeans hunt to the south, raiding parties will ravage Hebrew towns to the north, east and west. We'll flush the Hebrew army out into the open and destroy it."

"Suppose the Hebrews decide to wait us out, Uruk?"

"The Hebrew king must fight or be overthrown by his own people. Once he has committed to battle, we will corner his army with our infantry and slaughter it with our chariots."

"Before I approve anything, Uruk, you must show..."

"I have *already* approved his plan, Kaftor, as Supreme Commander."

"Then why bring us here today?"

"Each of the five kingdoms should be equally represented in the three raiding parties."

"I disagree. It's a Gath plan; Gath should bear the risk. Or is your courage lacking, Maoch?"

Achish recognized the dark look which swept over his father's face. Kaftor's infamous guile had put Maoch in a killing mood. If the King of Gaza could not be the Supreme Commander, he would incite an incident which would rupture the fragile Philistine coalition. Somehow, his father's burning rage must be cooled. Then Achish watched in amazement as Uruk reached over and gently laid his hand on Maoch's knee. The King of Gath met Uruk's eyes for a few tense seconds, before calmly nodding. After the dangerous moment passed, Maoch responded to Kaftor's challenge.

"Then I propose that Gaza, Ashdod, Ashkelon and Ekron provide equal numbers of infantry for the raiding parties, but Gath will provide all the chariots. Will that set everyone's mind at ease?"

The Kings of Ashdod, Ashkelon and Ekron readily gave their assent, but this display of cordiality did not deceive Achish. The three Philistine monarchs were content to allow Gaza to be the counterweight to Gath. It cost them nothing, and they could still pounce on whichever kingdom proved to be the weaker. Kaftor merely shrugged in resignation. Achish's heart skipped a beat when Maoch unexpectedly seized his collar bone in a bear-like grip.

"Achish drove off an entire Hebrew regiment with only a handful of men. There's no one better to command the raiding parties. Let's eat!"

Maoch's servants immediately began streaming into the tent, bearing all manner of delicacies and drinks. Any disagreement with Achish's hasty promotion was lost in the ensuing commotion. All the kings and generals, except Kaftor, were soon distracted by Maoch's alluring maidservants. However, Kaftor's funk quickly disappeared as he joined in the revelry. Achish participated half-heartedly, his mind already churning through strategies for the raids. When Uruk departed a few hours later, Achish excused himself to follow.

"Bedtime already, old man?"

"Yes, but someone is already warming my bed for me. I'm not that old."

"Seriously, Uruk, how did you gain my father's trust?"

"Ahhh...that's a secret. However, I'll tell you this much, Achish. Know that lower, front tooth Maoch is missing?

"Yes."

"I was the one who knocked it out."

"You should have died for that!"

"That's *exactly* what your father said. I replied that he *needed* someone who could knock him on his ass. Been with him ever since."

"What do you do for my father, Uruk?"

"Most men tell Maoch what he wants to hear. I tell him what he needs to hear."

"Does he always heed what you say?"

"Of course not, he's a king after all! But he listened today. That's how we duped Kaftor."

"But my father made concessions to Kaftor."

"Dog vomit! We expected Kaftor to raise hell, so Maoch suckered him into accepting Gath's chariots for the raiding parties."

"So, my father actually *wanted* his chariots in the field."

"Yes, Achish, but, even more, he wanted all his *infantry* in camp. Your so-called concessions give Maoch an edge over any of the other Philistine kings."

"Of course! None of the raiders will dare argue with me, not when Gath's chariots can run circles around them."

"The situation in Michmash will be even better. The other kings will each give up an infantry regiment for the raids. Maoch will have the single largest fighting force in camp."

"Except for the other cities' chariots."

"Chariots are open field weapons, Achish, useless in an encampment. Let the other four kings believe their chariots are safe and sound here. They're really under Maoch's thumb."

"It seems, Uruk, that we must subdue our Philistine brothers before we can defeat the Hebrews."

"It's always been that way. Don't worry. Your father will get exactly when he wants."

"Provided I handle the raiding parties properly."

"Raiding's easy, Achish. Just let your men have fun. The louder the Hebrews howl, the sooner their king will fight. But with three raiding parties, you'll need two other commanders."

"My man Davon is good with both chariots and infantry."

"That's one."

"What about that lieutenant who chased the Hebrews all the way to Gilgal with his chariot squadron? He's earned a promotion."

"I like him, Achish. You need a good head basher."

"I better round them up if I want to leave tomorrow."

"Why not today?"

"Why not?"

Chapter 32 - The Raid

So, on the day of battle, not a soldier with Saul and Jonathan had a sword or spear in his hand; only Saul and his son Jonathan had them. Now a detachment of Philistines had gone out to the pass at Michmash. Jonathan, son of Saul, said to his young armor-bearer, "Let's go over to the Philistine outpost on the other side". But Jonathan did not tell his father, the king.

From the Book of I Samuel, Chapter 13, verses 22 and 23 and Chapter 14, verse 1

The Israelite camp opposite the Michmash pass

Nathan's nightmare was back with a vengeance. His father. The forge. His mother and sister. The Philistine soldier. Every lurid detail was louder, bolder and bloodier than ever. The only constant was Nathan's inability to warn Jotham before the Philistine sword disemboweled his father. Nathan witnessed even greater anger than ever raging in Jotham's eyes as the man once more bled out. But at this fateful moment in the dream, Nathan experienced a violent shaking and heard a new voice.

"Nathan! NA-THAN!"

Slowly, Nathan's foggy mind began to churn. He became aware of the coarse blanket separating his back from the rough ground. Then Nathan roused from his heavy slumber when the frantic shaking resumed. As his eyes adjusted to the dim starlight, Nathan recognized Jonathan's face a few inches away from his own. Nathan broke the prince's tight grip on his shoulders and sat up. He spat the dust from his mouth and rubbed his eyes before speaking.

"It's still dark, so we must really be in some deep muck. Good news always waits until dawn."

"Hush, Nathan! You'll wake the men."

"What men? They've all deserted...the smart ones, anyway."

"Your pessimism will be the death of you."

"I like my pessimism just the way it is, Jonathan. And what are you so cheery about all of a sudden?"

"A plan came to me last night, one that will change everything!"

"Last night your plans were limited to curling up with a jug of wine."

"I know how to recapture Michmash."

Even through the gloom, Nathan discerned his friend was excited rather than intoxicated. Normally, he could have humored a drunken Jonathan until the young man drifted off to sleep, his mad venture forgotten. However, reining in an enthusiastic and sober prince might be impossible. Nathan sighed wearily.

"Jonathan, we already considered rushing the pass. Our soldiers wouldn't even reach the plateau."

"Only if the Philistines see our men coming, Nathan. So we eliminate the lookouts first. Then we slaughter the

Philistines like Gideon's three hundred slaughtered the Midianites."

"That's *not* what Gideon did."

"The principle's still the same."

"Their lookouts will still spot us coming."

"Not if we follow the gorge running beneath the northernmost cliff."

"So we're at the base of the cliff. Then what?"

"We climb it, of course."

"Jonathan, the name of that cliff is *Bozez*. That means *slippery* in Canaanite!"

"The Philistines don't expect us to come over the cliffs, Nathan. But we must leave now."

"It's dark."

"*Make the night your ally.*"

"Don't you quote Karaz to me, Donkey Boy. You want to cross a valley, traverse a gorge, climb a cliff and fight a battle. In complete darkness."

"It's not that dark, Nathan."

"And where will you get your soldiers?"

"I already have enough."

"Did Saul give your regiment back to you?"

"No, but I need only two men."

The night breeze from the desert became bone-chilling at that moment. Nathan shivered as he pondered the implications of Jonathan's words. His friend understood Nathan's dumbfounded expression and continued.

"Anymore more than two men would be detected. It's simple. Find the outpost's blind spot. Scale the cliff. Slay a few Philistines. Then you go back and fetch my father's army."

"What about you?"

"Someone has to stay behind in case they change the watch."

"What if there are more than *a few* lookouts?"

"We'll think of something, Nathan."

"Is this your penance for Geba, Jonathan? Getting yourself killed?"

"I plan to pay for my mistakes by living, not dying. Look...if this turns out to be truly suicidal, I'll call it off."

"Just like that?"

"And I'll never ask you for another favor."

"You always say that, Jonathan, but you never mean it."

"I just might this time."

"Why waste my breath? We both know you're going and that I'm going with you."

"Your loyalty is touching."

"Forget loyalty. If you walk us into a trap, I'll kill you myself."

"Careful, Nathan, poets never praise a hero with a lousy attitude."

"Before anyone writes songs about this little stunt, Jonathan, he'll have to clean us both up."

At the base of the cliff named Bozez

It did not take long for Nathan to feel his pessimism was justified. Jonathan's goal to ascend *Bozez* in darkness had been too aggressive. The first hints of dawn appeared while they were still negotiating the rough floor of the gorge. When the top of *Bozez* came into view, it was illuminated by the bright morning sun. Nathan shot the prince a reproving glance.

"Sun's up, Jonathan. Now what?"

"We find where their blind spot begins."

"How?"

"Keep walking until the Philistines yell at us."

"I hate this idea already."

"If they chase us, we run away."

"It begins to sound better."

"If they order us to come up, then we will."

413

"But, it only gets worse."

"Nathan, if we are outnumbered, the Philistines will come down after us. So we leave."

"I like that part, but the rest reminds me of rotten fish."

"If there are only a few, they'll be afraid to leave the safety of their perch."

"But, Jonathan, they'll know we're here."

"And we'll know where they can't see us. We go back down the gorge a little way and start climbing. The Philistines will think they scared off a couple of timid shepherds. It's sound reasoning."

"No, it's mostly guessing."

"Nathan, you're right. This is my responsibility. I have the sword, after all. Stay here. I'll toss down three stones after I've killed the lookouts. Then fetch my father and his soldiers."

"And if there is no signal?"

"No signal means that I won't be coming back."

"You'll cut your chances in half by going alone."

"Sounds like you want to come along."

"How could I tell Saul that I abandoned his son?"

"I never doubted your courage, Nathan."

"Stop it. You treat me like one of your donkeys."

"Well, it works, doesn't it?"

A sly wink from Jonathan caused Nathan to grin. He fell into step behind his prince without a word. Nathan never could resist the charms of his friend, even when death beckoned.

The Philistine lookout post atop the cliff named Bozez

Kelon was in a foul mood as the end of his four hour shift neared. Two Philistine lookouts were always posted at the top of *Bozez*, but after dark, one kept watch while the other enjoyed a nap. However, last night's rotation had paired Kelon with his squad leader, Dag. Kelon knew better than to ask the dour sergeant if he could sleep on duty. As Kelon stood at the cliff's edge, a movement directly below caught his eye.

"Dag! Something moved down there."

The sergeant jogged over from the rock where both men had propped their shields. They were patrolling along an open area on the cliff summit which gave a clear view for many miles. Like Kelon, Dag wore a helmet, mail armor and a sheathed sword while carrying a javelin. He looked down the slope where his soldier was pointing.

"See? Two men in the gorge. Should we tell the lieutenant?"

"No, I can handle this."

Leaning over as far as possible, Dag spoke in a booming voice.

"Look! The Hebrews have finally crawled out of their holes!"

Both men stopped and looked straight up at Dag. Surprisingly, they seemed to be waiting. After cursing their stupidity, Dag shouted again.

"What? You want something? Come up here, and I'll show you something!"

Both Hebrews immediately scampered back through the gorge the way they came. Dag smiled in satisfaction.

"Wasn't that easy? If they were spies, they learned nothing. Probably just bait for an ambush."

"Doesn't the lieutenant want prisoners for questioning?"

Kelon wilted under the withering look from the grizzled veteran. Dag could only shake his head at the inexperienced conscript. Their lieutenant would be annoyed to be awakened at this hour, especially since the man was not sleeping alone. That annoyance would turn to fury if the officer tramped out here only to find the prey had already fled. No, Dag would later report the sighting of two men who fled before any action could be taken. Dag chuckled to himself when he realized this was the best decision for everyone...even the two Hebrews.

At the base of the cliff named Bozez

Nathan jogged down the gorge after Jonathan until the summit of *Bozez* was no longer visible. He heard nothing except a morning breeze rustling the thorny brush. No calls for surrender. No sign of pursuit. Jonathan faced the slope and traced out a possible ascent with his finger. Nathan shrugged in response. Jonathan's choice was the best of a number of bad options. They studied the scattered crevices and sparse vegetation dotting the steep slope. Then Jonathan grabbed hold of a thorny bush and pulled himself upward using feet and knees. Nathan gripped a rocky outcropping with his toes and began his own climb. He made steady progress beside Jonathan; their presence betrayed only by some sliding gravel. Multiple abrasions caused Nathan to whisper through clenched teeth.

"So, Jonathan, how did you know what the Philistines would do?"

"It came to me in a dream."

"Why do I ask you questions? Your answers only upset me."

"Relax, Nathan. If I'm wrong, I'll apologize."

"You admit to being wrong? Hearing that would almost be worth dying."

The midmorning sun blazed over the pass by the time Nathan and Jonathan slithered onto the summit of *Bozez*. A bruised and bleeding Nathan half expected a band of grinning Philistines to be waiting. However, the same thorns which provided the two Israelites with so much misery also discouraged sentries from patrolling here. Both men breathed heavily and listened intently. The sound of voices soon gave Nathan a rough idea of their enemy's location. Nathan followed Jonathan to a spot where less than five feet of foliage separated them from a pair of Philistines. The two friends exchanged hand signals before Jonathan crept to the left while Nathan moved right. After allowing the prince sufficient time to get in position,

Nathan grabbed hold of two thorn bushes and shook them vigorously.

Dag was not alarmed by the rustling brush since wild goats often grazed on the sparse vegetation. Looking forward to the prospect of fresh meat, the Philistine aimed his javelin towards the movement on his left. Dag was therefore unprepared for a man bursting from the brush directly ahead. The Philistine lunged forward to skewer the Hebrew, but felt the javelin tip deflected by the man's sword. The sword blade traveled up the shaft, forcing Dag to drop his javelin as the Hebrew plowed into him at full speed. The Philistine landed flat on his back with the weight of the Hebrew crushing his lungs. The tip of the Hebrew's sword slipped between two of the small plates in Dag's mail armor. The last thing the Philistine felt was cold iron sliding under his breastbone and into his heart.

Nathan broke cover when the other Philistine shouted an alarm and raced to rescue his comrade from Jonathan. The man skidded to a stop at the sight of Nathan rushing forward with Karaz's rock encrusted club. As the second Philistine raised his javelin, Nathan flung the club at his opponent's head while in full stride. The Philistine easily dodged Nathan's weapon, but at the cost of lowering his own. This small disruption allowed Nathan to grab the javelin by the shaft and pull it from the Philistine's hand. While his opponent attempted to draw sword, Nathan pulled a small, bronze dagger from his belt and grappled with the man. As he worked his way around in back of the Philistine, Nathan remembered how butchers and priests could slay a huge bull. Nathan hooked his left arm around the Philistine's throat and slashed that same blood vessel with his dagger. The wounded Philistine suddenly kicked backwards with unexpected force, even though blood spurted from his neck with every heartbeat. Nathan landed on his own back, dazed by the impact, but still holding on until the quivering body lay still. A few seconds later, he looked up into the concerned face of Jonathan.

"What a mess! How much blood is yours?"

"None, but if you see any urine, it's mine."

"Honestly, Nathan, you can be such a baby."

"Said the man with the sword."

Nathan rolled the dead man off his chest and sat up. Grinning, Jonathan extended a blood covered hand and pulled him to his feet. The prince picked up the Philistine's sword and handed it to Nathan.

"Here. It's one less thing for you to whine about."

Both men's heads snapped around at the sound of shouting beyond the surrounding thorn bushes. Nathan surmised that the sentry's call for help had been heard in the Philistine camp. Nathan helped himself to his victim's shield and sword belt while Jonathan recovered the other Philistine shield. The young prince then hurried over to a break in the brush with Nathan close on his heels. They peered down a narrow trail winding through the thorn bushes, barely wide enough for one man. The element of surprise was lost, but Nathan knew they had to press on.

The Philistine camp overlooking the Michmash pass

After hearing the shout of alarm, Sergeant Sharuh called out, but was answered only with silence. The Philistine lookout post was one hundred yards from his platoon's camp, but the sergeant's view was limited to twenty yards by a barrier of man-high thorn bushes. Sharuh had wanted to clear out everything between camp and the cliff but was overruled by his lieutenant. The officer was decent enough on the battlefield, but the man was far too lax with camp security for his taste. The lieutenant's worst mistake, in Sharuh's opinion, was allowing his soldiers to sleep until midday. It was a lazy attempt to relieve the boredom of guarding this remote windswept rock. The officer used wine to dull his mind and women to warm his bed, habits gladly emulated by his platoon. The distress in Kelon's voice had been obvious, but Sharuh was uncertain what it signified. He was confident that the veteran sergeant Dag would report anything important. To be safe, he sent off the two men scheduled for the next watch. After both soldiers disappeared down the cliff trail, Sharuh still felt uneasy. He summoned the three sentries currently watching the camp and also ordered them to the lookout post. If no word was forthcoming, Sharuh would see for himself. Since most of the platoon was still sleeping, Sharuh roused another sergeant to turn out a squad of the least hung-over men.

Five hundred paces from the Philistine camp overlooking the Michmash pass

Nathan shadowed Jonathan down the trail that presumably led to the Philistine camp. They made slow, deliberate progress to avoid stumbling into an ambush. After a few minutes, Nathan heard voices approaching. He and

Jonathan backtracked to a bend in the trail offering concealment. Nathan peered out from the left side of the trail where he could see Jonathan crouching under a thorn bush ten paces ahead on the right side. Two Philistines soon appeared walking single file. Both men were armed similarly to the two lookouts, but with shields on their backs. As the first soldier passed by, Jonathan slashed the man's left ankle with his sword. The crippled Philistine collapsed on his back when the leg could no longer support him. Nathan burst from cover, leaped on the howling man and plunged his new sword into Philistine's exposed throat. Meanwhile, Jonathan was protecting Nathan's back. The other Philistine apparently thought he faced only one Israelite and failed to notice the prince rising up from the brush. Swinging his shield, Jonathan knocked the javelin from his foe's hands before chopping into the man's neck with his sword. The stunned Philistine fell prostrate on the ground, but crawled back up on his knees as blood poured from the awful wound. Jonathan pulled back his sword and promptly decapitated the man.

For a brief moment, both young Israelites stared at each other while breathing heavily. New voices immediately drove the fatigue from Nathan. When Jonathan pulled one Philistine's body under a thorn bush, Nathan swiftly dragged the other out of sight as well. The two Israelites resumed their hiding places. This time Nathan spied three Philistines as they came around the narrow bend in the trail, casually carrying their javelins. The lead Philistine noticed one of the hidden bodies just as he passed it. He immediately reversed his course and caused all three to bunch together. The other two Philistines knelt down to examine their dead comrade while the leader stood over them, with his back to the Israelites. Nathan felt his muscles tighten with excitement. His mentor, Karaz, could not have laid a better ambush. He timed his move with Jonathan's.

The Philistine camp overlooking the Michmash pass

Plest was in a sour mood this morning as he sat naked on his bedding. First, he had to listening to a babbling Philistine sergeant named Kallid. Also, a vein on the side of his head throbbed from too much cheap wine and sleazy women. The lieutenant from Gath was still trying to determine whom he had riled to earn such a rotten assignment. It was not so much the desolation of his rocky outpost overlooking the pass, as it was being removed from the few things which made campaigning endurable. The main Philistine encampment was well served by hordes of camp followers. These auxiliaries were not affiliated with any army, yet no Philistine commander dared take the field without them. Carpenters, blacksmiths and other artisans kept the soldiers' equipment in good repair. Those who dealt in wine, harlots and other diversions kept the soldiers in good spirits. Plest's predicament was that whenever he sought recreation, the best of everything was already taken. He just now realized last night's harlot had already slunk away. Ugly even in the dark, the woman had been a strictly *take it or leave it* proposition. More humiliating, he had been forced to pay in advance.

Plest grit his teeth and returned his focus to Kallid. The man was the least competent sergeant in his platoon, and Plest hoped to eventually palm the oaf off on some unsuspecting officer. It seemed that the platoon's senior sergeant, Sharuh, had ordered Kallid to assemble a squad to investigate some disturbance. Kallid rounded up the few men sober enough for duty and sent them off one or two at a time after Sharuh. Plest finally held up his hand to stop Kallid's rambling.

"So far, Sergeant, I have heard nothing that requires my attention."

"I just thought you should know, Sir."

"Well, if this was so important, why did Sharuh not tell me himself?"

"He thought you needed your sleep, Sir."

"So, Kallid, you woke me to tell me I need sleep?"

"But Sharuh hasn't come back yet, Sir."

"The man has two full squads with him. Now go away, Kallid, until you have some real news."

The sergeant's clumsy exit would have amused Plest at other times. He vowed Kallid's next assignment would be tending pigs. Plest sighed, crawled back in his bunk and tried to dream of being anywhere else but here.

Fifty paces from the Philistine camp overlooking the Michmash pass

Nathan was covered in blood, but thankfully little of it was his own. He and Jonathan had been engaged in nearly uninterrupted combat since scaling the cliff face of *Bozez*. Nathan knew they survived largely because the Philistines had come against them piecemeal. Such amateurish tactics allowed Jonathan to knock down their foes one at a time for Nathan to finish off. Now he paused beside Jonathan to peer from the thorn bushes at a rudimentary campsite. Nathan counted two tents, several smoldering cook fires and a handful of men lounging under the open sky. Jonathan took the furthest Philistine tent for himself and assigned the other to Nathan. They crept forward so that they were shielded from the rest of the camp.

Upon reaching his tent, Nathan clutched the fabric while carefully drawing his sword tip upward to split a seam from bottom to top. Nathan parted the opening just enough to see a lone man face lying face down. Needing to kill swiftly and silently, he cursed the clattering metal objects sent flying as he stumbled into the tent. The helpless Philistine cast a forlorn glance at his stacked weapons before screaming and fleeing outside. Nathan happened to gaze into a hanging bronze mirror and saw a blood covered demon staring back. He hurriedly threw back the tent flap in pursuit. Amazingly, the commotion had failed to rouse the camp. The sight of their naked commander sprinting downhill merely elicited ribald laughter from the score of Philistines lazing about the camp. Nathan saw only a single soldier who appeared armed. The rest were in various stages of inebriation and seemed unaware of Nathan. He quickly spotted Jonathan, but could only gaze in horror at what happened next.

The young prince burst howling from the other tent and leaped upon the armed Philistine. The startled man could not even draw his sword before Jonathan drove him face first into the dirt. Instead of fighting, the Philistine tried to crawl away as Jonathan straddled his back and hacked away. Philistine armor provided some protection, but the man quickly collapsed in a pool of blood. Nathan watched transfixed until the death of their comrade spurred the other Philistines into action. Many began staggering drunkenly toward Michmash, but those nearest Nathan scrambled after weapons. The only factor in Nathan's favor was that the men were all facing Jonathan. The closest Philistine clutched a sword while searching for a shield. Nathan chopped the unsuspecting man on the back of the neck and shouldered him to the ground. Ignoring the spurting blood, Nathan advanced on another soldier struggling to pull a javelin from his kit. The Philistine spotted Nathan and immediately tugged the spearhead free. However, Nathan easily parried the javelin aside before thrusting his blade under his foe's ribs. His final opponent was the easiest. The intoxicated Philistine had foolishly tried to don his armor, but succeeded only in entangling his right arm. After dispatching the man with a single blow, Nathan saw that Jonathan was the only other man standing in camp. Nathan counted four bodies around Jonathan and a dozen Philistines stumbling toward Michmash. The prince turned toward Nathan and croaked a single word.

"Water!"

A dazed Nathan nodded back and dropped his weapons in exhaustion. He began throwing aside blankets and sacks before uncovering a wine skin. He lifted the bag over his head and greedily gulped its contents, before spitting out the vile liquid. Nathan wondered how desperate a man must be to drink something more vinegar than wine. Jonathan called out again.

"Find anything?"

"Just some horse piss."

"See what's in the cart."

The sight of clay pots in the cart encouraged Nathan. He hefted one of the jars, heard liquid swirling inside and gulped a handful of sweet water.

"Found it!"

Nathan lifted the jar over his head and let a cool stream of water flow down his throat. His thirst satisfied, Nathan tilted his head forward, allowing the water to soak his hair and clothing. A rattling of the cart indicated that Jonathan had found his own jar. Tossing the empty vessel aside, Nathan hooked his arms over the side of the cart and leaned against it. He was too weary to even pull himself up. After a moment, Nathan began chuckling. He saw Jonathan cast a wary look in his direction.

"Have I missed something funny?"

"No, Jonathan. It's just, well...I'm too tired to sit down!"

It took Jonathan a few seconds to realize that he was hanging onto the cart the same as Nathan. The two friends stared blankly at each other before spontaneously bursting into laughter. Little sound came from their raw throats, but the cart trembled from the heaving of their chests. Nathan spoke once he could stop laughing.

"So much for surprise."

"It's not all gone, Nathan. The Philistines may know Israelites are up here, but not how many."

"They know there are only two of us."

"They know there are *at least* two of us."

"Still, a Philistine regiment will be here within the hour."

"Not if they think we outnumber them."

"So, Donkey Boy, how do you make two men look like an army?"

"We'll start by setting this camp ablaze. The smoke will look like the work of a large raiding party and get my father's attention."

"And after that?"

"We head for Michmash and cause some mischief."

"Just the two of us."

"Well, Gideon only had..."

"It is *not* the same, Jonathan! Make your plan and I'll follow it. Just quit bringing up Gideon."

They decided to torch both tents and toss in anything that would burn. Jonathan gathered hot coals from a cook fire while Nathan searched the supply tent for lamp oil. He found several full jugs and began splashing oil around the tent's interior. Nathan was about to soak down the other tent when a bright flash of metal caught his eye. He pulled away some blankets to reveal not one, but two shiny bronze objects. Nathan briefly admired their cunning craftsmanship, but set them aside since they were not weapons. He was about to continue with his mayhem when a faint memory suddenly blossomed into an idea. Nathan scrambled out of the tent clutching both bronze items while yelling for his friend.

"You want mischief, Jonathan? I give you mischief!"

Chapter 33 - The Slaughter

Jonathan said to his young armor-bearer, "Perhaps the LORD will act on our behalf. Nothing can hinder the LORD from saving us, whether we are many or just a few". His armor-bearer said, "I am with you heart and soul". So Jonathan climbed up on his hands and knees, with his armor-bearer right behind him. The Philistines fell before Jonathan while his armor-bearer followed behind and finished them off. In that first attack, they killed about twenty men in a small area. Then panic struck the entire Philistine army and the ground shook. It was a panic sent by God.

From the Book of I Samuel, Chapter 14, verses 6, 7, 13, 14 and 15

The main Philistine camp on the Michmash plateau

Kaftor was hosting a midday meal for the King of Ashdod and the King of Ashkelon when his field commander entered the luxurious pavilion. The King of Ekron was not invited, lest the gathering appear to be a conspiracy against Maoch, King of Gath. Of course, everyone recognized that as Kaftor's true motive, but Philistine politics still demanded a certain amount of subtlety. The King of Gaza waved his general over and listened without expression to the whispered report. He then inconspicuously slipped away as beautiful maidens brought in the next course.

"Show me, General."

"There, my King. Smoke rises from a cliff overlooking the western pass."

"Who is up there?"

"A platoon from Gath keeps watch."

"Perhaps the fools started a brush fire."

"Then the smoke would be spreading, my King. No, it is the Gath camp which burns."

"Summon your staff, General. Quietly."

Kaftor ground his teeth at this unexpected turn of events. The Philistine encampment was still peaceful, but more and more soldiers were nervously watching the distant fire. Kaftor sensed a crisis in the making. If the fragile Philistine coalition fragmented, Kaftor must seize the initiative before anyone else did. Yet taking the wrong action could be as destructive to as doing nothing. Then a small voice in Kaftor's head laughed and said he was overthinking the problem. The King of Gaza studied the situation from different perspectives before hitting upon the answer. *In all this confusion, the truth could be whatever I say it is!* While Kaftor hatched his scheme, Gaza's military leaders scurried to the side of their king. The commanders of four infantry regiments, the chariot corps and assorted mercenary units anxiously waited for orders. One Gaza regiment was off raiding Hebrew villages, but Kaftor assumed it could take care of itself.

"Prepare our infantry to move within the hour. No trumpets. No drums. The other kings must suspect *nothing*. Carry weapons, one day's food and water. Leave everything else."

"And the chariots, my King?"

Kaftor briefly pondered the general's question. Each city had separate campsites for its foot soldiers, but the Philistine horses all shared a common laager to simplify their feeding and watering.

"Bring only my personal chariot and escort squadron. Instruct our charioteers to stand by their horses. When the time comes to leave, detach one infantry regiment to clear a path for our chariots."

"Where are we going, my King?"

"All in good time, General. Now move."

Tension in the camp had risen steadily during Kaftor's impromptu conference. Kaftor was pleased; the confusion would mask the preparations of his infantry. As his officers dashed off, Kaftor detained Malia, commander of the mercenaries from Crete. Since the Cretans numbered fewer than three hundred, the man's self-chosen rank of general was rather pretentious. However, they were sufficient for Kaftor's scheme.

"Treason abounds, General. Soldiers from Gath will attack us."

"Our contract doesn't cover civil war, my Lord. That's extra."

"What a surprise. Say one tenth more? I want your troops to draw first blood from our Gath brethren. My soldiers can take it from there."

"That costs a lot extra."

"Another tenth then. "

"My men may want more."

"Please. We both know they will never see a shekel of it. Oh, and that *special job* we discussed? Do it now."

Kaftor returned to his pavilion to set the next phase of his scheme in motion. The feast was so raucous that he wondered if the other kings had even missed him. They had, of course.

"Where have you been, Kaftor?

"Yes, Kaftor, the host should never skip out on his own party."

"The Hebrews have captured the pass."

"That's a sick joke, Kaftor, even for a bastard like you."

"The Hebrews have lit a signal fire as proof of their possession. See for yourselves."

The Kings of Ashdod and Ashkelon ceased feigning drunkenness and followed Kaftor outside. By this time the smoke was so black that it was impossible to miss. Kaftor smiled as his fellow rulers swallowed the bait without question.

"We must retake the pass!"

"Yes, Kaftor, it's our only road home!"

"Impossible, my Friends."

"Why?"

"Maoch's soldiers will block our way."

"Why would they do that?"

"For the same reason his men allowed the Hebrews to enter the pass. It is why Maoch arranged for Gath troops to hold all the vital positions."

"Why would Maoch's men burn their own camp?"

"A message to the Hebrews: *The front gate is open!*"

"You're guessing, Kaftor."

"Open your eyes. Gath is in league with *the Hebrew king*!"

"Ridiculous! The Hebrews attacked a Gath garrison. That's why we are here."

"Don't you see? Maoch and the Hebrew king arranged a meaningless battle over an insignificant village with few losses to either side. Geba was *a ruse* to draw all of Philistia into a war under Gath's leadership."

"It's still groundless speculation, Kaftor."

"You want proof? Consider how Gath captured Michmash. The Hebrews occupied one of the greatest strongholds in Canaan. Yet, when Maoch's son approached with a single company of chariots, *the entire Hebrew army simply walked away!*"

"It doesn't matter how we got Michmash..."

"What matters is that we have been lured into a trap! The Hebrews are coming over the cliffs. Gath's army sits astride our only escape route. One is the hammer. The other is the anvil. I do not intend to remain in the middle."

"We should confront Maoch now, Kaftor. All of us."

"Do as you wish. Ignore my advice. Stay here and enjoy the fire. Leave the protection of your troops and visit the King of Gath in his tent. Ask Maoch if he is a *traitor*. I'm sure he will allow you to leave in peace."

Kaftor could almost hear the minds of the other two kings churning. Envisioning the future if their armies were destroyed. Considering how Gath and the Hebrews might divide up their realms. Fretting over the fate of their families. The King of Ashkelon slipped out of the pavilion first, followed seconds later by the King of Ashdod. Kaftor assumed they would both head for the King of Ekron. It mattered not a whit whether his tale of Maoch's treachery was true. *He would make it true.* Ultimately the Kings of Ashdod, Ashkelon and Ekron would accept Kaftor's truth for one simple reason. Given the chance, each would have made a similar bargain with the Hebrews. Israel...Philistia...Egypt...the pieces of Kaftor's plot were coming together nicely. The Philistine coalition was descending into chaos, but Gaza should emerge from it as the dominant kingdom. Pharaoh would have no choice but to accept Gaza's hegemony in Canaan. Kaftor had only to wait for his arrangement with the Cretans to bear fruit.

The King of Gath's tent on the Michmash plateau

"Maoch! Maoch! Wake up, you drunken dog!"

The King of Gath rolled over and surveyed his rumpled bed. It had been well populated last night, but now he seemed to be its only occupant. His eyes gradually focused on the rude figure hovering over his face. It was Uruk – his veteran scout, personal spy, trusted advisor and the best judge of wine in Philistia. No one else dared treat a king so roughly. Maoch would have strangled Uruk with his bare hands long ago, if only the man were not so damned useful.

"Too early, Uruk. Go away."

"It's midday. There's trouble."

"You handle it."

"The whole army is on the verge of panic. They need you."

"I'm drunk!"

"You can be drunk later, Maoch. Now get off your ass!"

"All right. I'm standing. Happy? Now what's the fuss?"

"There's smoke over the pass."

"You woke me for that?"

"Apparently the Hebrews snuck up on the plateau somehow."

"Where? How many?"

"No one knows. Rumors are spreading like locust."

"And my brother kings will believe the worst of them. That's more dangerous than the Hebrews."

"You must calm them before they bolt with their soldiers, Maoch. Need help dressing?"

"No, Uruk, I can manage. Find out what's really happening."

After Uruk took his leave, Maoch staggered naked over to a wash basin and plunged his head into the cool water. He stood dripping for a moment as he sorted through jumbled details from the previous day. The other four Philistine kings had submitted to his strategy. His son, Achish, was given command of three raiding parties before anyone could protest. The raiders had departed last night. Maoch now possessed the largest infantry force in the Philistine camp while Achish dominated the countryside with his chariots. Pleased with Gath's good fortune, Maoch had celebrated hard, only to wake and find it all slipping away.

The clinking of mail armor caused Maoch to turn towards the tent entrance. Instead of his bodyguards, four foreign soldiers walked in. Their shields identified them as mercenaries from Crete; the colored strips of cloth tied to their helmets belonged to the King of Gaza. Maoch was about to protest when he noticed blood dripping from their blades. *So much for my guards.* The wine was instantly flushed from Maoch's body as his fighting instincts were aroused. Maoch glanced at his weapons and armor neatly hanging on their racks at the far side of the tent. They might as well be back in his palace for all the good they were now. Maoch dug in his toes and coiled his body before leaping upon his adversaries.

On the trail to the main Philistine camp on the Michmash plateau

Nathan joined Jonathan in crawling to a rocky outcropping which overlooked the Philistine encampment. His head turned when the prince suddenly snapped his fingers and pointed at the trail. Over a hundred men were approaching from the enemy camp. To Nathan's horror, Jonathan leaped up from their shelter and called out in a strong, commanding voice.

"I am Jonathan, son of King Saul, Prince of Israel."

Cursing his friend's rashness, Nathan gripped his weapons, rose up and glared down fiercely on scores of....Israelites! Their fellow countrymen appeared startled by the unexpected sight of two blood-soaked demons. A plaintive voice from the rear of the crowd finally broke the awkward silence.

"Oh, bloody hell! What do we do now?"

None of the anxious faces were familiar to Nathan. It slowly dawned on him that he and Jonathan now faced a greater danger than the Philistines posed. Spies had reported Israelites in the Philistine camp. Death was the prescribed penalty for such treason, and the testimony of two witnesses would condemn them all. Nathan wondered how long it would take the traitors to realize that only two murders would ensure their safety. He searched for an escape route as Jonathan addressed the nervous crowd.

"Well, well. Philistine collaborators. You folks have a serious problem."

Nathan sighed. It seemed his friend could never do things the easy way.

"Naw, we got no problem. You're the ones with the problem."

Nathan beheld one of the renegade Israelites casually sharpening his dagger with a whetstone. Other men grew noticeably bolder in the tense silence which followed and gripped their weapons more tightly. Fortunately, Jonathan thrived in such moments. The audacious prince spoke with authority while leveling his bloody sword at the man with the dagger.

"What is your name?"

"Hamul."

"Hamul, my friend and I have just slaughtered a platoon of Philistines."

"So you say."

"Then let's get that settled right now. How many, Hamul?"

"How many what?"

"How many of you traitors must my man and I kill?"

"Is that supposed to scare us?"

"Quit stalling, Hamul, or we'll just start killing the nearest ones."

A few renegades around Hamul looked nervously at Nathan. He gave the men a wicked grin and was gratified to see them shrink back. An argument erupted when Hamul attempted to shove some of his reluctant companions forward. Nathan fought to maintain his fierce demeanor when Jonathan slyly winked at him. Confusion spread among the rogue Israelites until a formidable voice from the rear ranks shamed the men into silence.

"You Idiots! He's just playing with you!"

The crowd parted as a tall, rugged figure shoved his way forward. One look at the scarred, weather-beaten face told Nathan a dangerous warrior approached. The man paused only to give Hamul a contemptuous glance before shouldering his way past. He planted himself firmly in front of Jonathan with feet spread wide and hands on hips.

"You'll get no personal combat today, mighty Prince. Not when my archers can stand off and drop the two of you like plump pigeons."

"They're not your archers, Laban!"

Laban spun round at Hamel's outburst and swatted the dagger and whetstone from the shorter man's hands. Nathan found the combination of strength and speed to be most impressive.

"Your body is as slow as your mind, Hamul. Better let a man handle this."

Hamul knelt to pick up his weapon before slinking away. Laban raised an eyebrow while surveying the rest of the Israelites. Nathan saw many wither under the big man's gaze.

With his authority now firmly established, Laban confronted Jonathan.

"There is only one question, Prince Jonathan. What do you offer us for your lives?"

"That depends on what you need, Laban."

"What we need is protection for our families. We live in the lowlands of Judah. Desert raiders from Sinai ravage both Philistine towns and our villages. The King of Gath conscripted us to fight our common enemy and leaves us in peace. Now our families have food and safety, no thanks to King Saul."

"You're a long way from Sinai."

"The King of Gath wanted scouts. Anyone who refused was killed. So I ask again, Prince Jonathan. What do you offer us?"

"I offer forgiveness for your treason. I pledge to protect your families."

"Forgiveness and protection from a prince without an army. I know a better deal. "

"What?"

"Philistine gold for your head."

"The Philistines have turned on you, Laban. That's why you're skulking away from their camp. The Philistines are scared. When they get scared, they kill Israelites."

"You can hide in your mountains, Prince Jonathan. The Philistines will still be our neighbors."

"Then join me. Drive the Philistines away from your homes."

"Say, we accept. Then what?"

"We attack the Philistines. Now."

Nathan feared that Jonathan had finally gone too far as the crowd began to murmur. He sensed how deeply the promises of forgiveness and protection appealed to them. Unfortunately, Jonathan chose to break the spell by ordering them to attack the dreaded Philistines. Nathan was surprised no one had taken up rocks to stone them both. Instead, the renegade Israelites looked to a single man: Laban. The stakes were set. The time for argument was past. Everyone's fate would be determined by a battle of wills between Jonathan and Laban.

"The odds are greatly against you, Prince Jonathan. Promises from a dead man are worthless."

"I have a few tricks."

"Such as?"

"Come along and see, Laban. It will be great sport."

"Why not? I can always sell you to the Philistines later."

The encampment of the King of Gaza on the Michmash plateau

Four infantry regiments and twenty chariots stood ready in the Gaza campsite while Kaftor rejoiced. Malia, his Cretan mercenary leader, had just confirmed the assassination of King Maoch. Philistia's deceased supreme commander could no longer prevent Kaftor from returning home. Gath still fielded the largest army at Michmash, but Kaftor expected to be long gone before the leaderless troops could fully mobilize. No matter what fate befell the other Philistine kings this day, he would save his soldiers and his chariots. Kaftor would ensure that all blame fell on Maoch. Gath's territory would be divided between the other four Philistine kingdoms and Kaftor's intact army would ensure Gaza received the lion's share. All this would come to pass as long as the true reason for Maoch's demise remained a secret. Meanwhile, it was time to get his army moving. The Gaza commanders all snapped to attention at Kaftor's approach.

"Gath has betrayed us to the Hebrews. King Maoch will use his infantry to block our way home. General Malia!"

"My Lord!"

"Your Cretans will punch a hole through the Gath soldiers blocking the road. First Regiment!"

"My King!"

"Your troops will pass through the Cretans and advance on the Gath encampment. You are to keep the road open until Second, Third and Fourth Regiments have passed, followed by our chariots. Then follow as a rearguard."

"Shall I help the other kings escape?"

"No. That is their problem."

Kaftor strolled to his chariot while watching his officers carry out their assigned tasks. He summoned the commander of his escort while his driver helped him mount up.

"Instruct my Master of Horse to get his chariot corps moving."

A single chariot was soon flying toward the horse corrals. Kaftor noted the Cretan mercenaries in position at the head of the column. He thrust his arm forward and set the Army of Gaza in motion. Kaftor wanted no sounds to alert the other kings to his departure. Besides, unexpected trumpet signals would only cause confusion among the skittish Philistines.

The milling crowd quickly parted before the Army of Gaza. Kaftor positioned his chariot and escort squadron just behind his vanguard for the best view. He was amused that only the camp followers seemed to understand what was taking place. The soldiers of the other kings stood idly by while the merchants, tradesmen and whores closed up shop. Long experience had taught them how to recognize a retreat. The sight of the Gaza column roused the Gath camp, but only a single company presently guarded the road which descended through the pass and back to Philistia. As Kaftor expected, the Cretans attacked without hesitation, and the three hundred mercenaries made short work of the lone Gath company. The way was now open for his First Regiment to deploy and keep the road open. Kaftor did not expect a single Gaza regiment to defeat five Gath regiments. His men merely needed to disrupt their rivals until Kaftor's entire force escaped. Then the leaderless Gath troops would face the combined forces of Ashkelon, Ashdod and Ekron. The ensuing fratricide should leave Kaftor as the master of Philistia.

A nod from Kaftor to his driver set his personal chariot squadron in motion down the open road. They rode past the Cretan mercenaries taking a breather after their brief, but bloody, assault. Kaftor generously praised the Cretans in passing and received a salute from General Malia in return. He smiled a moment later in amusement. The mercenaries had indeed performed well, but their promised bonus would go unpaid. Maoch's death must never be traced back to the King of Gaza. Malia, his officers and the four Cretan assassins would not see tomorrow's sunrise.

The southern outskirts of the main Philistine encampment on the Michmash plateau

Nathan made a quick count of their new allies while advancing toward the noisy Philistine encampment. He and Jonathan now led one hundred and twenty-seven men; seventy-nine of whom were armed. They skirted the Philistine perimeter in search of a vulnerable point. Unexpected sounds and smells caused the Israelites to halt while their leaders scouted ahead. Crawling up beside Jonathan and Laban, Nathan gazed down on thousands of horses and countless rows of chariots. Thorn bushes had been cut and stacked to create five huge corrals. Hundreds of men were hastily preparing chariots for departure. Nathan heard Jonathan whisper to Laban.

"We strike here!"

"But there are ten of them for every one of us."

"Don't count men, Laban. Count weapons!"

444

Nathan also scanned the area carefully. Arms might be stored in the chariots, but none were visible. After a moment, Laban murmured an agreement.

"So they are unarmed. What now?"

"Build a small fire. Make torches for your unarmed men. Those with weapons will drive off the charioteers. The others will burn the chariots."

"Smoke will alert the Philistines."

"Smoke will alarm the Philistines, Laban. Wait for my signal."

"What signal?"

"You'll know it."

All was soon in readiness. The torch bearers waited around the around the small fire. The armed Israelites stood ready to attack. Nathan sensed Laban burned with curiosity over Jonathan's mysterious signal. He had a good idea what his friend had in mind, but said nothing. Suddenly, the enemy horses inexplicitly became restless and began racing around their corrals. Nathan feared the animals somehow detected the Israelites.

Then the earth literally fell out from under their feet.

Earthquakes were familiar to the inhabitants of Israel's highlands. Nathan had experienced several in his lifetime, but nothing of this magnitude. All the Israelites were knocked from their feet by the violent tremors. The shaking seemed to last an eternity before Nathan could finally he pull himself up and survey the scene. The Philistines below were either staggering around in confusion or attempting to quiet their horses. The other Israelites appeared stunned, but unharmed. Naturally, Jonathan was the first to recover his wits.

"What are you waiting for? Attack!"

The screaming Israelites fell on the unarmed Philistines, except for Laban. The veteran warrior simply stared at Jonathan in awe.

"How *the hell* did you do that?"

"That's my secret, Laban."

Nathan was about to make a sarcastic remark when a sharp look from Jonathan made him hold his tongue. One of Karaz's proverbs immediately came to mind. *If men call you a god, just keep your mouth shut!* He instead turned his attention to the battle below. Clouds of gray smoke billowed from the burning chariots, harnesses and wagon loads of fodder. The actual fighting was fierce, but brief since most Philistines simply fled. Afterwards, a visibly awed Laban approached Jonathan.

"What now, Prince Jonathan?"

"Nathan, empty your sack please."

Nathan grinned and dumped out the sack he had been carrying since burning the Philistine outpost. Two bronze trumpets lay glistening in the midday sun. Nathan knew they were Jonathan's mysterious signal, not the earthquake. The expression on Laban's face slowly changed from confusion to understanding.

"Do you know the Philistine calls?"

"Yes, Laban, but we need only one."

On the road from Michmash to Beth-Horon

Kaftor squirmed on the floor of his chariot, rubbing a shoulder bruised from being thrown against the iron border of its fighting compartment. Once the earthquake ceased, the driver helped the King of Gaza up where he could see. Three of Kaftor's infantry regiments had reached the valley floor before the violent tremors erupted. Half his men were still down and on the verge of panic. Kaftor wondered what effect the earthquake was having back at Michmash. He expected to see his chariot corps by now, but the pass was disturbingly empty. A new column of smoke, rising from the main Philistine camp itself, caught Kaftor's attention. He cursed when he realized it was above the chariot laager. Kaftor then heard a sound from Michmash that chilled him to the bone. It was a rarely heard Philistine trumpet call, used only in the most dire of circumstances. Its official title belied its fateful message. However, the common soldiers had devised their own name for it... *Run like hell.*

Silence reigned over the Michmash plateau for a moment. Kaftor then heard a faint sound, like a distant wave crashing against the shore, growing louder with each passing second. Absurdly, a flock of sheep raced down the pass, pursued by their shepherds and a gaggle of camp followers. However, these were soon submerged by the river of humanity which flowed after them. Soldiers from all five Philistine cities jumbled together in a mad dash through the pass. Kaftor could discern no recognizable formation, no identifying banner, and no obvious leader. The combination of the earthquake and the frightening trumpet call had reduced a disciplined army into a mindless mob intent only on survival. In that instant, Kaftor realized he would never again see his First infantry regiment or his chariot corps.

The sound of Hebrew shofars abruptly blared from the opposite side of the valley. Kaftor counted a mere six Hebrew companies advancing, but their organization now mattered more than the Philistines' greater numbers. Gaza's discipline still held, but other soldiers discarded their armor and scattered into the hills. Kaftor suddenly realized this cowardly behavior posed his greatest threat. If those panicked fugitives mingled with his Gaza regiments, their fear might infect his own soldiers. Kaftor quickly summoned his field commander.

"Get your men moving! Use the archers as a rearguard. Kill anyone who comes within fifty paces."

"Anyone, my King?"

"Philistine or Hebrew, kill them all! We must stay ahead of them both or we die."

Overlooking the Michmash pass

Nathan followed Jonathan and Laban to higher ground where they could admire their handiwork. The frantic activity in the pass reminded Nathan of ants swarming over a carcass. Thousands of Philistines jammed into a gap where twenty men abreast could not hope to pass. Philistines were trampled underfoot by the score. Some had stumbled while others fell beneath the blades of their impatient brethren. Nathan watched entire infantry companies march into this vortex, only to be torn apart by the ensuing crush. Camp followers driving their carts, oxen, sheep and goats contributed an additional level of chaos. It was indeed a glorious sight. Jonathan was extremely satisfied.

"Gather your men, Laban. Time to go hunting."

The former Israelite renegades were soon descending from the plateau along a narrow goat path. Jonathan again took the lead while Nathan brought up the rear. Laban casually dropped back and fell into step with Nathan. He thought the recent change in Laban's attitude was quite remarkable. The fierce warrior now showed great deference to Jonathan, someone he had considered slaying barely an hour before. After a few moments, the big warrior asked Nathan a question.

"The prince can't really summon earthquakes, can he?"

"If I said *no*, Laban, would you desert him?"

"Of course not! It means God favors him."

"What if God didn't send the earthquake for Jonathan's sake?"

"He's still the luckiest whore's son I've ever met."

When Jonathan later called an impromptu war council, Nathan felt Laban at his side. He suspected Laban sought to carve out a permanent role with the prince. Nathan wished the fierce warrior well, for the man had the makings of a good officer. They were encouraged by what they saw. Not only were Saul's six hundred soldiers in hot pursuit, but Israelite militia swarmed in from the nearby towns. Nathan pointed out a large Philistine formation marching over the horizon, but Jonathan decided to let them go. They were not ready to take on disciplined heavy infantry, especially when so many others were ripe for the picking. The remaining fugitives reminded Nathan of a flock of sheep evading a wolf. The members stayed together not to fight, but to reduce the chances of being singled out and killed. He suggested working around the edges of the enemy mass. This would keep the Philistines compressed and helpless while allowing individuals to be culled for slaughter.

"We should break up into small groups, Jonathan."

"You mean hunting parties, don't you, Nathan?"

"I do now."

"So, Laban, are your men up to it?"

Laban grinned viciously.

"We live for the hunt."

Chapter 34 - The Retreat

Then Saul and all his men assembled and went into battle. They found the Philistines in total confusion, striking each other with their swords. Those Hebrews who had previously been in the Philistine camp went over to the Israelites who were with Saul and Jonathan.

From the Book of I Samuel, Chapter 14, verses 20 and 21

On the road to Beth-horon, nine miles from Michmash

Achish found the first day of raiding the Hebrew countryside to be as easy and enjoyable as promised. Smoke rose above scattered Hebrew villages for miles around where he now stood in his chariot. Of the three Philistine raiding parties, the Prince of Gath had chosen to lead the western group. The other two were led by loyal Gath officers, and each commanded roughly fifteen hundred infantry and two hundred chariots. Though their infantry was provided by the other Philistine kings, the chariots all belonged to Gath. This meant Achish could literally run rings around any insubordinate infantry unit, although that appeared unnecessary. Pillaging did wonders for the morale of soldiers, no matter their city. The results had been good and the day was still young. Smoke columns to the north and east bespoke the success of his other raiders. Achish then noticed a look of puzzlement on the face of his chariot commander.

"Lord Achish, how many raiding parties were sent out?"

"Three. Why?"

The captain responded by pointing behind Achish. The distant column of smoke initially meant nothing to Achish, until he surveyed the horizon in all directions. It was then he realized a fourth area now burned, one in the vicinity of Michmash. Achish could find only one explanation. His father Maoch was under attack, either by an external enemy or an internal one. Perhaps even both. Achish swiftly evaluated the chariot captain waiting patiently at his side. With other senior Gath officers available, Achish realized this man would have to do. Achish thrust a finger forward and used his most commanding voice.

"You...you're a general now."

Achish paused to allow the captain a moment to absorb his unexpected promotion. He read skepticism in the older man's eyes. The veteran officer was undoubtedly wondering whether a teenage prince could really jump him two steps in rank. Achish considered that a good sign; the man was cautious. The captain's eyes momentarily flicked toward Michmash before he came to full attention.

"What are your orders, Lord Achish?"

"I'll depart with a chariot company for Michmash immediately. Command the brigade in my absence. Sound the recall, and collect your men."

"I think you'll need more than a hundred chariots."

"Agreed. Send the other chariot company after me as soon as possible."

"And the infantry?"

"Assume our army needs a safe route home. See that ridge west of this village? Assign the infantry from Ashdod to defend it. Have the others leave their armor and belongings behind; Ashdod can guard them. Bring the rest of your men at a quick march. Carry only weapons...food and water for a day."

"I'll leave within the hour, Sir."

"Good. Every thousand paces, station a score of infantry and archers to keep the road open."

"There might be problems on the road, Sir."

"Spit it out, General.

"I'm not the son of a king. Ashkelon, Ekron and Gaza may refuse my orders."

"Then show them this."

Achish's father had lent him a royal signet ring to expedite his capture of Michmash. He now pulled the ring from his finger and tossed it to the newly promoted general. As his chariot spun away, Achish called back to the astonished officer.

"And for the gods' sake, General, don't lose it!"

On the road to Beth-horon, three miles from Michmash

Hunting Philistines became almost too easy for Nathan. He merely had to follow the endless debris trail heading westward. First were the discarded shields and helmets, followed by scattered pieces of armor. Abandoned swords, javelins and bows began appearing after the second mile. Only

453

desperate men gave up their personal defense to gain a few extra steps on their pursuers. Nathan and his lightly armed companions settled into a disciplined trot which consumed long distances while preserving their strength. By focusing on Philistines who had broken away from the pack, Jonathan's band became the vanguard of the Israelite army. After the prince divided his company into groups of ten, the pursuit settled into a repetitive cycle. Each group of Israelites would latch onto a larger body of Philistines. As the distance closed, the fugitives would break into a sprint which bought them some time, but also splintered the herd. The Israelites continued their steady pace and picked off exhausted stragglers until none remained. Then Jonathan's men would move on to repeat this process again and again.

One man with a colored cloth streaming from his helmet caught Nathan's eye late in the day. When his victim made the fatal mistake of drifting to one side, Nathan raced forward to cut him off. The exhausted man still carried a sword, so Nathan approached warily. The stranger managed to fend off Nathan's first two sword blows, but not the third...or the fourth. As the dying man crumpled in the dirt, a shiny object rolled from his left hand. Nathan found himself gazing down on a huge jewel-encrusted medallion on an exquisite gold chain. The sight was so breathtaking that he almost missed his name being called.

"Come on, Nathan! You only have to kill him once."

Nathan turned to see the grins of Jonathan and Laban as they loped past. He scooped up his prize and hung it around his neck. Nathan was about to rejoin his friends when he heard sounds of crying. Walking a few paces to his left, he stared down into a shallow gully where a dozen Israelite men were busily looting three ox-carts. Sobbing came from several families huddled together under guard to one side. A dead body seemed to be the source of their grief. Nathan assumed the small clan served the Philistines and were now spoils of war. He was going to leave them to their fate when some objects being tossed from the carts drew his attention. Nathan instantly recognized the purpose of the hammers and tongs, as well as the value of the prisoners.

"Jonathan! Jonathan! Get your butt over here, Donkey Boy!"

An alarmed Jonathan and Laban raced over seconds later. The prince grew annoyed at the lack of immediate danger.

"It's very pretty, Nathan, but you could have shown me your new bauble later."

Nathan realized his friend was referring to the captured medallion. Shaking his head, he quickly apprised Jonathan of what he had seen. The prince immediately grasped the significance of Nathan's discovery. Assuming his most regal bearing, Jonathan led Nathan and Laban into the gully. The Israelite looters watched their approach suspiciously. One burly man hopped down from a cart and met them halfway.

"Well, what do *you* want?"

"I am Jonathan, son of King Saul, Prince of Israel. That is my Armor Bearer, Nathan. The big fellow is Laban."

"Good for you. Come back later; we're a little busy right now."

"Then I'll make this quick, Friend. I'm taking these carts and your prisoners."

"Are you now? Well, they belong to us. Spoils of war, honorably taken."

"The king decides the distribution of plunder. It's the law."

"Well, I may be ignorant of the law, Lad, but I can count. There're more men at my back than yours."

"I'm only going to say this once. Drop everything and leave. Now."

"All right. You've had your say. Get out before we...urk!"

Nathan was amazed by how swiftly Laban slipped behind the arrogant lout. The blustering threat had been interrupted when Laban slid the point of his dagger up the man's right nostril. Laban slowly tilted his blade until his hapless victim was standing on the tips of his toes.

"*Never* make Prince Jonathan repeat himself. Understand?"

"Yesh."

"Then say it."

"Yesh! Uh unnerstan."

A slight flick of the wrist was all it took for Laban to slice through the man's nostril and free his dagger. The howling leader clutched his bleeding nose with both hands and retreated toward his companions. The Israelite looters watched slack jawed while Laban carefully cleaned his knife before sheathing it. Nathan detected a hint of amusement on Laban's face as the fierce warrior strode toward them. A dozen cowed Israelites tripped over each other in their haste to escape the gully. Jonathan quietly praised Laban before moving to the prisoners.

"Who is your leader?"

A man in his thirties with a bruised face stepped forward. He gazed sadly at an old man's body lying a few feet away.

"My father is, or rather was. I am now."

"What are your people called?"

"We are Kenites."

"Why are you here?"

"We are iron workers. The Philistines use us to repair their weapons."

"And you agreed to this?"

"Philistines do not take *no* for an answer."

"Would you serve the King of Israel instead?"

"Would he take *no* for an answer?"

"He would not."

"Then we would be honored to serve him."

"Laban, arrange an escort to Geba for these people and their wagons. They are to be placed under the protection of a man named Karaz."

Ten of Laban's men were promptly detailed to deliver the Kenites to Geba. When Nathan followed Jonathan and Laban up out of the gully, they were confronted by a landscape barren of any signs of life.

"Is the battle over already?"

"I doubt it, Nathan. We've just drifted too far south chasing this last lot. Let's rejoin my father. Laban, what's the tracker in you say?"

"I'd cut across those hills until we reach the road to Beth-Horon."

"You expect my father to be there?"

"Who knows, but the Philistines will be there."

"Can we find food on the way? I'm starving."

"Follow me, Prince Jonathan. I have a treat for you."

On the Beth-horon road, six miles from Michmash

Achish's chariot crested a hill halfway along the road to Michmash when he spied Philistine infantry headed his way. He gave a few crisp orders, and twenty chariots sped forward to form a protective screen at the base of the hill. However, the bulk of Achish's two chariot companies remained concealed on the back slope. With his infantry trailing at least an hour behind,

Achish chose to be cautious. So many soldiers heading toward Philistia could only mean trouble. The Philistine column appeared to be composed of intact regiments marching in good order. However, Achish's keen eye soon noted the signs of a hasty departure. His most alarming observation was that only soldiers from Gaza were visible. Questions flooded Achish's mind. Where were the troops of his father and the other Philistine kings? Why were there no chariots screening the formation? Above all, why were Philistines in a place where they were of no use?

Lagging far behind the Gaza regiments, Achish spotted a new formation, composed of men from different Philistine cities. Even at a distance, it appeared more like a mass of refugees than an army. Achish needed to decide on a course of action before the Gaza vanguard reached the slope on which he now stood. He spotted Kaftor's royal banner and chariot trailing the leading Gaza regiment. Achish thought it typical of the King of Gaza to both hide in the center of his army and also have a ready means of escape. He quickly made his decision. Kaftor possessed five times his numbers, while Achish had greater mobility. He must seize the initiative. Aggressive action was the order of the day.

Kaftor nearly wet himself when Gath chariots surrounded his three infantry regiments. Hundreds of fighting vehicles neatly split into twin columns to race down both flanks of his soldiers. Kaftor's men halted without orders. The veterans knew their best defense was to hold fast in ranks. Kaftor felt his gut churn as the Gath chariot squadrons took up evenly spaced positions. The distance was slightly beyond the range of his foot archers, but well within the reach of the charioteers' composite bows. Kaftor noted a solitary chariot holding station at the hill summit and knew it could only be Achish, the son of his now dead rival. Kaftor now feared his fable might actually be true. Was Gath really in league with the Hebrews?

Achish's chariot advanced down the hill at a leisurely walk. The air grew still enough for Kaftor to hear the hoof beats of the prince's horses. As a further display of dominance, Achish rode between the platoons of the Gaza column, forcing men to lean against their comrades to clear a path. Achish pulled up about twenty yards ahead of Kaftor's small chariot escort. The King of Gaza gritted his teeth at the realization the young imp was expecting him to come forward like some beggar. Ordering his driver to advance, Kaftor vowed Achish would soon meet Maoch in Philistine hell.

"Kaftor! What has happened?"

The conversation started poorly for Kaftor. Ignoring protocol, Achish had addressed him as an equal. Apparently, the young prince thought hundreds of chariots allowed him to make the rules. Yet this was no time for Kaftor to bicker over etiquette. He could not afford a fight on unfavorable ground. Kaftor needed to reach Gaza before Achish learned of his father's death. So he resorted to evasion.

"I do not answer questions along a dirt road."

Achish rested one hand on his sword's hilt and firmly returned Kaftor's gaze. The king sighed when it became obvious the boy understood the power of silence. Perhaps deception would work. Kaftor averted his eyes and spoke in his best conspiratorial whisper.

"I am being discreet for your father's sake, Achish."

"Why would my father need your discretion?"

"It was rumored that Maoch sold us out to the Hebrews."

"My father fights Hebrews. Rumors are your style, Kaftor."

"Have it your way. Our camp was overwhelmed by Hebrews this morning. They came over a cliff *guarded by soldiers of Gath*. Your men gave no warning. They made no resistance. When Gaza, Ashdod, Ashkelon and Ekron tried to rally, we were *attacked by soldiers of Gath*."

Kaftor understood that he must take great care while spinning his web of exaggerations and lies. One slipup and an angry Prince of Gath could start a bloodbath. So far, Achish's face was unreadable.

"My father's men would have attacked only Philistine deserters."

"His soldiers fell upon us while *still inside the camp*. No one had a chance to desert."

"My father must have had a good reason."

"I wanted to ask him, but Maoch was nowhere to be found."

For the first time, Kaftor detected doubt in Achish's eyes. Of course, he had no business being a king if he could not sway a nineteen year-old boy. So it was disturbing to witness how quickly the prince regained his composure. Kaftor decided

461

to assassinate the young man sooner rather than later. Achish's next words chilled his blood.

"I have five hundred men holding the Beth-Horon pass."

Kaftor felt sweat form on his brow.

"I have another thousand on the road behind me."

Kaftor's jaw tightened involuntarily.

"They have orders to keep the Hebrews away so that your troops may proceed home unmolested."

It took all Kaftor's self-control to avoid giggling in relief. He spoke with renewed confidence.

"Hebrews are still harassing our stragglers, Achish. Your chariots could rescue them. You might even find your father."

On the Beth-horon road, four miles from Michmash

Nathan and Jonathan found that Laban could be tight-lipped whenever it suited the big man. The taciturn warrior ignored all inquiries regarding the mysterious treat during their cross-country jaunt. They crossed paths with many Israelite soldiers, and Nathan was shocked by the lack of fire in their eyes. The Israelite pursuit appeared on the verge of collapse. A chance to permanently break Philistine power seemed to be slipping away. The unexpected sound of faint buzzing interrupted Nathan's gloomy thoughts. He looked up to see a grinning Laban pointing to a tree where bees swarmed.

Honey!

The three men leaned forward to examine their tasty prize, only to be driven back by the hive's angry sentries. Jonathan quickly devised a solution. Holding his spear by the tip, the prince dipped its butt end into the tree and extracted a large section of honeycomb. Nathan watched enviously as his friend held the honeycomb over his head and allowed the golden liquid to drip into his mouth. A crowd gathered around the prince, but Nathan thought they appeared worried rather than jealous.

"Stop eating, you Fool! Are you insane?"

Nathan spotted an Israelite captain racing toward them. Laban growled and raised his spear, only to lower it at Jonathan's command. The officer stopped short when he came face to face with the glaring prince. The man appeared horrified by the honey dripping from Jonathan's chin.

"Recognize me, Captain?"

"Yes, Prince Jonathan."

"Don't you know how to talk to a prince?"

"Forgive me, but it is forbidden to eat any food before sundown."

"I've been fighting all day. I'm hungry."

"But your father, the king, bound the army with an oath this morning."

"What oath?"

"The king fears the Philistines will escape if the army stops for food. Any man who eats before sundown is to be executed."

"Look at your soldiers, Captain. They're collapsing from hunger! *My father has sinned against his people*! I ate a little honey and feel refreshed. Imagine how much greater the slaughter would be if our men had paused to eat a little food?"

"It is my duty to see that the king is obeyed."

"Are you really going to kill me over some honey?"

The captain's eyes grew wide with fear as Jonathan drew his sword. When a few men raised weapons, Laban sprang into a defensive stance beside Jonathan. Nathan's blood chilled as the confrontation began to whirl out of control. In that moment, he understood why Karaz had set him at Jonathan's side. Nathan stepped forward and raised empty hands.

"Captain, relax. No one is going to kill anyone."

"Who are you to decide that?"

"That's not important, Sir. What is important is your oath."

"What about it?"

"You swore not to eat until nightfall."

"So?"

"But you did not swear to kill anyone who ate. Did you?"

"Not specifically, but I assumed that..."

"You assumed a responsibility *which belongs to the king*. It's his oath, not yours."

This timely observation from Nathan ignited a dispute among the listening soldiers. Most men seemed to favor the Captain delaying judgment. Nathan felt an iron grip on his upper arm and turned to face an enraged Jonathan.

"I'm the prince. I don't need your help, Nathan."

"Calm down, Donkey Boy. The captain's not to blame. Take a good look at your soldiers. They just heard their prince reprimand their king. You frightened them...and me. It's time for a little diplomacy."

"You agree with this idiotic oath?"

"Tomorrow, everyone will be celebrating a victory and the matter forgotten. Unless you continue to publicly criticize your father."

"You're wrong, Nathan. The people may forget. My father won't."

"Then settle it with Saul in private. What's done is done. You can't get this day back."

Jonathan's eyes blazed, but Nathan refused to back down. His friend simply needed time to digest the unwanted advice. The loosening of the grip on his arm told Nathan that his counsel was being accepted. It helped to have Laban nodding in agreement. Jonathan finally grinned sheepishly and addressed the crowd.

"Take me to the king, Captain. Or did you swear an oath not to do that?"

Chapter 35 - The Trial

Now Saul's lookouts in Gibeah of Benjamin saw the Philistine army melting away in all directions. So Saul said to Ahijah the priest, "Use the ephod to ask God for guidance." After Saul spoke to the priest, the tumult in the Philistine camp grew even worse; so Saul said to the priest, "Stop. Withdraw your hand from the ephod." Then Saul assembled his soldiers and went to the battle.

From the Book of I Samuel, Chapter 14, verses 16, 18, 19 and 20

Now the soldiers of Israel were distressed that day because Saul bound the army under oath, saying, "Cursed be the man who eats any food before evening, before I have taken vengeance on my enemies." So none of the soldiers ate food. The army entered a wood; and there was honey on the ground. But Jonathan had not heard that his father bound the people with the oath; so he reached out the end of his spear and dipped it in a honeycomb. He tasted the honey and his eyes brightened. Then one of the soldiers said, "Your father bound the army under a strict oath, saying, 'Cursed be the man who eats food this day.'" But Jonathan said, "My father has made trouble for our people. See how my eyes brightened after I tasted a little honey. Our soldiers should have been allowed to eat freely today of the food plundered from the enemy! Would not the greater slaughter of the Philistines been much greater?"

From the Book of I Samuel, Chapter 14, verses 24 to 30

On the Beth-horon road, eight miles from Michmash

Locating Saul turned out to be a greater challenge than Nathan expected. Many Israelites knew where the king had been, but none could say where he had gone. When Laban suggested simply following the crowd, he and Jonathan agreed. The sun set long before they reached a stream where the majority of the Royal Army seemed to have just collapsed. As Nathan entered the camp, an uneasy feeling came over him. Hundreds of men rested in the darkness, yet there were few fires and no smell of cooking. He also noted an air of despair hanging over the soldiers. Jonathan sensed it as well.

"Nathan, I smell defeat, not victory."

"The men are tired."

"Even tired men can be proud. These reek of fear and shame."

"Let's find your father and get some answers."

A man rose from the shadows in response to Nathan's words.

"Jonathan? Prince Jonathan?"

"Who asks?"

"I serve Ahijah, the High Priest. He's been searching for you."

"Well, here I am."

"The High Priest must speak with you."

"Another time."

"The High Priest must talk with you *before* you see the king."

"About what?"

"Something for your ears alone."

Rather than insisting on being taken directly to Saul, Jonathan merely nodded. Laban was asked to wait with his men while Nathan and Jonathan followed the servant. The man led them to a grove of trees offering a measure of privacy. Ahijah was easily recognized by his ceremonial dress. The High Priest started to speak, but closed his mouth at the sight of Nathan. Jonathan tiredly shook his head.

"You can trust my friend. What's so urgent, Ahijah?"

"The king and I arrived to find this place in an uproar. Hundreds of hungry men demanding to eat the animals captured from the Philistines, but..."

"I heard about the oath, Ahijah."

"Well, no one had the forethought to organize anything. An orderly distribution of food became impossible."

"Let me guess. The men rioted."

"It was horrible, Prince Jonathan. Dozens fought over a single calf or even a lamb. Then, the abominations began."

"I thought the oath against eating ended at sunset."

"It was not that, Jonathan. Men ate meat raw. Without draining the blood. Without cooking."

"Horrible sacrilege to be sure, Ahijah, but it wasn't their fault. There must be some way to appease God."

"But there is more, my Prince."

"There always is."

"The king proposed night attack."

"Audacious and reckless. Why would my father even suggest it?"

"Some had begun to whisper the king was to blame for the tonight's sacrilege. A quick victory could end such talk, but your father might be gambling his crown. If the attack succeeded, they would praise Saul. If it failed, they would blame him."

"My father put himself in a difficult situation."

"I tried to offer Saul a dignified way out, but I only made things worse."

"How?"

"I suggested that we inquire of God whether to attack. No matter the answer, Saul would be blameless."

"Excellent advice, Ahijah."

"So I took the *Urim* and *Thummim* from the *ephod*."

"What was the answer?"

To Nathan's surprise, Ahijah lowered his head in shame. He heard pain in the High Priest's voice.

"Jonathan...*There was no answer*."

There was no sound except for a slight wind rustling the branches overhead. Nathan was stunned. Many times in Israel's history, a leader, be it judge, prophet or priest, had called upon the Urim and the Thummim to inquire of God. The answer could bring either good tidings or horrible judgment, but there had *always been an answer*. For God to ignore the *Urim* and the *Thummim* was unprecedented. Jonathan finally broke the silence.

"But there's more, Ahijah, isn't there?"

"When our lookouts reported a disturbance in the Philistine camp this morning, Saul told me to ask the LORD if we should attack. So I grasped the *Urim* and the *Thummim* inside the *ephod*. I started to pray. Then, the Philistines began fighting among themselves. Saul immediately ordered me to stop...before God answered. Then he went off to battle."

This latest revelation rocked Nathan more than anything else. The king had insulted the LORD by asking a question, and then not waiting for the answer! *What was Saul thinking of?* Nathan soon heard Jonathan answer his unspoken question.

"My father thought God might stop him. Why would he think that, Ahijah?"

"He feared God might give the victory to another. A king cannot tolerate a rival for his people's affections, even if that person is his own son."

"Ridiculous!"

"Not to the king. Tell me, Prince Jonathan. Why *did* you usurp your father's authority and attack on your own?"

"I wanted to help my father's cause by opening the pass."

"You could have shared your plans with the king."

"We were not on good terms then."

"So, like your father, you did not wait for permission. Well, Jonathan, your actions made Saul appear weak. You put *your name* on every soldier's lips. So how did Saul spend the day? Trying to regain control of the battle *from you*. That's why he made his men take that oath."

"Now I have more to tell, Ahijah. I ate honey this afternoon. Then I publicly condemned my father's oath."

"Some disgruntled captain already told Saul."

"Then it's time I faced my father."

"Perhaps you should wait. Saul has not been himself, lately. He may seek a scapegoat."

"Thank you, Ahijah, but please take me to him. Stay here, Nathan. I need to do this alone."

A worried Nathan went in search of Laban, but found it impossible to identify faces in the moonless night. A large bonfire came to life a short distance away. Nathan and the other Israelites flowed towards it like insects drawn to a flame. He soon came to a stream, barely ankle deep and only a few steps wide. The fire burned on the far bank, and soldiers began settling down along the gentle slope across from the flames. Nathan stepped over and past men until he reached the water's edge. Saul, Jonathan, Abner and a few officers stood beside the blaze. Nathan studied Jonathan's impassive features for a clue, but discerned nothing. The shallow stream acted as a boundary which kept the soldiers a comfortable distance from their leaders. Nathan was close enough to make eye contact with Abner, who then whispered something to one of his officers. The man looked directly at Nathan and then slipped away. Nathan thought it might have been the same captain who confronted Jonathan over the honey. He promptly forgot the incident when Saul stepped forward and called for attention in a booming voice.

"When Joshua led our fathers into this land, there was at a small city named Ai. But Joshua's soldiers fled before the men of Ai, and many died. God told Joshua that Israel's defeat was caused by the sin of one man, a man who had stolen gold dedicated to the tabernacle. Lots were cast to find the guilty man and execute him. Only then was the LORD satisfied and allowed Joshua to conquer Ai."

It seemed to Nathan that every man stopped breathing at the same time. He knew that Saul was angry, but the selection of this story seemed particularly ominous. His fears for Jonathan's safety grew as Saul pressed on.

"Once again, God denies victory to Israel because of sin in our camp. Once again, this sin must be rooted out and punished. I call your captains to stand before me. We will discover who has sinned. As surely as the LORD lives, that man will die... even if he is my son Jonathan. "

473

Saul's last words made Nathan ill. Dozens of officers gathered in front of their troops, facing the king. Nathan looked for the High Priest, but Ahijah was nowhere to be seen. It seemed Saul would avoid being embarrassed by the *Urim* and the *Thummim* again. Nathan suspected the verdict was already decided, yet Jonathan appeared resolute as his father continued.

"Your captains represent you while Jonathan and I represent the kingdom. General Abner holds a bowl containing two potsherds. One bears the mark for Jonathan and me. The other is marked for the army. By whichever one is chosen, God will indicate where the sin is."

The king raised his hands in prayer as the soldiers murmured their agreement. Nathan recalled Samuel rebuking Saul for combining the offices of priest and king, a folly now painfully obvious to him. Saul turned to Abner and reached into the bowl. The king extracted a single potsherd and studied it closely.

"The mark is Jonathan's and mine."

The silence held only until the soldiers realized they had escaped condemnation. Spontaneous cheers spread throughout the crowd, but Nathan did not join in. Jonathan's peril was the only thing on his mind. Nathan now understood the shameful conspiracy taking place. Israel had not been defeated. The story of Ai had nothing to do with the day's events. Excluding the High Priest from these proceedings was sacrilege. The soldiers would accept Saul's verdict because it saved their skins, a blatant bribe. The marking of the potsherds was never shown. Everything was left to Saul's interpretation, a man who had more at stake than anyone. Nathan's course was plain. If the

474

judgment went against Jonathan, Nathan would expose the injustice.

Abner returned the potsherds to the bowl and held it out once more for Saul. The king removed one and immediately held it overhead.

"The mark is Jonathan's."

Angry grumbling began in the dark and increased in volume as the soldiers slowly realized that the man most responsible for their victory was about to die. Yet, none of them made a move. It was difficult for even a good man to say *kill me instead of my prince.* As Nathan stepped forward, he felt his arms seized by two men as a sharp blade pricked his ribs. A familiar voice hissed in Nathan's ear.

"Go ahead, Boy. Try to shout."

Nathan turned his head to view the man holding the dagger. It was the *honey captain*, the same officer Abner had spoken to moments before. Obviously, Abner did not want Nathan disrupting the execution. No one else seemed aware of Nathan's predicament. The flickering firelight made the other soldiers blind to any movement in the dark. Nathan's lungs would be punctured before he could draw breath to shout. Nobody would even notice the small commotion. Jonathan now stood alone, but armed men were visible nearby. Saul strode within a few paces of his son and spoke softly. Nathan knew both men well enough to guess from their expressions what was being said. Saul seemed intent on domination while Jonathan responded with calm defiance. Each verbal exchange only increased the king's rage. There was venom in Saul's voice as he loudly pronounced judgment.

"May God deal even more harshly with me if you do not die, Jonathan!"

At a signal from Abner, four men advanced toward Jonathan with weapons drawn. Hundreds watched in horror as the spectacle unfolded. Nathan struggled against his captors even as he felt the blade slice into his flesh. He gasped as Jonathan tossed his sword to the ground and stared defiantly at the executioners. Abner's men halted a few paces from Jonathan, seemingly unprepared to kill an unarmed man. During this moment of uncertainty, a shout broke the night's silence.

"Should Jonathan die? The man who delivered Israel from the Philistines? Never!"

A fearsome figure stomped into the firelight. It was Laban. The big warrior boldly splashed across the narrow stream raising his spear. Scores of armed men surged after him to form a protective circle around Jonathan. Nathan recognized them as the Israelite renegades who had accepted Jonathan's pardon. The would-be executioners discreetly withdrew toward Saul. Laban pointed his spear back toward the multitude huddled in darkness and spoke again.

"Men of Israel, take with me a new oath. As surely as the LORD lives, not a hair of Jonathan's head will be touched. For what Jonathan did today, he did with God's help! How say you?"

Barely a hundred men now surrounded Jonathan, but their power was multiplied by a roar of acceptance from the rest of the army. There was much more to this rough peasant than Nathan expected. Laban was shrewd enough to realize that his fate was intertwined with Jonathan's. The man had convinced his companions that their protection would die with the young prince. Laban had saved Jonathan when Nathan was helpless to act. Saul, Abner, and their guards retreated to the edge of the firelight where the surrounding gloom seemed to diminish the king even further. Nathan believed in that moment Jonathan could have ordered Laban's men to kill Saul and no one would have interfered. Abner's henchmen holding Nathan chose this time to vanish. The initiative now lay with Jonathan and everyone, including the king, waited to see how he would use it.

In the end, Jonathan held the throng in suspense just long enough to demonstrate the extent of his influence. He spoke softly to Laban before crossing the stream, followed by his protectors. Taking their lead from Jonathan, the remainder of the assembly broke up. Nathan watched as Saul disappeared with his small entourage. He wondered whether the king recognized this final irony: Saul had called the assembly, but Jonathan had dismissed it. The king still kept his crown, but Nathan suspected Saul would have to wear it differently after tonight. A gruff voice interrupted Nathan's musings.

"Nathan, may I make a request?"

"You've earned the right to make several, Laban. And if I can't grant them, I'm sure Jonathan will."

The big man sheepishly bowed his head, but Nathan's respect for him only increased. Most men would be overcome by vanity after a performance like Laban's. Instead, his eyes humbly pleaded with Nathan.

"I've made some powerful enemies tonight. I'd gladly fight them face to face, but these are men who only strike from the darkness. I fear for my family."

Nathan nodded in understanding. It dawned on him that both he and Jonathan were in a similar position.

"How can I help, Laban?"

"Speak to Prince Jonathan for me. I wish to place my family under his protection. In return, my life is his."

"Jonathan will doubtless consider that an excellent bargain. I'll speak with him before I sleep. Expect his answer in the morning."

"That will sweeten my dreams tonight."

As Laban turned to leave, Nathan had a flash of inspiration.

"Wait, Laban. Can you find other men willing to serve Jonathan? Reliable men?"

"You mean...reliable like me?"

"Men like you are exactly what I have in mind."

"How many do you want?"

"How many can you get?"

"That depends, Nathan. Men like me are not good at following laws."

"As long as they have not committed murder, all will be forgiven."

"What if they had a good reason?"

"Then it can't be murder, can it? But they must be hard men, willing to die for Jonathan."

Nathan studied Laban's eyes. The reticent warrior was obviously deep thinker, someone who considered all the implications of an agreement. A frosty smile indicated his acceptance.

"Where should I send these reliable men?"

"Have them assemble at Geba before the next full moon. They are to report to a man named Karaz."

"This Karaz, will he be their commander?"

"Karaz will be their trainer. I expect Jonathan will appoint the best man from within their ranks as commander."

Laban's cheery expression showed he had no doubt who this commander would be. Neither did Nathan. The warrior winked slyly and departed on his recruiting mission. Alone again, Nathan fully felt his exhaustion. He desired only a brief conversation with Jonathan and a warm place to sleep. However, there was something which had to be settled first.

Once Nathan found his target, he patiently waited in concealment for the proper moment. It came when the *honey captain* walked to the edge of camp to relieve himself. Nathan rose from cover and drove his fist into the unsuspecting man's gut. The officer tumbled to the ground, wheezing as he struggled to breathe. Placing a foot on his victim's chest, Nathan seized the front hem of the man's garment and used his sword to slit it open up to the waist. Still unable to speak, the man stiffened as the cold, iron blade tickled his groin. The panicked officer tried to crawl away on his back, but Nathan still clutched the man's garment in one fist. Nathan then drew the tip of his sword lightly along his victim's exposed inner right thigh, just deep enough to produce a thin stream of blood. The man responded by noiselessly opening and closing his mouth like a fish pulled from water. Nathan withdrew his sword and leaned over until he felt the man's fetid breath.

"The next time you think to lay hands on me...remember this!"

Nathan sheathed the sword and stepped back to study the whimpering man lying in a muddy pool of his own urine. This was a clear message to Abner that neither he nor Jonathan was to be trifled with. Satisfied, Nathan went in search of Jonathan and a cozy spot to sleep.

Epilogue

And Saul said, "Come here, you leaders of my army, and let us find out what sin has been committed today. For as surely as the LORD who saves Israel lives, the guilty man shall die, even if it is Jonathan my son." But not a single one of the soldiers answered him. Then Saul said to his officers representing the army, "You stand over there, and my son Jonathan and I will stand over here." And the men replied to Saul, "Do what seems best to you." Then Saul prayed to the LORD, the God of Israel, "Give me the right answer." The lot fell on Saul and Jonathan, but the soldiers were cleared. And Saul said, "Cast lots between my son Jonathan and me." The lot fell on Jonathan. Then Saul said to Jonathan, "Tell me what you have done." So Jonathan said, "I merely tasted a little honey with the end of my spear. For that I must die?" Saul answered, "May God deal even more harshly with me, if you do not die, Jonathan." But the soldiers said to Saul, "Shall Jonathan die, the man who has accomplished this great deliverance in Israel? Never! As the LORD lives, not one hair of his head shall be harmed, for he did this today with God's help." So the soldiers rescued Jonathan, and he did not die.

From the Book of I Samuel, Chapter 14, verses 38 to 45

In Philistine occupied Beth-horon

Achish peeled off his sweaty armor and flung it across the filthy room he had just commandeered in the Gath outpost. Three solid days of raiding, retreating and fending off Hebrew militia would have exhausted any nineteen-year-old. However, he found the worst waiting for him at Beth-Horon. As Achish collapsed on a crude bed, he seethed over his recent confrontation with the other kings of Philistia. The ungrateful turds had assailed Achish with accusations of Gath treachery before he could even sit down. After vehemently defending his family's honor, he asked whose chariots had made the Philistine retreat from Michmash possible. In the embarrassed hush which followed, Achish demanded from each accuser the source of his information. One by one, the flustered kings retracted their accusations. The session ended with the galling admission that the true cause of the Philistine disaster at Michmash might never be known.

"Want some food, Achish? It's a little better than this piss they claim is wine."

Davon, Achish's adjutant, sat at the only table in the room and chewed a piece of pork. A prince normally enjoyed private quarters, but Achish required the counsel of his best officer. He was about to decline Davon's offer when his father's chief administrator, Abimelek, barged through the door. Achish was too fatigued to be offended by the lack of courtesy. He was not surprised that the *Archon* was already here from Gath. The man saw everything...just like a vulture.

"We have urgent business, Achish."

"That's *Prince* Achish to you, *Archon*."

"We're not in public, Achish. This is where affairs of state are really transacted. Your guest should leave us."

"It's all right, Abimelek. Davon is the new commander of my army."

Achish's spur of the moment announcement caught Davon with his mouth full of food. The soldier spat out some half-chewed meat before responding.

"What army? Our infantry has been annihilated!"

"Then build me a new one."

"From what? A single reserve infantry regiment and eight garrison companies? You might scrape together another regiment from the survivors of Michmash, but they have no weapons."

"Davon, you have a month to raise five full strength infantry regiments and three months to get them into the field."

"Only if your idea of an army includes thousands of boys holding sharp sticks."

"Turn the garrison troops into field infantry. Put the boys behind walls until they grow up. Recruit from our Canaanite laborers if need be. They're sturdy enough."

"That will give us one untried regiment, one demoralized regiment, one untrained regiment and two useless ones."

"I'm counting on your skill with men, Davon. Break up the reserve regiment. Two reserve companies will form the foundation of each new regiment. Distribute the other veterans and garrison troops as you see fit. Then add your boys and Canaanites."

"Diluting our strength is no answer, Achish. We need experienced soldiers."

"Conquer some of our smaller neighbors, Davon. That should blood your men."

"But many of them are allies."

"Then they won't much mind becoming subjects, will they?"

"The other kings may have something to say about that."

"Don't be so gloomy, Davon. They know Gath has the only credible chariot force left in all of Philistia."

"Even so, Achish, chariots are only as good as their infantry support. If our foot-soldiers are overrun, the chariots have nowhere to regroup. They'll have to scatter just to survive."

"I've considered that. Base the chariot brigades in our largest border garrisons. If Kaftor attacks from the south, our nearest chariots can harass his troops and destroy his supply train. Once we know Kaftor's line of march, we can concentrate the entire chariot corps against the Gazans."

"So, now you read minds, Achish?"

"It's not magic, Davon. Kaftor has the largest infantry force left in Philistia. The old jackal is drawn to weakness like a wolf to blood."

"Your chariot strategy is sound. Why the rush to buildup infantry?"

"We cannot wait for Kaftor to make an alliance with one of the other Philistine kings. Imagine Ashdod or Ashkelon also striking us from the west. Think of Ekron coming down from the north. Attacks from two different directions will finish Gath. They can besiege our outposts one by one, force us into open battle and destroy our army just as you have so colorfully described, Davon."

"Now I'm with you. Even a raw army can discourage invasion. But do we even have three months?"

"Kaftor is a master of conspiracy and intrigue, but he is no soldier. I expect him to first use those tactics at which he excels. His schemes will take time to bear fruit."

"Then I will build your army, Achish. Can I take some of the charioteers for officers?"

"Yes, but no more than fifty. We can't gut our most valuable asset."

"Half our infantry will still lack weapons."

"Leave that to me."

Achish and Davon both turned at Abimelech's unexpected interruption. The *Archon* had been observing their discussion without comment. Achish recalled it was Abimelek's custom to let military men complete their plans, before tearing them to pieces. He raised a skeptical eyebrow to the older man.

"Have you been skimming from the treasury, Abimelek?"

"My spies inform me that significant wealth will become available in six weeks."

"And what is the source of this windfall?"

"It's best if only I know the details, Achish."

"Fine, but it's your head if you fail. However, that cannot be why you are here, *Archon*."

"I need you to approve a list."

"What list?"

"All the people who must be killed before you can secure the throne."

There was coldness in Abimelek's eyes, but no malice, as he extended the list to his prince. Achish scanned through several dozen names and was intrigued by their variety. Relatives. Generals. Ministers. Nobles. Women. Infants. The *Archon* adroitly responded to Achish's puzzled expression.

"I already have men in place. You need only to add the royal signet."

"I did not realize an *Archon's* duties included selecting kings."

"If the throne does not interest you, Achish, I will trouble you no further."

"Answer me this, Abimelek. Out of all the uncles, cousins, half-brothers and full-blooded bastards, why choose me?"

"It is in my best interest that you become king."

"A most unexpected answer."

"Yet, you would be a fool to accept any other."

"There is no proof my father is dead. What if the Hebrews have him in chains?"

"Maoch is still finished as King of Gath. If you don't replace him, Achish, someone else will."

A moment's consideration was all that Achish required before walking to the table. Davon cleared a space among the dishes for the document to be laid. Achish removed his signet ring and stamped the symbol of Gath royalty on the death list. Somehow, the document felt much heavier as he returned it to the *Archon*.

"What happens now, Abimelek?"

"All executions take place the day after I return to the Capital. Some chaos is to be expected. A show of force around the Palace and in the larger towns should restore order."

"That's your job, Davon. You'll need more than chariots in the city. Can you take over the reserve regiment?"

"No problem. Its commander and I served together."

"The two of you will leave for Gath tomorrow and arrange my succession. I still have business here."

When Abimelek headed for the door with his deadly burden, Achish held out an arm to bar his way.

"Tell me Abimelech. Do you have a list with my name on it?"

The hint of a smile crossed Abimelek's lips. The *Archon* bowed deeply before exiting without a sound. Davon leaned back in his chair and gave a soft whistle.

"What a conscienceless bastard."

"Aren't we all, Davon? Besides, it's in my best interest to retain him as *Archon*...at least for now. Watch him until I arrive in Gath."

"I don't like the idea of leaving you here."

"Assign a good head basher as my aide."

"What about that wild-eyed chariot commander you've become so fond of?"

"He'll do. Leave me a chariot company as well."

"Just what do you have in mind, Achish?"

"I'm going back to Michmash and find out *what in the name of the gods* happened."

The abandoned Philistine encampment on the Michmash plateau

After sleeping on bare ground for so long, Nathan immersed himself in glorious comfort at Michmash. His new tent, former property of some high Philistine noble, was both plush and spacious. Nathan had enjoyed it since returning to the devastated enemy camp with Jonathan's band of volunteers. These tough Israelites had served the Philistines until Jonathan offered them a chance for redemption. They repaid their debt by fighting bravely at Jonathan's side and preventing an enraged king from killing him. Upon arriving at Michmash, the former renegades promptly cleared some drunken looters out of the two best tents before turning them over to Jonathan and

Nathan. Finding his new residence well stocked with food, Nathan ate his fill before falling exhausted into a wondrous bed. His next-to-last thought that night was how selfish it was to enjoy all this luxury while comrades still slept in the open air. His final sleepy thought was no one else would know, as long as he kept his mouth shut.

It was well past dawn when Nathan's eyes first opened. It was tempting to turn over, but he was anxious over Jonathan's plans. After allowing the broken Philistine army to escape, the Israelite fighters consoled themselves with the rich plunder at Michmash. It was as good a place as any for the inevitable showdown between Saul and Jonathan. Nathan strolled over to his friend's tent, but found it empty. As he ambled through the cool morning air, Nathan saw evidence of extensive looting. He stepped carefully over sleeping men still wallowing amidst broken wine jars. Several snoring drunkards sported expensive robes over their simple homespun garments. Nathan passed several groups of women carrying heavily laden baskets as if they were returning home from market day. Yet despite two days of plundering, much Philistine loot remained untouched. It effectively illustrated to Nathan the vast disparity between the Israelite and Philistine armies.

Nathan soon spied Jonathan seated on small boulder staring toward a distant cluster of tents. As he walked over, Nathan realized they were occupied by Saul's entourage. Jonathan was obviously deep in thought, so Nathan sat on the boulder next to his friend. Jonathan quietly smiled.

"I feared, Nathan, that you became lost in your huge tent. They could fit the Tabernacle in there."

"The Philistines go to war in great comfort. I'm seriously thinking of joining up."

"Well, at least wait until I sort things out with my father."

"Two nights ago, Saul wanted you dead. He might not be ready to make peace."

"My father has already sent me an invitation."

"When do we head over, Jonathan?"

"Not we, just me. Family conflicts are best resolved in private."

"Fine, give me time to gather Laban's men. We'll escort you there."

"No, Nathan. I'd be as good as declaring civil war if I arrive at the head of a personal army."

"At least wear your sword."

"And my armor, too. They must know a royal prince has come to call."

As Jonathan prepared to meet with his father, Nathan considered the irony resulting from the great victory over the Philistines. The Kingdom of Israel was never stronger...nor in greater peril.

****

Dear Reader:

I hope you enjoyed reading *A King to Rule*, the first book in my *Empire of Israel* series.

I would also greatly appreciate your writing a brief review on my book's detail page in Amazon. Your comments will provide feedback, so I can improve later books in the series.

This exciting Biblical saga continues in my second book, *A King to Fight*.

Thanks!

Dale Ellis

Made in the USA
Monee, IL
01 December 2020